Ethan Fox Books Presents

Triple Trouble: Ethan Fox Books 1 & 2 and add some Mayhem

3 Books in 1

ETHAN FOX BOOKS PRESENTS

TRIPLE TROUBLE: ETHAN FOX

BOOKS 1 & 2 AND ADD SOME MAYHEM

3 BOOKS IN 1

E. L. SEER

COVERS ILLUSTRATED BY JOHN COLLADO

The Ethan Fox Books Company
an imprint of The Ridge Publishing Group

To meet the author and learn more about the Ethan Fox Books original series
and E. L. Seer's books, please visit us at https://www.EthanFoxBooks.com.
Ethan Fox Books is an exciting new website from E. L. Seer that can be enjoyed
alongside the Ethan Fox Books series. You can discover behind the scenes
information about the author, learn more about your favorite characters, play
games, enter contests, and much more. It is FREE to join and use and is designed
to be safe for people of all ages. Subscribe to our mailing list, join our Caretaker
World Newsletter, join our KidsStagramCLUB, read all about us in The
Residential Daily Star, see updates at Ethan Fox Books KidsStagram blog at
https://www.KidsStagram.com, "like" us on our
Facebook.com/EthanFoxBooks page, or "follow" us on Twitter
@EthanFoxBooks.

Cover designs by: John Collado
Editor: Felicity Carter

Library of Congress Control Number: 2024923936

Seer, E. L.
Triple Trouble: Ethan Fox Books 1 & 2 and add some Mayhem 3 BOOKS IN 1
/ by E. L. Seer

ISBN 978-1-956905-45-8 (e-book)
ISBN 978-1-956905-44-1 (trade paperback)

1. Young Adult Fiction / Action & Adventure. 2. Young Adult Fiction /
Fantasy. 3. Young Adult Fiction / Mysteries & Detective Stories. 4. Young
Adult Fiction / Science Fiction. 5. Young Adult Fiction / Coming of Age. I.
Title. II. Series.

Print copies printed in the United States of America

This book is dedicated to my wife, Lori. Without her coaxing and inspiration, it would never have made it past a couple of wacky dreams and an old high school poem. She has been my wife, confidant, and cheerleader — she is my taletaddler.

Thank you, sweetheart.

ALSO BY E. L. SEER

Ethan Fox and the Eyes of the Desert Sand

Wordly Pagemore's Early Worm Activities & Games:
The Eyes of the Desert Sand Edition

Ethan Fox and the Shadow Princess

Wordly Pagemore's Early Worm Activities & Games:
The Shadow Princess Edition

Ethan Fox and the Kraken's Fury
Coming Soon

Mayhem in the Moongarden
Chapter Book

Received Mom's Choice Award, Moonbeam Children's Book Award,
Story Monsters Award, and Global Book Award.

CONTENTS

BOOK 1

ETHAN FOX AND THE EYES OF THE DESERT SAND

CONTENTS

CONTENTS

CONTENTS

BOOK 2

ETHAN FOX AND THE SHADOW PRINCESS

CONTENTS

C O N T E N T S

BOOK 3

MAYHEM IN THE MOONGARDEN

CONTENTS

Ethan Fox and the Eyes of the Desert Sand
Journey Map

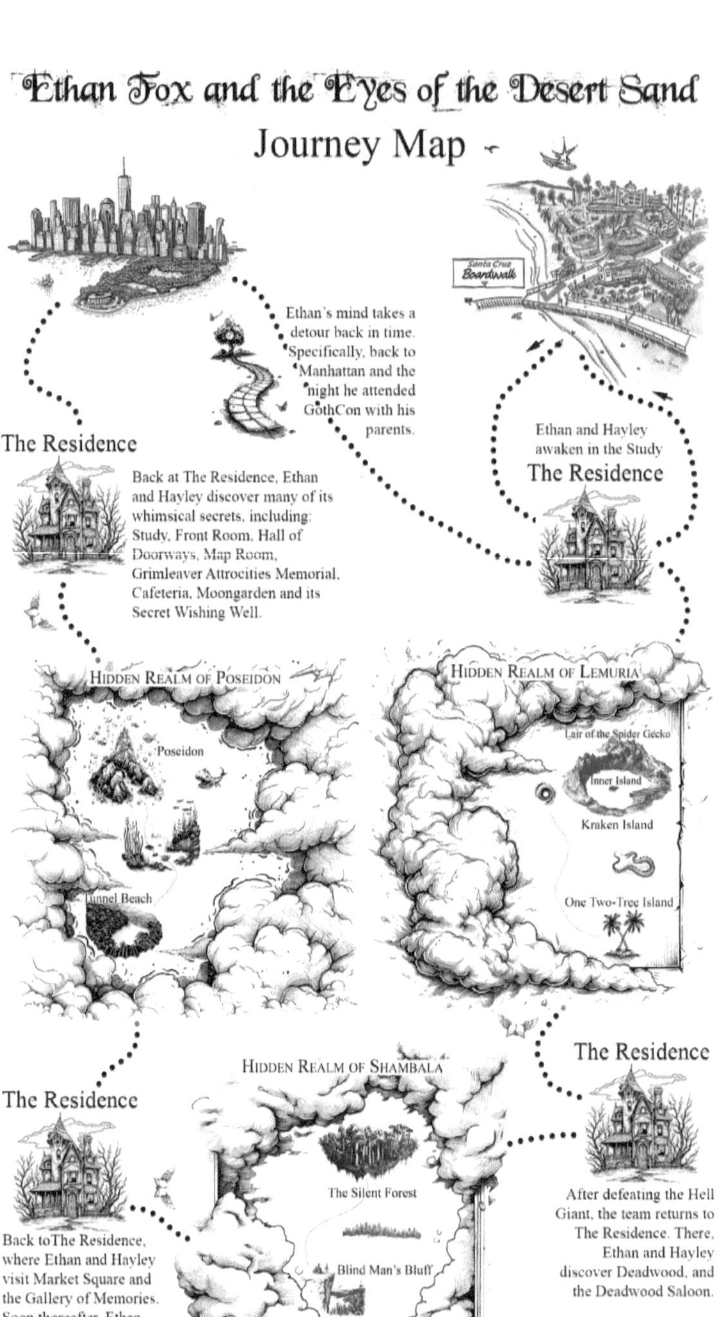

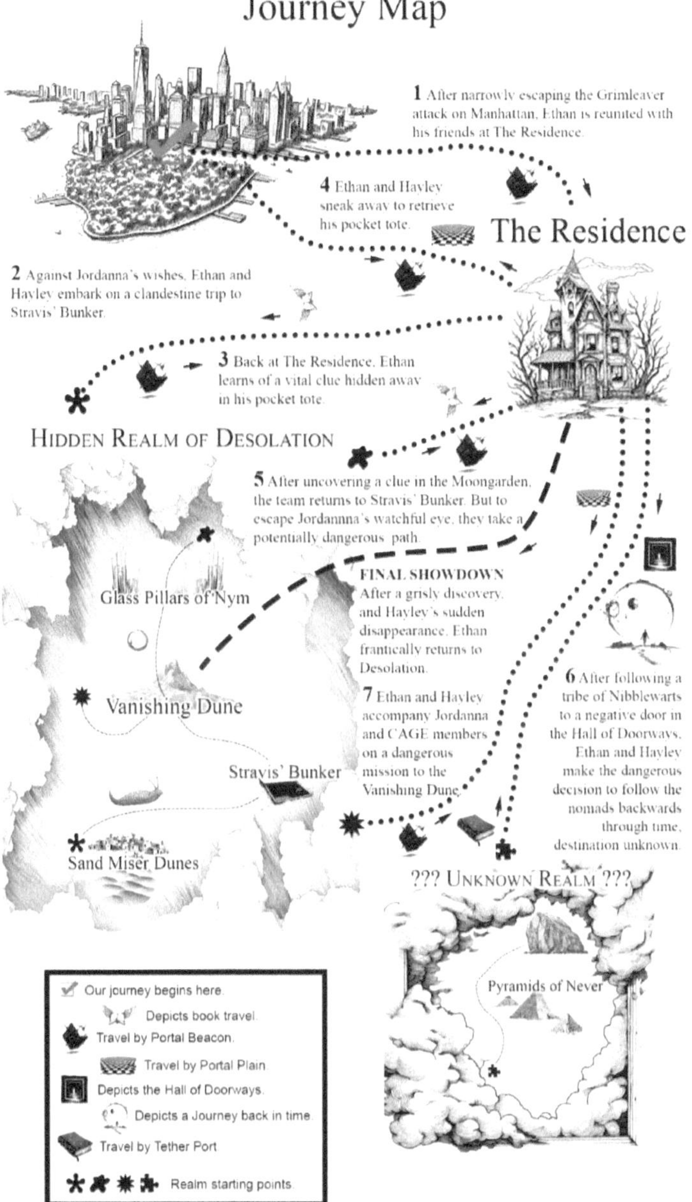

Ethan Fox and the Shadow Princess
Journey Map

1 After narrowly escaping the Grimleaver attack on Manhattan, Ethan is reunited with his friends at The Residence.

4 Ethan and Hayley sneak away to retrieve his pocket tote.

The Residence

2 Against Jordanna's wishes, Ethan and Hayley embark on a clandestine trip to Stravis' Bunker.

3 Back at The Residence, Ethan learns of a vital clue hidden away in his pocket tote.

HIDDEN REALM OF DESOLATION

5 After uncovering a clue in the Moongarden, the team returns to Stravis' Bunker. But to escape Jordannna's watchful eye, they take a potentially dangerous path.

FINAL SHOWDOWN
After a grisly discovery, and Hayley's sudden disappearance, Ethan frantically returns to Desolation.

7 Ethan and Hayley accompany Jordanna and CAGE members on a dangerous mission to the Vanishing Dune.

6 After following a tribe of Nibblewarts to a negative door in the Hall of Doorways, Ethan and Hayley make the dangerous decision to follow the nomads backwards through time, destination unknown.

Glass Pillars of Nym

Vanishing Dune

Stravis' Bunker

Sand Miser Dunes

??? UNKNOWN REALM ???

Pyramids of Never

Our journey begins here.
Depicts book travel.
Travel by Portal Beacon.
Travel by Portal Plain.
Depicts the Hall of Doorways.
Depicts a Journey back in time.
Travel by Tether Port
Realm starting points.

The *Ethan Fox Books* Company

Dive into the sands of adventure with "Ethan Fox and the Eyes of the Desert Sand," where every grain tells a story, and every dune hides a secret. As you traverse through Ethan's thrilling escapades, we invite you to extend your journey beyond the pages. For an exclusive peek behind the scenes, visit our official blog at: https://www.KidsStagram.com. Discover the depths of Characters, explore the vastness of Places, unravel the mysteries of Things/Events, and witness the Cutting Floor Scenes that make Ethan's world so vividly cinematic.

Your passion fuels our quest to bring Ethan and Hayley's adventures to the silver screen. If you're captivated by the idea of an Ethan Fox film, join our chorus of voices at our website at: https://www.EthanFoxBooks.com/Fan Page, and let's turn this vision into a panoramic reality!

BOOK 1

ETHAN FOX AND THE EYES OF THE DESERT SAND

E. L. SEER

INTO THE
RABBIT HOLE

Fun in the sun on the Santa Cruz Beach Boardwalk was just what the doctor ordered for the Fox family. It had been on Ethan's wish list ever since seeing it on the Discovery Channel. So, when his adoptive parents, George and Betsy Fox, asked him to choose a vacation destination, it was a no-brainer. It didn't hurt that California was the farthest on that list from their home in Manhattan – and after the events of the previous weeks, that was a good thing . . .

Ethan stood at a railing at the edge of the boardwalk and stared at the horizon while he waited for his dad. The fresh ocean breeze tickled his auburn hair as he squinted at the sun glistening off the waves. The ocean always brought Ethan a peaceful calm. Mesmerized by the waves, his mind raced as he imagined what sort of giant creature might burst up from the murky depths. Sometimes he'd even spot the odd whale or dolphin jumping, but so far today – nothing.

Ethan was of average height for a thirteen year old boy. He had brown eyes, straight reddish brown hair, and a freckled complexion. But unlike most boys his age, Ethan was not obsessed with videogames. He preferred to be outdoors.

He turned to scan the crowd, and a young girl caught his eye. He held his hand up to block the bright sun. She stood at a storefront, looking at her reflection in its window. She seemed sad, Ethan thought – like she was lost.

The girl turned and stared at Ethan as if she recognized him. The sun's rays glistening off her yellowish-blonde hair resembled a shimmering golden halo resting on her head. She wore a white sundress with yellow flowers that almost matched the color of her hair.

"Ethan – Ethan Fox!" shouted his father from the snack bar. "Come over here and give me a hand, will ya?"

Ethan turned and started towards his father but then paused to look back at the girl – but she was gone.

As usual, George had bought more junk food than he could carry, and when Ethan got to the snack bar, he could not believe his eyes. George had three jumbo hot dogs, four corn dogs, a large pepperoni pizza, two candied popcorn balls, three bags of cotton candy, and three bucket-sized sodas. Even for George, this was quite the bounty. An octopus would have a hard time carrying all that food.

By the time they carried all that grub to a nearby picnic table, Betsy was back from shopping.

"Wow, honey, you've outdone yourself as usual. How are we possibly going to eat all this junk?" Betsy said.

George smiled and winked at Ethan. "We'll manage."

Ethan's parents had an understanding. At home, Betsy made sure they ate healthy at every meal. While on vacation, she allowed them to loosen their belts, and for George that generally meant overindulgence and an upset stomach.

"I almost forgot," George said as he handed Ethan a handful of coins. "A man should always have a pocket full of change."

After lunch came Ethan's favorite part of the day – the rides. Ethan had done his homework and researched the rides to map out a plan of action. Their first stop was the Haunted Castle, followed by the Pirate Ship, Double Shot, Wipeout, and last but not least, the world-famous Giant Dipper.

Ethan's mom didn't like most rides, but she'd watch her two men have fun on the 'terror rides' as she called them. Betsy loved the carousel and the calm serenity it brought her. For now, her turn could wait until her two men tired out, and that might be soon at the rate they were going. They had hit all but one ride on Ethan's list and a few others for good measure, but they saved the best for last.

"That should challenge our tummies," his father said as he pointed up at the Giant Dipper.

Ethan gazed up at the enormous roller coaster. It got bigger and bigger as they neared.

"Ethan, you can skip this one," Betsy said, mistaking the excitement on his face for terror.

"Are you kidding? Can we ride it twice?"

"You two are going to throw up for sure, and then it's my turn on the carousel."

Two vomit-less rides later, Ethan and his father were ready for a break.

"That was awesome," Ethan said as he stepped off the platform. "When you get to the top – you can see over the ocean for miles."

"Yeah, and that big dip is a doozy. I almost lost my lunch the second time," George said.

"Have you two finally had enough?"

"After you – to the carousel, my dear," George said, motioning for Betsy to lead the way.

A sunflower yellow glow suddenly caught Ethan's eye, so he turned, and there she was again – the girl. She smiled, like she knew him.

"Hey, what are you looking at?" his father said from a distance. "Are you coming?"

"Be right there," he turned to answer. When he turned back, the smile drained from Ethan's face – the girl was gone again.

On the way to the carousel, George insisted that they stop for ice cream, so he and Ethan would have something to munch on while they waited.

"How in the world could you be hungry after that huge lunch?" Betsy asked.

The line for the carousel moved fast. Betsy stepped onto the platform and walked from horse to horse to study each one as if they were talking to her. She finally decided on a white steed with a blue saddle, its head cocked in a majestic pose. She had a bright smile on her face as she climbed into the saddle. Slowly the carousel spun and picked up speed as Betsy disappeared from George and Ethan's view. Ethan waited for his mother to reappear, but to his surprise, the girl appeared instead. She rode a white horse like the one Betsy had picked, and her bluish-green eyes were again staring at him.

They exchanged smiles each time the girl passed within his view. The connection was so evident that even his father took notice in between licks from his ice cream cone.

"Hey Tiger, you've got a live one there," George elbowed Ethan with a gentle jab.

The carousel slowed as the girl disappeared from Ethan's view, stopping in the same position as it had started.

"Go talk to her. I'll wait here for your mother."

Ethan jumped to his feet. He wasn't sure what to say or where he got the nerve, but he was going to walk up to her and start a conversation – there was something about this girl he was drawn to.

Ethan jogged around the carousel and carefully scanned the crowd. Having no luck, he studied the platform and spotted the white horse she had ridden. Disappointed, Ethan realized she was gone yet again.

Tired from a full afternoon of rides, games, and shopping, the Fox's were ready for some leisure time. And, of course, cheeseburgers, as his father insisted. After their third trip to the snack bar, the Fox's headed to the beach for a picnic. They hiked along the coast so his mother could find a patch of sand free of driftwood and sea kelp.

"Perfect," Betsy said as she spread a giant yellow blanket out over the sand.

Ethan's father wasted no time plopping down with his bag full of goodies.

"Cheeseburgers, anyone?" George said as he held up the bag. "I got enough for everybody."

"I'm sure you did," said Betsy as she sat down next to her husband.

Still full from lunch, Betsy and Ethan decided to share a cheeseburger and leave the remaining four for George.

"Your belly's gonna pop if you eat all those," Betsy said.

"No worries, honey, I've got one notch left on my belt. Besides, these are tiny little burgers."

The Fox's spent the next thirty minutes on their private patch of beach and nibbled away on cheeseburgers as they listened to the crashing surf.

"What's next?" George asked as he washed down his fourth cheeseburger with a gulp of soda.

"How about we wet our feet . . . like we used to . . ." suggested Betsy.

"You two go ahead," Ethan replied. "I may go for a walk along the beach if you don't mind." He wasn't in the mood to splash around in the water. He had other things on his mind.

George already had both shoes and one sock off.

"Suit yourself, but you're going to miss out on all the fun . . . I bet you didn't know your mother's a mermaid."

"Just be sure to stay in sight if you go on that walk," his mother said.

George struggled to lift his colossal frame from the blanket. Moments later, he and Betsy skipped off like childhood sweethearts.

"There they go – the *Beauty and the Beast!*" Ethan shouted.

"You're beginning to sound like your father."

Ethan's parents splashed around in the surf like playful sea otters. His thoughts returned to the mysterious girl on the carousel. "Who was she? What was her name?"

"My name is Hayley." A soft voice said from behind him, "You were watching me."

Ethan jumped to his feet and flopped around to regain his balance. He turned to see who spoke to him. It was the girl from the carousel.

"I-I-I wasn't watching you – you were watching me – weren't you?"

"I guess so," she said.

"Why?" Ethan asked as he blushed.

"I don't know . . . I don't remember anything before seeing you. I was just here. I don't remember where I came from or how I got here. I-I was just here . . ." she began to sob.

"Don't cry. I'll get my parents. They'll know what to do."

"At first, I was terrified among all those strangers, but then our eyes met, and it told me everything would be okay. I feel like I know you from somewhere. What is your name?"

"Oh, I'm sorry. My name is Ethan. What did you mean by 'it' told you everything would be okay?"

Hayley fondled the ring on her right hand. It was unlike any ring Ethan had ever seen. Made from a metallic black material and shaped like an infinity sign – ∞ – that bent so her finger could pass through both loops.

"It tells me things."

"It talks to you?"

"I know it sounds crazy. It doesn't talk, but sometimes it comes alive, like a snake slithering through my fingers. Then I just know what it wants me to know – it led me to you."

"That does sound crazy," Ethan said. "But I do feel like we've met before."

"Are those funny people your parents?" she asked, pointing at George and Betsy as they splashed in the waves.

"Yeah – but sometimes it seems like I'm the parent."

They both broke out in laughter. Hayley had an infectious laugh that made Ethan laugh even more.

"Strange – I don't know where I came from or how I got here but being with you makes me feel safe."

Hayley grabbed Ethan by the hand, and a rush of bliss overtook him – like a butterfly was about to fly up from his stomach and out his mouth. He nervously swiped his feet at the sand as they talked.

He drew something with his foot.

"That symbol," Hayley said. "What is it?"

"Nothing really, just a doodle I made up."

Hayley reached down to grab hold of his other hand as she faced him.

"Come on, let's go for a walk on the beach. I need to think things out," she said.

Hayley gently tugged at Ethan's arms, and they started down the beach. He didn't want this day to end. Ethan knew their strong connection was no coincidence.

"So," Hayley said as they strolled down the beach. "I've told you my secret. Tell me something about you – a secret you've never shared before."

Ethan thought for a moment. "I have two, so take your pick."

Ethan could not believe what he was about to tell her, but he felt compelled to do so.

Hayley was rubbing her ring finger. "Start with what that symbol really means."

"Your ring talking to you again?" Ethan said. "Okay, so it's not a doodle I made up. I have these."

Ethan held up his hands. Small white symbols glistened on the palm of each hand as if someone had tattooed him with shiny white ink.

"How did you get those?"

"I don't remember. The story is, my birth parents were in a cult before George and Betsy adopted me. The cult did this to me."

"That is quite bizarre," Hayley said. "What's your other secret?"

Ethan paused. "I have visions that come true," he blurted out. "I realize it sounds crazy."

"That doesn't sound so crazy. I have a ring that talks to me."

Ethan smiled at her attempt to comfort him.

"It's like a video in my head that always starts the same . . . I'm in the middle of the desert, and big blue eyes are peeking out from beneath the sand – they're everywhere. Then I'm somewhere else, watching as things happen."

"And they come true?"

"So far, they've all come true – all but one . . ." Ethan's voice trailed off.

They had walked for quite some time, and George and Betsy were no longer in sight. Ethan stopped.

"We shouldn't go any farther – I promised I would stay in sight."

"We have walked pretty far," she said.

They started back down the beach when Ethan spotted a seashell in the sand.

"A sand dollar," he said as he ran over to pick it up. Ethan handed the seashell to Hayley.

"They're supposed to bring you luck," he said.

"How beautiful," she said.

Hayley dusted the sand off the small disc-shaped shell and exposed a flower-like pattern.

As they continued down the beach, Ethan realized that it was now abandoned. He stopped to scan the area, but nothing appeared familiar, as if they were suddenly on a different beach.

Then, out of the corner of his eye, he spotted a bright blue flash. Ethan turned inland to check it out. A three foot tall blue rabbit with yellow polka dots stood upright at the edge of the beach. It appeared to be an Easter bunny with pastel pink shorts and red suspenders. Ethan rubbed his eyes in disbelief.

Hayley tapped Ethan on the back. "What is it?"

"Don't you see that?" Ethan asked and pointed at the strange creature.

"I don't see anything, but my ring is about to jump off my finger. You're the only one who sees it."

"It appears to be harmless enough. I'm going to take a closer look," Ethan said as he walked towards the creature.

"Wait for me."

As they neared the creature, Ethan could hear it as it waved and laughed like a mischievous child.

"Where is it?"

"Right in front of us."

The bunny stopped waving.

"Happy day Ethan Fox," said the bunny. "Are we having fun yet?" The rabbit sounded like a cartoon character with a nasal voice and giggled as if someone had just told a joke.

"Who are you, and how do you know my name?"

"Jasper I am, but many appreciate Ethan Fox."

"What do you want from us?" Ethan said.

"Jasper wishes to help."

"Do you know what happened to Hayley?"

"And what happened to Ethan Fox. Memories lost and destinies tangled. Jasper wishes to help."

"What do you know about my past?" Ethan asked.

"The answers you seek lie at The Residence."

Jasper scurried off towards an outcropping of rocks. He stopped and turned towards them and said, "The Residence awaits, Ethan Fox." Then Jasper waved and ducked behind the rocks.

"What did it say?" Hayley asked.

"Its name is Jasper," Ethan shouted as he followed in hot pursuit.

"Wait for me!" Hayley followed Ethan.

"He went behind these rocks."

They followed Jasper's trail, and what they found surprised them.

Ethan and Hayley stood at the top of a sandcastle staircase that descended into the dark wet sand.

"Do you see that?" Ethan asked.

"Yes – I wonder where it leads?"

"I don't know, but I'm going to find out. Wait here," Ethan said as he descended into the dark stairwell.

Ethan held out his hands to sense his way and the symbols on his palms began to glow.

Then in an instant, everything went black.

THE RESIDENCE

Ethan's head was fuzzy when he regained consciousness. He heard muffled voices and rustling as he lie on the ground, but now the room was silent. He stood and was now in a sizable study that reminded him of a room in a haunted mansion, except this one appeared clean and lived in.

At one end of the room stood a fireplace with an opening so broad Ethan could walk in standing upright. To the right, a thick golden book sat upon a pedestal. To the left stood a tall candelabrum with four white candles attached to the inside of a vertical circle. The candles pointed towards the circle's center, where a spherical replica of Earth rotated in place, as if held by invisible strings.

Ethan stared at the candles. Each burned a flame of a different color – red, green, blue, and yellow. Yet, unlike an ordinary candle, these defied the laws of physics. Each flame burned towards the tiny Earth replica as if holding it in place.

Ethan tiptoed towards the other side of the room. Tall floor to ceiling bookcases lined the walls to each side, and thousands of books sat on their shelves. On the far side of the room stood two doors, one to each side of a full-length painting that hung at the center of the wall. The portrait depicted an angelic woman hovering midair in a frosty ice wonderland. She wore a flowing white gown bathed in crystals.

"She's beautiful," a voice said, startling Ethan.

"Hayley," he said.

"Where are we?" she asked as she scanned the room in amazement.

"I don't know, but this place is familiar to me."

"Yes," Hayley said, "I've been here before too."

"Why did you follow me?"

"I didn't, somebody pushed me from behind, and then everything just went black."

"Everything just went black," a high-pitched voice mocked from somewhere in the room.

"She's beautiful," a different voice mimicked from another direction.

"Who said that?" Ethan said as he scanned the room.

"Who said that?" said a third voice echoed from yet a different direction.

"This isn't funny!" Hayley cried as she spun around on her feet.

"You do the *Hokey Pokey* and you turn yourself around. That's what it's all about," the voices sang in unison.

"Stop!" Hayley pleaded. "PLEASE, STOP!"

"They don't sound dangerous, more like a bunch of smart asses," Ethan reassured Hayley.

"Smart asses?" a voice replied, causing the others to giggle.

"You sound like an idiotic dork," Ethan baited the voice.

"I am not," the voice replied as the other two erupted in laughter.

"Newton is an idiotic dork – Newton is an idiotic dork," two of the voices chanted, teasing the third.

"I AM NOT!" an angry voice shouted back.

A book flew off one of the bookcases and startled both Ethan and Hayley.

"They sound like children," Ethan said.

"Children?" another voice said in a serious tone. "My dear child, your age is a mere tick of existence compared to us."

"That sounded like a grumpy old man," Hayley said.

She had caught on to Ethan's game.

"Linus is a grumpy old man," two of the voices sang out, mocking the third.

"So, we have Newton and Linus but not the name of the third dummy," Ethan said.

"Albert is a dummy – Albert is a dummy," Newton and Linus teased.

"Interesting choice of names," Ethan said. "We're tired of these games – show yourselves."

The room fell silent.

"Albert! Come here this minute!" Hayley ordered.

A red ball the size of an apple appeared on the table in front of them.

"Where did that come from?" Ethan was puzzled.

"Newton, come here now!" Hayley demanded.

A blue ball appeared next to the red one.

"Your turn Linus," she said.

A green ball appeared next to the other two.

Ethan and Hayley stared at the three balls on the table.

"Hey dummies, where did you go?" Hayley taunted, but the room remained silent.

"I have an idea," Ethan said.

A huge grin appeared on his face as he picked up the three colored balls and began juggling. He faintly heard three muffled voices as they laughed and screamed at the same time – like kids on a roller coaster. The voices grew louder as the balls began to grow and unravel.

Shocked by their metamorphosis, Ethan threw the balls into the air and jumped back. A loud popping noise echoed through the room, followed by flashes of colored light that blinded them at first. When their eyes cleared, the balls had transformed into three small creatures, each the color of their respective ball. The creatures were no more than two feet tall with tiny slits for noses and yellow cat-like eyes. They had devilish horns and rows of spikes that flowed down the center of their backs to the end of their forked tails.

Ethan studied the creatures in amazement.

They had long arms with loose skin underneath that attached to their bodies like a flying squirrel. Colorful gold speckled feathers covered all but their smooth-skinned bellies.

"I'm Linus," the green one said as he held his hand out politely.

"I'm Newton," the blue one extended his hand.

"You must be Albert," Ethan said as he shook each of their tiny hands. "My name is Ethan, and this is Hayley."

"You are Ethan Fox?" Linus asked.

"How do you know my name?"

"It's not every day a human shows up at The Residence," Newton said, "especially one named Ethan."

Ethan glanced at Hayley, who appeared distracted by something on the bookshelves.

"Ethan—"

"So, you've met RGB," a deep voice interrupted Hayley from across the room.

Ethan and Hayley spun around.

A tall man entered the room through the door on the left. He wore a long half-black half-white hooded robe and a red glove on one hand. The black side of his robe sported an emblem that resembled the candelabra near the fireplace. Four colored spheres: red, green, blue, and yellow surrounded a fifth – planet Earth. A transparent web-like casing encircled them all like a cocoon.

Unease overcame Ethan, like an invisible hand lightly teasing the back of his neck.

The hooded stranger kept his head down as he strode across the room. He slowly raised his head and lowered his hood with his red gloved hand. He brushed his long hair aside to reveal his face, and Ethan was shocked as he recognized the stranger – it was him!

"Stay back!" Ethan shouted as he jumped in front of Hayley to shield her.

Ethan's mind raced back to the events that began two weeks earlier . . .

ENTER SANDMAN

Silence filled the night air in the Fox household.

"I'm going to bed," Ethan's mom said.

"Goodnight," Ethan and his dad said.

"Hey, how'd you like to check out my new game idea?" said George to Ethan. George Fox was the creator of the successful *Dark Realm* video game series.

"Sure, Dad," he fibbed. Unlike most thirteen year olds, Ethan wasn't much of a gamer. He'd rather be outdoors where the real adventures happen.

"So, here's the idea—" George pulled an oversized sketchbook from his briefcase. "If a tree falls in the forest and nobody's around to listen, is there a sound? Of course." George answered his own question.

"I'm thinking of calling it, *The Ears on the Forest Trees.*"

"*The Ears on the Forest Trees,*" Ethan repeated.

The words resonated in Ethan's mind as he viewed George's drawings of a lush green forest with small nest-like huts that hung in the trees. Small appendages zig-zagged up the tree trunks – they looked like ears.

"What do you think?"

Ethan paused to gather his thoughts.

"So how are you going to explain a bunch of funny looking trees with ears?" Ethan laughed.

"Well—" George paused, "I don't know yet."

"This one is way strange, Dad," Ethan said.

Later that night, as Ethan lie in bed, his mind struggled to remember something. Like a thought was stuck on the tip of his tongue. Finally, he fell asleep only to wake up the next morning unrested.

Over the next several nights, the pattern persisted, and Ethan would lie in bed, unable to remember something buried in his memory. Yet each morning when he woke up, he felt closer to the answer.

"I've got to get some sleep tonight," Ethan thought on the fifth night as he lay counting sheep.

"What can't I remember?" he wondered as he picked up the notepad and pencil he had left on his nightstand.

He sensed a strange presence and sat up to scan the room. He was ready to confront the intruder and then . . .

Ethan walked in a vast desert as thousands of fist-sized blue eyes peeked from beneath the sand. They were watching him from everywhere, but the eyes did not threaten Ethan. They put him at ease like they were his protectors – Ethan fell asleep.

The next morning, he woke with the notepad and pencil still in his hands. He glanced down at the paper and saw writing on the tablet. Ethan's handwriting was evident, and his symbol appeared at the end.

"I don't remember writing anything," Ethan thought as he read the words:

The Eyes of the Desert Sand

On an old abandoned airstrip in a desert far away, lands an unknown flying saucer in the revealing light of day.

There are no creatures there to see it in this tortured barren land, no plant life there to feel it just The Eyes of the Desert Sand.

As the saucer doors swing open in a misty fog they see, a man from within the saucer from where could he possibly be?

Emerging from the saucer he steps down to the ground, pausing for a moment as he stops to look around.

He carries a flag of colors with shades from black to white, as he plants the flag into the ground it becomes a beautiful sight.

Returning to his saucer as quickly as he came, the doors swing shut behind him like a picture in a frame.

The saucer leaves undetected by the entire world at hand, unknown to all existence but The Eyes of the Desert Sand.

"Is this what I've been trying to remember?" Ethan wondered. "How come I don't remember writing this? I know – I'll show Dad. He always comes up with this kind of stuff."

Ethan headed downstairs to George's study with the notebook in hand.

"Come in," George hollered from within his study.

"Hey, Dad," he said and entered as George tossed a wadded-up piece of paper into a wastepaper basket. "Three pointer," George proclaimed with a grin. "What can I do for you, kiddo?" Ethan took the seat across the desk from his dad.

"You know all those weird ideas you dream up for your video games?"

"Yeah," George chuckled.

"Well – I kind of came up with one, but in a very creepy way," Ethan handed the notepad to his dad. The smile drained from George's face as he read the words.

"Where did you get this?" George asked.

"I wrote that in my sleep. I think your drawings jogged my memories about something from my past before the accident."

"Ethan, we've been through this . . ."

"Eyes of the Desert Sand – Ears on the Forest Trees," Ethan said. "Don't you see the similarities?"

"That's enough, Ethan. There is no mystery. You were in an accident and suffered amnesia before we adopted you."

"What about these?" Ethan said and held out the palms of his hands.

"We've been through that too. Your birth parents were part of a dangerous cult. They marked all of their children that way – end of story."

Ethan left the room disappointed, but convinced that his dad was hiding something.

Later that day, Ethan arrived home early from a friend's house and heard his parents upstairs arguing.

"Always showing him those stupid sketches – I knew you would jog something in his memory!" Betsy yelled.

"You're right, but I just wanted him to live like a normal child."

"I'm home," Ethan called out. He was not in the habit of eavesdropping.

The next few days were quiet around the Fox household. Ethan's parents were on edge, and it had something to do with his past. Whatever they were hiding, Ethan was going to get to the bottom of it.

Ethan was alone in the family room when a gloomy fog overcame his thoughts . . .

His mind raced and, in a flash, he was among the eyes in the desert. Another flash and he was in a dark auditorium with people all around dressed as ghouls, goblins, and other gothic creatures. His focus turned to a creature talking with two tall men dressed in tattered black robes. Chills tingled down Ethan's spine as he realized – they were vampires.

"Ethan," Betsy called from upstairs, "are you ready?"

Ethan's vision abruptly ended.

"Yeah, Mom – ready and waiting."

"Tell your father he needs to get ready."

"Sure, Mom—" Ethan headed to his father's study and found the door slightly ajar. He peeked in and saw George halfway up his bookshelf ladder holding a withered brown book with shiny golden writing on the cover. George pulled three books from the top shelf revealing a cubbyhole where he stashed the book away, replaced the three books, and climbed down the ladder.

"Dad," Ethan said after backing down the hall. "Mom says it's time to get ready."

George plopped into his desk chair and spun around, unaware of what Ethan had witnessed.

"I'll be up in a few minutes."

Tonight, was the third annual *Gothic Comic Book Convention*. Unlike other conventions, *GothCon* was only held at night at dark remote locations and attended by fans wearing all manner of nightmarish costumes.

George's *Dark Realm* video game series had been such a success that it spun off a comic book series, and those too had become successful. As a result, George was obligated to make an appearance for his loyal fans. But this year, George was also the keynote speaker, and that meant tonight was a family affair.

"I'm ready," George announced as he descended the staircase.

Upon seeing George, Ethan's eyes met Betsy's as she quietly giggled.

"You didn't tell us we're going to a costume party," Betsy joked as she eyed George's attire.

"I'm the keynote speaker. I've got a role to play," George said.

Only a die-hard gothie would appreciate George's outfit. A character from the *Dark Realm* series – Rubio, the Evil Minion of Krator.

Rubio's face was a tattered mass of flesh pieced together like a jigsaw puzzle over his exposed skull. He had no nose, only a hole where one should be. His shredded black jacket oozed with blood. Rusty chains wrapped around his waist – holsters for his blood-soaked hatchets. A spike pierced through his right hand while his left held a hook with an impaled rat that squirmed at the end.

"You went all out," Ethan said as they were leaving.

"Fitting attire for a creep-fest," Betsy said.

"Tonight, we ride in style," George boasted, taking Betsy's hand as their limo pulled to the curb.

The limo pulled in front of a dreary hotel. Dimly lit streetlights cast an eerie glow over the red carpet that led to the hotel entrance. Black lights lined the path making the carpet appear black under the darkness of night. They exited the limo, and applause erupted from the gathering crowd.

"He came as Rubio!" someone shouted as the crowd cheered.

"This place sure fits the bill," Ethan said as he glanced up at the two stone gargoyles perched at each corner of the rooftop.

Things were creepier inside. The floor exhibits resembled a giant graveyard, and burning crosses marked the entrance to each. Swarms of bats hovered overhead while headless zombies and other gothic creatures wandered the floor.

"I don't understand—" his mom whispered. "This is creepy. How can they be having so much fun?"

"They are some sick puppies," Ethan whispered back.

He scanned the crowd, and his gaze stopped at a strange creature. A sandman continuously reformed as sand spilled to the floor from its body to merge back into the pile at its feet. The sandman had vaguely defined facial features and two small pits where eyes should be.

"Quite a sandman costume," George said from several feet away.

"It looks so real," Ethan said as he followed his parents.

He glanced back as two tall figures in tattered black robes arrived. They spoke with the sandman and then spun around in unison as the sandman turned and pointed at Ethan. Chills shot up Ethan's spine as he realized they were vampires, and they were looking right at him just like in his vision.

"Time to head backstage so that I can prepare for my speech," George said in the nick of time.

Ethan breathed a deep sigh of relief as he closely followed his parents backstage.

"Ah, ah, all right. I'm with you," he muttered as the words froze in his throat.

After an hour backstage, Ethan finally talked himself down from freakout mode. The moment they had all been waiting for had arrived – George's keynote address.

"LADIES AND GENTLEMEN!" a voice boomed over the intercom. "IT IS MY PLEASURE TO INTRODUCE TO YOU THE CREATOR OF THE DARK REALM! THE ONE, THE ONLY – GEORGE FOX!"

Applause erupted from every corner of the convention hall.

"Break a leg," Betsy said as she smiled and stood on her tippy toes to kiss George.

"Knock'em dead, Dad," Ethan said as George walked towards the stage.

Ethan didn't understand all the fanfare, but as his dad took the podium, he was proud.

"Thank you for the bloody warmth you have shown, and welcome to my nightmare," George shouted to the crowd.

About a half-hour into George's speech, nature called.

"Mom, I'm going to go to the bathroom," Ethan said as he sped down a backstage corridor.

Halfway down the long corridor, he realized that the loud crowd noise had given way to a ghostly silence. Ethan shivered as a tingly chill rushed through his body like tiny ants crawling beneath his skin.

He turned around, and two dark figures descended upon him. The two vampires wrestled him to the ground and forced a bag over his head. Ethan felt a light gliding sensation like he was floating down the hallway. He shuttered at the cold sandpaper texture of their skin against his own. Ethan grabbed one of his attackers' arms and struggled to pry himself free – but he was helpless against their strength.

"Stay calm—" a soothing voice whispered inside his head.

A thunderous jolt abruptly freed him from his kidnappers' grasp as he thudded to the ground. He frantically tore the bag from his head and was face-to-face with not two but three tall figures. Ethan's heart thumped in his chest like a jackhammer as he faced his attackers. The two vampires made a hasty exit through a door at the end of the hall. The third figure stood over him and stared as if ready to attack. Ethan's body went ridged as he braced himself . . .

But a man, not a vampire, stood before Ethan. He wore a long half-black half-white robe and had a bluish-white complexion and long black stringy hair. His long pointy nose stretched from his narrow brows to below his thin upper lip. Ethan trembled as he stared into the stranger's devilish eyes, one green eye, and one bluish-grey with a moon-shaped pupil.

"What do you want with me?" Ethan asked as he and the stranger exchanged stares.

"Everything will be all right, Ethan Fox," the soothing voice said from inside his head.

Ethan could not tell where the voice came from, but he found it comforting.

"Ethan, are you all right?" Betsy's voice called out from the end of the corridor.

He turned towards his mother and screamed at the top of his lungs, "RIGHT HERE, MOM – I NEED HELP!"

But when he turned back to face his attacker, he was alone near the end of the corridor in front of a sign that read:

Men's Restroom

OUT THROUGH THE IN-DOOR

I've seen him before," Ethan said as he glared at the stranger.

"Him who?" Hayley asked.

"The man with the vampires who tried to kidnap me."

"Kidnap you?" Hayley questioned as she stared daggers at the robed stranger.

"I can assure you, Ethan Fox – it was not I who tried to abduct you," the stranger spoke in a low gravelly voice. "We've kept an eye on you, but we are not here to harm you."

"I saw you with the two others."

"Did you get a close look at your attacker?" the stranger asked as he approached Ethan.

"Yes – I saw you as plain as day."

"Then you should be aware of the differences," the stranger said as he bent closer to Ethan.

"Your eyes are brown, but his were creepy, and he didn't wear a red glove."

"My dear brother has joined the Grimleavers," the stranger said. "Mother will have to believe me now."

"Who are you?" Hayley asked. "And why would your brother want to abduct Ethan?"

"We will answer your questions in due time," the stranger said. "I am Daavic Ravenwood. We are well aware of Ethan Fox, but who might you be?"

"My name is Hayley, I think . . . I don't remember anything before seeing Ethan."

Daavic motioned towards the couch near the fireplace.

"Please, have a seat."

Ethan and Hayley sat.

"What are Grimleavers?" Ethan asked.

"The Grimleavers are an army of evil. Creatures devolved and enslaved to serve Victor Qruefeldt and help him fulfill his ultimate goal – world domination."

"Victor Qruefeldt," Hayley repeated. "I recognize that name."

Daavic shot Hayley a questioning glance.

"How do you know Ethan?" Hayley changed the subject.

"How indeed," Daavic turned his attention to Ethan.

"Roughly one human week ago," Daavic explained, "a sandman answered the call of an exhausted human child. He went about his business, sprinkling Z's to help the child sleep. But instead of falling asleep, the child proceeded to

write the words to a poem unknown to the human world—
"

"The Eyes of the Desert Sand," Ethan said.

"A sandman is a calm and quiet creature. Putting people to sleep is normally an uneventful endeavor. However, when something out of the ordinary occurs, they are very excitable. After witnessing Ethan Fox write the poem, the sandman traveled our world telling the story of the human child who wrote the words of a Creator."

"Sorry I can't help you. I don't remember writing that poem."

"What's the big deal about a poem anyway?" Hayley asked.

"Someone very distinguished wrote this particular poem, and it remains a great mystery. Ethan Fox has become a revered name to many in our world."

"That sounds like what Jasper said."

"Jasper?" Daavic asked.

"A blue rabbit creature we encountered on the beach. Hayley couldn't see Jasper, but I could. We followed him to a creepy staircase into the sand, so I went after him and woke up here."

"Ethan disappeared, so I went in for a closer view, and someone pushed me down the stairs from behind."

"Can you describe Jasper?" Daavic inquired.

"He resembled a child in a blue bunny suit with yellow spots," Ethan said. He held his hand a few feet above the ground, "He was about this tall and said his name was Jasper before he scurried away."

"Jasper, the blue taletaddler—" Daavic whispered to himself. "Is this the first time you've seen Jasper?" he asked.

"Yes," Ethan said.

"Jasper is a taletaddler," Daavic said.

Ethan sat with his hands relaxed comfortably in his lap. Daavic glanced down at his opened palm. An uneasy feeling crept over Ethan, and he quickly closed his hands.

"What is a taletaddler?" Ethan asked.

"Taletaddlers are a child's imaginary friend in the human world. They befriend human children and allow only that child to be aware of their existence. Taletaddlers are the world's greatest storytellers. Many of Earth's famous authors got their stories from taletaddlers."

"You've got to be kidding," Ethan said.

"Not at all," Daavic added. "J. K. Rowling had a particularly gifted taletaddler."

The flames flickered low, so Daavic approached the fireplace and reached into a bowl on the mantle. He plucked out a red marble with orange and yellow swirls and threw it at the base of the brick fireplace. A small inferno erupted and slowly rose from the floor, morphing into a little fire creature.

Ethan and Hayley watched as the foot tall fire creature jumped on a neatly stacked pile of logs and lowered its head to listen to the logs. The creature jumped to its feet and walked to the fireplace where it cradled its log like a mother cuddling her child. A faint whistle spewed from the creature and grew louder and louder. The small fire-being leaped into the fireplace with the log. The whistling stopped with a loud pop, followed by a red puff of smoke. They had landed perfectly into place on the newly burning fire. Then, as if getting into bed, the creature eased itself down on the log and melted into the burning fire.

"What was that?" Ethan asked.

"A firelyte," Hayley said. "The log will transform into a black firelyte diamond after it burns."

Ethan noticed a small pile of shiny black diamonds beneath the burning log.

"How did you know that?" Ethan asked.

"How indeed," Daavic said.

"I'm not sure. I just know."

"They are mine! I saw the humans first!" Albert shouted from across the room.

"No, you didn't – I did!" Newton countered.

"Irrelevant!" Linus rebutted. "I introduced myself first, so I own them."

"RGB – our guests belong to no one," Daavic said.

"What are those creatures, and why do you call them RGB?" Ethan asked.

"Pyrodevlins," Hayley said.

"Indeed," Daavic said. "Those little troublemakers are pyrodevlins. Albert, Linus, and Newton referred to collectively as RGB for obvious reasons, and because they normally find mischief together. There was a fourth that kept them in line – but Kepler's gone missing."

Daavic turned his attention to Hayley. "You, my dear, appear to have knowledge of our world."

Hayley fondled her ring, and Daavic took an interest.

"Interesting piece of jewelry. May I?" Daavic said as he reached out to take Hayley's hand.

"Very interesting indeed—" Daavic whispered to himself.

"I have more questions," Ethan interrupted.

"I've told you enough," Daavic said. "Come, Irvin will show you to your rooms. The Headmistress will answer your questions in the morning."

Daavic motioned towards the doors at the far end of the study.

"Rooms – I can't stay – my parents are probably worried by now."

"I'm sorry, but you cannot leave," Daavic said as he started towards the exit. "You may address your concerns with my mother."

Hayley followed Daavic. She placed her sand dollar on a study table, then turned and winked at Ethan.

When they reached the other side of the room, Ethan instinctively headed for the door Daavic had entered through, but as he reached for the knob, it vanished.

"You can't go out through the in-door," Daavic said as he opened the door on the right.

"The in-door?" Ethan pondered.

They entered the front room of the house.

"Wait. I forgot my seashell in the study," Hayley said.

"Run along and fetch your seashell," Daavic said.

Hayley turned to Ethan. "Come with?" she said as she grabbed Ethan's hand to pulled him along.

They reentered the study through the door on the left.

"How is that possible?" Ethan wondered. He reached for the knob, but again it vanished.

"Ethan, you can't go out the in-door."

"Why did you leave your seashell on the table? What are you up to?"

"I wanted to show you something I spotted before Daavic arrived," Hayley said. "I don't think you got those symbols on your palms from an evil cult." She walked to a bookshelf and pointed to a red book with black lettering. *Secrets of the Dark Realm* by Dakota Drakelan.

"How can this be—" Ethan said. His eyes widened as he stared at his symbol stamped prominently at the top and bottom of the book's spine.

"This place has something to do with my past," he said. "We should come back later and take a closer look."

A commotion broke out across the room as Hayley frantically chased after her seashell while Albert, Linus, and Newton enjoyed a game of keep away.

"They won't give me back my seashell," Hayley said as Newton tossed it to the waiting hands of Albert.

"I've got an idea."

Ethan ran to the fireplace and grabbed a handful of marbles from the bowl on the mantle. He rushed back to the table to Hayley's rescue.

"Catch," Ethan said as he pitched a marble at each of the mischievous pyrodevlins.

Newton held the seashell but panicked and threw it into the air as he reached to catch the marble.

"Got it," Hayley said victoriously.

"Not a firelyte capsule!" RGB screamed in unison. "We hate firelytes!" RGB threw their capsules to the ground, where they erupted into three small infernos that morphed into firelytes.

Ethan and Hayley were shocked as the firelytes each grabbed a leg of a wooden end table, hoisted it up, and whistled in unison as they marched towards the fireplace.

"Let's get out of here," Ethan said.

THE GRUMPLING

OF THE HOUSE

Ethan and Hayley returned to the dimly lit front room. It had a massive front door, ample enough for a small giant. A narrow black carpet stretched from the front door to the back of the room, where a tall black slab stood against the wall. A short spider-legged table sat at the center of the narrow carpet, a black leather couch with two end tables stood to its right, and two zebra-skinned chairs to its left. Dark hardwood floors encompassed the room.

"There's no ceiling —" Ethan announced, gazing up into the night's sky.

"It was there earlier," Daavic said, as if it was no big deal that a large portion of the ceiling was missing.

Ethan spotted a baseball-sized soap bubble floating above the spider-legged table.

"What's that?" he asked.

"We have yet to determine its purpose," Daavic said.

"A bubble only has one purpose," Ethan said. "Bubbles are for popping."

He approached the bubble and poked at it, but his finger went right through. He blew at it, but the bubble did not move.

"Must be a ghost bubble," Hayley said.

Ethan approached the staircase and gazed up. The stairs kept going up into infinity.

"Where does this lead?" Hayley asked as she pointed to a door under the staircase.

"That door is strictly off-limits," Daavic warned.

"I wouldn't go into a creepy basement anyway," Hayley said.

Ethan studied the wall opposite the staircase. The study stood to his left and another door to his right. A black chest of drawers stood at the wall's center. A small bench sat to the right of the chest, and to the left stood a giant mirror. Black marble material engraved with cryptic symbols framed the mirror.

"I bet that weighs a ton," Hayley said to Ethan.

Past the study door, a small green box sat atop a pedestal table that stood against the wall. Beyond that stood another door on the adjacent wall, a sign above read:

• THE HALL OF DOORWAYS •

"What is The Hall of Doorways?" Ethan asked.

"A hall with doorways," Daavic said. "I'm going to see what's keeping Irvin." He exited through The Hall of Doorways.

Out of the corner of his eye, Ethan spotted something green streak down the staircase. He turned as a large green moth fluttered through the air and landed on the wall at the base of the stairs.

He moved in for a closer look and spotted a green blob the size of a child's fist. Dark purplish eyes glared back at him and then blended into the wall and vanished.

"Did you see that?" Ethan asked. "A big green— something flew down from upstairs and landed here then disappeared." Ethan said pointing at the empty wall.

"Ethan, look—"

The phantom bubble drifted towards him as if attracted by an unseen force. It came to rest nestled against the wall where the moth had disappeared. The green blob reappeared, popped off the wall, and fluttered over their heads.

"I see it now," Hayley said. She chased the moth-like creature as it fluttered towards the back of the room.

"It wants inside that green box," Hayley said.

The tiny creature landed on the table and tapped three times on the side of the box. The lid swung open, the creature hopped inside, and the top swung shut.

"We have it cornered," Ethan said as he pried at the lid with his fingernails.

"It tapped on the box," Hayley said. She tapped on the side three times, and the lid swung open. "It's empty."

"No, it's blending again—"

"Ethan, the bubble," Hayley said as the bubble drifted towards them.

"Blasted tag-along," a muffled voice said.

The fuzzy green blob reappeared and popped out of the box, transforming in midair. A tiny green creature landed on the table in front of Ethan and Hayley.

"Gruggins McGhee, grumpling of the house, at your service," the creature said as he bowed and offered a handshake.

Gruggins was four inches tall with a mouse-like body and stubby arms and legs. His face was that of a grumpy old man, but tall cartoonish blue eyes softened his grumpy demeanor. A fat bulbous nose like Mr. Magoo's protruded from below his eyes. He had smooth skin on his face and belly, and short fuzzy hair covered the rest of his head and body. Brilliant colors accented his long moth-like wings – bluish-green with a purple and yellow eye pattern centered on each like the eye on a peacock feather.

"That dreaded bubble has followed me around for as long as I can remember," Gruggins said. He flopped back a tuft of his hair. "Every time I cloak, the pesky thing comes right to me. Throws a wrench into the whole cloaking thing."

The hair at the top of his head formed a tall pointy peak that bent forward under its own weight, like the top of soft-serve ice cream. Gold jewelry covered Gruggins from head-to-toe. Bracelets, anklets, and necklaces, as well as a chain that wrapped around his waist several times. Gruggins had bling.

Gruggins gazed up at Hayley, then to Ethan, and then back to Hayley. His cheeks puffed out as a wide grin appeared on his face. He fluttered off the table and onto Hayley's shoulder, where he hugged her neck.

"Miss Hayley finally returns," Gruggins whispered.

"How do you know my name?" Hayley said.

"Don't you worry, my dear," Gruggins said. "Your secret's safe with me – it's got you cloaked for a reason."

"Cloaked?" she asked, "what is that supposed to mean?"

"Not to worry yourself, whatever the reason, it will be revealed." Gruggins said with a calming smile. "Now then, who do we have here?"

Hayley gave Ethan a questioning glance.

"Gruggins, this is Ethan," Hayley said.

"There were rumblings we had unexpected guests," he said as he turned to Ethan.

Gruggins had a slight rasp in his voice. He fittingly sounded like a wise but grumpy old man.

"So, you're Ethan Fox," he said. "Ethan Fox this, Ethan Fox that, you're all I've been hearing about lately."

"I didn't mean to come here," Ethan said. "Please, can you tell me where I am – and how I can get back to my parents?"

"Are all humans this whiny? I'm sorry, but I can't help you."

"You've met our resident grumpling," Daavic said as he entered from The Hall of Doorways. "Are you being courteous to our guests?" he asked Gruggins.

"Always," Gruggins said.

"Irvin will be along shortly," Daavic said to Ethan and Hayley.

"Please Master Daavic, not that mush-mouthed morph-dork. I can't take his showboating theatrics. May I be excused?"

Daavic nodded.

"Thank you, sir," Gruggins said. "I bid you farewell," he bowed to Ethan and Hayley, fluttered to his box, jumped in, and shut the lid.

"Gruggins is easily annoyed," Daavic said, "and Irvin pushes all the right buttons."

"I don't think he likes me," Ethan said.

"Grumplings are leery of strangers, but he will warm up to you – eventually."

"Grumplings were nearly hunted to extinction by the leprechauns," Hayley said.

"Your memories appear to be returning," Daavic said. "Leprechauns fear the grumpling's ability to de-cloak the gold they've hidden. So, they hunt them, luring them with their favorite food – four-leafed clovers. Nearly finished them off until we stepped in and moved the grumplings – all except for Gruggins."

The sound of footsteps echoed from The Hall of Doorways.

"Gruggins McGhee is a goon faced flobbyknocker, and his father wears leprechaun slippers," a goofy voice said as the door burst open.

"Irvin – do not antagonize Gruggins," Daavic scolded.

"So, this is what humans look like – much uglier in person," Irvin said.

"Irvin, they can hear what you are saying."

"If you say so . . . Irvin McGillicutty at your service. Here to wait on you hand and foot as the Headmistress has ordered."

Irvin was nearly six feet tall with pale white skin that resembled candle wax. His smooth face had a vague definition, like a department store dummy. A black tuxedo with a bow tie and a rose corsage molded to his body as if a part of it.

"Irvin will show you a trick, but first, I have chores to tend to."

Irvin reached into his tuxedo and pulled out a tiny pouch. He tugged at a small string until the pouch grew to the size of a trash bag.

"I've been looking all over for this."

Irvin walked across the room and picked up a broom leaning against the wall. He opened up the now ample pouch and dropped the broom in, then tugged at a different string and the pouch shrank back down to pocket-sized.

"Cool—" Ethan said. "Awesome adventuring pack. What is that?"

Irvin looked at Ethan, then at the pouch, then back to Ethan. "A pocket tote," Irvin said with a smile. "And now, the moment you've all been waiting for—"

Irvin leaped into the air and morphed into a large egg with small arms and legs and facial features that resembled Mr. Potato Head. Landing next to Gruggins' green box, he sat perched at the edge of the table and rocked back and forth.

"Humpty Dumpty sat on a wall – Humpty Dumpty was a big fat klutz," Irvin said in a goofy voice as the egg slid off the table. Landing splat on the hardwood floor, the egg cracked open and transformed into a giant fully-cooked egg – sunny side up.

"How do you like your eggs?" Irvin asked as facial features appeared on the yolk.

"Scrambled," Hayley said laughing hysterically.

"However the lady likes," he answered as the egg transformed into scrambled.

"That was awesome. How did he do that?" Ethan asked as the pile of eggs morphed back into Irvin McGillicutty.

"Irvin is a mimic, a member of the shape-shifter family," Daavic said. "But unlike other shape-shifters, a mimic can only morph for a short time."

"Did you know that shnickyrooners and shnackleboxes and things like that," Irvin rambled, "they really only happen to old ice cream cones when giant tree turtles eat dirty diapers in a blue elevator of leaf monkeys making the leftover apple trees take the school bus?"

"Why is he talking like that?" Ethan asked.

"Who knows," Daavic said. "I've learned to ignore his jibber-jabber."

"Any final requests?" Irvin asked. "We've time for one more. Tell me the first thing that pops into your head."

"Tabby Cat," Hayley said.

Irvin morphed into a black cat.

"Tabby Cat," Hayley repeated.

The black cat changed into an oversized orangish striped cat.

"Tabby Cat," Hayley said with a smile.

As soon as the words left Hayley's mouth, a small metallic statuette of a cat appeared at her feet.

"Oh my," Irvin said.

"Where did that come from?" Hayley asked.

"Miss Hayley has summoned a copycat. It must belong to you, and its name is Tabby Cat."

"What is a copycat?" Hayley asked as she bent down to pick it up.

"A totem with exceptional powers. Only the true owner can command a copycat and learn its powers."

"But — I don't remember having one," Hayley said and frowned.

"Give it a try," Irvin prodded. "Spy an object and wish for a copy."

The copycat vanished, and a replica of Gruggins box appeared in Hayley's hand.

"How do I make it come back?" she asked.

"Repeat its name three times," Irvin instructed.

"Tabby Cat, Tabby Cat, Tabby Cat," Hayley said, and the copycat reappeared in her hands.

"Fun time is over. Take our guests to their quarters."

"Yes, Master Daavic. Follow me," Irvin said.

Irvin stopped at Gruggins' table, picked up his box, and shook it vigorously. "The leprechauns are coming, you flying green rat."

"Enough, Irvin," Daavic said.

"Come with me," Irvin said as he motioned towards The Hall of Doorways.

"I'll show you a flobbyknocker, you mush-mouthed, rubber-faced morph-dork!" Gruggins hollered as he erupted from his box. He raised a long tube to his lips, drew in a deep breath, and blew into the end of the blowgun. A dart zipped out the end and found its intended target, hitting Irvin square in the butt.

"AHHHHHHOOOOOOOWWWWW, the grumpy wart-moth shot me!" Irvin screamed and grabbed his butt. "I – I'm changing."

His screams grew louder as Irvin morphed into a purple goose-like creature with a bulldog's face and long clumsy antennas – Irvin was a flobbyknocker.

"Gruggins, what have you done?" Hayley asked.

"Don't worry. He'll change back in a couple of minutes," Gruggins chuckled.

"He does look funny," Ethan laughed as the two balls at the end of Irvin's antennas clanked together.

A few minutes later, Irvin morphed back into himself.

"W-w-where was I? Oh, yes – taking you to your quarters," he said as if nothing had happened.

They entered The Hall of Doorways and turned left. It was broader and taller than any hallway Ethan had ever seen. Huge doors lined both sides of the hallway with no space in between. Where one door ended, another began. Black carpeting covered the floor, and the mirrored ceiling reflected its darkness.

No lights were present, but a gigantic beetle-like creature clung to the ceiling. Bright purplish light radiated from its belly and reacted with the mirror. Light rained down several feet in each direction, abruptly ending in darkness – like an eerie invisible wall painted pitch black.

"Only use the numbered doors," Irvin said. "Except for the ones behind us, they are the negative doors, and they lead to the past."

The light beetle followed as they walked the hallway. Doors emerged from the darkness in front of them only to disappear into the blackness behind.

"Irvin, I need to get back to my parents. Can you take me to that door?"

"I'm sorry, Ethan Fox, it is forbidden. The Headmistress will meet with you in the morning, and then you will understand."

"But I can't stay."

"Here we are," Irvin said. "The sixth door on the left is for Ethan Fox, and the fifth is for Miss Hayley. Irvin has prepared very appropriate quarters for you."

"Thank you, Irvin," Hayley said.

"Loaded your Elemental Modulators myself," Irvin said. "Answer many of your questions the ELMO will."

Ethan entered a room that was exactly like his bedroom at home. Irvin had thought of everything. He spotted the ELMO device on his bedroom dresser.

"That might be of help," Ethan thought. Irvin said it would answer some questions.

The ELMO worked like an iPhone, so Ethan thumbed his way through the screens. Several apps grabbed his attention: The Residence Map, Caretaker Directory, Caretaker Training, and Hayley.

He pulled up The Residence Map and fingered his way down a virtual Hall of Doorways. The thirteenth door on the right caught his attention – the Map Room.

"That might tell me where we are," Ethan thought. "And how to get back to my parents."

"Are you there, Ethan?" Hayley's voice said from his ELMO.

"I'm here."

"Good, my ELMO has an Ethan App, and I guess it works," she said. "Have you sat on your bed yet? Mine is so comfortable."

Ethan approached his bed, and it transformed into a pillowy cloud that hovered a foot off the ground.

"You weren't kidding," he said as he eased himself onto the puffy cloud. "I bet these beds are sandman approved."

"Hayley, I studied The Residence Map, and this place has a Map Room. We might be able to find our way out of here."

"I – I don't want to leave. I feel like I belong here, and I think Gruggins recognized me. But I promise, I will help you find your way back to your parents."

"Good, I can use all the help I can get," Ethan said. "This can't wait till tomorrow. Let's go check out the Map Room now."

THE MAP ROOM

They followed The Hall of Doorways to the thirteenth door on the right, just as the ELMO had shown. They pushed through a giant doorway into an enormous room. Their eyes took several seconds to adjust to the darkness. They were in a vast circular room lit by dim floor lights that ran along the edges of the room.

"A dome room," Ethan said.

The walls curved inwards as they ascended. A thick blanket of fog hung high overhead. Towards the room's center, a small circle of light lit their way. When they neared the light, a black marble staircase came into view and disappeared into the layer of fog above.

As they approached the stairs, Ethan turned his attention towards the floor and froze mid-stride.

"Strike that – a sphere room," he said as he looked past his feet for the missing floor. The walls also curved down, forming a sphere. They were walking in midair at its cross-section.

"Like walking on invisible glass," Hayley said.

"This place is strange," Ethan said.

They ascended the staircase through the fog layer. Atop the stairs, they found themselves at the edge of a circular platform that sat dead center in the spherical room – like a crow's nest. At its center, a woman sat in a captain's chair with her back to them.

"Greetings," she said in a soft voice. "You must be Ethan Fox and Hayley – our mystery girl."

A petite middle-aged woman spun around and stood to greet them. She had sparkling blue eyes and a kind smile that put them at ease. Her smooth rosy cheeks were framed by silky long hair braided into thin strands of silver and black. She wore the same black and white robe as Daavic but a black and white butterfly with four spots colored red, green, blue, and yellow decorated hers. It fluttered around like a cartoon on the surface of the fabric.

"Irvin tells me you summoned a copycat," the woman said as she walked over and stood in front of Hayley. "May I examine it?"

"What's your name?" Hayley asked.

"I'm sorry, where are my manners," the woman said. "I am Jordanna Ravenwood, Headmistress of The Residence."

Hayley reached into her pocket and pulled out the small silvery statuette and handed it to Jordanna. Jordanna turned it upside down and studied its base. She let out a deep sigh and her eyes widened as a tear rolled down her cheek.

"What's wrong?" Hayley asked.

"My daughter's name was Hayley, too," Jordanna said, "and you've summoned her copycat." She held out the copycat to show them initials engraved into its base – H.R.

"Irvin gave this to her ages ago," Jordanna explained. "I thought it a silly toy until I witnessed what she could make it do. Hayley loved her Tabby Cat."

"You can have it back."

"Heaven's no, my Hayley's Tabby Cat chose you for a reason."

"What happened to your daughter?" Ethan asked.

"She went missing," Jordanna said, "exactly one century ago." Another tear rolled down her cheek.

"But it is curious," Jordanna said as she smiled. "You don't resemble or sound like my Hayley, but children don't show up here from the human world every day and summon my daughter's copycat. Especially children accompanied by Ethan Fox . . ."

"Where are we?" Ethan interrupted. "I have to get back to my parents, they'll be worried about me."

"Come sit," Jordanna said. "I'd like to show you something."

"Where do we sit?" Hayley asked.

Jordanna smiled and tapped at her ELMO device as she sat down. Two smaller chairs sprouted up on each side of the captain's chair.

"Come, sit—"

The platform began to disappear as they approached its center, and as Ethan sat, the floor completely vanished.

"—now recline back like this . . ." Jordanna said.

As Ethan and Hayley reclined back, their chairs disappeared too. They were floating in midair at the center of the empty spherical room.

The room walls transformed into a map of Earth – they were hovering inside a gigantic globe.

"This is cool," Ethan said.

Jordanna tapped at her ELMO. The globe rotated and zoomed to the United States. Two green dots appeared, one over New York and the other over California.

"This is what I wanted to show you."

She tapped at her ELMO again. The green dot over Santa Cruz zoomed towards them and transformed into a holographic screen that stopped in front of them. Ethan was comforted by the sight of his parents frolicking in the surf as Ethan had left them.

"We've been gone for hours," Ethan said. "They wouldn't take that long of a swim."

Jordanna turned to Ethan and put her hand on his. "Unlike in the human world, time is fluid here. The Residence allows us to go anywhere past and present. When you two arrived, a negative doorway opened. We can return you to precisely that moment at any time." Jordanna pointed at the screen. "I promise you – I will walk you to The Hall of Doorways myself and send you back. But first, we have other matters to discuss."

A river of calm rushed through Ethan's veins as he sensed Jordanna's sincerity. Then a gloomy fog overcame his thoughts, and in a flash, the eyes were watching him navigate a vast desert. Another moment, and he was alone on a beach walking towards his parents as they emerged from their swim and waved at him.

"Ethan, are you with us?" Jordanna asked as she squeezed his hand.

Ethan's vision stopped, and he snapped out of it.

"I – I understand," Ethan said.

Jordanna gave Ethan a quizzical gaze as she tapped at her ELMO. The Santa Cruz scene disappeared and was replaced by one from New York.

"Let's turn our attention to another matter," she said.

Ethan's bedroom appeared on the screen. A sandman morphed out from a wall behind Ethan and clung to it above his head to sprinkle Z's. Ethan seemed to fall asleep but then picked up the notepad next to his bed and started writing.

"You seem to be in a trance," said Jordanna.

"I don't remember any of that," Ethan said.

"Yet a moment ago, Hayley and I witnessed you appear as if you weren't with us. Like you were in a trance then as well."

"Well, I—" Ethan hesitated.

"You can trust her, Ethan," Hayley said as she rubbed the ring on her finger.

"I have visions."

"Visions – what sort of visions?"

"They always start the same, with me walking alone in the desert. Blue eyes are everywhere, peeking out from the sand watching me. Then I'm somewhere else watching as something happens – they almost always come true."

"The Seers – you've formed a connection," Jordanna said.

"Seers?" Ethan questioned.

"We don't know much about them. Never even knew of their existence until the unearthing of Stravis' journal told us of The Eyes of the Desert Sand, and the Hybrid—"

"Hybrid Child," Hayley said.

"What do you know of the Hybrid Child?" Jordanna asked with concern.

"Nothing that I can remember. It just rings a bell."

"Hybrid Child?" Ethan asked.

"Nothing to concern yourselves with. Just an unfortunate Caretaker scandal that occurred centuries ago."

"What do the Grimleavers want with Ethan?" Hayley asked.

"Good question. Something connects Ethan to our world, and if Victor is aware of what that is, that would explain his obsession with Ethan Fox."

"Obsession—" Ethan gulped.

"Ethan, I must ask something of you," Jordanna said as she gently put her hand on his. "Given what I've learned, I must ask you to stay. You will be safer here, at least until we learn what Victor Qruefeldt is up to."

Ethan pondered Jordanna's request. Returning to his parents might put them in danger. Besides, if he stayed, he might learn more about his past and what they were hiding.

"I'll stay," Ethan said.

"Thank you, and I promise your parents will never be aware you were gone."

The Headmistress stood up, and the floor reappeared as her feet touched the ground. She tapped her ELMO.

"We can discuss more tomorrow. Irvin with show you back to your rooms."

Moments later, Irvin arrived.

"Shnickyrooners and things like that," Irvin ranted as he ascended the stairs. "Did you know that blue lizard faced ice puppets are usually the only reason why light bulbs go out for lunch? And if it wasn't for the singing lips of frozen beetle arms then we never would know how the red trumpet bounces."

"Makes perfect sense, Irvin," Ethan said as he winked at Hayley.

"Shh – don't tell anyone why the little blobs of stinky white sock bubbles are still in the hall pantry next to the elephant poop," he whispered and smiled at Ethan as he had just found his new best friend. "Come – I will show you to your rooms," he snapped out of it.

"Here we are again," Irvin said. "Maybe this time you won't wander off. Trouble you will be in tomorrow – for wandering off."

"We're not in trouble," Hayley said.

"That's what they all say. I sure would like to be a fly on the wall when the Headmistress hands out your punishment," Irvin morphed into a giant fly and landed on Ethan's door. "It'll be curtains for you." The fly transformed into curtains that covered the entrance.

"Give up McGillicutty," Ethan said as he moved the curtains aside.

Upon entering his room, Ethan examined the apps on his ELMO. He found one about Caretaker training that explained their purpose on Earth – they were sent to nurture the human world. Black and white robed Caretakers all possessed the ability to evolve earthly creatures. They used this ability to maintain Earth's ecological balance and ensure that humans evolve naturally. It enabled them to evolve failing species that were important to the food chain, allowing them to survive when they otherwise would not.

Ethan touched the 'Hayley' app and heard her humming.

"Hayley—"

"I was about to call you," she said.

"Hayley, I studied the ELMO app that explains what the Caretakers do. They all have the power to evolve living things, but their laws forbid them from evolving humans . . ."

"Hayley – what were you humming?" Ethan asked.

"I'm not sure. I've had it in my head ever since we met."

"Sounds familiar—"

"What? I didn't hear you."

"Hayley, I haven't told you everything – I have no memory of anything before I was eight years old."

"What happened?"

"My parents' story is that I was in an accident, and until a week ago, I believed them."

"But you don't anymore?"

"No – I showed my dad that poem, and he freaked out. Then I overheard my parents arguing about me – they are hiding something."

"Our pasts, do you think they are connected?" Hayley asked.

"Jasper said something about our tangled pasts," Ethan said.

"I wonder—" Hayley said.

"Wonder what?" Ethan asked.

"I remember things about this place, and I'm sure I've been here before. But what is your connection?"

"Wish I knew," Ethan said.

"Well, I think we should work together to find out," Hayley said.

"I was hoping you would say that. I think we should start in the study. My symbol on that book isn't a coincidence. Maybe we can learn more about Victor Qruefeldt."

"Ethan – I was going to call you . . . I remembered something else about The Residence. There is a room here, a scary room that will tell us all about the Grimleavers."

Ethan pulled up The Residence Map on his ELMO and thumbed his way down the virtual Hall of Doorways.

"This must be it," Ethan said. "The Grimleaver Atrocities Memorial – let's go check it out."

A GRIM REMINDER

Ethan and Hayley met in The Hall of Doorways and made their way to the seventeenth door on the right. They entered a dimly lit room with row upon row of creepy life-sized statues on display. Some of the exhibits were massive and they stretched off into the distance as far as the eye could see.

"House of horrors," Ethan said. "Reminds me of a wax museum."

They approached a golden plaque that read:

**In memory of the brave Caretakers
who have paid the ultimate price in service to
humanity. May they serve to remind us of the
atrocities perpetrated by the Grimleavers.
We will never forget you.**

They crept into the dark room to explore. Light beetles clung to the ceiling and rained light down on each exhibit. Sets of two figures stood in each – a before and after. A gold plaque rested at the base to commemorate the victim.

"You were right about one thing," Ethan said. "This place is scary."

Ethan bent down to read a plaque:

In loving memory of Nicole Knight, survived by her husband, Nicholas . . . she was abducted and devolved into Earth's first vampire – the first of many vampires that now serve in Victor Qruefeldt's Grimleaver army.

The 'before' statuette of Nicole depicted a beautiful woman in a flowing white robe. She had a tan complexion and long ice blue hair that draped down her back between two elegant angel wings. Her facial features were soft and feminine except for the sharp canine teeth that peeked out from her pretty smile.

The 'after' version of Nicole showed a stunning contrast between good and evil. Grim-Nicole donned black hair and bat wings draped in black. Her tan complexion had faded to a dark grayish tone, and she had long, sharp vampire teeth and knife-like fingernails. Glowing red eyes glared back at Ethan as he studied what they had done to Nicole.

"Ethan, take a look at this one."

"This explains why all the doors are so huge," Ethan said as he joined Hayley at another exhibit that displayed a giant about twelve feet tall.

"His name was Gaball. They devolved him into a cyclops."

Gaball appeared to be a gentle giant with one enormous blue eye centered on his forehead. He wore blue jeans, a red plaid shirt, and snow boots. Gaball reminded Ethan of Paul Bunyan.

Grim-Gaball terrified Ethan and was much taller than before-Gaball – at least twenty feet tall. He wore pelts of fur stitched together to cover his body – like a caveman. A long sharp horn protruded from the middle of his head above his now black pupil-less eye.

Ethan peered down the long row of displays, and something caught his eye, another room with a bright light that shined towards them. He started down the row of statues, and a chill ran down his spine.

"Where are you going?" Hayley asked.

Ethan silently continued down the corridor, and as he drew closer, he could see into the room through a broad archway. He approached the backside of a statue well-lit from its front. The chills running down Ethan's spine intensified as he stared at the dark silhouette in front of him.

"What's wrong?" Hayley asked as she walked up behind him.

"It's him," he said. Ethan winced as he glared up at the figure of a tall man. Gargantuan protruding ears swept forward over his head like curved horns.

"Him who?" Hayley asked.

"Hayley, do you remember what I told you about my visions?"

"Yes."

"All but one has come true – and he's in it," Ethan said as he pointed at the figure.

They walked to the front of the statue and were shocked as they read the plaque:

Victor Qruefeldt

Once a respected Caretaker, Victor Qruefeldt is the founder of the Grimleavers. His murder of Odin Ravenwood and attack on the Hybrid Child are mourned in our hearts forever.

Victor later commissioned the Heldrik Vonn Grim puzzle box and has since committed countless atrocities by devolving earthly and elemental creatures into monsters. An army of evil to help in his crusade to enslave humanity.

To stop them, we have established CAGE, the Caretaker Anti-Grimleaver Enforcement team. Victor's crimes against the universe will not go unpunished.

"Hybrid Child—" Ethan said.

"Sounds like the Hybrid Child and Victor Qruefeldt are somehow connected," Hayley said.

Ethan looked up at the likeness of Victor Qruefeldt. He had piercing red inset eyes and wore a flowing black robe and army boots. Scars covered his disfigured face, and he had no hair. Bony ridges poked up all over his skull and gave his head a brainy appearance. Enormous ears were his most noticeable disfigurement. They protruded up and out and swept forward, coming to points over his head like large, tapered horns.

Ethan began to breathe heavily. "It's like a reoccurring nightmare and starts like they all do – with the eyes in the sand. Then I'm in a room with people around me. I'm not sure who they are, but he walks towards me. A bright light shines through an open door behind him, so only his silhouette is visible – until he gets closer." Ethan hugged his chest and backed away slowly as his teeth clattered.

"Maybe we've seen enough for now," Hayley said as she gently grabbed Ethan's arm to lead him away.

They entered the main gallery and veered right down a different row of exhibits. Someone was standing in the dimly lit corridor ahead. They approached and spotted a woman crying in front of a display. Not your average woman, Ethan realized as he glanced down at her coiled snake-like body.

"Was she family?" Hayley asked in a soft tone.

The woman's body rotated in place as her lower half uncoiled. She had brilliant blue skin accented by black swirls scattered over the length of her body. Her upper body was that of a slim woman's that tapered at the waist into an enormous snake body.

"Sss-she was my sister," the woman said between lashes of her black snake tongue. She had a gentle but hissy voice. A king-sized tear rolled down her scaly cheek and fell to the floor.

"I'm sorry," Hayley said.

"You must be Ethan and Hayley," the woman said. "I'm Brianna." She extended her hand.

"Yes," Ethan said as he shook her leathery hand.

"Nice to meet you," Hayley shook her hand too.

Brianna had pleasant facial features with long green tube-like worms for hair. They were as thick as licorice and moved and shimmered like satin. Tiny faces peeked out the ends and smiled.

"They say the pain sss-subsides with time, but it seems like only yesterday . . ."

Ethan glanced at the plaque and then at the exhibit. The before likeness looked like Brianna but with greener hues of blue. Ethan then turned to the after likeness. They transformed Brianna's sister Medusa into a hideous creature with an enormous serpent's body. Her vibrant colors had drained away to a lifeless grayish-green. Ethan grimaced as he gazed at the nest of black vipers with piercing red eyes that grew from Medusa's head.

"It's-sss why I joined CAGE," Brianna hissed. "We must stop them."

"You belong to CAGE," Ethan said. "Can you tell us about them?"

"We are a small team, at least CAGE leadership is small, but we have hundreds in the field. We've all suffered severely at the hands of the Grimleavers."

"The Grimleavers are very dangerous, so CAGE has an almost impossible task," Hayley said as she rubbed her ring.

"I will introduce you to more of us if you would like. Please join us for breakfast tomorrow, the eighth door on the left."

"We would love to," Hayley said.

BREAKFAST AND A TUSSLE

Ethan awoke bright and early and wasted no time calling Hayley.

"Hayley, you up yet?"

"Yeah, I've been up for a while."

"Let's start in the study today. We can follow up on the book with my symbol."

"I was thinking the same thing. We have time before breakfast."

They headed down The Hall of Doorways towards the study.

"Shnickyrooners and shnackleboxes and things like that. Have you ever seen a chocolate pig play ping pong underneath the fat noodle legs of a purple water rat?"

Irvin emerged from the darkness.

"No Irvin – but I'd love to," Ethan said.

Irvin smiled at Ethan's friendly response. "It's quite like the hair at the tip of a hockey puck's peach whiskers – but not quite as lonely."

"I think I'm beginning to understand him," Ethan whispered to Hayley.

Irvin carried a stack of newspapers in his arms.

"What have you got there?" Hayley asked.

"Hot off the presses, the first print edition of *The Residential Daily Star*. Would you like one?"

Irvin handed them each a copy.

"My very own idea. Caretakers have read the stupid app for centuries, but my new paper edition is the wave of the future."

"Thank you," they said.

"Got to run. I still have these to deliver before breakfast," Irvin said and disappeared into the darkness.

"Hayley, look—"

They studied the paper's front page, a tribute piece called: *In Remembrance of our Fallen Leader*s. A full-color picture of Odin and Ryvias Ravenwood accompanied the text. They were both handsome men and wore black and white Caretaker robes. Odin was slightly taller with long silver hair that fell below his shoulders. Ryvias resembled his dad Odin, but had long black hair and a darker complexion.

Ethan and Hayley read the article below the pictures. There weren't many details, but it did say that Odin Ravenwood was the second Caretaker headmaster. His friend, Victor Qruefeldt, stabbed him in the back so Victor could harvest the rib of the infant Hybrid Child.

"Why would Victor want an infant's rib?" Hayley asked.

"I don't know, but the story of the Hybrid Child keeps popping up everywhere."

The study sat empty when they arrived, so they beelined for the book with Ethan's symbol. He pulled it from the shelf and read the title out loud.

"*Secrets of the Dark Realm* by Dakota Drakelan. The Dark Realm—" he repeated. "My dad's videogame has a Dark Realm. I always thought he made it up."

Ethan turned to a page that described Dakota Drakelan.

"It says here that Dakota Drakelan is an expert on dark forces, the black arts, and creational sciences. He is a controversial Caretaker figure due to his belief in the existence of a hidden Dark Realm."

Ethan thumbed through more pages and stopped at one with pictures.

"These creatures are in my dad's game, he has connections to this place, and this is proof."

"Maybe we should talk to this Dakota Drakelan," Hayley said.

"Great idea."

Hayley spotted a title that caught her eye. *Weapons and Other Dangerous Inventions of the Chrysalis.*

She flipped through several pages and stopped on one that gripped her attention.

"Ethan, check this out," she showed him a picture of a small black metallic box. Hayley's infinity ring lay nestled inside. The paragraph next to the photo explained that the ring was a rift-key, crafted from the Hybrid Child's rib to power the Heldrik Vonn Grim puzzle box. Heldrik created only one – for Victor Qruefeldt. It was the most feared weapon in existence with known capabilities: soul reaping, rift jumping, teleportation, and instant death.

"Hybrid Child—" Ethan said. "Victor needed the child's rib for the rift-key."

"I wonder how it ended up on my finger? He must realize it's missing."

"He must, and we need to make sure he doesn't get it back."

Ethan and Hayley's findings disturbed them. They stayed in the study for another hour until Ethan's stomach growled.

"Sounds like somebody is hungry," Hayley said. "Brianna said they serve breakfast in room 8L."

"Yeah, let's go so that I can quiet my belly."

They entered a huge dining hall with white floors and a kitchen. The kitchen was a fully equipped chef's station, and in the dining area, tables were full of patrons that wore black and white Caretaker robes. An antique piano and bench stood against the wall. In the corner was a gigantic chair with legs that were nearly as tall as Ethan.

"Chef Irvin is slaving away," Irvin said from the kitchen as the top of his head morphed into a tall chef's hat.

"I'm pleased you came to join us," Brianna called out from a table. She sat coiled in a chair next to Daavic and another Caretaker as she waved them over.

Brianna and her tablemates politely rose to greet them.

"You've met Daavic," she said.

Daavic smiled and waved his red gloved hand.

"This is Nicholas Knight," Brianna gestured towards a tall man that stood to Ethan's left.

Nicholas had a muscular build and a tanned complexion, and piercing black pupils accented his pale blue eyes. He wore a long white robe with gold trim, and long white hair fell well past his shoulders. Behind his back, bulky angel wings protruded outside his robe.

"Hi—" Ethan stopped in mid-sentence, startled by the sharp canines that peeked out as Nicholas smiled.

"A pleasure to meet you," Hayley said with a smile.

"Unfortunately, Alexander Sturgis is on a secret mission, but Azron should be along sss-shortly."

"Alexander is always getting called away," Nicholas said. "Ever since he took over for old Dakota."

Ethan and Hayley looked at each other and then took their seats.

"Who is Dakota?" Ethan asked.

"A tired, crazy old man—" Daavic answered.

"He was our master of dark studies."

"He is Alexander's mentor," Nicholas said.

"Enough about that old coot," Daavic said.

"Are you all CAGE members?" Hayley asked.

"We are, and I for one am grateful," said Nicholas.

"As am I – to serve a noble purpose at such a terrible time has been lifesaving," Brianna said.

Nicholas nodded. "When I lost my Nicole, I thought life no longer had meaning."

"We viewed her statue in the Memorial," Hayley said. "She was beautiful, and what they did to her was horrible."

Ethan stared at Nicholas's teeth as a broad smile appeared around his pointy canines.

"Do I frighten you?" he asked Ethan. "Vamprils have no taste for blood – I can assure you."

"Vamprils once served as Caretakers in great numbers," Brianna said, "but after Nicole's abduction – only Nicholas remains."

The silverware on the table started to vibrate as the floor lightly trembled. A sizable shadow appeared as a small giant approached. He carried the huge chair to their table and sat. Even after sitting, he towered over the rest of their group. A section of the table rose to accommodate his height.

"Azron, these are our visitors – Ethan and Hayley, meet Azron," Brianna said.

Azron's enormous size took up nearly half of the table. He had scraggly black hair and thick whiskers that resembled burnt rice. Ethan gazed into the single oversized eye that bulged from Azron's forehead. He did not speak but greeted Ethan and Hayley with a friendly smile and gently offered his hand.

"Are you a CAGE member too, Azron?" Ethan asked as he shook Azron's pinky finger. But Azron did not speak and only smiled.

"You'll have to excuse Azron," Nicholas said. "Giants are shy around strangers, but he will warm up to you."

Irvin approached their table.

"If I may interrupt, Master Daavic. May I take your orders?"

"Certainly."

"I assume most of you will have the usual," Irvin said. "Brianna – one gopher ham and rat cheese omelet. Nicholas – one blood turnip, a side of buttermilk toad muffins, and a glass of dragon's milk. Master Daavic – two double-yolked eggs suns-up, waffled fish stick hash browns, and a dash of pickle dust. Azron – three platters of pancake leaves drizzled with melted peacock butter. Moonflowers sent a fresh pancake shrub just this morning."

Irvin turned to Ethan and Hayley.

"Our menu probably sounds strange," Brianna said.

Ethan's confusion must have been apparent.

"Our evolutioneer abilities allow us to grow plant-based foods into any concoction you might imagine – four-legged chickens, chocolate frogs – you name it."

"Our Mrs. Moongarden is quite the magician when it comes to growing things," Nicholas said. "Green fingers I believe the humans call it."

"Green thumb," Ethan corrected with a laugh.

The table broke out in laughter.

"Rest assured that no blood was spilled for your breakfast," Daavic added.

"What would our guests like?" Irvin asked.

"I'd like—" Hayley paused to think of something strange, "—an egg with three heart-shaped yolks, on a piece of apple toast, and a glass of blue peppermint milk."

"The number five," Irvin said as he smiled and jotted down Hayley's order. "And Ethan Fox?"

"I'll have . . . a piece of green chocolate toast, with two caramel yoked eggs on a bed of butterscotch leaves."

"Coming right up."

"Can I help?" Ethan asked as he stood and followed Irvin to the kitchen.

"Chef Irvin needs no assistance. I conjure flavors that make chef Ramsey jealous."

It amazed Ethan as he witnessed Irvin stir, shake, flip, sprinkle, and sort. Arms morphed from his body as Irvin showed off. He cooked every dish at once and needed no help doing so – Irvin McGillicutty had mad cooking skills.

A bowl of colorful cereal grabbed Ethan's attention. They looked like Fruit Loops, so Ethan slyly reached over and snuck a few. He turned away from Irvin as he popped them into his mouth. Delight quickly turned to disgust as these loops didn't taste like the sugary sweet flavor Ethan expected. These tasted like rotten fish and were slimy inside, so he spat them out.

"Ethan Fox ate grumpling food – Ethan Fox ate grumpling food," Irvin chanted as he handed Ethan a glass of water.

Their table erupted with laughter as Ethan gulped down the water.

"I thought grumplings ate four-leaf clovers," Ethan said.

"Four-leaf clovers are their favorite food," Daavic said, "but they like Rainbow Hoops too, especially Fish Gut and Snail."

Again, the table roared with laughter. Moments later – Irvin served breakfast.

"I can't believe this," Hayley said as her breakfast arrived. "Three heart-shaped yolks."

"Sure beats grumpling food," Ethan said.

The table erupted in laughter once again.

A four-armed woman with a red beehive hairdo interrupted their breakfast.

"Master Daavic," she said, "I am compelled to remind you of this morning's CAGE meeting – I am secretary after all, and attendance is most essential."

"Yes, Bella – we were just about to leave," Daavic said.

Bella had a yappy singsong voice that reminded Ethan of the nosey next-door neighbor type.

"I couldn't help but notice your breakfast companions. I've so looked forward to meeting our guests," she said.

"Bella Wentworth – Ethan Fox and Hayley," Daavic said.

"Pleased to meet you," Bella said. "I would love to sit down and chat – but duty calls, I must run along and prepare for the meeting."

Bella headed for the door but then stopped and turned back.

"I nearly forgot Master Daavic. My Boris has been missing for weeks now, so I think it's time for me to join CAGE in an official capacity."

"Bella, there is no evidence that Grimleavers even abducted your husband – but we can discuss this later." Daavic waved his hand and dismissed Bella.

"He's probably hiding in a closet somewhere," Daavic whispered.

The other CAGE members chuckled.

"We do have a meeting to attend," Daavic said.

"We wouldn't want to keep Bella waiting," Nicholas said. "She'll appoint herself CAGE leader faster than you can blink."

The breakfast room emptied by the time the CAGE members adjourned. Ethan and Hayley were finishing their meals when the piano in the dining area began to play. The piano appeared to be playing itself, but a small translucent figure was barely visible on the bench. Ethan's gaze met Hayley's as they realized the song was the one Hayley had been humming the night before.

"Who's playing that?" Hayley asked in a loud voice. She jumped out of her chair and approached the piano.

"How do you know that song?"

The music stopped as the creature bolted out the door to The Hall of Doorways.

Hayley pursed her lips. "Why did he run away?"

"Pepper is easily frightened, ever since his abduction," Irvin said. "Even taletaddlers are not immune to the evils of Victor Qruefeldt."

"Pepper is a taletaddler?" Ethan asked.

"Was a taletaddler."

"Where did he go?" Hayley asked.

"He normally runs to Gruggins when he is upset."

"I'm going after him," Hayley said.

Ethan and Hayley headed down The Hall of Doorways and heard a commotion as they approached the door to the front room.

"They're going to eat Pepper alive," the chants sounded as they entered.

It was quickly apparent that RGB were up to no good, but this time they had help. A teenage boy and girl with a ferocious four-legged pet were encouraging RGB to frighten Pepper.

"A burning fire-jay!" Albert shouted.

His forked tail rose, a red fireball formed between the forks, then shot out the end and transformed into a flaming red bird. The fire-jay zipped around the room and swooped at Pepper as a menacing screech erupted from the apparition.

"And a swarm of horned blue-goats!" Newton hollered as a blue fireball shot from his tail and exploded into a swarm of tiny blue-winged goats.

Linus shot a green fireball from his tail. "And a greenie meanie!"

The greenie meanie turned into a flaming green head that resembled something out of a *Ghostbusters* movie, but this one wore a menacing scowl and floated around directing obscenities at Pepper.

"STOP THIS NOW!" Hayley shouted.

Startled, RGB and the teenaged troublemakers turned to face their confronters as the flaming apparitions vanished in a puff of smoke.

The teen boy and girl approached Ethan and Hayley with their vicious pet.

"Look, Caden, our uninvited trespassers have come to join us," the girl said.

"We don't like trespassers. I should sic Malik on them," the boy said.

The teen's pet creature stepped forward, bared its sharp teeth, and growled at Ethan and Hayley.

Ethan looked into the creature's eyes. He held out his hands towards the beast, and the symbols on his palms began to glow. The creature stopped growling and walked to Ethan's feet, where it sat and let out a submissive cry. Ethan bent down and petted the animal.

"What kind of freak are you?" Caden said. "What have you done to Malik?"

"WHAT'S GOING ON HERE?" Gruggins erupted from his box. "Who is disturbing my nap?"

Gruggins directed his anger at RGB.

"Teasing Pepper again – I warned you, didn't I? If you ever did this again, I would think up a dreadful punishment!"

"Yes – Master Gruggins, we are very sorry," Linus said.

Newton and Albert nodded in agreement.

"If this happens again," Hayley said, "you will all spend the night locked in a box of firelyte capsules."

"No – not firelyte capsules," RGB cried out. They joined hands and bolted up the staircase. "Please, please, please . . ."

Their voices grew faint as they disappeared up the stairs.

"Well done," Gruggins said and smiled at Hayley. Then he turned his attention to the teen instigators.

"Blair Trabblemore, trouble follows you everywhere. Take your pet monster and leave immediately."

Blair Trabblemore wore a tapestry of red and black fabric wrapped around her slim body, arms, and legs like interwoven serpents. Her hair matched her wardrobe, crimson red strands braided with black. She had a pointed nose and chin, with eyebrows that curved upwards over her dark brown eyes. She was attractive, but wore a permanently wicked scowl – Blair Trabblemore was the original mean girl.

"We were leaving anyway – Grumpling," Blair said. "Can't stand the stench of humans."

Blair's boyfriend's name was Caden Stanley, a tall boy that towered over Ethan. He had blond hair, blue eyes, and high cheekbones. Caden was handsome with a sadistic streak – the perfect match for Blair.

Caden's pet Malik was a brutehound – a thick muscular dog-like reptilian with stubby legs. He resembled a prehistoric bulldog with razor-sharp teeth.

"Step aside—" Caden bumped Ethan on their way to The Hall of Doorways.

"You'll be sorry for that," Hayley said.

Blair faced Hayley. "What are you going to do about it?"

"Enough!" Gruggins ordered.

Blair, Caden, and Malik exited the room.

"How did you do that?" Hayley asked Ethan. "How did you calm that brutehound so easily?"

"I'm not sure. But – I could sense what that animal was feeling, and could speak to him."

"You were amazing," Hayley said.

"Who were those charming people?" Ethan asked.

"Blair Trabblemore, seems like I've disliked her forever," Hayley said and rubbed her ring finger.

"The Trabblemores are all mean," Gruggins said. "They blame your family for everything."

"Who's family?" Ethan asked.

Gruggins glanced at Hayley, then back at Ethan.

"Never you mind – nosy," Gruggins said.

A whimpering sound broke the tension.

"We still have work to do," Gruggins said.

They could barely make out the shape of Pepper cowering beneath the bench.

"Nobody is going to hurt you," Hayley said. "I'm sorry I frightened you. The song you played – I've heard it before," she said and then hummed the tune, "hmm-hmm hmm hmm-hmm . . ."

"It's working," Gruggins said.

Pepper emerged from beneath the bench and rose to his feet.

"Pepper, this is Hayley, and this is Ethan Fox," Gruggins said.

Closer up, Pepper wasn't as transparent. Tiny black specks swirled around his body – like flakes of pepper floating inside a body of clear gelatin.

"You're welcome," Ethan said to Pepper.

"You can hear him?" Gruggins asked Ethan.

"He thanked us for coming to his rescue," Ethan said.

"Evidently, Ethan Fox can speak with all manner of creatures," Gruggins said.

"Pepper can't speak?" Hayley asked.

"Not exactly. He communicates by manipulating the crystals within his body."

The specks arranged themselves into words on Pepper's chest.

"Greetings," Pepper said.

Then a sentence took its place, "Happy to meet Ethan Fox and Hayley." Pepper extended his hand as the black specks arranged themselves into facial features – Pepper smiled.

Ethan gently shook Pepper's hand, it felt like firm Jell-O and looked like that of a giant gummy bear.

"I'm happy to meet you," Ethan said.

"Ethan Fox might have some redeeming qualities after all," Gruggins said to Hayley.

Ethan noticed something in the front room had changed. The giant mirror had moved to a different wall, to the left of The Hall of Doorways.

"Wasn't that mirror over there before?" Ethan asked.

"Yes – and it's been here – and over there – and there," Gruggins said as he pointed around the room.

Ethan appeared puzzled.

"We have never moved it, yet it always finds someplace new."

"Well, my dear," Gruggins said to Hayley. "Off I go to my secret napping hole where nobody can find me."

Gruggins fluttered towards The Hall of Doorways. The door mysteriously opened, and he was gone.

"He doesn't like me," Ethan said.

"Gruggins has a kind heart," Pepper spelled out. "He's been a good friend."

Daavic entered through The Hall of Doorways and didn't realize Ethan and Hayley were in the front room. He proceeded to the basement door, pulled a skeleton key from his robe, and shoved it into the lock. Daavic paused and spotted Ethan, Hayley, and Pepper watching him.

"Run along," Daavic said as he opened the door and disappeared into the basement.

Hayley was rubbing her ring finger, but this time Ethan felt it too – Daavic was up to something.

Ethan and Hayley said goodbye to their new friend, and as they walked The Hall of Doorways, Ethan was pleasantly surprised when Hayley held his hand.

"You rubbed your hand," Ethan said. "Your ring told you something about Daavic, didn't it?"

"Nothing certain, just a feeling. I'm more interested in what Gruggins said to me. He said – the Trabblemores blame your family for everything. I think he was talking about my family, and he knows who I am."

As they approached their rooms, a rattling sound echoed from the darkness. The light from their light beetle merged with one above Bella Wentworth as she tapped on Ethan's door in rapid succession with each of her four hands. She was quite happy to see them.

"I've come to welcome you," Bella said. "Your arrival has rattled our CAGE," she continued, laughing at her own joke. "Caught our Headmistress off-guard, I'm afraid. Poor dear has been through so much."

Ethan realized that Bella loved to gossip and could be a treasure trove of information. He opened the door to his room and gave Hayley a wink.

"I'm glad you dropped by," he said and smiled. "What do you mean, she has been through so much?"

"Not for me to say, really – but the Ravenwoods have not fared well as headmasters. Jordanna is our first Headmistress after she took over for her dead husband, who took over for his dead father. Can you imagine losing a husband, daughter, and son all at the same time . . ."

"What happened?" Hayley asked.

"Damien Ravenwood killed his father – Headmaster Ryvias – and later abducted his sister Hayley."

"What happened to the daughter?" Hayley asked.

"She was never seen again. Damien is widely believed to have killed his sister too – but Jordanna, the poor dear, refuses to believe that."

Bella waved her four-arms around in dizzying hand gestures as she spoke.

"Damien is Daavic's brother?" Ethan asked.

"Yes," Bella replied. "Daavic witnessed the whole thing."

"Were Damien and Daavic close?" Ethan asked.

"Inseparable, they played in the Moongarden all hours of the day – used to drive Mildred crazy. When they grew older, something came between them."

"Mildred—" Hayley repeated.

"Mildred Moongarden," Bella said. "Old Moonshoes is a close friend of the Headmistress. She could tell you stories about those boys."

Bella blabbered off topic like a runaway freight train, and Ethan had heard enough, so he made up an excuse and told Bella they were late meeting Irvin to help with his chores.

After Bella's departure, Ethan and Hayley were left with a new avenue to explore.

"Mildred Moongarden," Hayley said. "Maybe we can learn more about Daavic and his brother from her."

"Can't hurt," Ethan said.

THE MOONGARDEN

Ethan and Hayley agreed to visit the Moongarden and then track down Dakota Drakelan later. They quickly found the Moongarden with the help of his ELMO – the twenty-first and twenty-second doors on the right.

They found themselves outdoors under a blue sky and scattered clouds. The Moongarden resembled a tropical garden with dirt walkways and picket fences that divided the numerous plant species.

"I've never seen such colors," Ethan said.

"Pleased you appreciate my labors – simply tickled," a voice said from behind a row of shrubs. "Tending to troubled butterfly shrubs has certainly put a bee in my bonnet."

Ethan's eyes scanned the lively shrubbery. Brilliantly colored flowers clung to the stems like butterflies; their wings opened and closed as if ready to take flight.

"Mildred Moongarden at your service," a woman said as she emerged from the shrubs.

Mrs. Moongarden was a short, plump woman with gray hair. She wore a flowered bonnet and had rosy cheeks and a kind smile. Circular glasses perched on her round face – she looked like someone's grandmother.

"My name is Hayley, and this is Ethan."

"More fun than a basket of daisies," Mrs. Moongarden said. "You must be very relevant – a negative doorway appeared after you, they tell me."

Ethan and Hayley looked at one another and then back at Mrs. Moongarden.

"You were adoring my Lisa," she said to Ethan.

"Lisa?"

"The butterfly shrub – silly. She told you her name, weren't you listening?"

"Mrs. Moongarden," Hayley said. "We spoke with Bella, and she said—"

"Bella Wentworth, a bantering Betty that one is, I bet she talked both your ears off."

"She did talk a lot," Hayley said. "She said Daavic and his brother used to play here."

Mrs. Moongarden's face lit up. "Oh yes, I haven't been reminded of the twins in quite some time."

"Could you tell us about them?" Ethan asked.

"I've rounds to attend, but you are welcome to tag along. I'll show you the boys' favorites."

A serious expression crept over Mrs. Moongarden's face.

"I must warn you though, do not wander off. Stick with old Moonshoes, and you'll be safe," she said and started down a dirt walkway.

Ethan and Hayley followed.

"That giant red flower must be the size of a car," Ethan said.

"Wendy is a withering froo," Mrs. Moongarden said. "Do you see the clusters of berries? Froo-berries are a delicacy, but very hard to come by."

As they approached the giant flower, Mrs. Moongarden smiled.

In the blink of an eye, the giant leaves beneath the flower snapped shut, encasing it in a balled up wad. The color drained from the green ball of leaves as they turned a grayish brown – like a giant wad of tree bark.

"And that is why she is called a withering froo," Mrs. Moongarden chuckled. "The boys would try to sneak up on Wendy and steal her berries. Damien was convinced they could, but Daavic grew tired of the challenge—darkness got into that one."

"Don't you mean Damien?" Ethan asked. "I thought Damien killed his father."

"Bigmouth Bella strikes again," Mrs. Moongarden replied. "Damien would never—"

"What's that odor?" Hayley asked.

"Smells like rain," Ethan said.

"Ozone – how delightful – we are in for a dilly of a treat."

Mrs. Moongarden hurried down the path, and they followed. She stopped at a group of small trees surrounded by a white picket fence.

"The scent of ozone always precedes the dance of the trembling nomads."

"Why are they fenced in?" Ethan asked.

"See for yourself," Mrs. Moongarden replied.

The trembling nomads resembled small penguin-shaped evergreens. They were three to four feet tall with small arm-like branches that hung at their sides. At their base, they each had two trunks that resembled legs.

"They look like little people," Hayley said.

"Why were they planted so randomly?" Ethan asked. "If you lined them up, they'd look like little soldiers."

Suddenly, the tiny trees trembled violently as if shivering. Then – all at once – their little arm branches rose as if shaking their fists at the sky. Their trunks popped out of the ground, and they ran around in random directions.

Ethan and Hayley laughed as the small trees ran about the pen bumping into one another only to bounce off and continue in a different direction.

"Bumper cars," Ethan said.

Then, all at once, the nomads stopped and dug their trunks back into the ground. Happy with their new locations, their arm branches returned to their sides, and they sat silently.

"That was so cute," Hayley laughed.

"Quite a hoot," Mrs. Moongarden added. "As you can see, trembling nomads do not like being arranged in neat little rows." She winked at Ethan.

"Mrs. Moongarden – what came between Daavic and his brother?" Ethan asked.

"I'm not exactly sure," she said.

They approached a wall of foliage with a dark tunnel. Mrs. Moongarden led them inside.

"Have you heard the story of *Jack and the Beanstalk?*" Mrs. Moongarden asked.

"Yes," Ethan said. "Fee, fi, fo, fum – are you taking us to a giant that eats children?"

They approached the end of the tunnel.

"No, but I will show you the beanstalk."

They exited the tunnel, and Mrs. Moongarden pointed skyward.

Ethan and Hayley's heads tilted back as they gazed into the sky. The beanstalk was three car lengths in diameter at its base. Its frame formed from thousands of intertwined vines – like a column of spaghetti hanging from a giant fork in the sky.

"Disappears into the clouds," Hayley said.

"Lois is a skyclimber vine," Mrs. Moongarden explained. "The 'swirling fan' pattern on her leaves are like a fingerprint, no two skyclimbers display the same pattern."

"Has anyone ever climbed it?" Ethan asked.

"I was getting to that. The boys tried, even though I forbade it. They were dear boys, but they did have an eye for mischief."

"What happened?" Ethan asked.

"I caught them and went to fetch their mother. They climbed down and hid for hours. I suspect they found a good hiding spot in the ruins."

"Can you show us the ruins?" Hayley asked.

"Certainly, they're up ahead," Mrs. Moongarden replied.

"Did they get into trouble a lot?" asked Ethan.

"They caused their fair share of mischief," Mrs. Moongarden snickered. "Created the zebra and giraffe I'll have you know."

Ethan and Hayley looked at each other.

"The boys were each assigned a species for evolutioneer training. One day Damien found his white horse species had evolved into a zebra."

"Daavic, I bet," Ethan said.

"Indeed," Mrs. Moongarden said. "When Damien learned his brother was responsible, he evolved Daavic's species into a giraffe."

"How did Damien find out?" Hayley asked.

"They never spoke a word about it. Neither why Daavic chose to deceive his brother, nor how Damien found out. Something had come between them, but they never spoke of why."

The path ended at a brick walkway that encircled a grass area with a fountain at its center. Beyond the courtyard to the right, a picket fence surrounded another grassy area. A willow swayed in the breeze, partially obstructing the view of a statue of a young woman. To the left sat the ruins of a stone castle where only a crumbling tower with a dark entrance still stood.

"I've saved the best till last," Mrs. Moongarden said. "The dancing angels are my personal favorite." She led them to the center of the courtyard.

Six plants surrounded the fountain. They had pumpkin-sized leaves at the bottom and long branches that rose above the fountain. Wilted lumps of tree bark sat atop the stems like balled fists.

"Withering froo flowers?" Ethan asked.

"They are a relative of the withering froo," Mrs. Moongarden smiled. "But they only emerge under specific conditions, and fortunately, I control the Moongarden."

She pulled out her ELMO and tapped at the screen.

"First, they need water to play in," she said as a fine mist sprayed from the fountain. "Next, we'll need a full moon."

Day turned to night, and within minutes the silvery light of the moon filled the sky.

"And now – we wait."

Moments later, the gray lumps began to unravel into elegant angel-like wings. The stems were budding with activity as the angels exercised their delicate wings, and a brilliant yellow glow illuminated them internally. Then – one by one, they took off – the dance had begun.

The dancing angels were hypnotizing and resembled butterflies but were more graceful. Their motion was fluid as they swiftly danced above the mist, and the light illuminating their bodies cast a circular glow where their heads might be.

"They have halos," Ethan said, proud of his discovery.

"A dozen candied fox tails for you."

The angels danced in a circular formation above the mist. One of the angels broke away and swooped into the fog illuminating the water from within like a bird in a cage.

As the angel danced in its watery cage, something spectacular happened. Water droplets hitting the angel's body would sparkle and bounce off into a shimmering cascade of gold.

"Pixie dust," Hayley said as she held her hand out to catch some beneath the fountain.

"Gold dust," Ethan corrected Hayley.

"Dancing angels do attract their share of leprechauns," Mrs. Moongarden smiled.

One by one, the angels took turns showering gold dust into the fountain until it overflowed. When they finished, snow of gold covered the ground around the fountain. The dance ended when the last angel rejoined formation. They returned to their stems and withered into ugly lumps.

"That was awesome," Ethan turned towards Hayley – but she was gone.

"NO, Hayley! NO!" Mrs. Moongarden screamed. She tapped her ELMO and the daylight returned. Hayley held a colorful golf ball sized fruit as she knelt at a vine that poked from beneath a white picket fence.

Mrs. Moongarden ran towards Hayley, who had a crazed grin on her face as she rose. She arrived and in one swift motion, swatted the ball from Hayley's hand. Another slap across the face broke her from the spell.

"What happened?" Hayley asked.

"You were in a trance," Ethan said as he rushed to her side.

"This is most disturbing – you nearly ate a petrified wood berry," said Mrs. Moongarden. "I'm sure I removed the fruit and pruned back all the vines."

"What would happen if she ate that fruit?" Ethan asked.

"She'd petrify – like Pandora," Mrs. Moongarden pointed at the statue under the willow where a wooden figure of a woman holding an open box stood. She had a crazed grin as Hayley had, and leafy vines grew from her feet in all directions – Pandora was the vine.

"She was alive," Ethan said. Chills crept up his spine as he realized what almost happened to Hayley.

"Yes," Mrs. Moongarden replied. "A petrified wood berry is irresistible once touched. The victim is overcome by the urge to consume it, which leads to petrifaction, vine growth, and eventually fruit pods."

"Ethan, did you see where the fruit landed?" Mrs. Moongarden asked. "I must track it down."

"This is what you are looking for, I presume," Daavic said as he emerged from the tunnel holding the colorful fruit in his red gloved hand.

"I trust such carelessness will not happen again," Daavic said to Mrs. Moongarden as he tossed the deadly fruit into the fenced area.

"I took every precaution," Mrs. Moongarden said.

"Obviously not enough."

"I can't imagine how this happened, but I will get to the bottom of this."

"I hope you enjoyed the tour," she said to Ethan and Hayley. "I'm sorry it ended with such sour apples."

"I had a wonderful time," Hayley hugged Mrs. Moongarden.

"Me too," Ethan said as he hugged Mrs. Moongarden too.

"I have something to show our guests – you are excused," Daavic said.

Mrs. Moongarden choked back tears as she hurried into the dark tunnel.

THE SECRET WISHING WELL

First, I would like to apologize," Daavic said. "I've been on edge lately, and I've mistreated you."

Daavic's admission surprised them both.

"So, how do you like the Moongarden?" Daavic asked.

"Awesome," Ethan answered.

"I love it," Hayley agreed.

"My brother and I played here nearly every day – and do you know what we found?"

"What?" Ethan asked.

"Not even Mildred Moongarden understands all its secrets. Many years ago, my brother and I became bored with the Moongarden until my brother had an idea – to climb the skyclimber."

Ethan and Hayley gasped as they gazed skyward at the mammoth vine.

"We didn't make it far before Mrs. Moongarden caught us. She was livid and went to tell our mother. So, we climbed down and hid in the ruins. Nobody ever ventured into the ruins because of the stories."

They hung on Daavic's every word.

"Stories?"

"Tales that something haunts the ruins. We hid for hours before poking around inside, and then we discovered it."

"Discovered what?" Ethan asked.

"A secret wishing well, hidden right here in plain sight."

Ethan and Hayley scanned the area.

"But nothing is here," Hayley said.

"Would you like to see for yourself?"

They both nodded in agreement.

"Follow me," Daavic said with a grin.

Daavic led them towards the partially standing castle tower. Stones had crumbled away at the top, leaving a jagged and uneven surface. As they entered, their eyes took a moment to adjust to the dimly lit interior.

"As you may have realized, it is quite dark in here. So naturally, the surroundings spooked us after a few hours. We pried at the stones on the walls to let more light in – and then we found this."

Daavic pulled a stone from the wall, and a pink glow emanated from the exposed hole. He reached in and pulled out a moon-shaped rock that glowed in the dark. He held it up, and its pearly pink texture glistened in the darkness.

"We were surprised to find this. It has such an irregular shape. Where would you imagine it goes?"

Ethan remembered seeing the shape when they entered. It matched a hole in the wall where a stone was missing.

"Right there," he said and pointed at the hole where a column of light peaked into the room.

"The honor is yours," Daavic said and handed Ethan the rock.

Ethan slid the rock into place, and the surrounding wall flattened into a smooth square panel. Four concentric circles etched into the panel before their eyes, exposing a pink glow. Symbols appeared evenly spaced within the circular bands. It resembled a dartboard with rings of characters around a small arrow pointing up in the bullseye.

Ethan and Hayley exchanged glances. They had both seen that one of the four symbols in the innermost ring was Ethan's.

"What is that?" Hayley asked.

"A selection dial or lock of some kind. We only tried a few combinations before we hit pay dirt."

Daavic spun the dials and lined up certain symbols with the arrow at the center. The symbols blinked, and suddenly they were able to see clearly in the dark.

"I can see all of a sudden," Hayley said.

"Me too," Ethan said.

"Dark light is what Damien called it."

Ethan pointed to a previously invisible staircase spiraling up the inner walls of the structure.

"Those stairs weren't here before."

"Shall we?" Daavic said and motioned towards the foot of the staircase. There was no railing, so they ascended the narrow steps slowly. The dark light lit their way to the top, where they found a dark tunnel. Dark light did not work inside, but the light at the end of the tunnel guided them, so they rushed through and quickly emerged into daylight.

Ethan rubbed his eyes as they adjusted. "What the—"

"How did we end up here?" Hayley asked.

They were back in the courtyard as if they had just stepped out of the stone ruins. Everything looked the same yet different – a wishing well sat at the center where the fountain had been, and the ruins were gone.

"I present to you – the secret wishing well."

Ethan and Hayley ran to the well, and Daavic followed.

The wishing well was crafted from a pearly-pink material. Solid gold trim and an assortment of inlaid black diamonds decorated the shell. The pink structure glimmered in the sunlight and from some angles threw out cold bluish hues.

"How beautiful," said Hayley.

"Quite, but there is much more to appreciate. The water in this well has curative properties, which is why I brought you here." Daavic turned to Hayley and smiled. "The well can restore your memory."

Daavic turned the well's crank with his red gloved hand. Rope gathered on its spindle, and a small wooden bucket with a golden ladle emerged. Daavic scooped up some water and held it in front of Hayley's face.

"No, thank you," Hayley said as she pushed the ladle away with her hand.

Daavic put the oversized spoon back in the bucket. "Suit yourself."

"On second thought," Hayley said as she picked up the ladle and gulped down a scoop of water.

Ethan wanted to take a drink too but didn't.

"That was fantastic, but I feel strange," Hayley said with a devilish grin.

"It doesn't work right away," Daavic said as he lowered the bucket into the well.

"Daavic—" Ethan said. "Can you tell us about the Hybrid Child?"

Daavic pursed his lips and bowed his eyebrows as he considered Ethan's question.

"The Hybrid Child is an abomination. Ever since the Seers intervened – he's been an idealistic symbol of hope for the foolish—"

Ethan and Hayley looked at one another as silence filled the air.

"Come – we've stayed long enough – we don't want people to hear voices."

"How do we leave?" Hayley asked.

"Simply step outside the circle," Daavic said as he walked towards the edge of the courtyard.

Ethan sat at the edge of the well and stared inside.

Daavic reached the edge of the brick walkway, turned around, took a step backward, and vanished.

Hayley followed Daavic. "Where did he go?"

Ethan glanced up as Hayley disappeared. He started after her but then stopped.

"It is a wishing well," Ethan said to himself as he dug into his pocket, fished out a coin, and flipped it into the well.

"Ouch—" a voice said from within the well, and a fluttering sound echoed up the shaft.

"Ugggggggggggg . . ." the voice said.

Gruggins fluttered up from the well carrying the bucket and ladle – surprising Ethan. He set them on the edge of the well and landed on the bucket's rim.

"Found my secret napping hole," Gruggins said as he jumped onto the handle of the ladle.

"Daavic showed us," Ethan said. "He and Hayley just left."

"Daavic—" Gruggins grumbled. "He and Damien used to bother me too. I thought I had everybody scared off with the ghost stories till those two showed up."

"It was you – you were the voice of the haunted ruins."

"It was me all right," Gruggins laughed but then stopped. "Promise me you will keep my secret."

"I won't tell anybody," Ethan promised.

"Drink to it," Gruggins said. He slid down the handle of the ladle into the bucket and stopped by catching his feet on the lip.

"Always parched after a good nap," Gruggins said as he scooped up a handful of water and gulped it down. He hopped to the rim of the bucket and peered at Ethan. "Drink to it," he said and pointed into the bucket.

Ethan scooped himself some water and drank.

"You better go, but don't forget your promise," Gruggins said.

Ethan exited where he had seen Hayley disappear. He reappeared in the courtyard where Hayley and Daavic were waiting.

"What was the holdup?" Daavic asked.

"I had to tie my shoes," Ethan said.

"We heard voices," Daavic said.

"Oh, that – I was trying to spook Hayley."

Daavic bought Ethan's explanation and escorted them out of the Moongarden.

AN OCEAN OF TROUBLES

After their tour of the Moongarden, Ethan and Hayley headed back to their rooms. On their way, they reencountered Irvin.

"Shnickyrooners and shnackleboxes and things like that," Irvin jabbered as he appeared out of the darkness. "You ever notice that wherever winged skunk rats play in the muddy popsicle drippings of fresh beetle dung there is always a piece of white pound cake dancing with a smelly old weasel troll?"

"I've never noticed that, Irvin," Ethan said.

Irvin smiled at Ethan. "Got you a present I did, a present for Irvin's new friend." He reached into his jacket. "Ethan Fox liked Irvin's pocket tote . . . so Irvin got Ethan Fox his very own adventuring pack." Irvin handed Ethan a small yellow pouch.

"Thank you," Ethan said with excitement. He tugged at the small string on the pocket tote to make it grow and then at the other string to make it shrink.

"Ethan Fox is already an expert," Irvin said. "Now then, the Headmistress would like a word with Ethan Fox and Miss Hayley. She is awaiting your arrival in the Map Room."

Ethan and Hayley continued to the Map Room.

"Ethan, I don't think Daavic did that to help me. My ring told me not to drink, but when I touched the ladle – I couldn't stop myself."

"Daavic was a little too friendly," Ethan said.

"Yeah, at first – but then he seemed angry when you asked him about the Hybrid Child."

"He did seem angry – but he also helped confirm one thing."

"What's that?" Hayley asked.

"The Hybrid Child has a connection to the Seers – like me."

They arrived at the Map Room, and as they strode over the invisible floor, Ethan trod softly.

"Please – have a seat," Jordanna said as they reached the crow's nest. "I trust you had a pleasant time in the Moongarden."

"I loved the trembling nomads," Hayley said as she took a seat. Ethan sat down, as well.

"My Hayley loved the nomads too," Jordanna said.

A loud noise interrupted as alarms sounded, and the Map Room came to life. The lights dimmed as Jordanna eased back in her chair. Ethan and Hayley did the same. The crow's nest vanished, and a detailed map of the globe enveloped the room, and this time two red dots flashed on the world.

"Tell us what we're looking at," Jordanna said to no one in particular.

"Troubles in the Pacific," a voice answered.

Ethan observed as Jordanna spoke to the Map Room. He realized the room had intelligence and an understanding of Earth's every interaction.

"Connect me with Fin. Poseidon must be aware of this."

"Certainly," the voice replied.

An image appeared in midair – a holographic window into a control room. An amphibious humanoid creature studied charts spread out on a table, and then he looked up.

"Fin Drenchler here – we've been expecting your call. Disturbing events have occurred, and the humans are very alarmed."

Fin's deep navy-blue color glistened with yellow highlights, and his oversized orange eyes bulged from his frogish face. Fish-lips and scaly fin-like ears protruded from his head. He had long webbed hands, and his smooth, shiny skin appeared wet.

"Elaborate," Jordanna said.

"First we have this," Fin said. A new window appeared with a live feed from a human news channel:

"Shocked Washington beachgoers bore witness this morning as killer whales washed ashore by the dozens. The death toll is climbing steadily as whales continue to wash ashore. One hundred eleven at last count, but it is how they died that has experts baffled. Many of them bitten in half, it appears. It's no wonder locals here are talking of sea monsters."

The news camera panned the long stretch of beach, and as far as the eye could see, mangled orcas littered the beach. Many had deep wounds, and huge chunks of flesh ripped from their bodies. Jordanna gasped.

"This could only mean one thing," Fin said.

Hayley rubbed her ring finger and then spoke loudly. "The Outpost – Inner Island is in danger!"

"The girl knows something," Fin said.

"Indeed, she does," Jordanna said. "What do you know of Inner Island?"

"Nothing I can remember, but you have to believe me – it's never wrong."

Jordanna glanced at Hayley's ring that silently slithered around her finger. "Your ring?"

"Yes, it tells me things," Hayley said.

"May I?" Jordanna asked.

"It won't come off. It doesn't want to," Hayley said as she tugged at the ring, but it tightened around her finger.

"Leave it alone. If it is talking to you, there is a good reason. It may help unravel the mysteries of your past."

"If I may continue," Fin interrupted. "Grimleavers have compromised our communications, so I suggest a face to face meeting."

Jordanna agreed.

"I will send a bubble-pod at first sun," Fin said. "Our safest mode of transportation for land dwellers."

"Fine, and I will contact the Outpost."

Jordanna studied Ethan and Hayley as she pondered something.

"I will include our guests in the under-party. They may prove useful," she said.

The windows disappeared and broke off communication.

"Patch me through to Commander Triplin."

Another window appeared, a pale man in a Caretaker robe answered.

"Triplin here. How may I serve you, Headmistress?"

"Has anything out of the ordinary occurred?"

"Nothing – all has been quiet."

"Are all three accounted for?" she asked.

"I checked on them myself less than an hour ago."

"Report immediately if anything unusual occurs," Jordanna ended the communication.

"Anything else?" she said to the Map Room.

"We've received word from Alexander," the voice replied. "He is reporting of Grimleaver chatter that Victor Qruefeldt has become fearful . . ."

"Fearful of what?"

"He did not elaborate, but our spies have sent word that Victor has received a leap-letter."

The Map Room quieted, and Jordanna turned to Ethan and Hayley.

"You two should get some sleep. Tomorrow you're in for an adventure."

Ethan and Hayley adjourned to their rooms, but neither could sleep a wink.

"Ethan – can I come over?" Hayley ELMO'ed.

"Sure, I can't sleep either."

Ethan was at his desk with an old fashion pen and inkwell when Hayley arrived. He was writing his symbol all over his pocket tote.

"What are you doing?" she asked.

"Trying to keep my mind off tomorrow. Besides, now we know whose pocket tote it is."

Hayley laughed.

"I wonder what a leap-letter is," Ethan said. "The Map Room said that Victor Qruefeldt had received a leap-letter."

"Don't ask me how I know this, but a leap-letter is a telegram from the future."

"Who would be sending Victor a telegram from the future?"

"Could be anybody, even Victor himself," Hayley said.

Ethan put the inkwell on his dresser with his pocket tote. He sat on his bed with his back against the headboard.

"I wonder where we're going tomorrow," Ethan said.

"Who knows."

Hayley laid down and rested her head in Ethan's lap. They both fell fast asleep.

Morning came, and a knock on the door woke them – it was Brianna.

"Rise and sss-shine, I've come to gather you for our journey."

Brianna escorted them to the study where Jordanna and Daavic were waiting.

"Brianna and Daavic will accompany you," Jordanna said. "You will book-travel to *Tunnel Beach* where a team of Seakeepers will escort you to Poseidon."

"Book-travel?" Ethan asked.

"I forget, we have first-timers," Jordanna said. "Some books in this room are extraordinary." She walked to the bookcase nearest the fireplace. The books all appeared the same – withered brown books with gold lettering. Ethan noted a resemblance to the one his dad had hidden.

"The books on this shelf are portals, and today's journey begins here," Jordanna pulled one from the shelf and held it up so Ethan and Hayley could see.

Tunnel Beach

"*Tunnel Beach*," Brianna read aloud. "Been quite some time since I've journeyed to Poseidon."

"I've never been myself. Thank you for accepting my request, Mother," Daavic said.

"About time you've taken more initiative. Fin's team will meet you on *Tunnel Beach*. Poseidon is their domain, so follow their orders and respect protocol."

"You speak of protocol, yet taking humans to Poseidon is against protocol," Daavic said.

Brianna's tail fluttered like a rattler. "Sss-stop questioning your Mother's authority."

"You've always questioned authority," Jordanna said.

An uncomfortable silence filled the air.

"Form a circle hand to shoulder – you must all be touching," Jordanna said as she handed the book to Brianna and stepped back.

"You may become sleepy but don't fight it."

Brianna opened the book and bright beams of light radiated from its pages. She stared into the light that shone on her face and snapped the book shut.

JOURNEY TO POSEIDON

Ethan woke up at the edge of a rainforest that nuzzled up against a secluded beach. Hayley sat in a patch of grass and watched as he slept.

"I thought you were never going to wake up," she said.

"Where are we?" Ethan asked as his arms raised and mouth stretched into a giant yawn.

"*Tunnel Beach* – don't you remember?"

Ethan struggled to his feet and studied his surroundings. The sight of Daavic and Brianna jogged his memory.

"The brown book—" Ethan said. "Hayley, my dad has a portal book that he keeps hidden in his office."

"We should tell Jordanna – we can trust her," Hayley said.

"She's not the one I'm worried about – Daavic is. Something's not right with him."

"I agree – I still can't believe I drank from that wishing well."

Brianna slithered towards them and cut their conversation short. Daavic held his ELMO up and gazed out to sea.

"They must have spotted something," Hayley said.

"Our boy is finally up?" Brianna asked as she smiled in her usual friendly manner. "First time is always the hardest, but you'll adjust."

"Have you spotted the Seakeepers?" Hayley asked.

"Yes – they'll be arriving shortly."

As they walked the beach, Ethan took in its beauty. They were on a fan-shaped beach with white sands that melted into the emerald waters. At each end of the beach, arms of foliage covered rock reached out to welcome the sea and form a broad cove.

"They're entering the shallows," Daavic said as they reached the water's edge.

Ethan scanned for signs of the approaching Seakeepers. Something had entered the cove and stirred up the water. There were several of them, making high arching leaps out of the water as they approached.

"Porpoises," Ethan said.

"Hydromorphs," Brianna corrected as five porpoises swam into the shallows and paused. They charged forward with the surf and beached themselves, the water receded, and the porpoises transformed. Their bodies rose from the wet sand as they morphed into humanoids.

"Sss-shape-shifters of the sea."

In humanoid form, hydromorphs displayed an impressive array of colors, each with a unique color scheme. Ethan recognized Fin Drenchler with his deep blue and yellow highlights.

"Welcome," Fin greeted the under-party as he walked onto the beach accompanied by two others. Two remained in the surf and alertly scanned the area. They were much larger than Fin and deep green with thick armored scales. They reminded Ethan of *The Creature from the Black Lagoon* – obviously Fin's security detail.

"I'd like you to meet my wife Lyn, and our son Gil."

Lyn was petite with floppy tadpole-like protrusions for ears. She had brilliant coloring like an underwater rainbow that appeared to Ethan like reef camouflage.

Gil was a mini-Fin with different colors – white with splotches of greens and blues and gold hints. He took an immediate liking to Hayley and smiled at her in a blatant display of affection.

"The bubble-pod will be arriving soon," Fin said.

A disturbance agitated the water as a hole formed several feet from shore. The gap grew more extensive and pushed towards the beach, forming two water walls that parted, creating a wet sandy walkway to a water tunnel.

"I will accompany you inside while my team swims along outside," Fin said as he motioned towards the tunnel.

"Might I swim along as well?" Brianna asked. "At least until we lose the light."

"Feel free. You can join us inside whenever you're comfortable."

Fin led them into the tunnel, where they entered a giant capsule of air. They stepped inside, and a firm buoyant surface met their feet like a giant waterbed.

"We'll walk to the nearest bubble port. The bubble port network is a series of depth portals we've installed. The depth drops off fast, so we won't need to travel too far."

As they walked along, the air capsule followed as they progressed deeper beneath the water's surface.

Crystal-clear water surrounded the bubble-pod and allowed them to view their surroundings. A beautiful underwater seascape with plant and animal life thrived in the tropical waters. Brianna's snake-like body adapted well to swimming underwater, so she and the Seakeepers swam alongside the protective bubble-pod. She looked like a cross between a mermaid and a giant sea snake.

The Seakeepers had transformed back into porpoises. Except for Gil, who had transformed into a boy in swimming trunks. Only his webbed hands and feet gave him away as he swam around outside the bubble-pod and performed stunts to gain Hayley's attention. Hayley finally took an interest as Gil motioned for her to come closer.

"What does he want?" Hayley asked.

As she approached, he blew bubbles from his nose, but instead of rising to the surface, the bubbles floated sideways and morphed into small seahorses.

"How cute," said Hayley.

"Big deal, they're just bubbles," Ethan whispered to himself.

Gil continued to blow bubbles in the shapes of fish, birds, whales, mermaids, and hearts that broke into smaller hearts.

"Enough flirting," Fin said to break up the fun. "We will be descending quickly from here."

Gil morphed into a porpoise and rejoined the others.

Brianna approached the exterior of the bubble-pod and pushed at the invisible barrier. She emerged inside like she was climbing out of a reverse water balloon – first one arm, then the other, followed by her head, body, and tail.

"Nothing like a refreshing swim."

Brianna dripped with water, but as each drop hit the floor, it absorbed back into the surrounding ocean.

They passed the edge of the underwater cliff, and the bubble-pod angled down like they were walking down an invisible staircase. As the light from the surface slowly vanished, the Seakeepers lit the way. Their bodies emitted a bright bluish glow that lit the bubble from the outside. Inside, Brianna provided light as the small tube-like worms on her head glowed a soft green.

They continued until they reached their destination. In the blackness of the deep, the team could hardly see, as bioluminescence didn't give off much light. What was visible as they got closer appeared to be a giant black cube that hung still in mid-water. It was much larger than the bubble-pod they were in. The Seakeepers disappeared beneath the cube and took their light with them. Everything got much darker as only Brianna's worm hair provided light.

The bubble-pod continued towards the cube on a collision course, but there was no collision when the time came. The bubble-pod melted into the cube, opening a hole in its side where a bright light shone through. The bubble-pod disappeared into the side of the giant cube taking the under-party inside with it.

They found themselves in a brightly lit room. The Seakeepers were already inside and in humanoid form. The cube appeared to be a furnished apartment with an instrument panel on one of the black walls.

"Bubble ports serve as remote quarters," Fin said as he walked to the instrument panel and hit buttons. "From here, we will take a series of slide tunnels. The bubble-pod is far too slow, so it will follow us down for your trip back."

The wall above the instrument panel came to life, and a giant map of tunnels appeared.

"The yellow line shows our path — only four depth portals away, but the changes in depth are extreme."

Fin punched one final button, and a broad tunnel appeared at the base of one of the walls. It resembled the bubble-pod they had arrived in, but a dim bluish glow lit the inside.

As they entered, the tunnel angled down at an increasingly steep incline until it became impossible to stand. The tunnel turned into a slippery slide as they zipped down its steep embankment. It was better than the wildest waterslide Ethan had ever been on. They slid for at least a minute before leveling off and ending at another bubble port.

They repeated the process three more times, each time journeying deeper into the abyss. As their slide down the final tunnel slowed, the blackness outside lightened. They rose to their feet and walked, and the tunnel grew brighter as they rounded a bend. The tunnel straightened, and a massive dome of light became visible, resting on the seafloor like a giant snow globe half-buried in the muck.

"What is that?" Hayley asked.

"An underwater city," Ethan said.

"Poseidon," said Daavic.

The tunnel curved towards the dome of light. When the team reached the light, there were no walls or barriers as Ethan had expected, only a dome of light encompassing the environment within. It was like walking from night into day with a single step. They were still inside a tunnel, only now it was brilliantly lit – like a tunnel inside a giant dome aquarium.

The surroundings reminded Ethan of a tropical coral reef, but this was much more spectacular. The visibility reached as far as their eyes allowed in the crystal-clear water. The golden sand on the ocean floor was the perfect canvas for the abundant sea life to glide above like an artist's brush. An assortment of creatures swam overhead. Giant seahorses swam outside the tunnel and were nearly big enough to saddle. Schools of V-shaped rays gracefully swam in perfect formation and turned in unison.

"I've never seen these types of sea creatures, and I watch a lot of Discovery Channel," Ethan said.

"No human ever has," Daavic said.

"Mermaids," Hayley said as she pointed to a group of three that gracefully swam by.

"Hydromorphs, actually," Fin corrected. "We often took merman and mermaid form when we first arrived in Earth's oceans, but several unfortunate human sightings convinced us of better options."

"How much farther to Poseidon?" Daavic asked.

"I thought this was Poseidon," Hayley said.

"Poseidon is over there," said Gil as he pointed and smiled at Hayley.

The tunnel angled down an incline, giving them a view through the ceiling above. Ethan gazed up at Poseidon, and it took his breath away.

Poseidon sat half embedded into the side of a seamount. The shimmering palace had been carved from an enormous pink pearl that was still partially intact. The palace structure appeared unfinished, but that was part of its allure. The spherical surface of the pearl abruptly ended where the palace began. It looked like someone had cracked open a giant round egg and erected a pink castle inside.

The tunnel ended at the base of a steep set of stairs that led to the palace. Many grueling moments later, they arrived at the top of the staircase. They found themselves in a foyer that led to a much larger room. The inside of the palace was as breathtaking as the outside. The doors, tables, chairs, staircases, and support columns were all sculpted from the polished pink pearl as if the entire palace were a single carved piece.

They entered a room with high ceilings and a grand staircase that fanned out at the bottom and forked at the top. Tall spiral columns decorated the interior from floor to ceiling like the inside of a giant seashell.

"Given the situation, we will start immediately," Fin said. "Please, follow me."

Fin led them through double doors to the right of the staircase. They entered the room and found the Seakeeper briefing team waiting. They sat at a pearlescent pink boardroom table, which was sculpted up from the polished floor.

Fin introduced his team, Brooke Troutland, and Marlin Trollwell.

Brooke was petite like Fin's wife, but her colors were more feminine with subdued pinks and whites, with magenta highlights that looked like lipstick. Brooke was in charge of the Pacific Ocean detail.

Marlin was Fin's right hand man. He coordinated Seakeeper operations, monitored human communications, and reported to Fin. Taller and thinner than the other Seakeepers, Marlin appeared to be a different species. He had long arms and legs and bigger webbed hands and feet. His head resembled a long smooth teardrop that forked at its tail end.

Everyone took a seat at the table. Ethan took out his pocket tote and fumbled it from hand to hand as he waited. He gazed around the room and spotted Fin staring at his pocket tote, then their eyes met.

"Ethan Fox, I've been hearing a lot about you," Fin said. "Would you stick around after the briefing so that we can chat?"

"Sure."

"Great – enough small talk, let's get started," Fin said. "First, we must take precautions." Fin held up an ELMO and scanned everyone in the room.

"What is the meaning of this?" Daavic protested.

"You will understand once we have briefed you," Fin said.

"Over the last two days, disturbing events have occurred," Marlin said. "Brooke will report the details."

A broad map appeared on the wall.

"The first event took place here," Brooke said and pointed to a flashing red dot. "Two days ago, a U.S. Naval submarine went missing. We intercepted their distress signal. The Navy has launched a search for their missing sub."

"Humans are always losing their naval ships," Brianna said.

"We located and cloaked the sub, but our findings are alarming. The hull was shredded down its entire length. Sadly, there were no survivors."

"No earthly creature could do such a thing," Brianna said.

"Exactly," said Fin.

"The second event occurred here, where it fed on a superpod of orcas," Brooke said as she pointed to a second dot.

"It can't be—" Brianna gasped.

"It can only be," Fin insisted. "They've released a kraken!"

"We have accounted for all three pups," Daavic said.

"Yet the evidence remains, only a kraken could cause such destruction. And there is more – we've tracked it to the *Mariana Trench* and discovered a series of tunnels."

Hayley rubbed her ring as it slithered on her finger. "It is searching for something – I warned you about the Outpost. Something is wrong!"

The room fell silent as everyone turned to Hayley.

"Indeed, you did, and I'm beginning to agree," Fin said.

Daavic shifted in his seat and appeared irritated at Hayley's participation.

"How do Grimleavers figure into this?" Daavic asked.

"That involves other unfortunate events and an old Seakeeper secret," Fin sighed. "Many years ago, when Ryvias was Headmaster, a Seakeeper named Newt Dripmore went missing."

"I recognize that name," Daavic said.

"I was the new leader of the Seakeepers, handpicked by Ryvias himself. I had reason to suspect foul play, so I decided to share our secret with Ryvias. A secret no Seakeeper had ever shared before – but I am about to share with you. Hydromorph blood is transmorphic."

"Transmorphic – no wonder you've kept that a sss-secret."

"What is transmorphic?" Ethan asked.

"It means if Victor Qruefeldt ever got his hands on a hydromorph – he would have the means to create an army of sss-shape-shifting vampires."

"Not exactly," Marlin said. "The effects wear off after a couple of hours. Regardless, this is not a weapon we want the Grimleavers to acquire."

"Which is exactly why I told Ryvias, I had a missing hydromorph – and there was a good chance the Grimleavers had learned our secret. I had to tell the Caretakers."

"Then why are we only learning of this now?" Daavic asked.

"Newt Dripmore was never found, and the Seakeeper secret died with Ryvias. We couldn't risk telling anyone else – until now."

"And how does this relate to current events?" Daavic asked.

"Two more hydromorphs have gone missing," Fin said. "Sal and Sil Finley, a husband and wife team. The Grimleavers have learned our secret – there is no question in my mind."

"Well, that explains the precautions," Brianna said. "We must return to The Residence immediately – we must tell the Headmistress of this news."

"The bubble-pod will not arrive for hours," Marlin said.

"Anything else to report?" Fin asked.

"We've received word from the field," Brooke said. "Our sources are reporting more of the same – the Grimleavers are worried that we will unlock the portals."

"If we have nothing else," Marlin said. "We will provide you quarters until the bubble-pod arrives. If you are hungry, a mess hall is close by. We have updated your ELMOs with maps of the palace."

The map on the wall disappeared, and the briefing was over.

"I will show you to your quarters," Marlin offered as he ushered everyone out of the briefing room.

Ethan stuck around after the briefing as Fin had asked. Their talk only lasted a few minutes, so Ethan used the ELMO palace map to find the way to his room. Along the way, he spotted Daavic sneaking down a hallway. Ethan was curious where Daavic was going, so he peeked at his ELMO map. Daavic was heading down the storage vault hallway, but when Ethan peeked down that corridor – Daavic was gone.

Ethan arrived at his quarters, and as expected, it was a replica of his bedroom at home; but now he had a waterbed. Hayley's room was next to his, so he knocked on her door. She answered and invited him in.

"What did Fin want?" Hayley asked.

"He was curious about the symbols on my pocket tote and wanted to know where I learned of Creator Stravis' symbol."

"You didn't tell him, did you?"

"Not exactly. I told him I had seen it on the spine of a book. But where have I heard that name before – Stravis."

"From Jordanna, when she said they learned of the Seers existence after unearthing Stravis' journal."

"Right, I remember now."

"Ethan, I have something to tell you. My ring has been teaching me—"

A knock at the door interrupted their talk. It was Brianna asking if they wanted to join her for lunch. They were both hungry, so they adjourned to the mess hall and shared a seafood tower. After lunch, the bubble-pod arrived, and it was time to go.

A DAMIEN SIGHTING

Upon their return, Brianna and Daavic rushed to brief Jordanna. Hayley returned to her room while Ethan decided to peruse the study for more research. Ethan was in the study for only a minute when his ELMO woke up.

"Ethan, I need to show you something. Are you ready?"

"Ready for what?"

Ethan's ELMO transformed into a small metallic cat. And in a flash, he was face-to-face with Hayley in her pink-walled bedroom — and she was holding two ELMOs.

"How did you do that?"

"I've been practicing. My ring has been teaching me how to use the copycat. It is capable of a lot of things. I don't even have to be in the same room or in view of what it copies. As long as I can envision the object, I can make a copy."

"But how did I end up here?"

"The copycat can teleport things too. And if I want, it can bring back anything or anyone touching the item."

"You should call it a swappy-cat," Ethan said with a smirk.

"Yeah, I guess," she laughed. "It can remember things too. Watch this—"

Hayley wiggled her pinky finger, and the copycat Ethan held turned into Gruggins' green box. Another wiggle of her pinky and it turned into a girl's hairbrush.

"It remembers the forms it had taken before," Hayley's face turned serious. "But here's where things get creepy. You might want to set it down."

Ethan set the copycat on the floor. Hayley wiggled her pinky, and this time the copycat turned into a small hairy creature about six inches tall. A small black gorilla-like creature with long hair, saber-like teeth, and piercing red eyes glared up at them.

The animal leaped on Hayley's bed and growled.

"That is a grindle," Hayley said, then she twitched her pinky, and the copycat returned.

"That creature was alive. I thought it only copied inanimate objects."

"Me too. Those were some shapes the copycat remembers. I don't think Jordanna's Hayley was the original owner."

"Jordanna said Irvin gave her the copycat," Ethan said. "Maybe it was Irvin's."

"Not Irvin – whoever owned it knew you."

"I don't understand," Ethan said.

"I haven't shown you yet," Hayley said. She wiggled her pinky, and a holographic image appeared in midair: the scene of a small cabin in the woods, where a man in a Caretaker robe stood on the porch with two boys. A teenage boy had his hand on the shoulder of a much younger boy – Ethan Fox appeared to be about five years old in the image.

Ethan gasped in disbelief.

"You had a brother," Hayley said.

"He's not my brother – he's my dad – George Fox."

Hayley's eyes widened.

"I wonder who the man is," Ethan said as he studied the scene. "Hayley – we need to talk to Irvin and find out who owned the copycat."

Hayley agreed, but they decided not to tell Irvin about the copycat's secrets. Instead, they would bring it up in casual conversation. Ethan touched the "Irvin App" on his ELMO.

"Shnickyrooners and things like that," Irvin said. "Butterfly trolls always meet their doom on the bald head of a flaming water hippo, and they never even get to lick the rosy lizard dew from the field of dripping rock monkeys."

"I saw that on the Discovery Channel," Ethan replied.

"Irvin McGillicutty at your service."

"Hi, Irvin – Hayley and I were wondering if you needed help delivering your newspapers today?"

"No one has ever offered to help Irvin before."

"I can't believe that," Ethan said. "You mean the pesky butterfly trolls don't help you cook the pickled whisker mushrooms?"

Ethan's double-talk perked Irvin up.

"Thank you, Ethan Fox. Irvin has made his delivery today. But if you'd like to come to Market Square – you can help me shop for Moonflowers."

"We'd love to help," Ethan said.

They met Irvin in The Hall of Doorways at the tenth door on the right. They followed a winding yellow brick road that led to Market Square. Along the way, Hayley pulled out her copycat and stroked it.

"Miss Hayley likes the copycat? The Headmistress told me she was happy her Hayley's copycat chose you."

"I adore it, but I think it may be broken."

She held the statuette up in her left hand, and it turned into Gruggins' green box, and then into a cat, and then the box, and then the cat . . . Hayley wiggled her pinky behind her back to fool Irvin.

"I hoped you could tell us where you got it, so I can have it fixed."

"Irvin purchased the copycat at Market Square. Irvin will speak with the merchant, the blistering hogwart of a scoundrel will fix the copycat."

Market square was around the next bend – an enormous flea market in the middle of a town square. Masses of people gathered around produce, and fruit stands, and tents filled with all sorts of goodies. A mix of humanoids and non-humanoids were present, bartering, and bidding on items from the merchants.

The town surrounded the market like a colossal U. Only the yellow brick road led in or out. Shops and cafes dotted the inner edges of town. Irvin bought Ethan and Hayley each a sugar-pickle soda and led them to a small courtyard.

"Sit tight while Irvin finds that scoundrel."

Ethan and Hayley sat at a table outside a small cafe. They sipped their drinks, watching Irvin until he got a safe enough distance away for them to follow.

"Sugar-pickle soda sounds nasty but tastes awesome," Ethan said as he glanced away from Irvin. "Hayley – isn't that Daavic – sitting with those two creatures?"

"Looks like him, and those are forest trolls. I wonder what he's doing here?"

Daavic sat across Market Square from Ethan and Hayley at a sister cafe. He was in deep discussion with the trolls, and they were laughing.

"They sure are laughing it up," Hayley said.

"Maybe that's Damien, and those are his wives," Ethan said.

"E-E-Ethan – it isn't Damien – Damien is right there."

Hayley's hand trembled as she pointed a few tables over. Damien sat intensely focused on his brother. Ethan and Hayley sat motionless and watched Damien watch Daavic. Damien snapped out of it and jumped to his feet, then he paused and turned to wink at Ethan before rushing off into the crowd.

"Ethan – we should tell Daavic!"

But when they turned towards Daavic, he was gone, and so were the trolls.

In all the excitement, they failed to follow Irvin – but that didn't matter because the scoundrel merchant had left town.

Irvin was sad, but Hayley convinced him that she had fixed her copycat. She showed him that it no longer exhibited strange behavior. They spent the next hour helping Irvin shop for Mrs. Moongarden – Irvin was grateful.

THE CRITTER

After delivering the items to Mrs. Moongarden, Ethan and Hayley said their goodbyes. Irvin was so happy he morphed into a giant smile to show how his new friends made him feel.

They headed back to the study to continue their research. Daavic sat at the desk near the candelabrum when they entered. He stopped what he was doing and locked something away in the desk drawer. Whatever he was doing was for his eyes only.

"To what do I owe the pleasure?" Daavic said.

"We thought we would browse the library if you don't mind," Hayley replied.

"Certainly – just stay clear of the portal books. We wouldn't want you to end up in a dark hole somewhere."

Daavic left the study. Hayley scanned the regular shelves, but Ethan made a beeline for the portal books.

"Ethan – we've been warned not to go near that shelf."

"Don't worry – I'm not going to touch anything."

Ethan studied the gold lettering on the spines and whispered the titles: *Frosthaven Gully, Nimble Narrows, The Straits of Borealis . . .*

Hayley joined him and read from eye-level down while he proceeded upwards. He reached the upper shelves and could no longer read the titles, so he used the nearby bookshelf ladder.

"Strange – the titles on the top shelf are written in symbols like on the secret panel in the Moongarden's ruins – and a book is missing."

Hayley looked up at Ethan. "Ethan – come down before you fall."

Ethan climbed down, and they returned to the regular bookshelves to browse more titles. The door slammed shut and interrupted them – Daavic was not in a good mood.

"I'll be needing the study – please run along."

They exited the study, and the front room was quiet. Hayley approached Gruggins' box.

"Gotcha!" Gruggins growled as he popped out of his box and scared Hayley half to death. "Oops, I'm sorry, my dear – hope I didn't frighten you."

"You didn't. I just wanted to ask you—"

"Been sensing a critter on the loose," Gruggins interrupted. "I thought it was a tribe of Nibblewarts the first time I sensed it. Passed through this room a moment ago, so keep your eyes open and holler if anything catches your eye." Gruggins disappeared back into his box.

"That mirror has moved again," Ethan said.

Hayley approached the giant mirror to investigate. It now stood against the staircase.

"Ethan – my reflection – that isn't what I look like. Is it?"

Ethan joined Hayley in front of the mirror. He was the same, but Hayley was a different girl with dark brown hair, and her infinity ring was giving off a faint glow.

"You don't look anything like that – but I have an idea of what's going on."

"What?"

"Do you remember when we met Gruggins? He said 'it' was cloaking you for a reason. I think your ring is cloaking your real identity."

Hayley held up her hand and peered at her ring. She tugged at it, and this time it slipped off easily – and Hayley's reflection changed.

"There you are," Ethan said and smiled.

Hayley stood in front of the mirror, taking her ring on and off watching her reflection change. Ethan wandered to the base of the staircase.

"I wonder what's up there," he said and started up the stairs.

"Ethan – don't go up there."

She tried to stop him, but he was halfway to the next floor already. He continued to the second floor and glanced around as he stood atop the first flight of stairs.

"Ethan – come back down here now!"

"A hallway there," he said and pointed to the right. "A huge dark room straight ahead, and another room over here." Ethan walked into the room to his left.

"ETHAN!"

She could hear him talking to someone.

"How'd you get here? You were just—" Ethan fell silent.

"Gruggins! Something's happened to Ethan!" Hayley cried out at the top of her lungs.

Gruggins emerged from his box and fluttered over to Hayley. He rode on her shoulder as she ascended the stairs.

"I won't let any critter harm Ethan Fox," Gruggins comforted her.

They entered the room and found Ethan on the floor unconscious. Hayley rushed over and knelt beside him. Gruggins hopped on Ethan's chest and examined his feet, hands, side, and backside after Hayley helped flip him over.

"Curious – that explains a few things," Gruggins said as he stuffed something into his pocket.

"What's wrong with Ethan?"

"Don't worry, he'll be okay – sleepy but okay," Gruggins said with a smile. He hopped onto Hayley's shoulder and produced a blowgun out of thin air. "This will wake him up long enough to get him to his room." Gruggins blew into the blowgun, a dart zipped out the end and landed squarely in Ethan's shoulder – he began to stir.

"Gruggins—" Hayley said.

"Yes, my dear."

"Do you know who I am?"

"Of course, but don't worry yourself – I won't tell a soul. It is cloaking your identity for a reason."

"I—" Hayley's words froze.

"You should tell your mother. The Headmistress has never stopped searching."

"Jordanna – Jordanna is my mother?"

Tears streamed down both sides of Hayley's face.

"You didn't know?" Gruggins said. "If I would have known—"

"You said it is cloaking me for a reason," Hayley interrupted as she stroked her ring. "We must keep this a secret, for now. I will tell my mother when the time is right."

"Agreed," Gruggins said. "I'm happy to have you back, Miss Hayley. I've missed you."

Ethan finally came around and was groggy when he woke up, but he couldn't remember anything. The trip back to his quarters went fast with Hayley's help. She draped his arm over her shoulder and acted as a crutch while Gruggins rode along for moral support. They plopped him into bed, and Ethan was out like a light.

A GIFT FROM JASPER

than could hardly see in the blistering sandstorm. He pushed forward as if guided by an invisible force. He had the strange feeling he was being watched, but that was not possible under such conditions. Ethan continued onward as the winds subsided. The heat from the sun made its presence felt, and soon the wind had stopped completely.

Ethan stood in a vast desert surrounded by tall dunes of sand. He scanned his surroundings and saw what was watching him. Deep blue eyes, thousands of them peeked out from the dunes of sand. They did not frighten Ethan but instead calmed him.

"Who are you? Why am I here?" He tried to communicate with them, but the desert was still.

A disturbance caught Ethan's attention as a sizable hatch slowly swung open from beneath the sand. A man emerged from within the desert bunker. He was tall and wore a hooded yellow robe. He strode across the sand, oblivious to Ethan or the eyes in the desert sand. The man knelt to pick up a brown book with gold symbols that shimmered in the sun.

A bright flash blinded Ethan, and he was abruptly somewhere else. A swift breeze blew back his hair and whistled through the branches of a nearby willow tree. Dirt with patches of crabgrass covered the ground on which the man in the yellow robe lie dying. He was older now, and blood from deep wounds pooled beneath his body.

A three foot tall blue bunny approached, walking upright, and knelt to hug the dying man. The man reached into his robe, pulled out the brown book, and handed it to the bunny as he took his last breath. Yellow spots appeared on the bunny's blue fur as it cried at the man's side. Ethan recognized Jasper and tried to get his attention, but words would not leave his mouth.

Another bright flash and Ethan was standing in his bedroom at home. Jasper held the brown book out to Ethan and pleaded for him to take it. A shadow on the wall caught Ethan's attention – someone was behind him, but he could not move. The shadow grew taller as it approached Ethan from behind. The tall devilish figure with thick swooping horns moved closer – Victor Qruefeldt was behind him.

Ethan burst out of bed and tried to catch his breath as sweat poured from his forehead. He pulled back the sheets to wipe his brow and found something. Under the covers lying near the foot of his bed sat a withered brown book with golden symbols. Ethan didn't understand, had his nightmare been real?

Ethan was still in shock from his dream. He reached for the ELMO on his dresser and realized that his pocket tote was larger than he had left it. Someone had opened it and was snooping in his room.

"Hayley, I need to speak with you."

"Finally, I have something to tell—"

"Hayley!" Ethan interrupted. "Come over now."

His tone must have alarmed her because she arrived in a flash. He explained his nightmare in every detail.

"It was only a dream," Hayley consoled Ethan. "Probably just a side effect from the dart Gruggins woke you up with."

"Hayley, I'm not finished. When I woke up, I found this," he said as he held the book up.

"That appears to be a portal book. How did it get here?"

"Beats me – but someone's been snooping in my pocket tote too."

"Do you think it could be the missing book?" Hayley asked as she rubbed her infinity ring.

"I can't be sure – but I'm not going to open it." Ethan set the book in his lap. "Your ring talking again?"

"Something is about to happen," she said.

The book came to life as the cover flipped open. The yellowish pages glowed as they flipped from page to page like a card dealer shuffling cards. When it finished, the book sat in Ethan's lap opened to page one.

"Ethan, the poem – The Eyes of the Desert Sand."

The opened book had not transported them anywhere, so Ethan flipped through the pages.

"The pages are blank," Hayley said.

"All but the first one, it looks like there were other pages, but someone ripped them out."

Wisps of yellowish light wafted from the book's pages and disappeared in wavy clouds of golden smoke. Ethan pulled his hands away as the book took over. The pages flipped forward then back as if searching for a specific page before settling on the first blank page. Writing appeared at the bottom as if written by an invisible author. Another poem was being written backward:

Cruel Intentions

He lurks in shadows to hide from the light,
With cruel intentions he feeds on fright.

An evil plan with dreams so dire,
The Silent Forest will burn with fire.

To find the key things must unfold,
At a Grumpling's feet a secret is told.

Four portals locked away so tight,
Unlock the door to begin the fight.

In evil deception the path will be laid,
through the back door the toll will be paid.

"Silent Forest—" Ethan said.

"Ethan," Hayley interrupted. "My name is Hayley Ravenwood – I am Jordanna's daughter."

Ethan's jaw dropped open. "But – how?" he said. "Jordanna's Hayley went missing one hundred years ago."

"I don't know how – but I bet it has something to do with this rift-key."

"How did you find out?"

"Gruggins – I asked him to keep my secret. And I would tell my mother."

"What are we going to do about this?" Ethan asked and pointed to the poem that had just appeared.

"I think we should talk to my mother about this – but I have to tell her the truth first."

"I have a feeling that she already knows," Ethan said.

A GALLERY OF MEMORIES

Ethan woke up bright and early. Someone slipped a note under his door. As he pulled the message from the envelope, a fragrant scent reminded him of Jordanna. The note read:

Dear Ethan,

We've made little progress in discovering why you were lured to The Residence. A new discovery has been brought to my attention that we should discuss. Please gather Hayley and meet me in the front room. I have something to show you.

Sincerely yours,

Jordanna Ravenwood

Ethan ELMO'ed Hayley.

"Jordanna sent me a message and wants us to meet her in the front room."

"Good, I'd like you to be present when I tell her."

They entered the front room, and Jordanna was standing next to the giant mirror that had moved again – this time to the right of the front door.

"That was fast. I'm pleased you rushed," Jordanna said with a smile.

"Your note sounded important," Ethan said.

"Please, follow me," Jordanna said.

"Wait—" Hayley said. "First, I need to show you something."

Hayley slowly approached her mother. A tear peeked out from the corner of Jordanna's eye as Hayley neared and slowly slid her infinity ring off her finger. Tears streamed from Jordanna's eyes as she fell to her knees and hugged her daughter.

"My Hayley – you haven't aged a day," Jordanna cried. "I suspected you were my daughter, but I couldn't risk exposing you. There were too many coincidences, but you've been cloaked for a reason."

Ethan wiped his wet cheeks as he witnessed the tearful reunion. Hayley and her mother embraced for several minutes before regaining their composure.

"Now then," Jordanna said. "We must keep this a secret until we know why this ring is cloaking you."

"That isn't a ring – it's a rift-key," Ethan said.

"Rift-key—" Jordanna repeated. "That would explain the time jump and cloaking ability."

Hayley put it back on her finger, and her reflection changed again.

"But – I still see my Hayley."

"It no longer regards you as a threat," Hayley said.

"Well then," Jordanna said with a smile. "Let us move on to matters at hand – follow me."

She opened the door to the left of the front door. A cool breeze rushed by and gave Ethan the chills. They followed a dark hallway that curved right. There were no lights or windows, but the light from the end of the hallway shone their way.

They emerged into an enormous room with very high ceilings and scaffolding around its outer edges. The place resembled a brightly lit aircraft hangar with white canvas walls that ascended eighty feet straight up. Hundreds of paintings randomly hung scattered along the walls like postage stamps. A small elf-like creature hung from a rope in front of each painting.

"Welcome to our Gallery," Jordanna said. "The Gallery catalogs happenings past and present."

A portly elf waddled up to greet them. He wore a black suit jacket with worn blue jeans and red sneakers. Much older than the rest, he had gray hair and round glasses perched upon his long-pointed nose.

"This is our curator, Dorkin Drumbles," Jordanna introduced. "Most of our gallery workers are forest elves, uniquely adapted for hanging in trees – we'd have a difficult time otherwise."

"Help out we do," Dorkin had a quirky voice that reminded Ethan of Yoda. "Monitor the artwork, collect and mount for display, a crucial task it is."

Ethan scanned the enormous room as the elves cut finished pieces from the walls and collected them. The cutaway canvas magically grew back like a healing wound. Many of the paintings were still being painted – by invisible artists. Next to each unfinished piece, an elf hung from a rope and patiently held a palette of paint. Floating brushes magically dabbed at the palette and painted on the enormous canvas.

"Take finished pieces we do – for determination," Dorkin said as he motioned towards the floor area.

Two areas divided the floor, and in one, a team of elves mounted finished works into frames. In the other, elves placed finished works on easels while three old hags hunched over and studied them.

"The Fates determine significance," Jordanna said and pointed to the old hags. "If deemed important, we move them to the viewing hall. Otherwise, we catalog and store them away."

"Who is creating the paintings?" Ethan asked.

"We do not know, but we have never questioned the validity of a piece's significance."

"Why I sent for you it is, significant the new painting is."

They walked to a corridor at the far side of the room. The viewing hall had hundreds of paintings on its walls. Small spotlights brightly lit each image. They were in no particular order but were all framed and engraved with a caption at the bottom.

As they continued, something grabbed Ethan's attention. A painting of a desert landscape with blue eyes peeking out from within the dunes. They were watching a man in a yellow robe hunched over a baby bundled in a blanket and laying in the sand. A hatch lay open behind the man exposing a staircase descending into the sand – the entrance to a desert bunker.

They rounded a bend, and the paintings stopped, and only blank walls continued into the distance. Dorkin pointed at the last painting in the hall that was covered by a sheet.

"This one it is," Dorkin trembled with excitement.

Jordanna unveiled the painting of Ethan and Hayley on the boardwalk the moment they had first spotted one another. Ethan held his hand up to block the sun while Hayley looked back at him.

"I don't understand. We've already been through that," Hayley said.

"It isn't always obvious at first. Inspect the scene. Does anything appear out of place?"

"Him – that man is watching Ethan."

"Indeed, he is," Jordanna said.

The man sat on a bench with his hands in the pockets of his brown trench coat. He wore a black wide-brimmed hat and dark sunglasses.

"That day was warm. Nobody in their right mind would have worn a coat," Ethan said.

"Do you think he's a Grimleaver?" Hayley asked.

"Possibly, but they rarely venture into the human world," Jordanna said.

"They did the first time," Ethan said.

"Yes, they did." Jordanna agreed.

They stared at the painting for several more minutes, but nothing new came to mind, so they adjourned back to the front room.

THE FOUR PORTALS

Jordanna sat in a chair next to the spider-legged table in the room's center, and Hayley sat across from her. The phantom bubble hung motionless above the table. Ethan studied the narrow black carpet that ran from the front door to the marble slab against the far wall. A smile formed on his face as his eyes followed the rug to the front door – curiosity got the best of him.

"If this is the front room," he said as he approached the door, "then what's in the front yard?" Ethan yanked the door open, and a bright light shone into the front room as he and Hayley's eyes grew wide in surprise.

A black and white checkerboard plane stretched in all directions like an endless tiled floor. The blue sky appeared vibrant in the bright sun – yet no sun was visible. Giant dead trees lined the horizon, and their leafless limbs reached towards the sky as if in agony. Four colored metallic spheres hovered several feet above the checkered plane.

"What are those?" Ethan asked as he pointed at the basketball-sized orbs.

"They are portals," Jordanna said.

The four spheres hovered side by side in a row, each held in place by an electric field of a matching color: one red, one green, one blue, and one yellow. The electric fields emanated from beneath the checkered plane and blasted up like colorful bolts of lightning.

"Portals to where?" Ethan asked. "I'm going to take a closer look." Ethan stepped through the doorway, but he didn't make it far. His body reflected into The Residence as if he had just walked in from outside.

"You've discovered the lock, and it appears to be still working," Jordanna said. "Let me demonstrate." A rubber ball appeared in her hand, and she tossed it through the doorway. The ball disappeared for a second and then zipped right back in as if thrown from the other side.

"They've locked the doorway to the four portals so no one can use them," Jordanna said.

The bright sunless day outside lit the front room as colored beams of light reflected off the metallic spheres and created a pattern that danced along the carpet. Ethan studied the curious pattern as he closed the door.

"Those spheres are portals to the elemental worlds of the Chrysalis. Atlantis, Ceres, Hades, and Zephyr – our home worlds."

"Caretakers are aliens?" Ethan asked.

"More like distant cousins – the elemental worlds are a coalition of planets united under the Chrysalis."

"Chrysalis?" Hayley questioned.

"The Chrysalis is the energy that surrounds the elemental worlds and shields them and any planet under our protection. Earth is currently under such protection."

"Why would Earth need protection?" Ethan asked.

"To make a long story short, The Destroyer – evil's ultimate. When The Designer finished his greatest design, he needed a world to house them. So, he called upon our Council of Elders to select four Creators. Each elemental world chose one – Driveous, Vraitor, Zamalador, and Stravis."

Ethan was beginning to understand – the emblem on their robes – the candelabrum – the red, green, blue, and yellow. All representative of the four elemental worlds of the Chrysalis.

"The portals are created as a side effect when we pull a finished planet into the Chrysalis – they serve to transport us to and from the elemental worlds. Upon extraction, the portals serve a different purpose."

"Why lock them?" Ethan asked.

"In Earth's case, a Great Exodus occurred, and creatures from our worlds migrated here in vast numbers. The Creators returned to fix the situation and prevent a repeat; the Creators locked the portals when they left. The lock will only open upon discovery of the portal prophecies as written in the Book of Creators."

"What are the portal prophecies?" Hayley asked.

"For the lack of a better term, they are a countdown if you will. A series of events will occur, and when the last of them has come to pass, we must perform 'The Ritual of the Pyrodevlins' or the Chrysalis will perish."

Hayley gasped at the thought, but Ethan remained silent as he retrieved his pocket tote and tugged at its string to make it grow.

"Mrs. Ravenwood, the portal books in the study, why do the ones on the top shelf have symbols instead of letters?"

"Someone's been snooping," Jordanna said as she smiled at Ethan. "The books on that shelf are extraordinary. The symbols are from the secret language of the Creators. I can't read what is on those books – no Caretaker can."

"Mrs. Ravenwood – the Silent Forest is in danger."

Jordanna smirked at Ethan's mention of the Silent Forest. "And what would you know of the Silent Forest?" she asked.

Jordanna listened closely as Ethan described his scary dream. Ethan reached inside his pocket tote. "I woke up soaked in sweat, so I pulled back the sheets, and I found this—" Ethan held up the book for Jordanna, and its golden symbols glowed in the dim light of the front room – Jordanna gasped.

"We thought it might be the missing book from the top shelf," Hayley said.

"May I?" Jordanna asked.

Ethan handed the book to Jordanna, but the symbols faded away as soon as it left his hands, leaving only the worn brown cover. Jordanna studied the book and gently flipped through the pages but then stopped.

"No, this is not the missing portal – but it is curious."

She handed the book back to Ethan. Once in his grasp, the golden symbols returned to the book's cover. He flipped to the poem page and gave it back to Jordanna as he described how the book came to life and wrote before their eyes. Jordanna read the poem and sat silently.

"For now, we will keep this between us."

Ethan and Hayley nodded in agreement.

"It appears you've received a significant gift, Ethan Fox. But until we are sure its intentions are pure, I will keep it for now. You and Hayley will accompany my team to the Silent Forest." She tapped her ELMO device. "Please have Daavic, Nicholas, Gruggins, Azron, and RGB report to the study at once."

THE HELL-GIANT

They rushed into the study, and the others soon joined. The in-door opened, and Ethan's gaze went up as Azron's enormous frame entered.

"I believe you've met Azron," Jordanna said.

"Hi Azron," Ethan and Hayley said.

The giant smiled and winked his single jumbo eye at them.

Jordanna briefed the team and told them she had reason to believe the Silent Forest was in danger.

"Certainly, you're going to tell us more," Daavic said.

"Do not question your mother's authority," Nicholas said, jumping to Jordanna's defense.

"You will book-travel to *Blind Man's Bluff*," Jordanna said. "You will camp cliff side. I've sent for Sol. He will fly you to the clearing in the morning when the winds are favorable. Any questions?"

"What is the Silent Forest?" Hayley asked.

"A hidden ecosystem created after the Great Exodus. The Creators created many secret ecosystems to house non-native species and hide them from the human world."

Everyone appeared surprised as Jordanna spoke openly to Ethan and Hayley.

"I've shown them the portals," Jordanna confessed, "I've told them everything."

The room fell silent.

"Daavic, you will take care of RGB. Keep them balled up until you need them. Unleash them on Nicholas' command. Gruggins, you'll ride along with Hayley. Azron, protect our guests and make sure they return unharmed."

"Mrs. Jordanna?" Linus asked.

"Yes, Linus."

"Do we have to stay balled up? We need to keep our eyes out for Kepler."

"Very well – but remain balled up until you reach the bluff."

Satisfied by her answer, RGB morphed into balls so Daavic could gather them up.

"Let's get on with this," she ordered.

Jordanna held out a portal book, and the cover read:

Blind Man's Bluff

She handed the book to Nicholas and stood back so the team could join hands.

Book-travel was much easier for Ethan the second time, and he woke up with the rest of the team. They were on a flat clearing at the edge of a high cliff that overlooked an ocean of trees. As far as the eye could see, lush greenery stretched into the horizon. Two hours had passed, and dusk was approaching by the time Sol arrived.

"Sol – our old friend is here!" RGB cried out. They had been scanning the horizon ever since their arrival.

Ethan followed Hayley and Gruggins to determine what RGB were looking at. An enormous bird of prey soared above the forest as if tickling his belly with the tips of the trees. Orange rays from the setting sun glistened off his silver feathers as he glided towards them. Ethan's hair blew back as Sol flapped his enormous wings and effortlessly touched down at the edge of the bluff. Sol's wingspan was as long as a school bus, Ethan thought.

"Sol," Linus said.

"We've missed you," Albert said.

"Happy to see you again," Newton said.

RGB hopped onto his back, and Sol turned his head and affectionately nudged them with his giant beak.

"What is he?" Ethan asked as he studied the giant raptor.

"Sol is the last of Earth's mighty thunderbirds," Nicholas said.

Ethan held his hand up towards Sol. The giant raptor bowed his head and studied Ethan. He gently nudged Ethan's hand with his beak.

"Yes," Ethan said and smiled at Sol. "Nice to meet you as well."

"You're communicating with him—" Nicholas said. "Well, well, well – there is more to Ethan Fox than meets the eye."

"Sol, did you bring the supplies?" Nicholas asked.

Sol bowed his head in acknowledgment.

"It appears you've met Ethan Fox," Nicholas said. "This is Hayley."

He bowed his head at Hayley.

Sol was a majestic creature that stood nearly as tall as Azron. Dark edges on his silver feathers made his shiny metallic finish resemble giant fish scales. Black and bronze feathers covered his head in a pattern that resembled the helmet of a warrior. Giant eagle eyes the size of saucers peered back at Ethan and Hayley over his yellow beak that hooked to a sharp point at the end.

Ethan gazed at Sol's enormous talons that reminded him of bent railroad spikes.

"We may be up against a Hell-Giant," Nicholas said. "Which means everybody must do their part." Nicholas looked at Ethan and Hayley.

"We're ready," Hayley said.

"Just tell us what to do," Ethan said.

Nicholas reached into the large saddle attached to Sol and pulled out two metallic objects that resembled giant spoons. He handed one to Ethan and the other to Hayley. Ethan wrapped his hands around the long round handle and gripped it like a lacrosse stick. Hayley followed Ethan's lead and held hers in the same manner.

"We must be in for one heck of a dessert," Ethan quipped.

"What are these?" Hayley asked.

"They are hydrosphere ejectors," Nicholas said. "Azron will demonstrate."

Azron blocked out the sun as he approached Ethan and Hayley. They gazed up as he held out an Azron sized ejector in precisely the same manner as Ethan had.

"Push button here—" Azron explained as he used his thumb to push a red button on the ejector's handle.

Ethan caressed the smooth handle with his fingers and found the button as he kept his eyes on Azron. He mimicked Azron and held down the button with his thumb. A small sphere of water grew in the bowl of Ethan's ejector. The hydrosphere grew to the size of a grapefruit.

"When balled-water stop – launch," Azron sprang forward and catapulted his basketball-sized hydrosphere into the air. The ball of water shot from Azron's ejector and continued to grow as it flew through the air, growing to the size of a truck before hitting the forest below.

"Awesome!" Ethan shouted as he launched a hydrosphere that sailed as if propelled by an invisible rocket and grew to the size of a mammoth boulder.

"Hell-Giant no like balled-water. Har, harr, harrr!" Azron roared.

Ethan and Hayley practiced for another hour, flinging hydrospheres into the forest. The progress they made in such short order pleased Nicholas.

Day turned to night, and the team gathered around a colorful campfire RGB had made. They were in a base camp of some sort, and oval huts resembling giant half-buried eggs circled the fire pit – two of the huts were big enough for Azron and Sol. After a dinner of grilled steaks – Caretaker style – the team retired to their cozy quarters.

They awoke early in the morning when the winds were favorable for the glide to the clearing. Sol would carry the team on his back. He was plenty strong to take them all, but Azron would have to fly separately.

Sol wore a saddle-like contraption with leather seats and straps they could hold when the team sat upon Sol's back. Daavic rode in front while Ethan, Hayley, and Gruggins sat in the back. Nicholas and RGB would fly themselves down.

Sol stepped to the edge of the cliff, bobbed his head, and leaped off. The view was beautiful as the forest slid by beneath them. Strong wind at their backs pushed them along like an invisible conveyor belt. RGB glided alongside at first but then decided to play.

"Weeeeeeeeeeeee," Linus rocketed ahead.

"Woooooo Hoooooo," Newton and Albert followed.

They played tag in the sky and chased one another, doing somersaults and loop-de-loops.

The glide lasted ten minutes before they sighted the clearing – a kidney-shaped meadow that tapered at one end. Sol made a quick descent and set down at its grassy center. The team dismounted as Nicholas and RGB landed nearby, and with a few flaps of his massive wings, Sol was off to fetch

Azron. The return to the bluff would take longer against the strong wind, but the team could waste no time and would enter the Silent Forest immediately.

At one end, a canopy of trees surrounded the meadow and formed a cave-like enclave – the Silent Forest entrance. Daavic led the way with RGB at his side while Ethan, Hayley, and Gruggins were behind them, and Nicholas brought up the rear.

You could hear a pin drop, Ethan thought – but not until someone decided to speak did Ethan understand what total silence really was.

"Mother has sent us on a wild goose chase," Daavic said.

No sound came out, yet Ethan could hear him – it was like dark light. Ethan pondered 'quiet sound' as they continued into the forest. But what it lacked in sound, it made up for in scent, Ethan thought as he breathed in the fresh smell of pine and other forest odors.

"It is a large forest, so we must explore to be sure," Nicholas said.

Thin beams of sunlight peeked through the thick cover of trees and dotted the forest floor. Colorful vegetation marvelously decorated the Silent Forest – much like the Moongarden. Several of the trees had appendages attached to them, and they looked like ears going up both sides of the trees – just like in his dad's sketches.

"*The Ears on the Forest Trees*," Ethan thought.

"They do look like ears," Hayley replied.

"You can hear me?" Ethan thought.

"Yes," Hayley answered.

None of the others were hearing Ethan and Hayley as the Silent Forest enabled them to communicate telepathically.

"I've seen them before in the sketches my dad showed me."

Ethan remained quiet, deep in thought.

No animal life was visible on the forest floor or in the trees above. The only signs of life were the ears on the forest trees and cocoon-like huts that hung high up in the trees. The team ventured deeper into the colorful lush forest.

A burning smell overtook Ethan's senses and suddenly an explosion of sound ruptured the silence. The forest's creatures flooded towards them – sprites, gnomes, jungle elves and forest trolls all joined the stampede.

"Something has breached the canopy!" Nicholas shouted above the noise.

The sound grew deafening as fire rampaged through the forest.

"As we feared – a Hell-Giant!" Nicholas announced.

The Hell-Giant was an enormous fire creature as tall as the forest itself. It resembled a giant firelyte with devilish flamed-horns and piercing black eyes. The monster ripped trees from their roots and tossed them aside in flames. Fire rained on the forest floor as the Hell-Giant stormed through the trees creating a vast clearing of embers in its wake.

"We've got to stop the beast before it has done irreparable harm," Nicholas said.

"Without Sol and Azron, that will be impossible. And without Kepler, the three pyrodevlins will barely be able to contain the beast," Daavic said.

"They will be along shortly, so unleash RGB now," Nicholas said. "If they can pull the beast into the clearing, Sol and Azron will spot us from above – it's our only hope."

"A ridiculous plan, you'll be sending us all to our deaths."

"Give the order!"

Daavic hesitated, but then obeyed, and bent down to give RGB their orders. The pyrodevlins darted into the clearing of embers that smoldered where a dense forest once stood. They raised their forked tails above their heads as brightly colored balls of energy grew between the forks. The baseball-sized sphere's shot out the ends of their tails and trailed streams of energy that remained attached to the pyrodevlins. They hit the Hell-Giant and wrapped around its arms and leg. RGB had lassoed the giant fire monster and were slowly pulling it into the clearing.

"Ethan and Hayley – you stay at the edge of the clearing and drench that beast with hydrospheres. Find a patch of forest that is not burning and use it as cover."

"It appears to be working – but they won't be able to hold the creature for long," Daavic said.

"That is why we are going to help them," Nicholas said.

Nicholas and Daavic ran to RGB and joined hands with them – a pyrodevlin to each of their sides. A bright glow emanated from the five of them as they worked together to tug the Hell-Giant towards the clearing.

It amazed Ethan how powerful the small pyrodevlins were as they wrestled the Hell-Giant. But they were tiring as the giant fire creature flailed back and forth, trying to break free.

Ethan and Hayley stayed at the edge of the clearing as Nicholas had ordered while Gruggins clung to Hayley's shoulder. They took turns launching hydrospheres at the fire beast, only ducking into the forest long enough to charge a new one. But aiming hydrospheres was more challenging than it looked, and none hit their mark.

"This isn't working. We need to be closer," Ethan said. He rushed deeper into the clearing and lurched forward with all his might launching a shot at the creature. The water boulder found the mark and landed splat upside the Hell-Giant's head. The fire monster glared down at Ethan.

"Nice shot!" Hayley cheered as she ran into the clearing near Ethan.

One of the giant's arms broke free as Albert lost his grip and the red energy lasso disappeared. He struggled to conjure up another energy ball as the Hell-Giant swung his free arm violently towards Ethan, and a huge fireball shot from the creature's hand.

"Duck!" Ethan shouted as he ran towards Hayley, dove, and tackled her to the ground. The heat from the fireball warmed Ethan's face as it roared over their heads.

"Are you all right?" Ethan asked Hayley.

"I'll be okay," Hayley jumped to her feet, lunged forward, and launched a hydrosphere of her own. This one hit the Hell-Giant in the torso and staggered it back.

Albert finally conjured up another energy ball and re-lassoed the Hell-Giant's arm just as Sol and Azron arrived. Sol swooped into the clearing, and Azron jumped from his back. The Hell-Giant kicked at a fallen tree with its free foot, and it ignited and blasted into the air like a rocket.

Ethan saw a red flash out of the corner of his eye. The flaming tree was nearly on top of him and Hayley when Azron swatted it away with his hydrosphere ejector. An explosion of water rained down and soaked Ethan and Hayley. Azron tossed aside the mangled ejector handle that survived.

Sol flapped his mighty wings to gain altitude above the Hell-Giant. RGB, Nicholas, and Daavic continued their tug of war battle to pull the monster into the clearing. Sol hovered above the creature flapping his wings harder and harder as he slowly drifted down. Sol's flapping intensified, and so did the wind he generated as thunder and lightning stormed from above. He was creating a storm over the Hell-Giant.

As Ethan viewed the action, he got an idea and held the palms of his hands skyward towards the Hell-Giant – his symbols began to glow. A strong sense of fatigue and agony overtook Ethan as he listened to the Hell-Giant's thoughts.

"He's weakening—" Ethan shouted at RGB. "Lasso his waist and pull him to the ground."

RGB followed Ethan's orders in perfect chorus. Newton stopped his energy stream and let go of the creature's leg so that he could re-lasso the creature's waist. Albert and Linus did the same as soon as Newton's beam was in place.

"Aim at its legs!" Ethan shouted to Hayley as he let loose with a hydrosphere that hit the monster square on its right leg.

RGB, Nicholas, and Daavic moved closer to the Hell-Giant to gain leverage and help them pull the creature towards the ground.

The team worked together in perfect unison, and the monster was hurting. RGB were tiring, too, as the color drained from their bodies and their lassos grew thinner. Sol's storm intensified, and together they were pulling the Hell-Giant to the ground.

Then in a final act of defiance, the monster lunged up and swiped at Sol with both arms. He hit one of Sol's wings and almost knocked him out of the sky, but Sol was too strong and regained control as the Hell-Giant fell to its knees. Rain from Sol's storm and Ethan and Hayley's hydrospheres drenched its flames as the Hell-Giant slowly melted away. When the battle was over, a giant firelyte diamond the size of a pumpkin was all that remained of the Hell-Giant.

Ethan stood at the center of the clearing with Hayley and Azron nearby. He gazed skyward and spotted a single giant feather floating in the air – it would land somewhere deep inside the Silent Forest.

"Thank you, Azron. You saved us," Ethan said.

Azron grinned at Ethan. "Hell-Giant no like Ethan Fox. Har, harr, harrr!"

Ethan turned towards Hayley, and something caught his eye. It was Damien, crouching near a bush holding two giant firelyte capsules the size of baseballs.

"DAMIEN – HE DID THIS!" Ethan shouted at the top of his lungs.

Azron, Nicholas, and Daavic gave chase to the retreating culprit. RGB and Gruggins stayed with Ethan and Hayley as Sol circled overhead. Several minutes later, they returned empty-handed – Damien had escaped.

Nicholas sent RGB to scout the remainder of the forest – just in case. After a quick dart about, they returned to report all was quiet. The team journeyed back into the forest on their way back to The Residence, and Nicholas stopped them at the 'ears' of the forest trees.

"Damien has alerted the forest creatures, they'll be attacking anything that doesn't belong in the forest. He won't be able to surprise them again," Nicholas said.

"Agreed, but speaking of forest creatures, I saw no grumplings in that stampede," Daavic said.

"No grumplings are present," Gruggins said, "they have left the Silent Forest."

Gruggins pointed to a bulky thatch of shrubs and waved his hand in a circular motion. The shrubs transformed into a complex of small box-like structures. "They've abandoned their village."

"Where did that come from?" Ethan asked.

"It was there all along, hidden in plain sight by a grumpling's cloak," Hayley said.

"Can't be too careful, even in the Silent Forest," Gruggins said.

"Where did they go?" Daavic asked.

"I couldn't tell you," Gruggins replied.

DEADWOOD SALOON

Upon their return, Jordanna called an emergency CAGE meeting. Ethan and Hayley were happy for the break and quickly decided it was time to find Dakota Drakelan. But first, Ethan had something else he wanted to check out, so Hayley followed him to the front room.

"Where are you taking me?" she asked.

"Back to the Gallery," Ethan said. "A painting in the exhibit hall caught my eye, and I need to learn more about it."

Ethan and Hayley entered the enormous gallery, and Dorkin Drumbles quickly greeted them. "May I help you?"

"Maybe," Ethan said. "I saw a painting in the viewing hall and was wondering if you could tell me about its significance."

"Of course, Dorkin understands significance of all pieces in the viewing hall."

They strolled down the long hallway and Ethan glanced at each piece as they passed by.

"Right there, that one," Ethan said and pointed.

They stopped in front of the painting, and Ethan read the picture's plaque:

Creator Stravis, Savior of the Hybrid Child.

"Very significant, this one is . . . thwarted by the Seers, Victor Qruefeldt was. Teleported the Hybrid Child they did, teleported to Stravis for looking after. Healed the Hybrid Child, Stravis did, and marked him with his symbol. Marked him right here."

Dorkin pointed to the palm of his hand. Ethan's face turned warm, and his heart began to race.

"Th-Thank you, Dorkin – you've been a great help."

Dorkin flashed a muted grin at Ethan and returned to the Gallery. Ethan held up his hands, stared into his palms, and the symbols began to glow.

"Ethan, do you understand what this means?"

"Yes – I do – I am the Hybrid Child."

"That would explain Victor's obsession with you."

Ethan remained silent for several minutes. He made Hayley promise not to tell anyone – even Jordanna – until he could digest the revelation.

They ventured back to The Hall of Doorways to search for Dakota Drakelan. Finding out where he lived was simple with the ELMO and The Residence map. Dakota lived at a place called Deadwood, the twelfth door on the right. They were near the eleventh doors when they heard voices coming from the darkness ahead.

"Malik, come back here," Caden Stanley ordered.

"Probably caught a whiff of those human brats," Blair Trabblemore said. "My father says the Headmistress has furnished them with quarters. He thinks she is a fool for taking in humans."

Ethan quietly opened the eleventh door on the right and pulled Hayley inside. They didn't have time for another confrontation with the hostile Caretaker teens. They found themselves in a dark entryway to another room, and light peeked through a closed curtain.

"Ethan Fox spotted him with two hell-pods, Mother – Damien is working for Victor Qruefeldt, as I've always said."

Ethan recognized Daavic's voice as they had inadvertently entered the CAGE meeting room.

"Daavic reports the truth," Nicholas affirmed.

"Well then, I've been in denial for far too long," Jordanna said in a solemn tone. "If Damien has sided with Victor Qruefeldt, I will deal with him as a Grimleaver."

The room fell silent.

"We can't overlook the news of the grumplings," Nicholas said.

"What about the grumplings?" Jordanna asked.

"They've abandoned the Silent Forest," Daavic said.

"Why would they risk capture by the leprechauns?" Brianna asked.

"Indeed," Jordanna said. "We are left with more questions than answers."

"How did you know Mother?" Daavic asked. "Who told you the Silent Forest was in danger?"

"Let's just say that my source is beyond reproach."

"You're going to get yourself killed, Mother!"

"Enough, Daavic!" Nicholas said.

The room again fell silent.

"Moving on, Fin has reported a theft at Poseidon. The culprit stole several items from the storage vault. Whoever did this used our presence as a distraction – it occurred during our visit."

"What was sss-stolen?"

"Fin will report back when he learns more – but we all understand the importance of Poseidon's storage vault. It was the only place considered out of Grimleaver reach."

"Victor Qruefeldt become bold," Azron said.

"On top of all that," Jordanna said. "We've lost contact with the Outpost. A team will depart for Kraken Island at first light."

The room fell into a stony silence.

"I've yet to decide who will accompany me," Jordanna said. "I will make arrangements and send word once my decision is final."

"You can't be suggesting – no headmaster has ever joined a mission," Nicholas said.

"I will contact you all when my decision is final," she concluded.

Ethan and Hayley slipped back into The Hall of Doorways undetected.

"Hayley, I think Daavic had something to do with the theft. When I returned to my room after talking with Fin, Daavic was sneaking around, so I followed him. He ducked down the storage vault hallway, and I lost him."

"That does sound suspicious. We should keep a close eye on him."

They entered the twelfth door on the right, and it opened to a small town right out of the Old West. Night was falling as they entered Deadwood. They stood on a dirt path that angled left and widened to the road into town. To the right, a plane with tumbleweeds rolled into the distance where a mountain range spanned the horizon. Directly in front of them was a hill with a narrow dirt path that wound its way up to a dark house at the top.

"That spooky old house is where Dakota Drakelan lives," Ethan said.

A candle burned in a window next to the front door. Ethan's eyes traced their way up the narrow dirt path as they arrived at the base of the hill. He thought a curtain moved in the window. Ethan lunged forward and fell to the hard dirt ground.

"Did you see that, Blair? The clumsy human tripped over his own two feet," Caden Stanley said as he stood over Ethan.

"Leave him alone, you bully," Hayley rushed to Ethan's defense, but one push from Blair sent her crashing to the ground next to Ethan.

"She's just as clumsy as he is," Blair Trabblemore laughed.

Ethan rose to his feet as an odd sense of calm overtook his body, and he took in a deep breath.

"Don't worry, Hayley," Ethan sighed. "Caden was just about to apologize."

Caden swung his fist at Ethan's head but inexplicably fell to the ground.

"Did you see that, Hayley?" Ethan asked. "The clumsy bully fell over his own two feet."

"Sic him, Malik!" Caden ordered as he jumped to his feet.

Malik bared his razor-sharp teeth and growled, but Ethan raised his glowing palm, and the brutehound stopped with a whimper.

"Ethan – isn't that a grindle?" Hayley asked as she pointed at Blair's feet.

A small hairy gorilla-like creature appeared on the ground near Blair's feet. The grindle glared up at Blair with its beady red eyes and bared its sharp teeth.

"Aaaaaaaaaaaa!!!!" Blair screamed as she jumped behind Caden to shield herself from the tiny creature. She tugged at Caden's arms from behind and backed away from Ethan and Hayley.

"This isn't over," Caden said as he and Blair backed away – but they stopped when they backed into Azron. He had been watching from the road into town. Caden and Blair retreated out The Hall of Doorways.

"Troublemakers no like Ethan and Hayley. Har, harr, harrr!" Azron howled as he motioned for Ethan and Hayley to follow him. "Come—"

They followed Azron into town. A row of Old West style buildings lined the dirt road that ended at a red barn at the end of town. The chatter of a boisterous crowd echoed from the building on the left. It had swinging doors, and a sign in front of the building read:

Deadwood Saloon

Azron pushed the swinging saloon doors open with a swipe of his giant hand. The doorway was tall, but he still needed to bend down to avoid bumping his head. The crowd got quiet as everyone turned to view who had entered, then the chatter resumed.

RGB were on a small round table in the middle of an extensive seating area. They jumped up and down and danced around in circles chanting.

"Dragon's breath, dragon's breath . . ."

Ethan and Hayley followed Azron to a table at the end of the L-shaped bar. A single enormous chair and several normal-sized ones surrounded the table, so they took a seat.

"Ethan – how did you do that? How did you dodge Caden's punch and make him fall?"

"I have no idea, everything slowed down, so I stepped aside and gave him a nudge."

Azron studied Ethan and Hayley as they conversed.

"Great move with the copycat," Ethan said. "That grindle nearly scared Blair out of her shoes."

"Blair has always been frightened by grindles."

Azron bent down closer to the table. His face crinkled as matchbook-sized teeth peeked out from behind an ear to ear smile.

"Ethan Fox friend of Seers – Ethan Fox, a friend of Azron," he whispered.

"Friends," Ethan said and returned the smile.

"Azron CAGE member," he said. "Azron brother Gaball become cyclops – twice size Azron."

"I'm sorry," Ethan frowned.

"Terrible what they did to him," Hayley said.

Brianna and Nicholas arrived and were surprised to find Ethan and Hayley with Azron.

"Dragon's breath, everybody?" Brianna asked.

"Do they have sugar-pickle soda?" Hayley asked.

"Sure," Brianna said and smiled at Hayley. "Same for you, dear?" she asked Ethan.

Ethan nodded.

Brianna returned to the table carrying an enormous goblet of dragon's breath for Azron. A bartender followed with two normal-sized goblets.

A thick fog wafted from the goblets of dragon's breath. Ethan stood to peek inside Azron's enormous goblet. A glowing purple liquid bubbled beneath the layer of fog.

The sugar-pickle sodas arrived in the grasp of a small, winged dragon equipped with a basket. The tiny dragon landed on the table next to Ethan and Hayley.

"Two sugar-pickle sodas," the dragon said.

"This is Tinx," Brianna said. "Tinx, meet Ethan and Hayley."

"A pleasure to meet you," Tinx said.

Tinx was a winged pixie-dragon about four inches tall and six inches long. Her lizard-like skin was peach colored with white swirls.

"If you need anything else, just ask," Tinx said as she smiled and then flew off to continue her aerial deliveries.

"To the successful dousing of a Hell-Giant," Nicholas said as he raised his goblet. "You two performed admirably in the face of impending danger," he said to Ethan and Hayley.

They clanked their drinks together and gulped away.

"Ahhhhh – nothing like the clarity that comes from that first sip," Nicholas said.

"What brings the two of you here?" Brianna asked Ethan and Hayley.

"We came with Azron. After we had a run-in with Blair Trabblemore and her bully puppet Caden."

"I will speak with the Trabblemores," Brianna offered. "They've sowed trouble for far too long."

They made small talk for another round, but Ethan sensed what was really on their minds – who was accompanying Jordanna to Kraken Island?

They exited the Deadwood Saloon, and Brianna stepped off the wooden sidewalk and turned to say something but stopped dead in her tracks. Her black tongue lashed out and whipped wildly as she began to speak.

"Ssss-send for help—" Brianna struggled to spit out the words as she pointed at the saloon sign.

"What's wrong?" Ethan asked. "You haven't seen a raven before?"

"Not a raven," Nicholas said. "That is a grimtailed dread, and wherever they are seen—darkness follows."

DARKNESS
FOLLOWS

Grimtailed dread was a fitting name for this creature. It was larger than a raven and looked more dead than alive. An opaque white film covered its eyes, like that on a dead fish. Tattered feathers clung to its body like someone had put it through a shredder. The only evidence that this bird was alive was its beating heart visible through a gaping wound in its abdomen.

"Contact Jordanna at once while I fetch RGB. Azron, you and Brianna protect the children at all costs," Nicholas ordered.

Brianna called Jordanna on her ELMO. Azron took up a position next to Ethan and Hayley while Nicholas ran back into the Deadwood Saloon.

"CAW-CAW—" the grimtailed dread shrieked. It bobbed its head and then took flight and sailed past Dakota

Drakelan's house over the planes. The dread disappeared, and a swirling gray vortex appeared in the sky. A strong wind gusted from its black center as the vortex grew larger. It resembled a small hurricane turned sideways in the evening sky. Tumbleweeds blew through town as the gusts grew stronger, and then the wind stopped, leaving only an eerie calm.

"Send a sss-security detail at once."

Nicholas rushed through the swinging doors, and RGB were right behind him, eager for action. They stared up at the swirling vortex, and the stillness in the air was unsettling – like the calm before the storm.

Thunderous noises erupted from the vortex as creatures flooded from its blackness. Vampires swarmed the sky, gliding on enormous bat wings. Vicious flying monkeys carried stones, and giant horned birds dropped off ground troops – armored trolls armed with staffs that spewed blue bolts of electricity. An army of trolls assembled on the planes outside of town – they were preparing to attack.

"RGB, protect the children," Nicholas said.

RGB darted into a triangle formation around Ethan and Hayley.

"Let them bring the fight to us," Nicholas shouted as he stretched out his wings. "Brianna, you and I will concentrate on the air assault. Azron will handle the trolls, and RGB will handle anything that gets by our defenses."

Nicholas flapped his bulky angelic wings and swiftly took to the sky. Brianna and Azron started down the road out of town. Brianna took a position at the edge of town while

Azron continued to the planes to greet the approaching trolls.

The flying monkeys dropped enormous stones on Azron from above, but he dodged and swatted the stones with his massive hands as he ran towards the trolls. Nicholas swooped in behind the monkeys and ripped the wings from the ones he could catch. Brianna had an attack of her own as the tube-like worms on her head pointed skyward and glowed. Green pulses of light shot at the monkeys' eyes and blinded them instantly. With each shot, the worms lost their glow, only to regenerate and shoot again. RGB shot fireballs at the monkeys as they continued the onslaught.

"We've got to do something to help," Ethan said. He couldn't sit by idly while the CAGE members risked their lives to protect him.

"I've got an idea," Hayley said. She pulled out her copycat, and it morphed into a hydrosphere ejector.

"Here, you launch farther than I do," Hayley said. She handed it to Ethan, and he lobbed water boulders at the incoming attackers.

Azron arrived at the army of trolls as they leveled their staffs at him and fired. The jolts of blue electricity struck Azron but did little more than anger him. He swung his arms like giant clubs sending trolls flying in all directions. Wave after wave of trolls attacked, but they were no match for Azron.

As the battle raged on, Brianna and Nicholas handled the attacking squadron of flying monkeys, but the bulk of Grimleavers in the sky had not yet attacked. The vampires viewed the battle from above, hovering in a tight formation as if protecting something – a chill crept up Ethan's spine.

"Take this—" Ethan said to Hayley as he handed her the hydrosphere ejector so she could take over the launch duties.

"What's wrong?" Hayley asked.

Ethan did not answer. He raised his palms skyward, and they began to glow as he fell into a trance. Ethan was somewhere else for about a minute before he snapped out of it.

"He's here!" Ethan cried out. "Victor Qruefeldt is here!"

The swarming mass of vampires hovering in the sky broke formation. They were attacking, and they headed straight towards Ethan and Hayley.

"RGB!" Ethan shouted, and the pyrodevlins turned to face Ethan.

"Albert, Linus, Newton – take the attack to them – up there. They will overwhelm Nicholas without you. You must help him." Ethan said and pointed at the approaching vampire swarm. The pyrodevlins understood and took to the sky like three guided missiles.

"Hayley, I have an idea," Ethan said. "Dakota Drakelan – I think he will help. Do you think you can make it up that hill while Brianna and I cover you?"

"No problem," Hayley said as she handed the ejector back to Ethan, and they ran towards Brianna.

RGB were much faster and nimbler than the attacking Grimleavers. They could dart between the vampire swarm and hit them with bursts of energy from their forked tails.

Between RGB and Nicholas, vampires were raining from the sky.

"Brianna—" Ethan shouted as they approached her from behind.

"You two should be with RGB."

"No time for that—" Ethan interrupted. "They're helping Nicholas. Hayley is going to run up that hill and ask for Dakota Drakelan's help while we provide cover."

Brianna peered into the sky. Between RGB and Nicholas, the vampires had their hands full, but there were too many of them. She glanced up the hill and then to Ethan.

"Super idea," Brianna said. "Hurry up that hill, girl."

Brianna and Ethan provided cover as Hayley zig-zagged up the hill. Ethan glanced out to check how Azron was doing, and a battalion of much larger trolls was sneaking up on his flank.

"Azron's in trouble!" Ethan screamed.

"Ogres!" Brianna shouted back. "He doesn't see them. They'll tear him apart!"

Brianna aimed her worm-beams at the advancing ogre army.

"My beams are of no use—" Brianna cried. "I'm too low on energy, and they're too far out."

"I've got an idea," Ethan said as he flipped his hydrosphere ejector upside down.

"Bowling for ogres!" he shouted as he rolled a hydrosphere with all his might.

The ball of water hit the ground and rolled like a bullet car speeding across the plane, gathering dust as it grew into a gigantic ball of mud. Ethan launched three more before the first one went SPLAT. One by one, the giant mudballs hit their mark and left the army of ogres wallowing in an ocean of mud – like a giant litter of pigs.

"Nice bowling," Brianna shouted back to Ethan with a wink.

Ethan stopped and glanced toward Dakota Drakelan's place. Powerful bolts of lightning burst skyward from behind the house.

The vampires turned around as if an unheard voice had called them. They were heading towards the vortex – the Grimleavers were retreating.

The giant horned birds swooped down to pick up the trolls while vampires collected their fallen brothers. The Grimleavers were disappearing into the vortex as the Caretaker security detail arrived. There was not much for them to do but witness the Grimleavers retreat.

Nicholas and RGB landed beside Ethan and Brianna. Hayley ran down the hill to join them. They stood and viewed the retreat as they fought to catch their breath. The thud of giant footsteps filled the air as Azron approached.

"Azron no see ogres," he said as he gazed down at Ethan. "Ethan Fox save Azron. Azron owe Ethan Fox life."

"You owe me nothing."

Azron studied Ethan and blinked his sizable eye as a smile formed on his lips.

"Ogres no like Ethan Fox. Har, harr, harrr!"

Ethan, Hayley, and Brianna all laughed with Azron, but Nicholas was deep in thought.

"My tactics were all wrong. If RGB hadn't joined me in the air, you'd have all perished."

"Ethan Fox saved the day when he sent RGB to help you . . . and Hayley to sss-solicit Dakota Drakelan's help."

"Brilliant decision," Nicholas said to Ethan. "I guess I owe you one as well."

Ethan smiled, then turned to Hayley.

"You found Dakota Drakelan?" he asked.

"Dakota Drakelan?"

"Yes – when you ran up the hill for help," Ethan said.

"I – I don't remember. The last thing I remember is running up the hill."

"Dakota no want be found," Azron said.

"What happened to you?" Hayley asked Ethan. "You fell into a trance."

"The Seers – I had a vision, and vampires overran us, so I told RGB to help Nicholas when they attacked."

Nicholas and Brianna exchanged glances at the mention of the Seers.

"Beyond reproach indeed," Nicholas whispered to Brianna.

"Something else happened – after the vision, I sensed Victor Qruefeldt and could sense his thoughts. He's frightened – terrified of the Caretakers unlocking the portals."

"Sss-surely, Victor understands that it is beyond our control."

The calm silence returned as the last Grimleaver disappeared into the vortex. A strong gust of wind sucked the tumbleweeds in the opposite direction. The vortex was shrinking, and within an instant, it was gone.

"What I'd like to find out is where did that dread come from?" Brianna asked.

Brianna contacted Jordanna to report what had happened.

"I trust you thwarted the attack without much difficulty," Jordanna said.

"More or less," Brianna said. "But how did you know?"

"Because it was not an attack, it was a diversion. Report to the front room at once – and bring the others."

The team rushed to the front room. Jordanna was picking up the pieces of Gruggins' crushed box when they arrived.

"Daavic tried to stop him—" Jordanna said, "a struggle ensued, and Daavic gave chase, but I'm afraid he's escaped to the Moongarden."

"Stop who? What happened here?" Nicholas asked.

"What has happened to Gruggins?" Hayley asked with concern.

"Damien – he's abducted Gruggins," Jordanna answered.

LAIR OF THE SPIDER GECKO

The Grimleavers had used the attack as a distraction so Damien could abduct Gruggins. But why? It didn't make sense, and Hayley took the news especially hard.

"Ethan Fox communicates with Seers," Nicholas said to Jordanna. "No doubt the boy is your secret source that is beyond reproach—"

"This must remain a secret. You will speak of this to no one."

"The boy can also sss-sense Victor Qruefeldt's thoughts."

"I'm not crazy – you have to believe me," Ethan said. "He believes you can open the portals, and that terrifies him."

Jordanna studied Ethan, her eyebrows raised as she pursed her lips.

"But we cannot, and even if it were possible, I cannot think of a reason why we would. Discovering the portal prophecies is the normal order according to the Book of Creators . . ."

Daavic returned to the study. Although he had chased Damien to the Moongarden, his brother had given him the slip.

"I've made my decision," said Jordanna. "Nicholas, Ethan, and Hayley will accompany me while the rest of you find Gruggins. We depart for Kraken Island at first sun."

"But Mother, this is preposterous," Daavic protested. "We should abandon the mission altogether."

"We must learn what has happened to the Outpost," Nicholas said.

"I've made my decision," Jordanna said.

Ethan woke to find his pocket tote had once again been disturbed, but this time the intruder had knocked over the inkwell, and small peanut-sized footprints trailed ink across the dresser. Whoever had snooped in Ethan's room was small.

Jordanna was alone in the study when Ethan and Hayley arrived. She held out the poem book for Ethan. He reached out, and Jordanna grasped his wrist with her free hand. She slowly rolled Ethan's hand over, exposing the small white symbol in his palm. Jordanna released her grip and grinned at Ethan as she handed him the poem book.

"You've been given an extraordinary gift. You are an essential part of what is to come, Ethan Fox."

Nicholas arrived shortly after that. Hayley wanted to stay with the others to find Gruggins, but Ethan convinced her they should stick together. They'd book-travel to *One Two-Tree Island*, a micro-island in the middle of the Pacific. Fin would send a team of seaskippers to take them the rest of the way.

This time Jordanna did the honors. She opened the portal book, and in a flash, they were gone.

Ethan woke to a soft breeze tickling his hair as the sun glistened off his forehead. He was the first to awaken this time. *One Two-Tree Island* was a small patch of sand no bigger than a basketball court. Two palm trees stood at its center and leaned across one another in a perfect figure X – the only thing missing was the message in a bottle.

The others awoke shortly after Ethan. They scanned the horizon for Fin's greeting party, an approaching hydromorph cracked the smooth glassy surface of the water as it breached. A lone porpoise swam towards the small island. Four humps beneath the water's surface followed along like approaching speed bumps. The porpoise surfed to the edge of the beach, morphed mid-swim, and waded the last few feet.

"I'm Wilbert Frye," he said.

Wilbert was yellow and white with orange markings. He was much smaller than the other hydromorphs they had seen. Wilbert Frye was a pygmy hydromorph.

"Four seaskippers as requested," Wilbert said as he pointed at the strange sea creatures.

The seaskippers glided effortlessly below the water's surface. They resembled giant stingrays with longer wings and shorter bodies – like underwater stealth bombers. The seaskippers were navy blue with red circles scattered across their enormous wingspan.

"Ever ridden a seaskipper?" Wilbert asked.

"Never," Ethan said.

"That would make us all," Jordanna said.

"They are easy-peasy to ride – I'll show you," Wilbert said and motioned Ethan to the surf.

Two seaskippers joined them at the water's edge. Wilbert stepped on one's back where two foot-shaped orifices swallowed Wilbert's feet to his shins – like ski boots.

"Gross, the inside is all gooey," Ethan laughed as he slipped his foot in.

"Now, lean back and steer," Wilbert said.

Ethan thought Wilbert was going to fall as he leaned back, but a thick flap of seaskipper skin popped up beneath his rear like a captain's chair. Two long antennas whipped around from the front of the seaskipper. Wilbert caught one in each hand and steered like they were a horse's reins.

Riding seaskippers was relatively easy, as Wilbert had promised. Besides, they didn't need to steer as the seaskippers had already plotted the way to Kraken Island. They glided over the ocean as if skiing behind an invisible boat while the seaskippers skimmed along beneath the water's surface. They quickly lost sight of *One Two-Tree Island* and were alone in the middle of the Pacific.

"How much farther?" Hayley called out. "I don't see any sign of land."

A giant hole formed in the water, wide enough to drive a bus into, so the seaskippers headed right for it.

"I think you spoke too soon," Ethan shouted to Hayley.

"Hang on tight," Jordanna called out.

The seaskippers expertly navigated into the giant swirling funnel and descended at a steep angle. Spiraling down the edges of the tunnel, like they were skiing down the inside of a giant straw. The tunnel leveled out and angled towards the surface. Everything got brighter as they approached the light at the end of the tunnel and neared a dead-end; a brightly lit wall of water.

The seaskippers joined formation one behind the other in a single file. Then one by one, they catapulted their riders at the wall of water and broke formation.

Ethan hit the water like he had jumped from a cliff. He found himself swimming in a small lagoon surrounded on three sides by thick foliage. The fourth side was a small beach that ended at a cliff that circled the island. A dark cave was visible at the base of the cliff.

"The only way to the island's interior is through that cave," Jordanna said.

"We'll need sunlight crystals," Nicholas said.

Nicholas walked to the base of the cliff and hammered at a gigantic boulder. He chipped off pieces, picked through the pile of rubble, and returned with four dirty crystals he washed in the lagoon. They shimmered like diamonds as he laid them out on a handkerchief.

"Sunlight crystals store the sun's rays," he said to Ethan.

Nicholas gathered the sunlight crystals and handed them each one. As they reached the entrance of the cave, Nicholas disappeared inside and emerged with four lantern enclosures. He opened one up and put his sunlight crystal inside. They all did the same.

"Sunlight crystals emit sunlight," he said as they entered the cave.

The crystals fired up and lit the cave like a propane lantern. The cave was straight and narrow but widened as they reached a fork in its path.

"We must take the path to the right," Jordanna said. "A fearsome creature lives within this cave – the path to the left is home to the fabled spider gecko."

They continued to the right, but a cave-in had blocked the path.

"We should fear the worst and prepare for a dangerous journey," Jordanna said.

"Agreed, we'll have to risk the other tunnel. The children will be safe at the lagoon. We will send for them once we've reached the Outpost."

"No – you can't leave us behind at the first sign of danger," Hayley said.

"Besides, you might need us," Ethan said.

"I understand your disappointment, but I won't risk your safety – we will send for you shortly."

Ethan and Hayley were back at the beach, and Nicholas and Jordanna had ventured into the lair. The spider gecko slept most of the time but always woke up hungry, Jordanna had explained.

Nearly an hour had passed, and Ethan and Hayley were impatient.

"Something's not right," Hayley said.

"Your ring again?"

"No, just an intuition that my mother brought us along for a reason."

"I've been thinking the same thing. When Jordanna gave the poem book back to me, she saw my palm symbols and said I was an important part of what was to come."

"They need our help, Ethan. She must have felt strongly about that, or we wouldn't be here."

Ethan and Hayley scooped up their sunlight crystals and retraced their way to the fork, where they ventured into the lair of the spider gecko. They trodded lightly and made as little noise as possible. The cave opened to a chamber the size of a living room. Their lanterns did not light the entire chamber, so Ethan veered left while Hayley explored right.

"Ethan," Hayley whispered.

Ethan peered across the chamber to determine what she had found. A pirate's remains were pinned to the cave wall in a sitting position, held in place by thick webbing. The skeleton wore tattered clothes and clutched a jeweled dagger in his hand.

Ethan hurried to Hayley's side, and a glittering patch of gold materialized on the cave wall; a circular pattern of gold flakes above the remains.

"Somebody must have hidden that there," Ethan said in a muted voice.

"The gold is hiding something," Hayley said.

Ethan scratched at the gold, and it flaked away, uncovering a black crest embedded in the cave wall. He pried at the crest with his fingers, but it was in too deep.

"Use this," Hayley said as she handed Ethan the dagger she had removed from the skeleton's hand.

Ethan pried the crest from the wall and held up the cantaloupe-sized object crafted from black marble-like material. As he moved closer to his lantern, a vague outline of symbols became visible engraved into its surface. One symbol inscribed into each quadrant – and one of them was Ethan's.

"Stravis' symbol, I wonder what the other ones are," Ethan said as he stored the dagger and crest in his pocket tote.

They continued to the end of the chamber, where the cave narrowed. The darkness ahead was stone silent, so they crept along quietly. They arrived at the next chamber, and a pungent musty scent filled the air as they entered. It reminded Ethan of an enormous gymnasium with high ceilings. White oblong sacs clung to the walls like water balloons, and bluish fluorescent light glowed from within each one. Thousands of them lined the walls of the giant chamber.

"They're eggs of some kind," Ethan whispered.

"My ring is crawling again . . ."

They were at the center of the chamber when wisps of yellow light emerged from Ethan's pants. The poem book came to life inside, so he retrieved his pocket tote and drew it open. He held the book out in his empty hands, and the pages flipped to the first blank page where a poem eerily appeared on the glowing page. The poem read:

Creepy Crawlers

Dark and dreary comes the night.
We lose our way in fear and fright.

Loud and crunchy noise prevails.
It all begins with slugs and snails.

Death that's black is all around.
So use your light but make no sound.

For if you run away with fear,
Creepy Crawlers will be near.

Ethan finished reading the poem when a crunchy crawly sound began to reverberate through the cave. Something rustled on the ground around them, so Ethan held his lantern out and bent down to see black bugs covering the chamber floor. Slugs, snails, beetles, scorpions, centipedes, worms, and crickets crawled over themselves. They were much larger than any Ethan had seen before, and they had them surrounded.

"AAAAAAAAAHHHHHHHHHHHHHH!" Hayley let out a piercing scream.

"Shh," Ethan said. "The poem said not to make a sound."

Ethan swung his lantern at the creepy crawlers, and they backed off as he pushed forward, making sweeping motions with his lantern.

Hayley regained her composure and joined Ethan with her lantern.

"STOP!" Nicholas called out from across the chamber.

"Listen carefully – place your lanterns on the ground and stand between them, then do not move a muscle."

Hayley's scream had alerted Nicholas and Jordanna, as they stood on a ledge at the end of the chamber at an entrance to another tunnel.

They obeyed as Nicholas slammed his lantern against the cave wall. The sunlight crystal fell to the ground, so Nicholas scooped it up and spread his wings to take flight. He circled overhead, looking for a sweet spot in the mass of black death below.

"Close your eyes," Nicholas said.

He broke into a dive and smashed the crystal into the black mass. A blinding flash of light enveloped the chamber as the bugs ignited into a blue inferno and vaporized. Nicholas landed beside them.

"You were foolish to come after us," Jordanna said.

She jumped off the ledge then stopped as a sound filled the cavern. Ethan, Hayley, and Nicholas spun around to view what was making the creepy clicking sound. The noise came from another tunnel high up on the chamber wall. An enormous spider gecko emerged from the dark tunnel. The creature resembled a car-sized scorpion with spider legs and gecko feet as it crept down the cave wall.

"Take the children and find a way up that shaft," Nicholas said. "I will hold off the monster with the sunlight crystals."

Ethan and Hayley ran to Jordanna as Nicholas smashed their lanterns and retrieved the two sunlight crystals.

Jordanna led them down a narrow tunnel. They arrived at another small chamber that was dimly lit by the luminescence of spider gecko eggs. A thin ray of light beamed down from a shaft at the end of the chamber. They were at the bottom of a well that led to the surface.

Jordanna scanned the walls looking for a way up. A rope ladder lay at her feet – someone had thrown it in from above. They continued searching but found nothing on the smooth rock walls.

Nicholas entered the chamber.

"I hoped you'd be gone by now. I only stunned the beast," he gasped. "I can't say I like our chances."

"Can't you fly the ladder up the shaft?" Ethan asked.

"My wingspan is far too extensive. I would never make it up that shaft."

"I know what to do," said Hayley.

She pulled a squishy glowing egg from the cave wall. The sac was the size of zucchini and jiggled like Jell-O. She squeezed the end, and slimy green goo squirted out. She squeezed every last drop of goo from the egg sac and slipped it over her arm. It fit like a sock at first but then sucked itself snug against her skin. Her arm began to grow longer as her fingertips morphed into suction cups. Hayley had grown a gecko arm.

The others were speechless as Hayley continued with her other arm and legs. She was halfway up the shaft before they understood what she was up to.

"Follow Hayley," Nicholas said, "The creature will be coming."

He shattered the remaining lantern, and Ethan and Jordanna were outfitting themselves with gecko limbs when they heard the creature return – click-click-click.

The beast emerged from the tunnel and was a blackish-purple with a gecko head with six black spider eyes. Three tails hung over its head like a scorpion, two web spinners, and a long one in the middle for shooting dagger-like spikes at its prey.

Jordanna and Ethan started up the shaft wall.

Nicholas threw the remaining crystal at the creature's feet, and a blinding flash filled the chamber, causing the beast to retreat into the tunnel.

Nicholas squished eggs to outfit himself with gecko limbs. He was on his last limb when the spider gecko crept back into the chamber. He started up the shaft with the creature in hot pursuit.

Ethan and Jordanna emerged from the shaft into a bright and sunny day. If Nicholas could reach the sunlight, the spider gecko would not follow. Hayley found a thick coil of rope to tie around a nearby tree.

Nicholas clumsily made his way up the shaft. The spider gecko closed in as its three tails spit like machine guns. Streams of web trailed out the spinners while spikes zipped out from the middle tail. A stream of web narrowly missed Nicholas' head, but the next one ensnared his foot in its grasp. He lunged forward and broke free, but one of his gecko legs pulled off. Nicholas was losing his grip.

Hayley finished tying off the rope. Ethan and Jordanna helped her carry the heavy coil to the edge of the shaft. The spider gecko was nearly upon him when they tossed the rope.

"Grab the rope, and we'll pull you up," Jordanna yelled.

The rope was just outside of Nicholas' reach. The spider gecko was bearing down on him when he made one last desperate move. He lunged up in one sweeping motion, and his gecko limbs nearly tore off, but his effort was just enough as he grasped the rope.

The spider gecko lurched forward and spat two spikes from its long middle tail. One struck Nicholas in the meat of his thigh. He was using his last bit of strength as they hauled him up. When he reached the top, Nicholas lost consciousness.

KRAKEN ISLAND

Nicholas had a death grip on the rope when he reached the top. Jordanna removed the barb and revived him with water from a canteen. He appeared weak, but Jordanna explained that vamprils have a healthy metabolism, and it would take time for the poison to do its damage.

"There's nothing more I can do," Jordanna said. "We must get him to the Outpost."

"I'm too weak to fly, but if you fashion a crutch, I will walk," Nicholas said.

They were at the top of a cliff that overlooked the interior of the island.

Ethan and Hayley helped Jordanna search for a branch they could use to build a crutch.

To the right, a narrow path carved its way down the inside of the circular mountain range like the threads of a bolt – that was their way down. The mountain range encircled the island's interior like a giant bowl. A land-locked lake filled the bowl, and a landmass stood at the lake's center – an island within an island. A column of smoke rose from the small island.

"Inner Island," Jordanna said. "We must proceed with caution."

They made their way down the narrow path as Nicholas struggled but managed with the help of the crutch. An hour later, they had reached the bottom as the trail ended on a small rocky beach with a sign in the middle that read:

Private Notice from Inner Island:

To raise the bridge of water, it takes a special stone. A five hopper is required to make it ring the tone. Skip not once to see it through, it takes two skips from me to you.

"A riddle," said Ethan.

"One of Commander Triplin's extra precautions," Jordanna said. "He mentioned extra measures, but he never gave me any details."

"Let's see," Ethan said as he pondered the riddle. "I think it is talking about skipping a rock. I used to skip rocks with my dad – a five hopper is five skips."

Ethan looked for a rock to demonstrate.

"There is a trick to skipping rocks. The flattest ones skip the best."

He picked up a rock shaped like a used bar of soap. He walked to the water's edge and pitched the rock low and parallel to the water. Ethan's rock sank the second it touched the water and didn't skip a notch.

"Bad throw, needs to skim along the top," Ethan said.

Hayley searched for rocks too, and Ethan found a pile of flat slate. He was on his fourth unsuccessful attempt before Hayley found her first rock. She approached the water with a perfectly round rock.

"They have to be flat, that one will never skip," said Ethan.

"The sign says, 'a special stone,'" Hayley said, "haven't you noticed most of the rocks on this beach are flat?"

She launched an underhanded softball pitch at the lake, and the stone bounced off the water's surface like a ping-pong ball off a concrete floor – a three hopper.

"Ouch, I got told," Ethan laughed.

"Give one a try," Hayley handed Ethan a round stone.

He launched the rock straight up into the air, and it landed with a thud and hopped five times before sinking.

A loud gong sounded from Inner Island and rang in their ears like a hearing test. The water bubbled like in a kettle on a campfire. Pillars of water sprouted in the distance, and one after another, they sprang up like pegs in a cribbage board. Two rows of water columns stretched across the lake to Inner Island – piles for the forming water bridge. A river of water rushed across the top and calmed to a smooth glass surface that rested atop the pilings. Fish swam within the structure of the liquid bridge.

"A bridge," Ethan said. He ran onto the bridge, and it easily held his weight.

"Come on," he said as he stopped and splashed into the lake below.

Hayley reread the sign, and a deviant smile grew on her face – Ethan was about to get told again.

"It takes two skips from me to you," she read.

She skipped up the ramp to the platform of water and kept skipping in circles.

"You have to skip, and you can't stop," she said.

"Well done, my dear," Jordanna said.

Nicholas was barely able to walk, let alone skip across the long bridge – but with his wings and crutch together, he was able to lighten his weight and mimic a skipping motion.

As they reached Inner Island, Nicholas collapsed.

"Shnickyrooners and things like that," he murmured.

"What's wrong with him?" Hayley asked.

"He's growing weaker and has become delirious," Jordanna said. "We'll have to help him the rest of the way."

Jordanna draped Nicholas's arm over her shoulder. Ethan took the other.

They were at the edge of a thick jungle where a well-traveled path led into the green wall of growth – they had found the way to the Outpost.

They came upon an extensive clearing with a cluster of tall trees at its center. The abundant branches hid a collection of structures with bamboo stairways and bridges that connected seven tiers of huts. The sight reminded Ethan of a Disney treehouse he had once seen.

They arrived at the towering trees that held the Outpost. A giant bonfire became visible – the source of the smoke that billowed from the island. Piles of vampire bodies lay stacked near the bonfire; and a woman knelt, crying, while a tall man threw another vampire into the flames – they wore black and white Caretaker robes. Jordanna called out to Commander Adam Triplin and his wife Trudy.

"What happened here?" she asked.

"They surprised us and killed my entire staff before we even knew what hit us," Commander Triplin said. "They were Grimleavers – but they could shape-shift."

"Hydromorph blood," Jordanna said. "They've learned of its transmorphic properties and are using it as a weapon."

"They were nervous and kept talking about Victor Qruefeldt's fear that the Caretakers would somehow unlock the portals."

"This isn't the first time I've heard that," Jordanna said.

"They sabotaged our communications – we were helpless – until they came and killed them all."

"Who came? Who are they?" Jordanna asked.

"I-I-I don't know – they were unlike anything I've ever seen."

Nicholas collapsed as Jordanna and Ethan laid him down gently. Jordanna knelt by his side as he was about to lose consciousness.

"Vamprils are near," Nicholas said in a barely audible voice.

"Where are your medical supplies?" asked Jordanna.

"Ethan, the poem book," Hayley said as her ring slithered around her finger.

CHAPTER TWENTY-TWO

Ethan retrieved the book like a pro as it sprang to life. Jordanna looked on with keen interest as the pages flipped to the first blank page. Writing crawled up the page then they read the words:

The Plight of the Vamprils

A proud but troubled species, secluded and alone.
Vampril wings take flight; they come to save their own.

Dark disturbing secrets, the story will be told.
Feeding on blood of vampires, so ruthless and so bold.

Devolved of spirit, weak of mind.
Like fallen angels, running blind.

The dangerous path they've chosen could surely be their end. Two outcomes, one forsaken, be it enemy or friend.

"This can only mean one thing," Jordanna said.

She held her palms to her temples as if in pain. Then she stood, extended her arms, and spoke in an amplified voice.

"He will die without your help. He does not deserve to die."

Her voice echoed through the island. There was no reply, but then sounds thundered from the distant mountains as angelic figures flew towards them – vamprils.

They landed near the bonfire and walked towards Jordanna in a V formation. All seven of them were female.

"Valeska, I wish we were meeting under better circumstances," Jordanna said.

The vamprils wore flowing white robes, and Valeska Vandercort was the tallest of the group – she was their leader.

"Tend to him," Valeska ordered, and the vampril women rushed to Nicholas' side.

"Where are the others?" Jordanna asked.

"A terrible thing happened," Valeska said. "We never considered they could hunt us so easily. The Grimleavers have a nose for vampril blood – only four of our men survived."

"You could have come back," Jordanna said.

"We thought we had found a place of safety here, but they can shape-shift now – we won't be safe anywhere."

"He's in bad shape, but hopefully, we've treated him in time," one of the vampril women said.

The sound of splashing came from a nearby inlet on the other side of the trees. Jordanna and Valeska walked towards the disturbance, and Ethan and Hayley followed.

"We've been taking care of the pups," Valeska said. "Since the attack on the Outpost, we've been feeding them."

They came to a ramp that led into a small cove where two sea creatures frolicked in the water like seal pups. The playful young animals hobbled out of the water to greet the approaching people.

The kraken pups had cute faces with big brown eyes and long lashes. They were dark bluish-purple with the body of a massive seal, but much longer and their tails tapered at the end like an eel. They walked on a row of elongated pectoral fins that were floppy at the ends like immature tentacles.

"Where is the third?" Jordanna asked. "Commander Triplin said they were all accounted for."

"As I was saying, we've taken care of the pups for nearly a week. The commander you spoke to was a Grimleaver. They held Commander Triplin and his wife captive when they arrived and took the pup. Some stayed behind to carry on the charade until . . ." her voice trailed off.

"The Commander spoke of someone killing the vampires. Did you witness who killed them?"

"I know who killed them. When I said only four of our men had survived, that was not entirely true. Romulas and three others killed the vampires and fed on their blood — they've become bloodfiends."

"Why would your husband do such a thing? Romulas is a noble man."

"We were on the run and helpless, so Romulas hatched a plan. They would bait a vampire, overpower it and feed so that they would turn bloodfiend. That would make them strong enough to become the hunters and kill every last Grimleaver."

"Then the bloodfiend theories are correct," Jordanna said, "vampire blood transforms vampril DNA."

"The reality is worse than theorized — they've become monsters," Valeska said. "I worry of what is to come when they run out of Grimleavers to feed on."

Nightfall was approaching, so they decided to stay at the Outpost. The tree huts were mostly unharmed and would provide ample shelter. Nicholas was in good hands with the vampril women, and Jordanna and Valeska helped burn the rest of the vampire remains.

Ethan wondered why the vampires didn't burst into flames under the sun's rays – like in the movies. Jordanna explained that real vampires avoid light because their eyes favor darkness.

In the morning, they would bury the dead and repair communications. Commander Triplin and his wife would remain at the Outpost with Valeska and the vampril women. Jordanna, Ethan, and Hayley would return to The Residence and dispatch a team to retrieve Nicholas and the injured vampril men.

UNEXPECTED GUESTS

When they arrived back at The Residence, Jordanna wasted no time calling a meeting of the Caretaker Council. They would meet in the Map Room in four hours.

Ethan and Hayley were in Ethan's room, discussing the trip to Kraken Island. Ethan retrieved his pocket tote and pulled out the jeweled dagger and mysterious black crest.

"This knife must be worth a fortune," Ethan said as he examined its jeweled handle.

"I'm more interested in the crest," Hayley said. "Somebody hid it there for a reason."

"You're right," Ethan said as he stuffed the dagger back into his pocket tote.

Ethan held up the crest so that they could view it in the light, but it slipped from his hand and fell to the ground, landing with a heavy metallic clang. The crest did not break – whatever it was made from was very strong.

"I wonder if we might learn something in the study," Hayley said.

Ethan agreed. He returned the crest to his pocket tote, and he and Hayley headed to the study. When they entered, RGB were arguing.

"RGB stands for Really Great Blue," Newton said.

"Rat Germ Blue maybe, but not very great," Albert said.

"It means Red Goat Baby," Newton said.

"Or Red Geek Booty," Linus said.

"No – RGB means Ranting Green Brat," Albert shot back.

"You're all wrong," Hayley interrupted, "it means – Really Good Boys – so be Really Good Boys and quit bickering."

"We're sorry," Newton said.

"You are correct," Linus agreed.

"No problemo," Albert added.

Ethan and Hayley adjourned to the bookshelves to search through the reference books. They were looking for anything about knives, weapons, symbols, or emblems. No sooner had they started, then RGB began to bicker again.

"I remember, it means Rotten Grump-face Blue," Albert said.

"Ethan, can I inspect the crest?" Hayley asked.

Ethan retrieved his pocket tote and pulled the black crest out, and the room got quiet. RGB stopped bickering and stood side by side, staring at Ethan with wide eyes.

"How did Ethan Fox come to possess the Creators' crest?" Linus asked.

The pyrodevlins hopped onto the study table, knelt, and held their hands out.

Ethan started towards RGB but tripped and fumbled the crest. It flipped up into the air and hovered for a moment before floating towards RGB. As the crest reached their tiny outstretched hands, RGB each grasped a quadrant, and the symbols began to glow in each of their colors as RGB fell into a trance.

Ethan approached as RGB held the glowing crest above their heads. The symbols glowed bright red, green, and blue, but the fourth remained black. As Ethan reached the table, the black symbol began to glow yellow, and wisps of golden light emerged from Ethan's pocket.

"Something's happening again," Hayley said as she rubbed her infinity ring.

Ethan retrieved the poem book and held it in his open hands. The book took over, but this time it flipped to the torn-out pages. The first torn-out page grew and reconstructed itself as the fourth symbol of the crest glowed a brighter yellow. There was already a poem on this page, and it read:

The Odyssey Begins

The journey's just begun but evil's planned ahead.
Behold a Realm of Darkness where the living become
dead.

Its minions lurk in silence among the breeding horde.
Awaiting the arrival of an evil dark Grimlord.

Creator from a chosen world this warning you must fear.
Be careful who you trust as darkness will be near.

But the future runs eternal, and a savior will arrive.
A long lost Hybrid Child, feared dead but still alive.

Creator from a chosen world protect it at all costs.
A Moment in Eternity, will tell you when you're lost.

"What does this mean?" Hayley asked.

"I don't know – but this one is not a new passage and it sounds like Creator Stravis was the intended audience."

"Yeah," Hayley said, "and if the future is now – you are here to save us."

The poem book calmed, and RGB awoke from their collective trance. They set the crest down on the table, and it snapped apart effortlessly and melted away, leaving four black symbols that were now separate.

"The Hybrid Child has arrived," RGB said in unison. "Your journey has begun, Ethan Fox."

"What journey?" Ethan said. "What are you talking about?"

"Red Gas Buffalo, that is what RGB stands for," Newton said.

The bickering resumed as if nothing happened. Ethan gathered up the symbols and poem book and tossed them into his pocket tote.

"What just happened?" Ethan asked Hayley.

"I have no idea," Hayley said as she rubbed her ring finger. "But I'm getting a strange feeling."

RGB's bickering stopped.

"Master Daavic," Newton said.

"He's not happy," Linus said.

"Let's hide," Albert said.

Three colored streaks flashed in front of Ethan's eyes, and RGB were gone.

"We should hide, too," Hayley said.

She pulled at Ethan's arm and led him to the floor behind the couch. Daavic entered the study, slammed the door, and strode over to his desk.

Ethan and Hayley peeked over the couch as Daavic unlocked his desk drawer and stared at the contents. He pulled out a yellow journal and read for several minutes before returning it to the drawer. He retrieved a skeleton key from his robe and tossed that into the drawer too.

Daavic then took out a pen and paper and wrote a long note. He stuffed it into a fat oblong envelope and scanned it with his ELMO. Bright red beams danced up and down its length until it transformed. Long thin, wiry wings sprouted from the ends of the envelope and flew it away – right through the out-door.

Daavic's ELMO sounded an alarm, so he answered.

"We have spotted Damien in the Moongarden," a voice said. "He was seen scaling down the skyclimber."

Daavic locked his desk and stormed out of the study.

"Did you hear that," Ethan said, "they spotted Damien in the Moongarden."

Hayley's interest was somewhere else.

"Ethan, did you see that?"

"Yeah – I wonder what's in that yellow journal that he finds so interesting. And what was with that flying—"

"No, Ethan, I was talking about the key. Daavic used that key to open the door underneath the staircase. He's hiding something in that basement, and my ring is telling me so."

"Are you thinking what I think you're thinking?"

"I have an idea," Hayley said as she reached into her pocket and pulled out her copycat.

"Tabby Cat, Tabby Cat, make me a copy," Hayley said as the copycat vanished from her hand and the skeleton key appeared.

"Let's go find out what's down there," Hayley said.

The key fit like a glove, and a musty odor wafted up from the dark cellar as Hayley pulled the door open. A creaky sound filled the air and sent chills down Ethan's spine. Hayley flipped a switch, and a dim light flickered down the narrow staircase, barely lighting their way. Ethan's heart raced as they reached the bottom of the creaky wooden staircase. They were in a dark, dingy room with workbenches on each wall. The sound of dripping water emanated from blackness at the back of the room, and then a rustling noise filled the air.

"Do you hear that?"

"Yes, I think it is coming from over there," Hayley said as she pointed at a tall domed cylinder covered in black fabric.

"Looks like a birdcage," Ethan said as he approached.

"I've got a bad feeling about this," Hayley said.

Ethan tugged at the fabric, and the cover fell away as blood rushed to his head.

"CAW, CAW, CAW—"

The grimtailed dread's shrieks filled the damp air as Ethan and Hayley backed away slowly.

"It was Daavic," Ethan said. "He opened the vortex and is helping his brother."

"We should warn my mom and the others."

Ethan felt something move around in his pocket. His pocket tote was unraveling itself, so he set it down on a nearby workbench.

"You're growing on me," said a voice from within. "I'm starting to like Ethan Fox, or should I say – Hybrid Child."

A small green head emerged from the pocket tote.

"And a how do you do to you," Gruggins McGhee said with a smile.

FAMILY REUNION

Gruggins! We've been worried," Hayley cried. "How did you get into Ethan's pocket tote?"

"Been there all along," Gruggins said.

Ethan and Hayley gave each other a glance.

"How did you escape?" Ethan asked.

"I didn't escape, Master Damien let me go. I've followed Ethan Fox since the day he arrived."

"The negative door," Hayley said. "You went through the negative door that opened up when we arrived."

"That ring of yours talking again?" Gruggins said. "Followed Ethan Fox around and slipped into the pocket tote after bumble-head Irvin gave it to him."

"Why would Damien let you go?" Hayley asked. "He and Daavic are scheming with Victor Qruefeldt."

"Not all is how it appears to be," Gruggins said.

Ethan was leaning against the workbench. Gruggins rubbed his hands together and put them on Ethan.

"I remember," said Ethan. "You were at the top of the stairs and shot me with a dart."

"A harmless sleeping dart – I'm sorry for that," Gruggins said. "I couldn't let you blow my cover. I didn't want me to find me. Imagine my surprise when I found my dart stuck in your butt."

Gruggins held out a small golden dart with "G.M." monogrammed on the shaft.

"Confused me at first, but then I figured things out. I wasn't sensing a tribe of Nibblewarts outside my box – I was sensing me."

"It all adds up," Hayley said, "Ethan thought someone was snooping in his room – but you were just coming and going from his pocket tote."

"And the gold dust appearing on the cave wall," Ethan said. "That was cloaked leprechaun's gold, I bet."

"You're figuring things out quickly," Gruggins said.

"Why did you hide in my pocket tote?" Ethan asked.

"We needed to make sure you were safe," Gruggins said, "and to find out what you would learn along the way."

"Who is we?" Hayley asked.

"Do you trust me?" Gruggins asked.

"Yes," Hayley replied.

"And you, Ethan Fox?"

"Yes."

"Then there's someone I want you to meet," Gruggins said and hopped onto Hayley's shoulder.

They locked the basement and followed Gruggins' directions to the twelfth door on the right. There was daylight in Deadwood as they strode into town, and the Saloon was nearly empty as the bartender stood at the bar reading *The Residential Daily Star*. Gruggins directed them towards a stranger sitting at a table in a dimly lit corner. Ethan felt a tingle at the back of his neck, and then a voice spoke up in his head.

"Stay calm, Ethan Fox," the soothing voice said. It was the same voice he had heard when the vampires were abducting him.

As they neared the stranger, Ethan saw him clearly as his eyes adjusted to the dark. He wore a brown trench coat, a black wide-brimmed hat, and dark glasses.

"The stranger from the Gallery painting," Hayley said.

They sat at the table. The stranger's head tilted towards his goblet of dragon's breath. Gruggins hopped from Hayley's shoulder.

"Enjoying yourself?" Gruggins asked. "I've spent days holed up in a stuffy pocket tote."

"Moments for me," the stranger said. His voice was soft but gritty and sounded familiar to Ethan.

Gruggins turned to Hayley.

"Your brother is a good man," he said.

"But the grimtailed dread," Hayley replied. "You saw for yourself – Daavic is helping the Grimleavers."

The stranger's head rose slowly, and stringy black hair fell around his face as he removed his hat. He pulled the glasses from his face to expose his eyes – one deep green, the other bluish-grey with a moon-shaped pupil.

"He's talking about your other brother," Damien Ravenwood said.

Hayley's eyes widened, but she stayed seated. Ethan jumped from his seat and started for the door when the voice spoke up again.

"It was I, Ethan Fox," the calm voice said, "Damien Ravenwood saved you from the vampires."

Ethan immediately realized whose voice was in his head – Damien was his guardian angel. He stopped and returned to the table.

"He has misled you," Damien said. "Daavic has done a masterful job of framing me, but he made one grave mistake."

"We witnessed you with two hell-pods," Hayley said. "You tried to burn down the Silent Forest."

"Do you remember Market Square?" Damien asked. "Do you remember those trolls laughing as Daavic spoke with them?"

Ethan and Hayley nodded.

"Forest trolls only laugh when frightened," Damien said. "Daavic gave them three hell-pods – but unfortunately, they ignited one before I was able to stop them."

"He is telling the truth," Gruggins said.

"I'm still not sure of my brother's motivation – but in the end, it was the perfect set-up. There I was, holding two hell-pods as a party of Caretakers looked on. I couldn't exactly explain my way out of that one."

"Why did you abduct Gruggins?" Ethan asked.

"I was running out of options and needed an ally. Someone had to believe me, and only a grumpling can see through such lies and deception. I was fully prepared for Gruggins to fight me tooth and nail – but imagine my surprise when he came along willingly."

"Willingly?" Hayley questioned.

"Yes – once I figured out that the critter outside my box was me. It made sense that I'd soon be jumping timelines."

"We never did trust Daavic," Ethan said.

"He showed you the secret wishing well – didn't he?" Damien asked.

"Yes – he said a drink would heal my lost memories."

"He lied," Damien said. "The water in that well steals memories. Daavic tried to ensure you would never remember. I bet he didn't offer Ethan Fox a drink, did he?"

"How did you know that?" Hayley asked.

"But I did take a drink—" Ethan interrupted. "I shared one with Gruggins."

"That is how you ended up with my sister's memories," Damien said to Gruggins. "You all shared a drink from the same bucket."

"I don't understand," Hayley said.

"The well swapped your memories. When Daavic and I discovered the well, we drank from it – and I ended up with some of his memories, and he with mine."

"That's how you found out Daavic evolved your species into a zebra," Ethan said.

"Yes, but in your case, the swap was three-way, and Gruggins ended up with my sister's memories of Daavic, helping Victor Qruefeldt kill our father."

Hayley didn't appear surprised by Damien's revelation.

"Master Damien," Gruggins said, "there are other developments we need to tell you about."

Ethan and Hayley got themselves a sugar-pickle soda while Gruggins filled Damien in on what he had learned.

"What now?" Hayley asked upon their return.

"We need a plan," Damien said.

Ethan's mind raced through the events of the past few days – he was formulating a plan.

"I've got it – but it may be risky," Ethan said.

"Let's hear it," Damien said.

Jordanna had called for a meeting of the Caretaker Council, and hundreds of Caretakers looked on from the packed lower half of the Map Room. Jordanna, Daavic, and the CAGE team floated above them.

Ethan, Hayley, Damien, and Gruggins had slipped in to observe from the shadows of the mid-section entryway.

"I've called this meeting to fill you in on recent events," said Jordanna. "We will start with the Grimleavers. We've received reports of chatter from various sources. Victor Qruefeldt has become increasingly fearful of us unlocking the portals."

Muffled voices filled the room.

"Open-em up!" shouted a voice from the crowd.

"The Book of Creators clearly states," said Jordanna. "The portals will only unlock upon discovery of the prophecies – we have no key."

"Their fear makes perfect sense. Secluded from the elemental worlds they stand stronger," said Brianna.

"So, the Grimleavers have become more aggressive," Daavic said, "to distract us from accomplishing something we cannot possibly accomplish."

"Yes," Jordanna said. "Unless – there is another way."

"If they fear it, we should unlock the portals," a voice yelled out.

"Find the key!" cried another as others followed along.

"Find the key! Find the key!" the crowd chanted.

"Moving along," Jordanna hushed the crowd. "We've received word from Fin regarding the break-in at Poseidon – the stolen items were from Stravis' bunker."

Muffled discussion filled the room again.

"They are still investigating, but Stravis' journal was among the stolen items."

"Stravis' journal," Ethan whispered. "That has to be the yellow book Daavic has locked away in the study – just as I suspected."

The crowd grew louder.

"The Grimleavers have attacked the Outpost and abducted one of the pups. Fin believes a kraken is on the loose."

"How could they attack the Outpost?" asked a voice in the crowd.

"The vamprils held witness," Nicholas said. "They were hiding on the island and confirmed another of Fin's suspicions. The Grimleavers are using hydromorph blood – it is transmorphic."

Muffled voices erupted again.

"We've lost many vamprils – and some have become bloodfiends," Jordanna said.

The voices grew louder.

"Why release a kraken?" someone in the crowd yelled.

"Grimleavers are not foolish enough to devolve an earthly kraken!" another chimed in.

"Another of those nagging questions," Jordanna said.

"Isn't it obvious?" a voice shouted above the crowd. "They freed a kraken to wreak havoc so you would send a team to Poseidon."

A stranger emerged from the shadows above the crowd – he wore a brown trench coat. Ethan and Hayley were at his side with Gruggins on Hayley's shoulder. Damien took off his hat and glasses, and the room erupted with noise as the crowd recognized the man who killed their beloved leader.

"SECURITY, TO THE MAP ROOM!" Daavic screamed into his ELMO. "ARREST THIS MAN IMMEDIATELY!"

Daavic pointed his red gloved finger at his brother, his face pink with anger. The room grew silent.

"I know what they've been up to, Mother – I know what he's been up to!"

Damien pointed back at his brother.

"SEIZE THAT MAN," Daavic ordered as security entered the room.

"I didn't come alone, we can help you, Mother – but we must speak in private."

The security detail surrounded Damien and the others, and slowly closed in.

"WAIT – I will hear what my son has to say."

"But Mother—"

"Daavic – you are dismissed."

BROTHER DEAREST

Ethan's plan was coming together. They had planted a small snooping device atop the study bookshelves before crashing the Council meeting. Jordanna, Damien, Gruggins, Ethan, and Hayley were in the front room huddled over Ethan's ELMO display, watching as Daavic paced around inside the study.

RGB were arguing over a book in a three-way tug-of-war.

"OUT! LEAVE AT ONCE!" Daavic yelled.

RGB dropped the book and were gone in a flash.

Daavic took a seat at his desk and leaned back deep in thought. He unlocked the drawer and retrieved a yellow book; an old dusty journal with tattered edges. He held it up and studied its cover – and then Daavic vanished.

He reappeared a few feet from Hayley, and the yellow journal in his hands morphed into a small metallic kitty.

Daavic threw it to the ground. Hayley's Tabby Cat had returned to her owner.

"Looking for this brother?" Damien said as he held up Stravis' yellow journal.

"I've been giving it a read, fascinating, the writings of Creator Stravis. He tells of his distrust of Zamalador, his friendship with Jasper, and how he saved the Hybrid Child."

"Enough of this nonsense, you must arrest him, Mother."

"I didn't make the connection myself," Jordanna said. "When Ethan Fox told me of his dream – of the blue and yellow taletaddler – I didn't consider that it might be Jasper."

"But you did, dear brother – and you had your Grimleaver buddies release the kraken. You needed it to sow destruction so you could journey to Poseidon to steal the journal. Fin had to request a face-to-face meeting with the secret he kept."

"YOU CAN'T BELIEVE HIM!"

"Victor Qruefeldt's obsession with Creator Stravis is well documented," Jordanna said. "He insists that Stravis is still alive. After Stravis' death, Jasper disappeared. If Victor learned of Jasper's appearance, he might consider it proof of Stravis' survival as well."

"Mother, you can't believe these lies."

"You insisted on the assignment," Jordanna said as the room quieted.

"You also sent trolls to burn down the Silent Forest," Ethan said.

"And don't forget about the grimtailed dread he has hidden in the basement," Hayley added.

"Lies! All lies! I swear to you, Mother! He's the one who abducted Gruggins."

"I didn't abduct Gruggins – he came along willingly. And imagine our surprise dear brother, when Gruggins began having flashbacks – memories that could only be our sister Hayley's."

Daavic's body tensed, and a defeated expression swept over his face.

"You made one grave mistake," Damien said. "You recognized the rift-key on our sister's hand – so you took her to the wishing well to erase her memories. You couldn't chance her remembering what you did to her. But what you didn't know—"

Damien paused, and Jordanna hung on his every word as tears welled in her eyes.

"What you didn't know was that Gruggins and Ethan shared a drink with our sister. Gruggins now holds our sister's memories – memories of you helping Victor Qruefeldt kill our father."

Jordanna glared at Daavic.

"What wishing well?" she asked Damien.

"A secret place in the Moongarden, the well holds extraordinary powers, its water churns memories. Gruggins was in the well and intercepted the bucket, and shared a drink with Ethan. Gruggins received my sister's memories – memories that he views differently than she did. The interesting thing about grumplings, they have many special abilities and can see through a cloak of deception – they perceive the truth.”

“What are you saying? What did Gruggins see?”

“He witnessed Victor Qruefeldt kill my father. Victor used hydromorph blood to disguise himself as me – the Grimleavers learned of the hydromorph secret long ago.”

Jordanna turned to Gruggins, and he gave a confirming nod.

“How did Victor kill my husband?”

“A Heldrik Vonn Grim puzzle box,” Damien said. “There was a struggle, and Ryvias grabbed the puzzle box and dislodged the rift-key.”

“Hayley witnessed me killing Ryvias. She ran to his side, and before he died, Ryvias put the rift-key on her finger. Later, she witnessed Daavic and Victor plotting in the Moongarden, and they spotted her.”

“HE MADE ME HELP HIM! He said, we would all suffer if I didn’t – a fate worse than death!”

“That night, Victor sent Daavic to kill our sister with the puzzle box. Missing its rift-key, the puzzle box did not work as expected and transported Hayley through time and space to Ethan Fox – the Hybrid Child.”

Wisps of golden light lashed from Ethan’s pocket. He retrieved his pocket tote and then the poem book. Gruggins glanced at the cover and mumbled. Ethan gave Gruggins a questioning glance as he opened the book.

“Read it aloud,” Jordanna said.

Ethan’s palms glowed as he read the poem:

The Hybrid Child Returns

Behold the Hybrid Child, his journey has begun.
Born of pure intentions beneath the desert sun.

His path is stalked by darkness as evil is abound.
But lightness shines upon him in the friendships he has
found.

The next step must be taken, and choices must be made.
To bypass the natural order and guide him from the shade.

The portals shall be opened but only by his hand.
Welcome Hybrid Child, from the Eyes of the Desert Sand.

Daavic removed his red glove exposing a bony gray hand
that looked dead. He smirked, and his demeanor abruptly
changed.

"We didn't know the rift-key was missing," Daavic
admitted. "Or your dear Hayley would be ashes."

"What has happened to you?" Jordanna cried. "You're a
monster—"

"Why does Victor fear the portals?" Damien asked.

"The Grimlord fears nothing – he wants the portals
open, to expose the Hybrid Child and leave him vulnerable."

"All the chatter we've been hearing," Jordanna said.
"That has all been a ruse – to motivate us to unlock the
portals."

Daavic let out a sinister laugh.

"Here's an interesting passage," Damien read from Stravis' journal:

". . . my distrust of Zamalador deepens by the day. I fear he may tamper with the natural order. Thus, I've taken countermeasures and created a back-door to unlock the portals. The Seers will make sure that only the Hybrid Child can set things in motion . . ."

"But we were hearing about the Grimleaver chatter long before Daavic stole the journal," Ethan said. "Fin even reported it at the meeting in Poseidon."

"I wasn't sure what it was at the time," Hayley said, "but we witnessed Daavic send a leap-letter in the study. Victor may have learned of all this the moment Ethan and I arrived."

Daavic erupted in a devilish laugh.

"Kudos dear sister – I should have cut out your tongue the moment I recognized that rift-key."

"If Victor wants the portals opened," Jordanna said, "then they must remain locked."

"No—" Ethan interrupted. "I must unlock the portals – the Seers are telling us that."

"He's right," Hayley said as she rubbed the rift-key.

Ethan peered at Gruggins as he perched on Hayley's shoulder, and the phantom bubble floated above his head. Ethan opened up the book of poems and studied the pages.

"I think I've found the key," Ethan announced.

UNLOCKING THE PORTALS

F unny thing about grumplings, they have many special abilities," Ethan said. "They can even read the secret language of the Creators."

Ethan held the poem book up so Gruggins could view the cover. "Can you read that Gruggins?"

"Of course – can't you? Gruggins replied. He read:

A Moment in Eternity

Ethan read from the book:

Creator from a chosen world protect it at all costs.
A Moment in Eternity, will tell you when you're lost.

Ethan paused to let the words sink in.

"This book – *A Moment in Eternity*, has been telling us when we're lost."

"Of course," Jordanna said. "It warned the Silent Forest was about to burn. And on Kraken Island, it told us the plight of the vamprils, and helped me realize that Nicholas was right – and they were nearby."

"It also warned Ethan and me about the creepy crawlers."

"Stravis was the Creator from a chosen world. In my dream, he gave this book to Jasper, and Jasper gave it to me. I think this book holds the key."

"What are you suggesting?" Jordanna asked.

"The book just told us that we—" Ethan paused. "That I, must bypass the natural order and open the portals. Then there's this:

To find the key things must unfold,

at a grumpling's feet the secret's told.

Ethan walked to the front door and opened it. Bright, colorful beams of light shimmered off the metallic spheres and created a pattern on the floor, a trail of tiny footprints that led down the narrow black carpet. They resembled the ink trail Gruggins had left on Ethan's dresser.

"At a grumpling's feet, the secret's told," he repeated and pointed at the pattern. "Gruggins, would you do the honors?"

Gruggins fluttered off Hayley's shoulder and landed on the carpet at Ethan's feet. He walked the trail of footprints –

a perfect match for his feet. The phantom bubble followed Gruggins as he walked towards the black marble slab at the other end. Damien moved the coffee table that stood in Gruggins' path. As he continued, a golden pedestal appeared where the table had been. Symbols were etched on its surface:

A Moment in Eternity

"The phantom bubble follows Gruggins because it is attracted to gold," Hayley said.

"Yes, and when Gruggins isn't around, it hovers over this pedestal – and if I'm right, this should do the trick."

Ethan placed the poem book on the pedestal, and it began to glow as it melted away, and their shapes morphed together. When the transformation was complete, a knee-high golden pyramid stood in the room's center. A hole bored down through the top of the small monument.

"Where did the book go?" Hayley asked.

"I have no idea," Ethan said.

A golden rod swiftly rose from within the hole and as it grew taller, a small saucer formed at the top. The staff grew to three feet tall before it stopped. The phantom bubble floated towards the staff and came to rest in its saucer, where it solidified into a flawless crystal sphere.

"The footprints," Ethan said.

The colorful trail of light disappeared from the carpet as the light reflecting off the portals changed direction. A laser-like beam blasted from each of the four spheres: one red, one green, one blue, and one yellow. The beams aimed directly at the newly formed crystal and entered at the same spot – but emerged split into their respective colors like a prism. Four small colored symbols projected on Daavic's robe as if the crystal were decoding a signal.

"Step aside," Damien moved Daavic from the beams path.

The beams zipped across the room and projected larger symbols on the four corners of the marble slab. They grew brighter and intensified as they etched into the black slab, and then the beams stopped.

Ethan and Hayley looked at each other as they recognized the symbols etched into the slab, the symbols from the Creators' crest.

"Now what?" Damien said.

"I think we know," Hayley said.

Ethan retrieved the four black symbols and handed them to Damien.

"Where did you find those?" Jordanna asked.

"In the lair of the spider gecko, cloaked in leprechaun's gold," Hayley said. "If Gruggins weren't with us, we would have never seen it."

Damien approached the black slab and placed the symbols into their respective corners – a perfect fit. When the last symbol was in place, the slab sank into the floor like a piece of ice melting on a hot stove. It disappeared and exposed the empty wall.

"The Creators must have put that there to project the lock," said Damien.

They turned their attention to the front door.

"What are you waiting for? Give it a try, Mom," Hayley said to Jordanna.

Jordanna held out her hand, a ball appeared, and she handed it to Hayley. "I want you to be the one."

Hayley threw the ball through the door, and it zipped right back – the portals were still locked.

Ethan caught the ball as it bounced by him. He glanced back at the wall where the slab had stood.

"Hayley, you silly girl, you can't go out through the in-door."

Everyone turned to Ethan. The giant mirror had moved itself to the empty wall the slab had left – it had finally found its place. The mirror reflected the portals on its surface like it was the front door.

Ethan threw the ball through the mirror, and it bounced onto the checkerboard plane and rolled past the portals.

"You did it – you unlocked the portals," Hayley said.

The basement door burst open, and a damp, musty odor overtook the room. Loud shrieks echoed up from the basement.

"CAW, CAW, CAW."

The grimtailed dread's call was unmistakable as a black lifeless form swiftly navigated up the stairwell. "CAW, CAW." The dread circled overhead and then broke into a dive that ended near the giant mirror.

A small vortex appeared and swallowed the dread in its path. But the vortex wasn't there to let something out – it was there to let someone enter. Victor Qruefeldt stepped through the growing vortex with the grimtailed dread perched on his shoulder.

"Bravo, Ethan Fox. I couldn't have done better myself."

Victor clapped his hands in applause.

"You've made a grave mistake coming here," Jordanna said as she stepped in front of Hayley to shield her.

"Young Ethan Fox has done us a great service – or should I say, Hybrid Child," Victor said. He scowled, and his eyes glowed red as he stared through Ethan.

"All has happened as the Grimlord has planned," Daavic said.

"I'm sorry, Daavic – but your secret is out. You're of no use to me any longer."

"But Master, I left Poe in the basement as you ordered, and I've been a faithful servant for all these years."

"Poe, tend to Daavic's demise."

"But I'm loyal!"

"CAW, CAW," the dread screeched.

Daavic begged for his life. "Please, I beg of you, Master!"

"CAW, CAW," the dread leapt from Victor's shoulder, flapped its wings, and circled overhead where the ceiling was missing.

"I CAN STILL BE OF SERVICE MASTER!"

The dread dove at Daavic and whizzed by his face leaving a small black vortex behind. Jordanna started towards Daavic to help, but Damien wrapped his arms around her.

"That is a death vortex – it would kill you," Damien said.

A ray of light shot out from the center of the vortex and scanned the length of Daavic's body. Daavic slowly turned transparent – he was dematerializing.

"IT BURNS – AAAAAAAAAAHHHHHHHHH – IT BURNS!"

Daavic changed shape like a blob in a lava lamp. His head smooshed into an oblong blob as the death vortex reduced Daavic to a swirling mass of screams. The vortex sucked him in like a vacuum cleaner as the dread swooped through the vortex and returned to Victor's shoulder.

The vortex was gone. Daavic was gone – Daavic was dead.

Damien and Jordanna stood emotionless. They had just witnessed the demise of another Ravenwood – another Caretaker dead at the hands of Victor Qruefeldt.

"You'll pay for this," Damien started towards Victor, but Jordanna hugged him tighter.

"Have you ever seen a Heldrik Vonn Grim puzzle box?" Victor asked.

He reached into his robe and pulled out a shiny black cube.

"Heldrik invented a very effective weapon, but it isn't nearly as useful without its rift-key."

Victor peered at Hayley and raised his arm. Hayley's infinity ring unraveled and flew across the room into his waiting hand.

"Makes sense it sent you to Ethan Fox," Victor said to Hayley. "I had the rift-key fashioned from his rib after all."

Victor roared with an evil laughter.

Hayley gasped at the loss of her ring, and Ethan could tell it perturbed her. He glanced at her, and she pursed her lips and smirked – then winked.

"As much as I'd love to stick around, Victor said, "I've got a Hybrid Child to kill, and a human world to pillage."

The top of the puzzle box opened. Victor dropped the rift-key in, and the top sprang shut. He took a step towards Ethan, and Jordanna and Damien stepped in his way.

"I sensed you the moment you arrived from the human world," Victor said to Ethan. "When they interfered in our first meeting, the Seers joined our consciousness. I spent centuries wondering what happened to that connection, and Stravis' journal tells the story."

Ethan looked at Damien and the others, and smiled. Then he looked Victor Qruefeldt in the eyes and stepped towards him.

"You obviously haven't read the words of Creator Stravis," Ethan said with a confident grin. "If you had, you would know that you can't kill me. Stravis spells it out, as clear as day."

Victor raised his arm, and the yellow journal flew from Damien's hands into his. He flipped Stravis' journal open, and the book turned brown with gold letters. A bright light beamed from the book's pages into Victor's face, and he vanished.

IN THE BEGINNING

Jordanna held a lengthy meeting of the Caretaker Council following Daavic's death. Damien and Hayley sat as CAGE members. They made Ethan an honorary member due to his role in opening the portals and vanquishing Victor Qruefeldt, not to mention that he was the Hybrid Child – a beacon of Caretaker hope.

Nicholas, Brianna, and Azron were leery at first but gave Damien a warm reception after learning the truth. The news of Daavic's death saddened them, but learning of his betrayal was even harder for them to hear.

After the meeting, Jordanna called the CAGE team to the study but gave no reason why. Gruggins was a no show, but Ethan and Hayley arrived after the others. Jordanna had news from the elemental worlds and was eager to get started.

"We've received information from the Council of Elders," Jordanna said, "it explains why Victor Qruefeldt was so eager to open up the portals. The lock on the portals served more than one purpose."

"What other purpose does a lock sss-serve?"

"It prevented Grimleavers from entering the human world. The Creators implemented a unique mechanism that utilized a marker they added to Earth's atmosphere – the marker attaches to non-earthly creatures."

"Wouldn't that include us?" Nicholas asked.

"Their mechanism can make the distinction between good and evil. The scheme wasn't perfect as Grimleavers could enter the human world, but only for a short time before dying."

"That explains how I dissuaded the vampires from abducting Ethan Fox so easily," Damien said.

"And why they rarely ventured into the human world," Nicholas added.

"The portals also acted to disrupt Victor's connection to the Hybrid Child," Jordanna said. "The connection remained severed as long as Ethan Fox stayed in the human world."

"But now all those protections are gone," Damien said.

"Yes, and our job just got a lot more difficult," Jordanna said.

"Ethan Fox saved the day with his brilliant plan," Damien said.

"Indeed, and I'm still not sure how you all pulled it off," Jordanna said. "How were you able to disguise a portal book as Stravis' journal?"

"I asked Gruggins to cloak a portal book with a grumpling's cloak," Ethan said. "After that, Damien just had to make the switch at the right time."

"By the way—" Damien interrupted. "Where did you send Victor?"

"*One Two-Tree Island,*" Ethan said. The room erupted with laughter. "What's so funny?" he asked.

"Grimleavers all hate the light," Damien said. "But Victor is from Hades, so he has a natural dislike of earth, wind, and water as well – and you sent him to a sunny, breezy desert island in the middle of the ocean." The laughter continued.

"Sorry to break up all the fun, but I do have other disturbing news to share," Jordanna said.

"Tell us, Mother," Damien said.

"The lock on the portals shared a linked duality with the prophecies."

"What on earth is that supposed to mean?" asked Nicholas.

"It means that they shared a two-way cause and effect relationship. The Book of Creators foretold a list of prophecies that, once discovered, would unlock the portals. That, in turn, would set things in motion and the prophecies would come to pass. The list would act as a countdown indicator, so we know when to perform the extraction ritual."

"I hope you're not saying what I think you're saying," Damien said.

"I'm afraid unlocking the portals has set things in motion. The prophecies will come to pass, and with no list, we won't have any idea of when to perform the ritual. We must find the prophecies . . ."

"Well then, we've got our work cut out for us," Damien said.

"Does that mean you've decided to accept?" Jordanna asked.

"Yes, Mother."

"Accept?" Nicholas asked.

"I've asked Damien to take on Daavic's role, and serve as my number one and eventual replacement."

"Congratulations, Master Damien. I'd hoped to learn such news," said Gruggins from the study table. He'd been in the room all along, cloaked and napping right beside them. "You didn't think I'd miss the festivities, did you?"

Gruggins hopped onto Hayley's shoulder. "Woke up when I heard my name," he whispered into her ear.

"Glad you showed up, Gruggins," Brianna greeted. "I have a question for you."

"Well, don't choke on it," Gruggins said.

"Why would the grumplings leave the Silent Forest? Where would they go?"

"That is two questions, and I don't have an answer to either. They were happy in the Silent Forest, and there is only a handful of other places they'd be safe."

"Kraken Island for one, but the vamprils are adamant the grumplings are not present," Jordanna said.

"That reminds me," Ethan said. "Why would the Grimleavers abduct one of those cute little pups? How could one of those wreak havoc?"

"The Creators designed Kraken Island to keep kraken pups in their infant state," Jordanna said. "Kraken pups are cute indeed – but on Earth, they grow into giant sea monsters."

"Shnickyrooners and things like that," Irvin's jabbering quickly took center stage. "Have you ever measured the green strip of bacon lips that normally gets reserved for picture frames? You'll often find loads of toad rubbish taped between the pink envelopes of skunk odor that hangs from the fiberglass chair."

"I'm going to miss your keen insights," Ethan said.

"How does Ethan Fox know?" Irvin asked. "I was told to keep it a secret."

"How did I know what?" Ethan asked.

"That it is time for you to leave," Jordanna said.

"You can't let him leave – he is no longer safe," Hayley said.

"Irvin will miss Ethan Fox."

"As will Gruggins McGhee," Gruggins said. He hopped from Hayley's shoulder to Ethan's and gave him a small hug on his neck. "I enjoyed hanging out in your pocket tote – on-the-go adventurer you are. Irvin called that one right."

"We can't send him back," Hayley argued.

"I'm sorry, dear," Jordanna said. "I promised Ethan we would return him to his parents, and I am sure he is missing them by now."

"But that was before we knew," Hayley said. "Before we learned he is the Hybrid Child."

"Damien will keep a close eye on him," Jordanna said.

"I've already made arrangements," Damien assured Hayley. "I have a full detail that will covertly guard over him. And the Map Room has been put on full Hybrid Child alert. If a Grimleaver comes within a mile of Ethan Fox, we will welcome them with extreme force."

"But I don't want him to leave!"

"Don't worry, Hayley. I'll be fine. I am the Hybrid Child, after all." A tear fell from his eye.

"Will I see any of you again?" Ethan asked Jordanna.

"You are the Hybrid Child, and I am confident the Seers will make sure that we meet again. For now, you mustn't speak of your time here – not even to your parents."

"My parents," Ethan repeated. "How did I end up with them? I still have so many questions about my past."

"I'm sure you do, so here is what I have learned. You were born in the desert, at the site of Stravis' bunker. Alexander and Tiffany Sturgis are your birth parents. When you were a year old, Victor Qruefeldt attacked you, and the Seers intervened. They teleported you to Stravis, who healed and looked after you. You reappeared centuries later with Stravis' symbol etched into your palms, and you hadn't aged a day. Ryvias and I learned of you then, and we decided to move you to the human world. Ryvias and I agreed not to be told of the details. Only those close to you would know your whereabouts. But that was over a century ago, and I have no idea of how you ended up where you are today . . ."

"Who were they?" Ethan asked. "Who took me to the human world?"

"I only know of Alexander Sturgis and Dakota Drakelan," Jordanna answered. "But they spoke of others."

Ethan stood quietly, pondering his mysterious past.

"If you've no further questions," Jordanna said. "Irvin will escort you to the negative door – your parents will never realize you were gone."

Ethan made his way towards the out-door. The Caretakers lined up, so he could say his goodbyes to each of them on his way out. The Caretakers were huggers, even Azron, who sat quietly listening.

"Azron miss Ethan Fox," the giant said as he knelt and gently enveloped Ethan in his hands. Azron picked Ethan up, held him snugly against his chest, and set him back down.

Brianna and Nicholas said their goodbyes as well, followed by Damien and Jordanna.

Hayley was the last in line. She tried to choke back the tears – but as Ethan approached, she lost it. Tears streamed down Ethan's cheeks as he looked into her eyes. They fell into each other's arms and hugged. Neither of them wanted that moment to end, but Ethan understood it had to. "Hmm-hmm hmm . . ." Ethan hummed into her ear. He hummed the tune Hayley hummed to herself their first night at The Residence.

"We will meet again, I promise," he whispered.

"Me too," Hayley whispered back.

"Say goodbye to Mrs. Moongarden," Ethan said.

They broke from their long hug, and Ethan followed Irvin through the out-door. They entered The Hall of Doorways and turned right, towards the negative doors.

"The negative third door on the right," Irvin said as they arrived. Irvin saluted Ethan as he pulled the door open – Irvin wasn't a hugger.

"Shnickyrooners and shnackleboxes," Ethan said.

Irvin gave him a wink as he stepped through the door.

Ethan saw purple and green pin-spots in the darkness. He felt lightheaded, and then he was back on the beach, staggering forward as he tried to overcome his dizziness. He almost lost his balance and bumped into something. Ethan's eyes came into focus just in time to turn around and witness Hayley falling down the staircase on the beach.

"It was me all along – I pushed Hayley down the stairs," he said to himself.

Ethan walked down the beach and pondered the events of the previous week. Would he ever see Hayley and the rest of his new friends again? The Seers would see to it, Jordanna had told him.

The Caretakers had their hands full now. The Grimleavers were sure to make their presence known in the human world – not to mention the adult kraken on the loose. Would the Grimleavers come after him again? Jordanna and Damien were sure they would try. He was the Hybrid Child, after all, and that was sure to put Ethan atop Victor's naughty list.

Ethan now knew what his parents were protecting him from, but many mysteries remained. How did Ethan end up with George and Betsy? And how did his dad come to possess one of the portal books?

Ethan would keep the secret as he had promised. He would not discuss his time at The Residence with anyone, not even his parents.

He ran down the beach to where he had left his parents more than a week ago. George and Betsy had just finished frolicking in the surf and were walking back to the beach blanket. Betsy realized Ethan was gone and scanned the beach. She spotted him and pointed him out to George.

"Go for a walk along the beach, Tiger?" George shouted.

"Yeah, Dad, just a short one," Ethan answered with a smile.

Ethan was back with his parents just as the Seers had shown him, and he had missed them more than they would ever know.

TWO DAYS LATER

Two days had gone by since Ethan Fox had left The Residence. In the study, Jordanna and Damien were discussing strategy on finding the portal prophecies and the Grimleaver onslaught they were sure would be coming to the human world. Hayley entered the study wearing a half-black half-white Caretaker robe.

"What makes matters worse is the Heldrik Vonn Grim puzzle box," Damien said. "We've never dealt with such a weapon and know nothing about it—"

"About that," Hayley interrupted, "I forgot to tell you."

She smiled and held out her hand. The infinity ring was on her finger. "Never steal a girl's favorite jewelry."

"But how?" Jordanna asked.

"Your copycat," Damien said. "Very clever, sis. You have no idea how many lives you've saved."

There was a knock on the study door, and Dorkin Drumbles rushed into the room.

"Headmistress Ravenwood, a development there has been. A most unusual painting, completed it has."

Jordanna, Damien, and Hayley accompanied Dorkin to the Gallery's viewing hall. Dorkin wobbled over to the piece and pulled back the cover.

He revealed a painting of a dark alleyway dimly lit by an overhead streetlamp. A pitch-black shadow figure of a young woman stood near a trash bin. Her eyes glowed yellow as she reached her black arms out towards a young boy. The boy was facing the shadow-being and held his glowing palms out towards her.

"The boy is Ethan Fox," Hayley said. "I wonder who the shadow girl is?"

"Good question," Jordanna said.

"Whoever it is, she's making my ring crawl."

Jordanna, Hayley, and Damien stared at the painting in silence.

"Well now, this is a first," Jordanna said, "the Gallery has never predicted the future before."

"What do you mean?" Damien asked.

"Look—" Jordanna pointed at an event poster on the alley wall. "That flyer says – Tonight's Performance. But the date is months away – this has not happened yet."

BOOK 2

ETHAN FOX AND THE SHADOW PRINCESS

E. L. SEER

A BITE OF
THE BIG APPLE

The cold night air nipped at Ethan's nose as he stepped into a taxi at New York's Times Square. He gazed out at the crowded mass of tourists enjoying the circus-like atmosphere under the bright lights and towering billboards. Street performers were dressed in their usual flamboyant costumes and performing for the city's visitors to vie for their money. While his parents talked beside him, Ethan quietly cataloged his favorite characters in attendance: Spiderman, Superman, Ironman, Godzilla, King Kong, and even a magician masquerading as Harry Potter.

But then a vampire character in the crowd caught his eye, interrupting his fun thoughts. The homemade human costume looked cheesy – but it was enough to jolt his train of thought back to his time at The Residence.

"I wonder what she's doing right now," Ethan thought.

Nearly a year had passed since Jasper lured him and Hayley to The Residence and introduced them to the strange Caretaker world. Things had almost gotten back to normal since he returned home – but that didn't stop him from thinking about his time with the Caretakers and all the friends he had made. Ethan had kept his promise and told nobody, not even his parents George and Betsy, of his adventures. But things could never truly return to normal now that he knew he was the Hybrid Child and connected to the hidden Caretaker universe.

Well, he sort of knew. Nobody had explained what it meant to be the Hybrid Child or where his memories had gone. Ethan's adoptive parents hid his past by explaining away his lost memories and the shiny white symbols etched onto the palms of his hands. Their story was his birth parents were members of an evil cult who marked their children in that manner, and he later suffered amnesia after a car accident. He still had so many questions, and the answers could only come from The Residence – but he felt at ease and had a strange feeling he would see his friends again soon. He settled back into his seat and watched New York flash by.

Miles away and far above the city streets, a dark figure in a black robe stood atop a high-rise building, looking down at the bustling crowded streets. An evil laugh erupted from the silhouette and echoed over the city as his warm breath met the frosty night air and billowed out like smoke from a bull's nose. The stranger's army boots stepped over a dead rat as he made his way to a stone statue of a gargoyle at the corner of the rooftop. He rubbed his hands together, and they began to give off a hot red glow as he reached out to place them atop the cold stone statue.

Moments later, the stone gargoyle moved beneath his touch and slowly animated into a living, breathing monster with a rugged scaly hide where stone used to be. The newborn creature turned and peered up at its master with ruby red eyes that glared with laser-like intensity.

The master turned to face a tall female vampire who stood in front of a dozen more animated gargoyles, drawn from their stone homes around the city. She wore a tattered black robe, slit down the back and sides to allow her batwings to emerge, plus a thick red rope wrapped around her waist to fasten everything in place. She had long pointy ears, dark grayish skin, and deep red eyes. Her long black hair draped down her backside and nearly touched the ground.

"Go, Norell, take our new children and join the others," the dark figure said in a low gnarled tone.

"Will you be joining in on the fun?"

"I wouldn't dream of missing out," the master said. "But our party is not yet complete. I have a graveyard or two to visit before the festivities begin. Join the others and await my arrival."

Norell edged forward as massive batwings grew from beneath the back of her robe. The newborn gargoyle jumped from the side of the building and joined the others behind Norell. She stretched her wings out, and the small battalion of gargoyles did the same.

"All hail the Grimlord," she said and then ran to the edge of the building and jumped off, followed by her gargoyle companions.

The taxi rolled to a stop to drop the Fox family off a few blocks away from their favorite Italian restaurant. Ethan and his parents George and Betsy Fox often went out on the town for a Broadway show, followed by dinner – but tonight was a celebration—Ethan's fourteenth birthday. Their routine was to eat a late dinner after the show and discuss their opinions about the performance. Betsy always asked the taxi driver to drop them off several blocks from their dinner destination. She was a stickler for making sure George got at least a short walk in before what would become a belt-loosening feast followed by at least one dessert.

Saturday night was busy, and the crowded streets crawled with people from all walks of life. The sounds of the city reverberated off the surrounding high-rises; car horns honking, sirens singing, and people shouting above one another filled the air. The Fox family strolled down the busy sidewalk – oblivious to what was happening above.

High above the bright city streets, the light faded to darkness atop the tall buildings that tickled the belly of the skyline. Norell, the female vampire, hopped onto the raised edge of the building and scanned the neighboring rooftops. Hundreds of glowing red eyes glared back. A small army of vampires stood at the edges of the surrounding skyscrapers as the gargoyle battalion circled in the dark sky above.

Norell walked along the narrow edge of the building and stared down at the people walking the streets. But she focused her interests on one particular threesome of people as they entered their favorite Italian restaurant on schedule.

The Fox family entered the restaurant, and the owner greeted them warmly, and escorted them to their usual seats. Ethan's eyes took a moment to adjust to the dim room lit only by the candles from each table. The dining area was nearly empty as usual for this time of night. But Ethan knew that was part of Betsy's plan to minimize embarrassment when George inevitably decided to play the "crack Ethan up game."

Betsy stood to excuse herself for the ladies' room, when a busboy arrived with three glasses of water, each with a slice of cucumber floating on top. George waited for a moment to make sure Betsy was out of sight. He fumbled around in his coat pocket with one hand and plucked two cucumber slices out with the other. A wide grin swept across his face as he ducked under the table. Moments later, a loud wallowing noise rumbled from under the table.

"I am Charlie, the Walrus man of Wiltor. I am here to speak with Ethan Fox!" A loud voice growled as George emerged from beneath the table.

Ethan erupted with laughter at the sight of George's face. A rubber walrus nose with whiskers and tusks covered the bottom half of his face, and cucumber slices stuck to his eye sockets to look like enormous green eyes—George was a Walrus man. Ethan was still laughing when Betsy returned from the ladies' room.

"What's with all the laughter? Is your father being silly again?" She approached George from behind – unaware of his crazy masquerade. Betsy quietly sat down at the table and turned to face her husband. Startled by his face, she let out a high-pitched shriek and turned bright pink. Even in a dark, nearly empty restaurant, George could embarrass his wife.

"Looks like your father's been to the joke shop again. Well, at least one of my men is growing up."

Once the antics were over, dinner arrived, and the Fox's enjoyed a relaxed meal discussing the night's events and how much they enjoyed the show. After dinner, they each ordered only one dessert – but George finished his and half of Betsy's. They paid their bill and left the restaurant for another walk up the street, where Betsy insisted taxis were more abundant.

Norell spotted the Fox's emerging from the restaurant across the street and far below her perch on the roof's edge. She jumped from her roost and walked to the center of the rooftop, where a group of vampires stood awaiting orders.

"I wonder what's keeping him," she said to no one. "If he doesn't arrive soon, we will miss our window."

"CAW, CAW, CAW," the shrieks rang out, announcing the arrival of a sizable raven circling overhead and slowly descending. The raptor had tattered feathers, exposed bones and organs, and the eyes of a dead fish. In fact, this bird was not a raven at all. It was a grimtailed dread and was more dead than alive.

"Poe is here," Norell said, "our master has arrived."

The dread swiftly broke into a dive towards the rooftop and pulled up into a quick loop maneuver causing a small swirling vortex to open near the vampires. The whirling disturbance grew darker and fuller as bright jolts of electricity danced out from its center. A black army boot poked out as Victor Qruefeldt stepped through the vortex to join his Grimleaver army.

Victor Qruefeldt was the master and creator of the Grimleavers and the archnemesis to Ethan's Caretaker friends at The Residence. During their previous encounter, Ethan had outsmarted the Grimleaver leader, making him look foolish. And that left Victor with a particularly strong disdain for young Ethan Fox.

"All hail the Grimlord," Norell said.

"All hail the Grimlord," the vampires echoed from the rooftops.

"Master, you've arrived just in time," Norell said. "The target is on the move."

"Has the devil's swarm arrived?" Victor asked.

"We've seen no sign of them."

"They'll arrive shortly," Victor said with a grin. "Their tiny wings slow them down – but they are eager for their first taste of human blood."

Midnight was approaching, but the streets were still bustling with people as the Fox's strolled towards their destination. An untied shoelace nearly tripped Ethan, so he stepped off the sidewalk onto a small patch of grass in front of a high-rise hotel. His parents kept walking; unaware he had stopped behind them. Ethan knelt and tied his shoe – but as he finished, a sudden eerie quiet overcame him, and time slowed to a crawl. The symbols on his palms started to tingle, and the hairs on the back of his neck felt like crawling ants.

"All hail the Grimlord," voices cried out in Ethan's head.

"He's here," Ethan said aloud. "Victor Qruefeldt!"

An explosion of sound shattered the silence in Ethan's head as a bus roared onto the sidewalk through a crowd of pedestrians, and crashed into a giant lamppost, barely missing him. Victims flew in all directions as a shower of sparks bathed pedestrians now running for their lives. The crash cut Ethan off from his parents, who were now being shepherded away with the frightened mob.

"If they had stopped to wait for me, they'd be dead," he thought.

Ethan gazed at the pedestrians across the street, standing and watching the commotion. Thunderous sounds of shattering glass abruptly filled the air. Ethan gazed up at a formation of stone gargoyles flying kamikaze-style right into the sides of the buildings above the crowd. Shards of glass rained down on the unsuspecting spectators, impaling many of them as chaos overtook that side of the street.

Vampires swooped down and randomly picked people off, hoisting them into the sky, and using them as human artillery to drop on the scattering crowd below. Ethan ducked behind a bush near the crash to hide from their view as he gathered his thoughts. Moments passed, and most of the mob dispersed from the area. The sound of screams slowly quieted, and Ethan emerged from the bush. He backed away from the heat of the now burning bus and slowly scanned his surroundings. A deep sense of angst overcame him as he took in the surrounding carnage. But then his palm symbols tingled, an eerie calm returned to his head, and the voice spoke up again.

"I am not yet finished with you, Ethan Fox. You must stick around for my encore."

"I'm not afraid of you!" Ethan shouted at the sky. "I'm not afraid of you—Victor Qruefeldt."

A mob of people ran back up the street, in the opposite direction from where they had just run. Ethan ducked into the entrance of a long dark alley at the side of the hotel. The sound of the running mob quieted, replaced by a loud, low-pitched hum. Ethan stepped out of the alleyway to look down the street, and his heart skipped a beat. Masses of slow-moving people walked awkwardly down the middle of the road, groaning. The scene reminded Ethan of a *Walking Dead* episode.

"Walkers," Ethan whispered. "Zombies creep me out."

Looking for his parents would have to wait till after he avoided becoming a zombie main course. Ethan turned and ran down the dark alley as fast as he could. Cool bluish light from a lamppost dimly lit the back corner of the alleyway near the backside of the hotel. Ethan stopped when he reached the light so he could scan the area. The alleyway ended but continued left around the back of the building. Ethan strode around the well-lit corner where a lamp hung above a door at the back of the hotel. A spacious trash bin and several random trash cans stood up against a cyclone fence opposite the hotel – but beyond that was more darkness. He turned towards the door and noticed a flyer for an upcoming event posted on the textured concrete wall by the door. But the light flickered a few times and went out, leaving only the lamppost's moon-like glow.

Ethan was reading the flyer when his palms started to tingle, so he raised his hands to look. The bright white light emitted by the glowing symbols bathed his face. The symbols spun in his palms several times and stopped abruptly, pointing to his right – like animated cartoon compasses. Ethan pivoted to his right, and the symbols followed to stay pointing in the same direction. He lowered his hands, and that's when he saw her.

Standing between him and the trash bin was the dark silhouette of a young woman – but this was no ordinary woman. She was pitch black from top to bottom and outlined by a glowing blue aura. Her face, body, and clothing, all consisted of the same glossy substance that caused her shining yellow eyes and blue aura to cast a glow giving her a liquid sheen. A golden necklace wrapped around her neck was clearly visible against her blackness. A swirly eye-shaped pendant hung from the chain against her upper chest.

"It's you," Ethan said and stepped towards her. "I've been seeing you in my dreams."

Her mouth moved like she was trying to speak to Ethan, but he did not understand the unusual sounds she made.

"I'm sorry, I don't understand what you are trying to say."

She raised her arm and pointed up at the wall behind him. He turned to look at what she pointed to and jumped back at the sight. A horde of small dragon-like creatures clung to the wall glaring at Ethan with piercing green eyes. Swarms of them swooped down from the darkness and hovered in front of the others. They were pitch black like the woman but had blue swirl patterns covering their bodies. Ethan backed away as the tiny dragons slowly advanced toward him. Then, all at once, the creatures stopped moving and opened their mouths. The dim yellow glow inside slowly grew brighter and brighter.

The hairs on the back of Ethan's neck crawled as time seemed to slow, and a bright burst of energy erupted from the dragon's mouths like laser beams. Ethan dove towards the woman in black, who promptly vanished and reappeared between him and the tiny monsters. The blasts from the dragon horde absorbed into her blackness like water into a sponge.

"Thank you," Ethan said as he hopped to his feet.

But the menacing horde continued clinging to the walls, glaring at them as they recharged their energy beams. The woman in black spun around and looked at the garbage cans behind Ethan. One of the cans swiftly levitated into the air and launched towards the horde of miniature dragons causing them to scatter and swarm in all directions. The woman looked at Ethan and pointed to the door to the building. It swung open, and a bright light flooded the alleyway as if inviting him inside. He hurried in, but stopped and turned to thank his savior – but the shadow woman was gone.

Ethan shut the door and hurried down a long corridor towards the front of the hotel. He proceeded through a door that led to the hotel lobby, where crowds of people were barricading the doors as others stood glued to the windows watching the commotion outside. He could hear the wailing sirens of ambulances, and the whirring blades of television and rescue helicopters, as the city reacted to what had just happened.

Ethan found a nearby restroom to splash water over his face and catch his breath after his harrowing experience. He finished washing his face and leaned against the sink with his arms as he stared into the mirror.

"Where are the Caretakers?" he whispered to himself. "They must be aware of this."

A small green blob appeared on the mirror, like a wad of gum, and popped off. A three inch tall creature landed on the sink in front of Ethan. Its fuzzy green face looked like a grumpy old man with tall blue Tweety Bird eyes.

"Of course, we know of the situation," Gruggins McGhee said. "I've come to escort you back to The Residence."

Ethan refused to go at first. He was still anxious and insistent on finding his parents before going anywhere. Gruggins tried to reassure him that his parents were already under Caretaker protection and the Grimleavers weren't after them anyway. But when that didn't work, Gruggins resorted to casting a grumpling enchantment on Ethan. It would alleviate his anxiety and temporarily cause him to forget about the plight of his parents. It was Ethan's safety that was of paramount importance – and The Residence was the only place that could ensure it.

Gruggins rode cloaked on Ethan's shoulder and directed him farther down the alley behind the hotel. He widened his eyes to make his way in the darkness of night as the eerie quiet told him they were alone.

"How can you see your way down this dark alley?" Gruggins asked.

"I don't know, I just can."

Gruggins uncloaked himself and held his tiny left hand out. He pointed his right index finger down at his palm and swirled it in a circular motion. A globe of light popped up out of nowhere and hovered over his palm, lighting the alleyway around them.

"You'll have to teach me that trick," Ethan said.

"I'd have to turn you into a grumpling first," Gruggins said as he scanned their surroundings. "A little farther down."

Ethan continued down the alley as Gruggins' glowing orb lit the way.

"Our destination is right up ahead here." Gruggins pointed to a beat-up old tire leaning against the fence at the back of the alley.

"What are we supposed to do with that?"

"Didn't you learn anything during your stay at The Residence? That, my dear boy, is a portal beacon and our ticket home."

Gruggins instructed him to touch the dirty old tire with both hands. Ethan was initially reluctant and wondered if Gruggins was punking him – but the sound of a distant scream interrupted the silence, reminding him of the dire circumstances of the night. He knelt next to the tire, placed his hands against the cold hard rubber, and they vanished in a flash.

BACK TO THE RESIDENCE

The tire transformed into a hefty crystal ball in Ethan's hands. The glassy sphere balanced on the point of the upside-down cone attached to the bottom. Ethan's eyes squinted shut in the bright sunless blue sky hanging over the black-and-white checkerboard they were kneeling on. Ethan recognized the portal plane from his prior visit to The Residence. He spun around to scan the horizon where tall lifeless trees stood, reaching for the sky with jagged arm-like branches. The portal spheres floated behind him, held in place by colored electric fields.

"Blue for Atlantis, green for Ceres, red for Hades, and yellow for Zephyr," Ethan said as he named the elemental worlds.

"Enough of the history lesson," Gruggins said.

Ethan turned as a doorway appeared out of nowhere and opened slowly. Blue sky, a checkered floor, and a tree-lined horizon framed the outside of the doorway. But inside was the front room of The Residence—the entrance to a world within our own.

They entered the front room, where Ethan's reflection stared back at them from the sizable mirror across the room. He remembered throwing a ball through the mirror and watching it bounce out onto the portal plane when he unlocked the portals.

"Well, kiddo," Gruggins said, "this is the end of the line for me. I'm beat after all the excitement. Time for a well-deserved nap."

"Where is everybody?"

"Dealing with the mess we just left, I'd imagine. Mush-mouth will be along shortly, I'm sure. You can wait here or in the study." The front door shut as Gruggins fluttered off Ethan's shoulder. He vanished into a tiny brown box on the table near the study door.

Ethan's eyes were adjusting to the dimly lit front room. He gazed towards a door at the back of the room. The sign above read:

• THE HALL OF DOORWAYS •

Movement near the base of the door caught Ethan's attention, so he moved in for a closer look. Tiny red eyes peered back at him as a hairy black creature came into view. The animal was almost a foot tall with a thick body, short legs, and arms that hung to the ground. Ethan studied its face as they stared back at one another. Horns grew from the sides of the creature's triangular head and curved forward like bull horns. Long sharp canines protruded up from its drooping lower jaw.

A loud bang erupted from the study and startled the creature. It moved towards the door and shrank smaller with each step. Upon reaching the door, the wee-sized critter was tiny enough to squeeze underneath and escape into The Hall of Doorways.

Ethan quietly entered the study to investigate and immediately stopped in his tracks to witness the scene. The fact that RGB were up to no good did not surprise him. Albert, Linus, and Newton, the three mischievous pyrodevlins were collectively referred to as RGB because of their respective red, green, and blue colors – and because they normally stirred up trouble as a unit.

This time, they were at the base of the bookshelf wall that ran the room's length. RGB were looking up at three books hovering over their heads. They were frantically lunging at the books, trying to snatch them from the air.

"I almost got mine," Albert shouted.

"No, you didn't," Linus rebutted.

"I'll catch mine first," Newton insisted.

RGB's antics reminded Ethan of old videos he'd seen of *The Three Stooges*. He stood quietly as one book floated down teasingly close to Albert's head while the other two rose higher. Linus and Newton turned their attention towards

Albert as he lurched up at the book above his head. But the object of Albert's desires swiftly jumped out of his grasp as the other two books came crashing down on the unsuspecting heads of Linus and Newton.

Ethan witnessed the process cycle several times, and RGB fell for the same trick every time. Then something caught his eye. A small green caterpillar stood atop the bookshelves directly above RGB. Its tiny arms moved like a puppeteer's controlling the books. Ethan smiled as the little creature waved his arms gracefully like a maestro conducting a symphony. He laughed and caught the creature's attention.

The books hovering over the pyrodevlins slowly drifted lower and changed shape as they fell. Then, all at once, RGB lunged up and grabbed their prizes.

"Got mine," Albert said.

"Me too," Linus replied.

"I snatched mine first," Newton added.

Albert, Linus, and Newton's yellow eyes grew round as golf balls as they realized what they held.

"Oh no—" Albert yelled.

"Not again," Linus shouted.

"Run for the hills!" Newton screamed.

RGB tossed the reddish marbles into the air, and in a flash, darted past Ethan and out the study door. Ethan recognized the firelyte capsules and dove in a futile attempt to catch them before they could ignite. He crashed to the floor beneath the marbles that hovered in the air and slowly morphed back into books.

"Nothing to worry about," a soft silvery voice said. "I would never give RGB a real firelyte capsule. I wouldn't want them burning down the place."

Ethan hopped to his feet and approached the small caterpillar creature now on a lower shelf directly in front of him.

"Wordly Pagemore, at your service, Master Ethan," he said and extended one of his many tiny arms.

"You know my name," Ethan said as he shook his puny hand.

"Everyone at The Residence has heard of Ethan Fox. I was away on business during your last visit."

Wordly was a four inch bookworm with round nerdy glasses over his baby blue eyes. He was bluish on top, fading to green in the middle, and yellow at the bottom. Oval red rings with yellow centers lined his sides.

"I'm happy to meet you," Ethan said. "That was quite a show you put on."

"RGB are naive and easy to fool."

"Yeah – well – I saw them take down a Hell-Giant last time I was here."

"Good point. I've heard the stories and shall proceed with caution in the future."

Wordly turned towards the still floating books, and with the wave of a hand, they returned to their respective slots on the bookshelves.

"Now then, how may I be of service to Ethan Fox? I'm the resident bookworm. I oversee the Caretaker Arts & Literature archive. If you require information of any sort, I'm your worm. Anything written, drawn, or painted, and I can likely find related information."

"Wow, that's quite the resumé," Ethan said. "Thank you – but I'm only here to wait for Irvin."

"Shnickyrooners and things like that," a voice said from outside the study.

"Speak of the devil," Wordly said. "Until we meet again, Ethan Fox, I will leave you in Irvin's capable hands." He squeezed between two books and disappeared into the shelf.

"Have you ever noticed how big fat toad ears always run through traffic during the leftover pizza underpants?" Irvin ranted as he entered the study. "I've always been amazed at how smart the noodle whiskers sound when they eat frozen beetle lips."

"I wonder that all the time," Ethan answered. "Great to see you again, Irvin."

"Master Ethan," Irvin said, breaking out of his nonsensical rant. "Irvin is happy Ethan Fox is here too!"

Irvin McGillicutty was the butler of The Residence – but his duties didn't end there. He was also the chef, tailor, handyman, and assistant to the Caretaker headmistress. Irvin was a mimic, a species with limited shape-shifting abilities that he used to maximum effect. His appearance reminded Ethan of a living department store dummy wearing a black pinstriped tuxedo with a red rose corsage.

"I've become quite the student of human behavior since your last visit," Irvin said. "I monitor their television channels and follow the news, TV shows, reality shows, and cartoons. But my favorites are the mini shows played during the breaks."

"The commercials?"

"I guess, they don't have names – but I remember most of them." Irvin's face morphed into a cartoon rabbit. "Silly rabbit, Trix are for kids." Then a leprechaun. "Lucky Charms, they're magically delicious." Then a tiger. "Frosted Flakes, they're Grrrrreat!"

Ethan roared with laughter at Irvin's cereal commercial impressions.

"I am sorry for being late, Master Ethan. I was informing Miss Hayley of your arrival."

"She knows I'm here?"

"Sure does," Irvin said as a grin swept across his face. "Giddy as a flobbyknocker she was when I told her. Asked me to stall so she could get all prettied up."

Ethan's face felt flush and warm, and his heart thumped at the thought of seeing Hayley. Then he noticed Irvin staring at him, his head tilted like a confused dog, and his face slowly turned pink to mimic Ethan's.

"Looks like Miss Hayley isn't the only one who's giddy. Don't worry. She'll be along shortly."

Minutes felt like hours while Ethan waited for her arrival. Finally, the study door swung open, and Ethan's heart skipped a beat as Hayley entered the room. Ethan recognized the white sundress with yellow flowers she was wearing from the day they met at the Santa Cruz Beach Boardwalk. Her golden hair was longer and wavier, but glistened as if the sun shone into the study. Her penetrating bluish-green eyes met Ethan's gaze as she ran across the room. He opened his arms, and she softly fell into them and wrapped hers around him. They hugged for at least a minute before anyone spoke.

Irvin stood quietly watching but then broke the silence.

"I don't understand the hugging thing – but it sure seems all the rage these days."

Irvin wisely decided to give Ethan and Hayley their privacy and left to continue his daily chores.

"I've missed you," Hayley said. "We've all missed you."

"I missed you too. I've thought about you every day since I left – and I've been away almost a year."

"We have so much to catch up on. A lot has happened around here," Hayley said. "Come, we can talk along the way. My mother has summoned us to the Map Room."

They turned towards the exit when Ethan noticed something different about the study.

"The out-door is missing."

"Yeah, it disappeared after you unlocked the door to the portals. We're not sure why, but my brother Damien has a theory. The idea is the lock on the portal plane was causing the duality, and when you unlocked it, the door reverted to normal."

Hayley escorted Ethan out of the study and into The Hall of Doorways. They held hands and slowly walked the hallway under the eerie glow of the light beetle that crawled with them on the ceiling above.

"Wait, I need to get something off my chest," Hayley said as she stopped and faced Ethan. "I haven't had a friend to confide in since you left."

"What's wrong?"

"My mother – she's overly protective and won't let me go anywhere or do anything she deems dangerous."

"Well, she did lose you for a long time. Her reaction is normal for a parent who searched for their daughter for a century."

"Of course, you're right. But when it comes to me, Mother deems everything dangerous – yet I'm ready to start Caretaker training soon."

"Be patient. She'll come around and see things your way eventually."

"You are always able to make me feel better," Hayley said with a smile.

"You do the same for me. I think that's part of our destiny."

Hayley's smile widened, and her cheeks grew rosier.

"While we're getting things off our chest," Ethan said and paused. "I have something that's been bothering me for nearly a year."

"What is it?" Hayley asked.

"Everyone here makes such a big deal out of me being the Hybrid Child. But nobody ever stopped to explain what that means. What the heck is a Hybrid Child, and what's so special about it?"

"I—I don't really know either," Hayley replied. "I always assumed it meant you were half-human half-Caretaker."

"That's what I thought too—at first. But now I'm not so sure. Something tells me there's more to it than that."

"Well, I say we work together and do whatever it takes to find out."

"I was hoping you'd say something like that."

Ethan smiled, glanced down, and noticed the black infinity-shaped ring on Hayley's hand.

"I see you're still wearing the rift-key," he said. "I knew you'd get it back when I saw the look on your face after he stole it from you."

She held out her hand, looked at the ring on her finger, and smiled.

"It hasn't spoken to me since the incident. But that's okay. It's sentimental to me for other reasons."

Hayley grabbed Ethan's hand, and they started back down the hallway.

"So, what else is new?" Ethan asked.

"Well, I am getting some of my memories back."

They walked towards their destination slowly, made small talk, and enjoyed one another's company. They felt like no time had passed since their last time together, and their bond was more vital than ever.

They entered the Map Room and strode over the invisible floor at the midsection of the spherical room. They heard Damien and Jordanna talking as they reached the stairway's base to the crow's nest at the room's center.

"The Grimleavers are honing their craft," Damien said. "They've learned to reanimate dead humans and stone statues."

"If we are to believe the reports," Jordanna said. "They sound far-fetched, even for Victor Qruefeldt."

Ethan and Hayley stepped onto the crow's nest, causing the platform's floor to appear. Jordanna and Damien were sitting in captain's chairs at its center.

"You can believe them," Ethan said, "I witnessed them myself. Reanimated stone gargoyles flew into buildings to shatter windows over the crowded sidewalks – and masses of zombies walked the streets. That's when I ran."

"Ethan, my dear," Jordanna said. "I'm so happy you've come to visit us again."

"Yes, but too bad your visit has come under such dire circumstances," said Damien.

"But that's not all," Ethan continued. "Victor Qruefeldt was there. I felt his presence and was able to communicate with him. It was like some sort of telepathy. I could hear his thoughts, and he could hear mine."

"Has anything like that ever happened before?" Damien asked.

"Kind of, last time I was here," Ethan replied. "But that was nothing like this; this time we were able to talk like we were right next to one another."

"Interesting," Damien said. "I suspect your connection has been there all along. Likely a result of your very first encounter."

"What did Victor say to you?" Jordanna asked.

"Nothing of substance. He was taunting me and told me to stick around for the encore. That's when the zombies showed up, and I bolted."

"Anything else you can tell us?" Jordanna pressed.

"Yes, I saw her," Ethan said. "The woman in black from my dreams. She warned me about a swarm of miniature black dragons stalking me, and when they attacked, she saved me from being fried by their energy blasts."

"He's using the pixie-devils," Damien said.

"Pixie-devils?" asked Ethan.

"Yes, Victor's latest victims were devolved from Tinx's relatives."

"More importantly," Jordanna said to Damien. "The painting that arrived in the Gallery after Ethan's departure has come to pass."

"Indeed, it has," Damien replied.

"The dark spirit woman you encountered," Jordanna said. "You've seen her in your dreams?"

"Yes, I've had the same dream many times since I was last here," Ethan replied.

"Can you describe it?" Jordanna asked.

"I'm in a giant room. It's pitch black, and I can't see a thing until she appears in front of me. Her blue aura and glowing yellow eyes barely light the area around us. I'm not afraid; I feel comforted by her presence. We stare at each other, and she tries to speak, but I can't understand her. Suddenly, I'm able to see in the dark and can see all around us. We are alone in the room – but I feel someone watching.

Something evil is watching us, and I can tell she feels its presence too."

Ethan paused to catch his breath.

"Then what happens?" Damien asked impatiently.

"Then the dream ends and I wake up."

"The evil presence you feel, is it Victor Qruefeldt?" Jordanna asked.

"Before, I couldn't tell who it is," Ethan replied. "But now, after today's encounter, I'm sure it's him."

"Interesting," Damien said, and then the room grew quiet.

Jordanna and Damien exchanged glances and tensed up as if they were hiding something.

"Moving along," Jordanna said. "There is one more important matter to discuss. I must ask you something about your prior stay at The Residence."

"Okay, ask me anything."

"During your visit to Poseidon, Fin Drenchler asked you to stay behind after the briefing. Do you remember?"

"Sure."

"Do you remember your conversation with Fin?"

"Um, uh, not exactly," Ethan answered. "I remember shaking his webbed hand after everyone left. He reminded me of a blue *Creature from the Black Lagoon*, but not as scary. After that, my memory is fuzzy."

"That doesn't surprise me," Jordanna said.

She tapped at the screen of an iPhone-like device called an elemental modulator, or ELMO for short. A holographic window popped up like a theater screen hovering in midair.

"Maybe this will jog your memories," she said as a video of the meeting played.

Fin approached Ethan slowly and asked him to retrieve his pocket tote. Ethan handed the tiny pouch to Fin, who studied the symbols written on the outside. Fin handed it back to Ethan but grabbed his wrist and turned his hand to look at his palm. The symbols on Ethan's palms glowed yellow as he fell into a trance. His eyes glowed yellow too and opened full as he spoke to Fin just as the sound cut out and the recording ended.

"I—I don't remember any of that."

"It appears Fin suspected you were the Hybrid Child," Jordanna said. "But what you said to him remains a mystery."

"As does Fin's whereabouts," Damien said. "Fin Drenchler has gone missing."

"Missing," Ethan repeated.

"Yes, missing," Jordanna said. "Nothing to concern yourself with. We will find him. But if you do remember anything, please tell us immediately."

The long night of danger, chaos, and mystery exhausted Ethan. He was happy to visit his friends at The Residence – but he was also worried about what happened to his parents in the crowd. Damien and Jordanna reassured him George and Betsy were safe and the Caretakers were in control of the situation after the attack on Manhattan.

Hayley escorted Ethan down The Hall of Doorways to his room. She explained, she now had her own living quarters in Zen city, but would stay in her old room next to his while he was around.

Ethan entered his room and found it surprising to see it was identical to his room at home—even his most recent changes were reflected. Irvin made sure to leave Ethan his own ELMO device on his dresser as well. Exhausted, Ethan plopped down onto his bed; it transformed into a soft pillowy cloud, and he fell fast asleep.

Ethan strolled through a dark cave that grew darker as he ventured deeper. An eerie clicking sound echoed out of the blackness in front of him as a tingling sensation crawled down his back like tickling from an invisible hand. He opened his eyes and recognized the ceiling of his room – but the soft pillowy cloud he was on reminded him, he was at The Residence.

Ethan sat upright and stretched his arms over his head when he heard the sound again. The clicking noise from his dream was in his room, coming from under his bed. He moved to the edge and leaned over the side to peek beneath the floating cloud he was on. Two glowing yellow eyes met Ethan's and startled him—sending him crashing to the floor. He hurried onto his hands and knees and peered underneath the now regular-looking bed – but nothing was there.

"Click, click, click," the noise started again – but this time the sound came from above his head and behind him. He glanced up at his dresser, where a small creature stood next to his ELMO device, staring down at him. The critter was nearly eight inches tall with a deep-purple egg-shaped body covered with spikey fur. It had long thin ostrich-like legs, and curving horns that spiraled up behind its bulging yellow eyes at the top of its head. Its body was nearly all mouth, and four tentacle arms covered with hooks protruded from the sides.

"Click, click, click," the sound came from a sizable black insect the creature had trapped in one of its tentacles. The creature's mouth widened into a smile, exposing sharp shark-like teeth as it sprawled open to gobble down the insect in a cacophony of crunches.

Ethan sat frozen on the floor as he and the creature stared at one another for what seemed an eternity. His ELMO rang, startling the tiny monster into hopping off the dresser and landing on the floor by the door. The creature flattened out like a pancake and slid underneath, escaping into The Hall of Doorways.

Ethan quickly jumped to his feet and answered his ELMO. It was Hayley.

"Meet me in The Hall of Doorways, and hurry," he said as he gave chase. He entered the hallway and spotted the creature disappearing into the blackness to his left. Realizing the futility of pursuit, he waited for Hayley to emerge from her room.

"What's with all the excitement?"

"There was a monster in my room under my bed."

"A monster under your bed," Hayley repeated as she crinkled her forehead and furrowed her brows.

"I know it sounds crazy, but this isn't the first one I've seen. When I arrived, there was one in the front room – but that one was a different kind."

"Well, we did have a Ravisher infestation in the Moongarden. But I'm not aware of any monsters lurking around The Residence."

"Come on," Ethan said and started towards the Map Room. "We can tell your mom about them too."

Hayley stopped and gave him a questioning look.

"I need to speak with her anyway," he said. "I remembered an important detail about the dark spirit woman."

"Okay, we'll go speak with her, but please don't tell her about the monsters. She'll never let me near you if she thinks monsters are following you."

"Deal," Ethan said with a smile.

They entered the Map Room and immediately overheard Jordanna and Damien talking like they had never left.

"We control the portal plane," Damien said. "The Grimleavers have limited access to the human world—limiting their attack and retreat options."

"I agree – but we must stay focused and continue searching for the portal prophecies."

They stepped onto the crow's nest platform, and Damien spun around in his chair to greet them.

"Back so soon—"

The Map Room came to life, and its alarm cut him off.

"Incoming transmission, Headmistress," the room said, "I have confirmed the message as level one."

"Onscreen," Jordanna said, and a full holographic screen popped up.

A tall, robed man with angelic wings and vampire teeth stood next to a blue-skinned woman with a snake's body and bright green hair that was alive. Ethan recognized them as Nicholas and Brianna.

"What have you found?" Jordanna asked.

"We've uncovered a base of operations," Nicholas said. "A warehouse in the meatpacking district in New York City. They've cleared out the last of the vampires and other Grimleaver soldiers. But we have found another victim, Boris Wentworth – and he's alive."

"The Grimleavers were holding him captive as Bella had feared," Brianna added.

"What is his prognosis?" Jordanna asked.

"He's weak and malnourished," Brianna said. "But we expect he will make a full recovery."

"That's strange," Damien said. "Why would they take him to the human world and hold him in a warehouse?"

"I agree," Nicholas replied. "There is no rhyme or reason to it."

"Regardless, this is great news," Jordanna said. "Wrap things up and return to The Residence. We will inform Bella of the good news."

"There's one more thing to report," Nicholas said. "We hear chatter of Grimleaver activity in other cities around the globe. The humans have only reported minor disturbances thus far, but they may be planning more attacks."

"Send all updates to the Map Room as they come in," Damien said. "We will monitor the activity in real-time from here."

"Good work," Jordanna said.

The screen disappeared, and the spherical room lit up into a giant globe of Earth with them sitting inside at its center. Yellow blips of light began popping up in random cities on the map surrounding them.

"Well, there you have it," Damien said. "He orchestrates an attack on Ethan's birthday – and now we uncover a secret lair in the human world. As I've been saying, Victor Qruefeldt is planning something."

He pulled a yellow journal from his half-black half-white robe and studied its pages. Ethan recognized Stravis' journal from his previous visit. As he had learned, Earth was created by four Creators from the elemental worlds, and Stravis was the Creator from the yellow world of Zephyr.

"Agreed," Jordanna said, "but your obsession with the journal is becoming a distraction."

"I've been studying it, Mother, and I think I've deciphered some of Stravis' encoded entries."

"The Grimleavers are spreading us thin as things now stand. We can't afford your continued focus on that book."

"But Stravis' journal is not just a book, Mother. It is the writings of a Creator, and we can learn a lot from such a gift if we know what to look for and where to look."

"But that's my point, Damien. We do not have any idea where to look. So we will focus on what is real—the Grimleavers have infiltrated the human world and are attacking humans."

"I won't drop this, Mother. We thought it crazy for Victor to have wanted the portals open—yet he did. The whole notion is crazy unless he had help on the other side. And if I'm right, we will need all the help we can get."

"You are stubborn like your father," Jordanna said as a proud smile slipped onto her lips. "All right, I will indulge you this once—what have you learned?"

"Stravis wanted to protect this information, he encoded some of his entries, and I think I've cracked the code on some of these markings. I believe they are timestamps, and some of them are dated after the Creators locked the portals."

"Interesting," Jordanna said. "That would suggest Stravis stayed behind when the other Creators returned home. But we were already told that by the Council of Elders, so you have learned nothing new."

"Yes," said Damien. "But don't you find it odd that nobody has bothered to question why? Why would Stravis stay behind? We know he is strongly connected to the Seers and helped them save the Hybrid Child."

Jordanna, Damien, and Hayley all turned their gaze toward Ethan.

"I believe some of these encoded entries are about Stravis' dealings with the Seers. I believe he stayed behind to help them – and I think he lived in his desert bunker to serve them."

The room fell silent, so Ethan blurted out what was forefront on his mind.

"Can somebody please explain to me what a Hybrid Child is?"

Jordanna turned towards Ethan and studied the intense look on his face as she pondered her answer.

"We don't know for certain," she said softly. "It is the term used in the writings and stories passed down through the ages. I suppose only the originators of those truths know for certain."

"Great, so in other words, I need to ask the Seers," Ethan said.

"What we know for certain is the Hybrid Child is special," Jordanna continued, "and plays an important role in what is to come. The survival of Earth and the elemental worlds depends on it—depends on you."

"Yet another reason to study Stravis' writings more thoroughly," Damien said. "The answers could be right here in this journal."

"What became of Stravis' bunker?" Ethan asked.

"Humans discovered it," Jordanna said. "They unearthed the bunker and made off with most of its treasures. We may never have found out if not for an unfortunate accident."

"What happened?" Hayley asked.

"A young woman stumbled upon a box. She opened it and found something dangerous inside."

"Pandora," Hayley said. "She found a petrified wood berry."

"Yes," said Jordanna.

"What happened after that?" Ethan asked.

"We sent in a team. Alexander Sturgis cleaned up the mess and ensured no humans would discover it again."

"Alexander Sturgis—" Ethan repeated the name of his birth father.

"Yes," Jordanna said. "Your mother was present as well. Alexander took Tiffany on that mission, and you were born."

Ethan's face felt flush, and he grew antsy. He had tried to avoid thinking about it for George and Betsy's sake. But the mere mention of his birth parents caused a flood of emotions to rush through his mind.

"They might have missed something," Ethan said. "We should go to the bunker and have a look."

"Alexander is the best we have," Jordanna said. "He missed nothing."

"I agree with Ethan," Damien said. "I'd like to examine Stravis' bunker for myself."

"Have you forgotten what we learned during Ethan's last visit?" Jordanna asked. "The portal prophecies are out there somewhere and finding them must be our priority. We cannot afford to lose sight of that."

"But Mother—"

"I forbid you to return to the bunker!" Jordanna commanded. "I have entertained this nonsense for long enough. We have real Grimleaver problems to deal with – and we must find the portal prophecies before it's too late."

The room fell into an uncomfortable silence. Ethan's mind became distracted, so he and Hayley left without discussing what he had remembered. He returned to his room to sulk and ponder his next steps. Hayley's attempts to cheer him up fell on deaf ears, but she understood. He still didn't have the answers he was seeking. Between that, his concern for George and Betsy, thoughts of his birth parents, not to mention his strange encounter with Fin – it consumed his thoughts.

The sound of singing outside his door awoke Ethan from his thoughts.

"Hotdogs, armored hotdogs, what kind of kids eat armored hotdogs," Irvin sang out loud.

Ethan opened the door to witness the spectacle that was Irvin McGillicutty.

"Fat kids, bratty kids, kids with dirty socks. Dumb kids, smelly kids, even kids in cuckoo clocks."

Ethan roared with laughter at the sight of Irvin, who had morphed into a giant hotdog with arms and legs and a smiling face. He was there to cheer Ethan up on Miss Hayley's orders.

"Shnickyrooners," Ethan said.

"Shnickyrooners, and shnackleboxes, and things like that," Irvin said.

"Thank you, Irvin. I needed a good laugh."

"I've been meaning to stop by," Irvin said as he morphed back into his pastie-white self. "I've brought Master Ethan a gift – like the ones on TV." Irvin rummaged through his pocket tote and pulled out a bright orange toy gun.

"A water pistol. Thank you, Irvin. I haven't seen one of these in forever."

"Irvin modified this one himself. Added a hydro-generator so you won't run out of water as quickly as the human ones."

Ethan pointed the toy pistol into the darkness and pulled the trigger. Water squirted out like a kid's water gun.

"Cool," Ethan said, trying to sound convincing.

"That's nothing," Irvin said with a proud grin. "That was on the lowest setting. The knob on the side adjusts the power, and you could put out an inferno with the highest setting."

"Well, I—"

"No need to drone on thanking me. Sorry, but I must run along, Master Ethan—toodles."

Ethan started back towards his room but stopped and knocked on Hayley's door instead.

"Was he able to cheer you up, I hope?" she asked as the door swung open.

"A little," Ethan said. "I'm still worried about my parents, even after all of the reassurances—"

"I understand why you'd feel that way," Hayley said. "Last you saw of them; they were in danger. But I can assure you if my mother says they're safe, they are safe—trust me."

"Yeah, you're right, I guess," Ethan said. "My mind is racing on overdrive after our last discussion with your mom and brother."

"I'll say," Hayley replied. "You even forgot to tell them whatever you went to tell them in the first place."

"Oh yeah, I guess I did," Ethan said. "It wasn't anything major. I just forgot to tell them about the golden necklace the black spirit woman wore. It held a large swirly eye-shaped pendant that glistened against her chest."

"Yeah, that doesn't sound like anything major to me either."

Ethan stared at the ground and grew quiet again.

"Okay, out with it," Hayley said. "What else is bothering you?"

"It's just—seeing that video of my encounter with Fin—it makes me wonder. Maybe something I said led to his disappearance. I don't remember anything – but seeing myself fall into a trance like that makes me feel somehow responsible."

"Well, you shouldn't—"

"Hear me out," he said. "I have no idea where to start, but I need to do something. Somehow, Fin suspected I was the Hybrid Child before anyone else did. And now I learn that Stravis stayed behind on Earth, maybe to help the Seers. I can't shake the feeling that my past is also a part of it."

"Yeah," Hayley said and nodded.

"We know I'm connected to the Seers."

"And?"

"And I was born at Stravis' bunker. That's where everything started for me."

"Are you saying what I think you're saying?"

"If Jordanna isn't going to let Damien investigate the bunker, I will."

Hayley's cheeks bunched into a broad smile.

"I was hoping you would say that. I'm tired of being overly protected. I'm ready for some adventure."

"Really?"

"You didn't think I'd let you go alone," she said. "But how do we find Stravis' bunker?"

"I don't know, but I know who might."

"Wordly Pagemore," Hayley said.

"Wordly Pagemore," said Ethan.

STRAVIS' BUNKER

After agreeing on a plan of action, all they needed to do was find Wordly Pagemore's whereabouts. Hayley pulled out her ELMO and tapped on the screen. A list popped up with the names and locations of all inhabitants currently at The Residence.

"He's at the archive," Hayley said.

They hurried down The Hall of Doorways and entered a dimly lit warehouse that reminded Ethan of a Home Depot with the lights out. The ceilings were twice as tall as any he'd ever seen, and rows of giant racks lined the floor as far as his eyes could see.

"He's probably in there," Hayley said and pointed to a small office.

"What is this place?"

"A storage facility, where we archive all Caretaker art and literature. The study contains only a small sample of Caretaker literature, chosen by Wordly, of course."

They entered the well-lit office where Wordly stood on a desk under a reading lamp. He was studying a ledger as the pages magically turned by themselves.

"And the art, where does that come from?" Ethan asked.

"The Gallery," Wordly said. "The archive houses all pieces rejected by the Fates. At least that is how things are supposed to work."

Ethan recalled seeing the three old hags in the Gallery on his previous visit. It was the Fates job to use their clairvoyance to determine a painting's significance.

"Hi, Wordly," Ethan and Hayley said in unison.

"How may I be of assistance?"

"Well—"

"I'm studying for Caretaker training," Hayley said, cutting Ethan off. "And one of the questions asks about traveling to Stravis' bunker."

"Interesting, I write the Caretaker training questions and I do not recall writing that one."

"Well—I—um—"

"No need to explain," Wordly interrupted. "I was a rebellious teenager once."

"So, how might someone travel to Stravis' bunker?" Ethan asked.

"You could have just asked that in the first place," Wordly said and smiled.

"Well, how would we?" Hayley asked.

"One would first book-travel to *Sand Miser Dunes*. From there, one must inquire at the nearby shantytown. But beware, as that town is home to thieves and criminals looking to hide from civilization."

"What would one inquire about?"

"One would seek out KaaFoo, a one-armed desert nomad who wears a patch over his eye. KaaFoo will decide if the traveler is worthy of continuing the path."

"Thank you, Wordly," Ethan said.

"Yeah, thanks for the information," Hayley said and then paused. "You—you're not going to tell my mother about this—are you?"

"No. I couldn't even if I wanted to," Wordly replied. "As the resident bookworm, my directive is to disseminate information, no questions asked."

"Really?"

"Yes, really. You are protected by worm-client privilege, and the Headmistress would never ask me to break that trust."

They started to head out of the office when Ethan spotted something on a shelf behind the desk.

"That looks familiar," Ethan said and pointed at a wooden box with cut vines protruding from it.

"Is that—"

"That is Pandora's box," said Wordly.

"The petrified woman in the Moongarden was holding that," Ethan said.

"I remember," Hayley said, "when I nearly shared her fate."

"Yes," Wordly said, "and now we know why. Someone enchanted the box to eject petrified wood berries. We discovered its secret recently – so Mildred had it sealed and moved here for safety."

"What happened?" Ethan asked.

"After a recent infestation, Mildred found a petrified Ravisher in the Moongarden."

"Why would someone enchant a wooden box?" Ethan asked.

"One can only surmise, but Mildred has her suspicions."

"Sure would have saved Grubner a lot of headaches," Hayley said. "If he knew petrified wood berries worked against Ravishers."

"Grubner?" Ethan asked.

"You haven't met him yet," Hayley replied. "Grubner is a dwarf who works in the Moongarden. He's become Mrs. Moongarden's right hand man."

Ethan and Hayley dashed to the study so they could book-travel to *Sand Miser Dunes*. Caretakers often used book-travel to teleport to the many hidden realms scattered throughout the human world. Doing so required the use of special portal books found on a specific shelf in the study. They hurried to the shelf of brown books with golden letters on the cover and perused the titles. Ethan ran his hands over the books on the shelf to his left, pulling some out and looking at them, and then re-shelving them. He searched through more books, faster and faster.

"The book is missing," Ethan said as he frantically scanned the shelf a third time. "We must find it; I need to see where it all started for me."

"Must be here somewhere. I remember seeing the title before," said Hayley.

"Is this what you're looking for?" A petite girlish voice said from somewhere in the room.

Sand Miser Dunes

Ethan scanned the room and saw nothing, but then a tiny, winged dragon fluttered down from atop the bookshelf above their heads. She carried a brown book in her claws and set it down gently on the reading table at the other end of the room.

"Planning a trip, are we?" she asked.

"Tinx, what are you doing here?" Hayley asked.

"Rebelling against an over-protective headmistress," said Tinx. "Does that ring a bell?"

Tinx was a winged pixie-dragon with peach and white swirled lizard skin.

"I remember you," Ethan said. "From the Deadwood Saloon, you served us sugar-pickle soda."

"Likewise," Tinx said as she smiled and bowed to Ethan.

"I don't understand," Hayley said. "You're a CAGE member now. Why would you rebel?"

CAGE was short for Caretaker Anti-Grimleaver Enforcement. A special group of Caretakers focused on fighting against Victor Qruefeldt and his army of evil Grimleavers.

"Yeah, the newest CAGE member due to the atrocities committed against my family. But according to the

Headmistress, I am too small and delicate for the dangers of fieldwork."

"Oh, I understand now," Hayley said.

"After what they did to my family, I can't sit around and do nothing. So, I'm going with you."

"I understand too," Ethan said. "I had a dangerous encounter with the pixie-devils, I've seen what they turned your loved ones into."

"When I learned of your return—when I heard Ethan Fox was back at The Residence—I knew it was only a matter of time before the two of you would be seeking answers. So, when Damien asked me to keep an eye on you, I followed you and listened to your conversation with Wordly. Being small does have some advantages."

"My brother is keeping tabs on us?"

"Yeah, he wanted me to let him know the moment you showed up in the study and book-traveled."

"And are you going to tell him?"

"Of course not. I'm going with you."

Ethan and Hayley gazed at one another and nodded in agreement.

"Well then," Ethan said, "let's get a move on!"

Tinx stood atop Ethan's shoulder as he and Hayley joined hands and fumbled with the brown book to flip its cover open. They stared into its pages as a blinding bright light sent them spiraling into darkness.

They awoke in a field of small, perfectly round dunes of sand. Ethan stood up and scanned the horizon. He spotted a small town in the distance, so they set off on foot. Nearly an hour later, they reached the small village of canvas tents and wooden shacks thatched together for shelter.

They stopped at the edge of town before entering. It reminded Ethan of an old western movie as they started down the street while the town's people eyeballed them intently. They walked into the heart of town – and an unruly-looking gang of locals immediately greeted them. They were tall with tattered brown clothing, whiskered faces, and missing teeth.

"Y'all are not welcome here," the group's leader said.

"We don't want any trouble," Ethan said.

"We are looking for somebody," Hayley added.

"Nice ring," one said and pointed at Hayley's infinity ring.

"We'll be taking that," another said.

"We'll be taking everything," the leader said.

"You're not taking anything from anybody," Ethan said and stepped in front of Hayley to shield her.

Ethan squinted at the bright sun behind the strangers, but a shadow abruptly moved in like a giant raincloud. He gazed up and smiled at the one-eyed giant he recognized standing behind the gang of robbers. Damien stepped in front of Ethan and faced the strangers.

"As the boy said, you'll not be taking anything. Is that understood?"

The gang of thugs turned and peered up at Azron, blocking out the sun behind them. Azron was a one-eyed giant that stood at least twelve feet tall, a member of the soleyed dwarf-giant species. He and Damien were fellow CAGE members. The thugs turned back to Damien, who stood smirking with his arms folded. His long half-black half-white Caretaker robe presented a look of authority.

"We meant no harm," one said.

"We were only joking," the leader said. "We'll be going now."

The thieves slowly backed away from Damien and Azron, then turned and ran like scared mice.

"Azron, am I glad to see you," Ethan said.

"Robbers no like Ethan Fox. Har, harr, harrr," Azron roared as he gently patted Ethan on the head.

"You were foolish to come here alone," Damien scolded them and then turned to Tinx. "And what have you got to say for yourself?"

"I came along because I'm fed up with being overly protected. I wanted to be a part of something real."

"How did you know we'd come?" Hayley asked.

"I learned from watching you two. When you get together, you don't take no for an answer. So, when Mother forbid us from visiting the bunker, the look on your faces told me all I needed to know."

"That's why you told Tinx to spy on us," Hayley said. "You wanted us to come."

"Well," Damien said with a smirk, "since you two were so foolish to make the trip. I had to come after you. But who's to say you didn't make the journey to Stravis' bunker before we could stop you."

"Who's to say," Hayley agreed and smiled at her brother. "We need to find KaaFoo."

"Follow me," Damien said.

He led them to a brown tent near the end of town and disappeared inside. He emerged with a one-armed man with an eye patch several minutes later. The man handed Damien a small disc-shaped object and pointed behind his tent.

Damien walked into the desert and waved for them to follow. He continued for several hundred feet, stopped, and threw the disc onto the desert sand.

"Our ride will be along shortly," he said.

Moments later, the ground trembled, and Ethan saw a significant disturbance in the sand moving towards them.

"What is that?"

"A giant sand slug, if I'm not mistaken," Hayley said.

"Correct, sis, you've been studying."

The disturbance slowed and drew closer, and the ground calmed as the oblong pile of sand came to rest directly in front of them. The mound grew taller, and the desert poured off the sand slug exposing brown armored scales along its back and sides. The front half of the giant slug held seats saddled into position behind two long antenna-like eyes protruding from its head.

"What about Azron?" Ethan asked. "That's not big enough to carry him."

"Don't worry about Azron," Damien said. "He grew up on Hades and is well adapted for traversing the desert."

"Azron hell-walker," Azron said and thumped his chest.

Damien made sure Ethan and Hayley were adequately seated before seating himself. The sand slug jolted into motion and sailed along the surface of the sand like a jet boat. Tinx darted around like a playful hummingbird searching for nectar. Azron stood in place to let the rest of the party get a head start.

"What's he doing?" Ethan asked, staring back at Azron as he disappeared into the distance.

"He'll be along shortly," Damien said with a grin.

Azron squatted down and launched skyward like the Hulk. He flew several hundred feet into the sky before falling and landing gently back on the desert surface. Azron continued Hulk-vaulting his way across the desert landscape and caught up with them quickly.

"Look," Hayley said and pointed up at the horizon to an enormous dune.

"What is that?"

"That is the great vanishing dune," Damien said.

"I read about that somewhere," Hayley said. "If you approach close enough, the dune disappears. Some say a desert mirage is the cause; others say the dune is real but protected by the desert harpies."

Ethan's palm symbols suddenly distracted him. They were glowing white and pointing at the giant mountain of sand. His eyes moved back and forth between his hands and the dune as he watched his symbols follow the mirage across the horizon. But then he nearly slipped off the sand slug.

"Whoa there," Damien said as he quickly grabbed Ethan by the arm to stop his fall.

"Are you okay?" Hayley asked. "We almost lost you."

"I—I'm okay." Ethan peeked down at his palms, but they were no longer glowing.

"Here we are," Damien said after nearly an hour of uneventful dune-surfing.

The sand slug stopped to let them off. Tinx landed on Ethan's knee while Azron gently sat on nearby sand. Damien hopped off and pulled out his ELMO device. He tapped the screen and spun around in circles to scan the area. A black metallic pole poked up from beneath the sand and stopped at six feet tall but then shortened and grew into a widening rectangle that repelled the sand. The rectangle continued to shorten and grow until disappearing into the sand and exposing a sizable hatch hidden beneath the desert.

"I could use a hand with this," Damien said to Azron.

Azron approached the bunker door, and Ethan immediately realized he would not be joining them inside. The generous handle appeared small in his hands as he lifted the heavy iron hatch, exposing a dark stairwell into the sand.

"Remind you of anything?" Hayley asked Ethan with a deep grin.

"Hang tight. We won't be long," Damien said to Azron.

"It's getting hot out here," Ethan said. "Will he be okay in this heat?"

"Har, harr, harrr," Azron roared. "Azron from Hades, this desert cold like ice—Har, harr, harrr."

Tinx rode on Ethan's shoulder as he and Hayley followed Damien down the dark staircase. Damien tapped at his ELMO as they reached the bottom, and light shone on the dusty dingy cavern they were now in.

"Doesn't look like much," Damien said.

The room was mostly empty but for an old wooden table and benches. Ethan spotted a small object lying beneath one of the benches.

"What's that?" Tinx jumped onto the table as Ethan bent down to pick up the miniature capsule.

"Be careful, Ethan," Hayley said. "Remember what happened to Pandora."

"Let me see that," Damien said, and Ethan handed it to him.

"This proves Fin Drenchler has been here."

"What is that?" Ethan asked.

"A hydration capsule," said Damien. "Used by hydromorphs when they are away from water for extended periods."

"Why would Fin come here?" Tinx asked.

"Good question," Hayley said. "This is the last place I would expect Fin to go."

Hayley's attention moved to the back of the room, where she spotted something.

"What's that on the wall?"

Damien and Ethan followed Hayley to the jagged rock wall at the back of the cavern. She pointed at a flattened-out area where someone engraved a hand-sized symbol into the rock.

"Interesting," Damien said as he examined the engraving.

Ethan's hands tingled again, so he stepped away from Damien and Hayley to take a peek. His palm symbols were glowing faintly and pointing towards the staircase. Ethan walked to the base of the stairs and glanced up into the bright light of day. A three foot tall blue bunny-like creature with yellow polka dots was standing atop the staircase, waving at him—it was Jasper.

"I—I'm gonna check on Azron," said Ethan and started up the stairs.

Ethan reached the top of the stairs and followed Jasper right past Azron, sitting in the sand. Azron's eye followed Ethan as he continued into the desert – but then he stood and followed quietly to ensure the Hybrid Child's safety.

Jasper continued into the desert for several hundred feet but then stopped and turned to face Ethan.

"They want you to have it back, Ethan Fox," Jasper said in a cartoonish voice. "The Hybrid Child's journey has only just begun."

Ethan was suddenly walking in the middle of a cold, fierce sandstorm. He squinted his eyes as he struggled to move forward but felt compelled to continue as if he was searching for something vital.

Azron stood behind Ethan and watched him stand as if alone in the warm sunny desert. Then Ethan threw his arms up to shield his eyes and slowly stumbled forward. He stopped abruptly, dropped his arms, and spun around to scan his surroundings.

"Ethan Fox feel okay?" Azron asked.

"That sandstorm, you didn't experience it?"

"Azron, no see phantom storm."

"And Jasper? I suppose Jasper wasn't here either."

"Azron, no see Jasper."

"Yeah, I didn't think so," Ethan said, sounding defeated. His head drooped as he looked to the ground and spotted a brown book with shimmering golden symbols on the cover. It lay in the sand between his feet – so he knelt to pick it up. His spirits lifted.

"What about this?" He asked as he held up the book.

"Azron, see book."

"Jasper said they wanted me to have it back."

"Seers speak to Ethan Fox," Azron said.

Ethan and Azron headed back towards the bunker – but along the way, a strange feeling overcame Ethan as the sky dimmed and storm clouds formed overhead. Azron stopped to gaze up at the previously blue sky, and that's when it happened. The black form of a woman appeared from out of nowhere. She was less than twenty feet away, and her shiny black sheen, and golden pendant necklace glimmered in what was left of the desert sun. The sky quickly darkened as the clouds continued to grow. The woman's eyes glowed bright yellow as she motioned at them and pointed into the desert behind them.

"Do you see her?" Ethan asked Azron as he pointed at the black apparition outlined by a blue aura.

"Azron see shadow spirit."

"She saved me before," Ethan said. "I think she's warning us about something."

Ethan spun around to see where she was pointing, and Azron did the same. They saw a significant disturbance dredging up the sand as it moved towards them. It was still far away but approaching quickly.

"Whatever that is," Ethan said, "it's heading this way, and I doubt it's a welcoming committee. We need to warn the others."

Ethan turned to thank the dark spirit woman – but she was gone. He hurried back to the bunker while Azron stayed put and kept his eye on what was coming.

"I think we're all in danger," he yelled into the bunker. Damien, Hayley, and Tinx emerged quickly to witness the commotion.

"Ethan, your symbols, what is happening to them?" Hayley asked.

Ethan glanced down at the symbols on his palms. They had come to life like a cartoon again. They were glowing red and spinning, but when he flattened them out, they stopped and pointed towards the approaching danger like compass needles.

"I don't know. They've been acting strange lately. But there's no time for this now. Danger is approaching." He turned and pointed out the disturbance in the sand. "I think a monsoon is coming."

"That's not a monsoon," Damien said. "It hugs the desert floor too closely."

"Desert harpies," Tinx said.

"But they never leave the vanishing dune," Hayley said.

"Well, they have now," said Damien.

He held up his ELMO and stared at the zoomed-in display of approaching harpies. The desert harpies were hag-faced sand creatures with mermaid bodies. They swam in and out of the dunes like porpoises over ocean waves. Their shapes merged in and out of the churning sand as if formed from the desert itself.

"Shelter," Azron said, pointing at the bunker. "Azron, take care of harpies."

"They're very dangerous," Tinx said. "They bury their victims in torrents of sand. He'll suffocate."

"Azron, be okay."

"We'll have to take that chance—good luck, old friend," Damien said and directed the others towards the bunker.

When the vast school of sand creatures arrived, they concentrated solely on Azron. They circled him and took turns jumping at his head, back, and torso, exploding into shards of glassy sand when they hit. Azron swatted many away with his giant mitt-like hands – but he was vastly outnumbered, and a wall of sand quickly grew around him.

"We've got to help him," Ethan said. "They must have a weak spot."

"Water," Tinx said. "They hate water."

Ethan glanced at Hayley, and his eyebrows arched high.

"Hayley, your copycat! Summon a hydrosphere ejector like you did at Deadwood."

"But I don't have my copycat, and Tabby Cat won't hear me call to her from inside a hidden realm."

The smile drained from Ethan's face, until he remembered something. He handed Hayley the poem book, reached into his pocket, and pulled out the toy water pistol Irvin had given him.

"I hope Irvin's modifications work."

Ethan spun the power dial and took off towards Azron, who was now buried to his neck in glassy sand. Ethan aimed the pistol at the swirling mass of churning desert near Azron's feet and pulled the trigger. A powerful jet of water erupted from the tiny barrel and nearly knocked him to the ground. But Hayley had followed him and arrived just in time to brace Ethan's back and help him stay upright. The small orange toy performed like a water cannon, dousing the harpies until they melted into a mud-like soup of water and sand. The wall of glassy sand melted away from Azron as the harpies wailed in pain, retreated, and disappeared into the surrounding desert.

"Arrrrrr," Azron groaned.

Shards of glass covered those parts of his arms and neck not protected by clothing. He tried to extract them with his giant fingers but was only poking them in deeper.

"Stop your whining," Tinx said as she flew over and gently landed on his shoulder. "Your giant sausage fingers aren't going to help."

Ethan and Hayley spent the next hour scouring Azron's arms and neck, looking for glass shards while Tinx removed them with her tweezer-like front teeth.

"Well, I hate to break up all the fun, but the time has come to return to The Residence," Damien said.

Azron stood and stared down at Ethan.

"Ethan Fox save Azron again," he said.

"You would have done the same for me. Besides, those harpies looked thirsty, didn't they?"

"Har, harr, harrr," Azron roared. "Harpies no like Ethan Fox—har, harr, harrr!"

"That was very brave of you," Damien said.

"That wasn't bravery. Tinx told me about their dislike of water."

"You didn't know if Irvin's modifications would even work – yet you still charged a swarm of harpies with what you only knew to be a harmless child's toy," Damien said. "I call that bravery."

Ethan turned to Hayley with a questioning look.

"Where is your copycat?"

"On a secret mission. I might tell you about it when you tell me where this came from?" Hayley held up the brown poem book for everyone to view.

"I saw Jasper again," Ethan said.

"So, your little friend came bearing gifts, did he?" Damien said.

"Yes."

"What did he say?" Hayley asked.

"He said my journey has only just begun."

"Well, that's an understatement," said Damien. "By the way, did any of you think to bring a portal beacon?"

Ethan, Hayley, and Tinx all shook their heads.

"That's very careless, you're lucky Azron and I were around—this time. Let this be a lesson to you all, the number one rule that all Caretakers must live by, when traveling the protected realms—or anywhere outside The Residence for that matter—always bring more than one portal beacon along. You never know how many you might need in a pinch."

Damien held open the right half of his Caretaker robe to display an array of small pockets stitched to the inside lining. He reached his hand inside a pocket, pulled out a small black cube, and tossed it to the desert floor. The portal beacon morphed into a crystal ball standing atop an upside-down glass cone that grew tall enough for them all to reach.

"I never go anywhere with less than three – but often carry more. Now then, let's get home."

CREATURES OF THE DARK REALM

Ethan's eyes squinted nearly shut in the bright sunless light of the portal plane. The eerie sight of endless checkerboard stretching in all directions under the clear blue sky was an oddity he cherished. They entered the front room of The Residence, and the sound of Gruggins' angry voice greeted them.

"Come back here, you rock-eating roaches," Gruggins shouted as he shook his fist in the air. He was standing at the edge of his table, looking at the ground, but nothing was there.

"What's wrong, Gruggins?" Hayley asked and ran to his side.

Gruggins gazed up at Hayley and the grumpy scowl on his face melted into a smile.

"Those dastardly Nibblewarts are interrupting my nap for the millionth time. They've been on the move lately, coming through in caravans, and they always stop to chant below my table."

"Nibblewarts believe grumplings symbolize good luck," Tinx said from her perch on Damien's shoulder. "Their chanting is a gesture of admiration and goodwill."

"Yeah, well, I'll give them some of my goodwill, all right," Gruggins said and shook his fist again. "Always droning on about the Shadow Princess—"

The beeping of Damien's ELMO cut Gruggins off.

"They are awaiting us in the study," Damien said. "And by the tone of her message, the Headmistress is unhappy."

Hayley, Damien, Tinx, and Azron turned towards the study – but something had grabbed Ethan's attention, and he stood listening to Gruggins' rant.

"The Shadow Princess has returned," Gruggins said as the others walked away.

"Ethan, are you coming?" Hayley asked. Ethan backed his way towards the study but kept his eyes on Gruggins.

"The Shadow Princess delivered us from evil, the Shadow Princess will lead the chosen one, Shadow Princess this, Shadow Princess that . . ."

Ethan reached the door to the study and turned towards the others.

"You can sit this one out," Damien said to Azron, "go take care of those wounds – and I'll cover for you."

Damien opened the door and led the way into the study. Ethan glanced at Gruggins as he stepped into the study.

"If I hear one more word about the Shadow Princess or the Nibblewart prophecies—"

The study door closed.

Jordanna sat behind the desk in the center of the back half of the room. Nicholas stood by her side with his expansive angelic wings on full display, protruding from under his white robe.

"What have you to say for yourself?" Jordanna said, glaring at Damien. "How can I expect others to trust in your leadership if I can't—"

"Damien didn't do anything. I did this, Mother!"

"But I've made it perfectly clear," Jordanna said. "You are not to—"

"Yes—you've made it perfectly clear you will treat me like a child – and I can no longer think for myself."

The room fell silent for several moments as Jordanna and her daughter exchanged glares.

"You've made your point," Jordanna said and turned to Damien. "Fill me in on the details."

"Well," Damien said and hesitated, "After our discussion in the Map Room, I suspected these two would venture to Stravis' bunker. I sent Tinx to keep an eye on them, but when she didn't report back, I learned she went along with them. That's when Azron and I went after them."

"Tinx, what have you got to say for yourself?"

Tinx jumped from her perch on Damien's shoulder and darted over to land on Hayley's.

"I insisted upon joining them because I needed to be a part of something real."

"But I've made you a CAGE member. You are a part of something. Why would you disobey?"

"My reasons are not unlike your daughter's. I'm sorry, Headmistress, but you've been overly protective of me because of my size."

The room fell silent again.

"Continue," Jordanna said to Damien.

"We caught up with them in the shantytown. After that, it was my decision that we continue to Stravis' bunker."

"Of course, you predicted your sister would be insubordinate," Jordanna said and smirked. "I bet you even counted on it – so don't think you've put one over on me."

"I'm sorry, Mother, such a lapse in judgment will not happen again."

"Moving along. What did you find?"

"We found this," Damien said as he showed her the hydration capsule.

"Interesting," Jordanna said. "But what would Fin be doing at Stravis' bunker of all places?"

"That's what I asked," Hayley said.

Jordanna glanced from Hayley to Ethan and the book in his hands.

"It appears the Seers took the opportunity to return their gift to you."

"Yes. Jasper appeared and led me through a phantom sandstorm where I found it buried in the sand at my feet."

"The Seers have reached out to you once again," she said and turned to Hayley. "And the Hybrid Child's exploits will undoubtedly include you. I understand I must come to terms with my motherly instincts."

Jordanna paused then continued.

"Anything else to report?"

"The desert harpies attacked us," said Tinx. "For some reason, they saw fit to leave the site of the vanishing dune and attack us."

"The Shadow Princess," Ethan said. "She appeared again, and this time Azron saw her too."

Hayley's eyebrows bunched as she shot Ethan a questioning look.

"She warned us that the harpies were coming."

"Interesting," Nicholas said. "We've still not received any reports of such a woman—inside or outside of the human world."

"Which brings us to other matters," Jordanna said. "Fill them in on Grimleaver activity."

"Reports are coming in from across the globe. Small random sightings are occurring with regularity. Thus far, they are nothing more than minor annoyances – but the humans have reported seeing vampires, zombies, and otherworldly creatures."

"It sounds like they are trying to spread us thin," Damien said.

"My thoughts exactly," said Nicholas. "They are trying to distract us from something."

"They are distracting us from searching for the prophecies, and they are doing a good job of that. We are spread thin, so I will not tolerate any more rogue missions like today's."

Damien nodded in agreement – but Ethan, Hayley, and Tinx were quiet.

"Might I suggest," Damien said, "we catalog the time and location of each and every event and search for a pattern. No matter how careful they've been, there is bound to be a pattern hidden in the chaos."

"Good thinking," Jordanna said. "Nicholas, task a team of scholars to start immediately."

Hayley asked Jordanna to excuse them from the remainder of the strategizing session – and she agreed. Tinx stayed behind, eager to learn more about what the Grimleavers were doing.

The day had been very long, and midnight was nearing, but neither Hayley nor Ethan had eaten – so they beelined down The Hall of Doorways to the Caretaker cafeteria. The room was dark and empty when they entered, but Hayley tapped at her ELMO and lit up the large white room.

"Irvin's not around to serve us," Hayley said. "But the wall pantry he had installed is always stocked with food."

Ethan scanned the room looking for a pantry and then gazed at Hayley with his eyebrows wrinkled.

"Follow me, and I'll show you," she said.

She walked past the kitchen to an empty area where no tables, chairs, or anything stood. There was only a tall, blank white wall.

"All you have to do," Hayley said, "is concentrate on what you're hungry for and put your hand on the wall like this."

She held her hand against the wall, and a rectangular section lit up around it. When she removed her hand, the lit up area opened like a hatch exposing an opening where a plate of hot spaghetti stood waiting.

"Reminds me of a replicator."

"A what?" Hayley asked.

"The wall pantry is like the replicator in *Star Trek*," he said.

"Star Trek?"

"Yeah," Ethan explained. "*Star Trek* is sort of a universe of its own. It started as an old TV series but has grown into movies, books, and more series."

He placed his hand against the wall, and moments later, his small pizza appeared—just the way he liked.

"Boy would George love to have one of these. Mom rarely lets us eat pizza at home—"

Ethan fell silent. He and Hayley adjourned to a table where they sat and quietly nibbled away at their midnight snacks.

"You seem distracted," Hayley said. "Is something still bothering you?"

"I just keep picturing them in my head," he replied. "My parents, surrounded by a frightened mob, being rushed down the street against their will. They were probably worried sick about me."

"Well, they know you're safe now," Hayley said.

"Yeah, I know – but I just can't shake the feeling."

"I understand," Hayley said. "Let me think about it. I may have an idea."

A meatball rolled off Hayley's plate and Ethan pulled a pizza slice away from his mouth creating a stringy bridge of cheese to stretch between them. They broke out in laughter – but it quickly subsided and silence filled the room as they each took another bite.

"Your mother seemed upset," Ethan said to change the subject. "She tried to hide it – but I could tell."

"Me too. I hate making her sad, but she's become suffocating – and when you came back, I knew it was time to take a stand."

"Yeah, well, you took a stand all right—"

"Why did you call her the Shadow Princess?" Hayley asked, cutting him off mid-sentence. "Before, you referred to her as the woman in black – but this time you called her the Shadow Princess."

"Did you hear what Gruggins was shouting about when we arrived in the front room?"

"Not really. My mind was wandering. I was more worried about what I would say to Mom."

"He was angry with the Nibblewarts," Ethan explained. "They keep disturbing his naps, and all they talk about lately is the return of the Shadow Princess."

"Yeah, so what," said Hayley. "The Nibblewarts are always blabbering about something. Nobody listens to them or takes anything they say seriously."

"A truth that falls upon deaf ears is true to no one," Ethan said.

"Where did you come up with that philosophical nugget?" Hayley asked.

"I—I don't know. It just popped into my head."

"Well, it is a good point. I never thought of it that way," Hayley replied. "The Nibblewarts could be telling us the meaning of life, and nobody would listen."

"Don't ask me how, but I'm sure they are talking about her. She is the Shadow Princess and has returned to lead us to something."

"Lead us to what?"

"I don't know," Ethan said. "But she's trying to tell me something."

"Well, Gruggins seems to hear a lot from the Nibblewarts," Hayley said. "Maybe we should talk to him about them."

"Great idea, we should—" the words froze in Ethan's mouth as he quietly pointed at something moving near the door to The Hall of Doorways.

A tiny insect-like creature squeezed in beneath the door and slowly grew bigger.

"Do you see that?" Ethan whispered.

"What is that? I've never seen anything like that."

"Act like we don't see it," Ethan said.

He and Hayley continued making small talk as they sneakily kept track of the creature out of the corner of their eyes. It was the size of a guinea pig and looked like a black scorpion covered with red lines in a shattered glass pattern. But this was no scorpion. Its head consisted of one giant yellow eye and two small nose slits. Two arm-like appendages grew from the sides of its head, each holding another eye that swiveled independently to scan the area. Instead of a stinger, this creature had a mouth at the end of its tail that reminded Ethan of *Predator*. The fangs clapped repeatedly as sharp finger-like bones outside its mouth bristled inward like inviting fingers.

"Is that what you've been seeing?" Hayley asked.

"That's the third one I've seen, but they've all been different."

"Have they all been this scary-looking?"

"Yeah, but they're not coming to harm me. The one under my bed even smiled at me before it chowed down on a big creepy bug."

Suddenly, the poem book came to life atop the cafeteria table and scared their little visitor away. It flipped open as wisps of golden whimsy wafted from the pages and turned to the first blank page. A poem wrote itself up the page backward. The passage read:

Creatures of the Dark Realm

They revel in the darkness, and hide from view of light.

As they slither, creep, and crawl, while staying out of sight.

CREATURES OF THE DARK REALM

Not all of them are evil, and some have earned free will.

They protect the Hybrid Child, from those who've come to kill.

Most Creatures of the Dark Realm were born of ill intent.

But some serve a different master, who's taught them to repent.

Ethan and Hayley read the poem over and over carefully and sat in silence for several minutes pondering the Seer's cryptic words.

"Creatures of the Dark Realm," Hayley repeated.

"Yes, it rings a bell with me too."

"I recall where we've seen something similar before," said Hayley. "The book in the study with your symbols, it was called *Secrets of the Dark Realm*."

"I remember, written by Dakota Drakelan. He lives in the scary old house on the hill outside Deadwood."

"Yeah, he has a reputation for being creepy. He was the master of dark studies when Grandpa Odin was the headmaster. We must pay him a visit," Hayley said.

"I agree," Ethan said. "The poem book wants us to learn about Creatures of the Dark Realm and he is our best place to start. But it's late, so we'll have to wait till morning."

"No, we'll go now," Hayley said. "Dakota Drakelan is a retired dark master. Everything I've read about dark masters says they are night people and normally sleep during the day."

"Even better."

They agreed, there was no time like the present, and they were both eager for answers. They pondered the poem in silence as they finished their snacks and cleaned their plates—then they were off.

They stood at the base of the hill and stared up at the silhouette of the meager house against the blackish-blue morning sky. Only the light of a half-moon shining from behind the house lit the winding path leading to the front porch. Ethan started up the narrow path, and Hayley hesitantly followed closely behind him.

"This is creeping me out," she said.

"Nothing to be afraid of," Ethan said in as bold a tone as he could muster. Truth be told, he was a little creeped out too, but he continued up the hill anyway. As they drew closer, Ethan saw a small dark blob run into the house through the front door that was slightly ajar. Moments later, a curtain in the front window moved.

"Do you see anything?" Hayley asked. She was walking behind Ethan and held onto his belt loop to help guide her way in the darkness.

"N-Not yet," Ethan fibbed.

Ethan stepped onto the porch and paused at the partially open front door to muster his nerves. Hayley joined him and stood at his side, staring into the black crevice leading into the house.

"Are you sure?"

Ethan took one step forward and pushed at the door with his hand. It creaked its way open, slowly exposing the total blackness of the house's interior.

"Trick or treat," said Ethan. "Is anybody here?"

"Well, well, well," a deep gruff voice said from inside. "Guess I finally got yer attention. Come in, please."

Ethan stepped inside the dark house. A snapping sound clicked, and a series of candles lit themselves one by one around the room. Hayley stepped into the house and stood by Ethan's side. An older man with long grey hair, a goatee, and a bushy mustache sat in a recliner in the corner of the room. He grabbed a beat-up brown cowboy hat and placed it atop his head as he stood to greet them. He wore a long duster-style overcoat and a worn leather vest.

"Good thing too," he said. "I was fresh outta nice ones ta send."

"Are you Dakota Drakelan?" Ethan asked.

"The one and only—last I checked."

"Pleasure to meet you. I'm Ethan—"

"Yeah, yeah, I know who ya both are. Ethan Fox, the Hybrid Child, an yer the long lost Ravenwood kid."

"Well, you don't have to be rude," Hayley said. "Ethan was only being polite."

"You've got your mother's spirit," Dakota said.

But Hayley's attention was elsewhere as she looked around the room at the various oddities. In particular, she focused on the candles burning around the room. Only, they were not candles at all, and they were alive. Small stick creatures with the tops of their heads burning and their arms held up as small flames burned their hands. A look of horror reflected from their tiny faces as bullets of sweat poured down their sides, and they grimaced in pain.

"You're hurting them!" Hayley shouted at the top of her lungs.

"An yer grandmother's," Dakota said.

"Stop it, put them out now!" Hayley insisted.

"Alright, alright, calm down, was only for effect anyway."

Dakota smiled, snapped his fingers, and the burning candle creatures vanished. Various antique lamps around the room flickered on to replace the candlelight.

"Definitely a Ravenwood woman," Dakota said.

"Where did they go?" Hayley asked.

"Back to where I summoned 'em from," Dakota said. "And for your information, those little liars were not'n pain. They're fakin grief to feed off ur sympathy."

"I—I'm sorry," Hayley said.

"Well, that's a first," Dakota said and smiled at Hayley. "I'm told you're quite the promising student. If you read page 115 of my book, you'da learned about candle-grifters."

"Well, I—I'll be sure to put that on my reading list."

"About your book," Ethan said. "The one titled *Secrets of the Dark Realm*."

"Yeah, what about it?"

"The symbols on the spine," Hayley said.

"Symbols?" Dakota questioned.

"Yes, Stravis' symbols," Ethan said and held up his palms. "Symbols that looked like this."

"Oh, that," Dakota said. "Met him once, made quite the impression."

"That's it?" Ethan asked.

"Yep."

"So, did you send the little monsters?" Hayley asked.

"They're not monsters. They're friends. We categorize many'a the world's creatures as monsters based on appearance alone. It's all'a matter of perception."

"Are you saying there are no monsters?" Hayley asked.

"Oh heavens no. There are monsters in this world as sure as the nose on ma face. But not all scary creatures are monsters. You can come out now—"

Dakota snapped his fingers, and three tiny creatures crept out from beneath a couch, miniature versions of the ones stalking Ethan. They grew as they crawled across the room, growing to about eight inches tall.

"Are they shape-shifters?" Hayley asked.

"Not exactly. I've taught 'em various dark techniques to help 'em help me."

The tiny critters stopped at Dakota's feet and turned to face Ethan and Hayley.

"Balder, Gilly, an Skronk," Dakota said as he pointed to them. "Meet Ethan an' Hayley."

Ethan and Hayley waved and said hello, and the creatures smiled and curtsied to acknowledge them.

"Are they from the Dark Realm?" Ethan asked.

"These ur the ones I rescued. But their kin are still in that god-forsaken place."

"What is the Dark Realm?" Hayley asked.

Dakota tensed up, and his demeanor immediately got serious.

"It—It's whur happiness goes ta die," he said, and the room fell silent.

"Why did you send them?" Hayley asked, breaking up the silence. "Why did you send your friends to capture Ethan's attention?"

"Because he's in danger. There'za dark presence at The Residence. Fact is, they been protecting ya since ya first arrived. That's how they caught all those."

Dakota pointed at a sizable, covered enclosure in the corner of the room. He motioned with his left hand, and the cover flew off, exposing a brightly lit aquarium. Inside, a hoard of at least twenty palm-sized black insects crept over one another. They were black beetle-like insects with protruding thorny legs and barbed appendages angling forward over their sharp giant mandibles.

"Those look like the creepy bug one of your friends ate," Ethan said.

"I told ya not to eat 'em," Dakota said to the creatures. "Okay, spill the beans. Which one a ya ate a death scarab?"

The creatures slowly shrunk smaller at the sound of Dakota's scolding, and then they each raised an arm or leg.

"Did you say death scarab?" Hayley asked.

"I'll deal with ya later," Dakota said to the creatures and turned back to Ethan and Hayley. "Yeah, someone's been releasin 'em in The Residence. Releasin 'em everywhere Ethan Fox goes from the looks'a things."

"I've read about death scarabs," Hayley said as her face paled, "a pinprick of their venom kills instantly."

"It does indeed," Dakota said. "We captured these since ur arrival, not countin the ones they ate, of course. Someone's out to getcha."

The room fell silent again. Hayley paced around the room and appeared deep in thought. She stopped abruptly and studied something in the colorfully decorated fish tank at the other end of the room. Ethan noticed too – and quickly approached the tank alongside Hayley.

There was only one fish in the tank, swimming frantically in circles. But as Ethan got close, he could tell the fish was not a fish at all. It was a tiny porpoise blowing shape bubbles from its blowhole. A string of bubbles blew out and hovered mid-water before slowly floating towards the surface. As they rose, the bubbles morphed into letters spelling out the words: HELP ME!

"I've never seen such a small porpoise before," Ethan said.

"Why is he calling out for help?" Hayley asked.

"Um—oh yeah—about that," said Dakota. "There'za perfectly good explanation fer that."

Ethan and Hayley's eyes stayed glued to the small porpoise that turned towards them and stared directly at them. Its eyes grew larger, and its nose shortened as its skin changed color. The porpoise slowly morphed into a navy-blue colored aquatic humanoid with yellow highlights and bulging orange eyes.

"Is that—"

"What is Fin Drenchler doing in your fish tank?" Hayley asked in a stern, condemning tone. "Let him out of that tank immediately!"

Dakota approached the tank and fished Fin out with a small net. He placed him on the dusty wooden floor. Tiny Fin hopped out, peered up at Dakota, and shook his webbed fist at him.

"I was fixin to set 'em free soon enough. Held him here fer his own good I did."

"Free him now!" Hayley ordered.

Dakota held his hand out over tiny Fin and mumbled unintelligible gibberish as he moved his hand in a circle. Fin sprouted quickly and grew like a time-lapsed flower. He rose to over six foot tall and turned to face Dakota.

"What is the meaning of this? I will inform the Headmistress of your despicable actions."

"I meant no harm by it. Ya come poking around, asking questions ya had no business ask'n. Trapped ya for yer own good."

"My own good—"

"Was only holdin ya till I could discuss matters with someone. Meant ta let ya go, but then all the commotion started, and Ethan Fox came back."

Dakota pointed at Ethan, and Fin's anger quickly melted away. He bowed his head to Hayley, turned to Ethan, and changed the subject.

"Ethan Fox – am I glad to see you. Do you remember anything about our last meeting?"

"Um—no, but Jordanna showed me part of a video. I fell into some sort of a trance and spoke to you."

"You spoke in tongues," Fin said. "I believe you spoke in the voice of Stravis himself."

"I don't remember any of that. What did I say?"

"I'm not quite sure. You spoke in the language of the Creators, from what I could tell. I couldn't understand what you were saying – but felt a strong presence that I believe was Stravis."

"Is that why you visited Stravis' bunker?" Hayley asked.

"Yes," Fin replied. "Let's just say that after my encounter watching the ghost of Stravis possess Ethan Fox—it piqued my interest. I spent months researching Creator Stravis and his connection to the Hybrid Child. But my efforts came up mostly empty. I couldn't even find a mention of what a Hybrid Child even is."

"Tell me about it," Ethan said.

Dakota seemed very uneasy with their conversation with Fin. Ethan suspected Fin might be more forthcoming if Dakota weren't present. So he suggested to Hayley that they escort Fin back to the Map Room to tell Jordanna of his return. They left Dakota's creepy house, and along the way, continued their talk with Fin.

"Why did you visit Dakota in the first place?" Hayley asked.

"Stravis' symbol on the spine of his book for one," Fin replied. "But you already know that."

"Yeah, but it sounds like you had other reasons," Ethan replied.

"I did indeed. Years ago, when I was first recruited to become the Seakeeper leader—Headmaster Odin summoned me to The Residence to meet with him."

Ethan recalled his visit to Poseidon, the Seakeepers homebase. Seakeepers were the ocean-going equivalent of the Caretakers. Watching over the human world's oceans for the betterment of mankind.

"Upon my arrival," Fin continued. "I witnessed the end of another meeting Odin was finishing. I didn't see all the attendees, but I saw Dakota Drakelan and Creator Stravis— and Stravis was carrying a baby wrapped in a Caretaker blanket."

"That had to have been me," Ethan said.

"I suspect it was," Fin replied. "The timeline seems right, though I found no information on when Stravis received you."

"That also matches the painting we saw in the Gallery," Hayley said.

"Yes, it does," Ethan said. "Which means I still have business to discuss with Dakota Drakelan."

"Be cautious with that one," Fin said. "You saw how he reacted to me asking questions."

"Fin's right," said Hayley. "We can't just go storming up to his house asking questions."

They arrived at the Map Room and delivered Fin to Jordanna. He had been away from Poseidon for too long and was becoming weaker by the hour. But she'd make sure he received a hydration capsule to regain his strength for his return to Poseidon.

ESCAPE TO NEW YORK

Ethan slept like a log after the previous day's events, and by the time he finally woke up, Hayley was gone from her room and not answering her ELMO. He dressed and headed for the study to check if she might be there. When Ethan entered the front room, Irvin was hard at work, dusting and cleaning.

"Hi, Irvin," Ethan said. "Have you seen Hayley? She's not answering her ELMO."

"Miss Hayley is in the Moongarden," Irvin said. "She may have blocked incoming messages. They are performing a very delicate procedure requiring utmost quiet. That is why Irvin is forbidden to join them. Irvin can't keep his big trap shut—as Gruggins always says."

Irvin's face drooped, and his mouth morphed into an exaggerated frown.

"Shnickyrooners and Shnackleboxes," Ethan said. "I heard that loon turtles were walking upside down on the roof of the rabbit's French toast."

Irvin quickly perked up, and the frown on his face spun into a smile.

"Yes," Irvin said, "and they always wash the poopy diapers of the lawn mower's sausage lips by the side of the baker's trousers."

Irvin stood upright, stopped dusting, and turned to face Ethan with a straight face.

"Thank you, Master Ethan. Nobody has ever tried to cheer Irvin up before."

"That's what friends do."

"Ethan Fox is a good friend. But Ethan Fox should be in the Moongarden with Miss Hayley and the others. Go — Irvin is cheered up now—thanks to his friend."

When Ethan arrived at the Moongarden, the entrance area was quiet, and not a soul was around. He quietly entered and walked the path towards a giant red flower on the ground ahead. Right on cue, Wendy, the withering-froo, balled up into a huge bolder of bark to protect her precious froo-berries. He continued along the path and gazed up at the skyclimber that fell from the clouds like an enormous rope of vine tethered to the sky. His gaze traced its way down the immense beanstalk to a gigantic figure climbing up its side. He stopped to watch and heard shouting in the distance, coming from the back half of the Moongarden. He ran along the path to a dark tunnel boring through the tall wall of foliage that split the Moongarden.

Ethan emerged from the tunnel and slowed to a crawl as he quietly approached the small crowd of Caretakers gathered at the base of the massive vine. Hayley stood between Nicholas and Mrs. Moongarden while a group of seven dwarfs stood in front of them. They were all looking up at Azron, who Ethan could now tell was the climber.

"What a rosy surprise," Mrs. Moongarden said. "Ethan Fox has chosen to join us – delighted as daffodils I am."

"What's going on?" Ethan asked.

"One of the trembling nomads," Mrs. Moongarden said. "Escaped the pen and wandered up Lois' side. The poor dear has been stuck there for months."

"Escaped. How?"

"Ravishers," Hayley said. "They infested the Moongarden and set fire to the nomad pen."

"Indeed, they did," Mrs. Moongarden said. "If not for Grubner's quick thinking, I wither to guess what else may have happened."

Mrs. Moongarden motioned to one of the seven dwarfs who was fidgeting. He reminded Ethan of one of Snow White's little friends.

"Let me introduce you to Grubner Trowel."

Grubner stepped forward and held his hand up to Ethan as his cheeks turned bright pink.

"Grubner, this is Ethan Fox."

"Grubner has heard the stories of Ethan Fox. Grubner is pleased to meet the Hybrid Child."

"Happy to meet you too. And who might they be?"

Grubner turned and gazed at his brothers as his cheeks flushed a deeper red.

"They are my brothers. Grabner, Gribner, Grobner, Gripner, Gropner, and Daryl."

Grubner's brothers stepped forward and surrounded Ethan, who shook their tiny hands as they expressed their admiration. A thundering sound interrupted the introductions.

"Azron, reach nomad!" Azron's voice echoed over the Moongarden.

"I'll be right up," Nicholas shouted to Azron. He stepped away from the crowd, tied a rope around his waist, and stretched his ample angelic wings as wide as they would open.

"Okay, everybody," Mrs. Moongarden said. "It is important we all remain silent while I entice the little dear into uprooting."

"Ready?" Nicholas asked.

Mildred tapped away at the screen of her ELMO and hesitated.

"Go!"

Nicholas flapped his wings, soared into the sky, and within seconds he was hovering next to Azron, who patiently clung to the side of the skyclimber. They witnessed the operation in silence as the trembling nomad quivered at Azron's side while Mildred stared at her ELMO screen. She raised her hand, and Azron gently plucked the nomad from Lois' side with two fingers. He held it out to Nicholas, who quickly lassoed its trunk legs and secured the rope tightly. Azron dropped the small evergreen, which dangled from Nicholas' waist as he circled overhead and slowly glided towards the ground. Azron Hulk-leaped from the side of the skyclimber and landed with a thud several feet from the rest of the crowd. They quickly made their way back through the foliage tunnel and stood by the nomad pen when Nicholas swooped in and gently set it down with the other trembling nomads.

"Whip-dilly-doodles," Mrs. Moongarden said.

Most of the crowd stuck around and made small talk as Grubner entered the pen to remove the rope around the lassoed nomad. But Hayley had other ideas and tugged at Ethan's shirt sleeve to draw his attention. She nodded sideways towards the back of the Moongarden where they had just been. They quietly slipped away and headed back through the dark tunnel.

"I need to show you something," she said as they emerged from the tunnel.

Hayley led him past the skyclimber towards the courtyard near the back of the Moongarden.

"I've been doing a little research," she said as they passed the fountain at the center of the courtyard and proceeded into a vast field of ruins. "I've been trying to learn about the history of this place."

"What's to learn from a heap of old stone ruins?" Ethan asked.

"Lots of things," Hayley replied. "What were they before? Who built them? Who destroyed them, and why?"

"But why does any of that matter now?"

"Because whoever built them also built the spin dial Daavic showed us."

"Good point. What have you learned?"

"I haven't been able to find much information on them. It's like somebody erased their past. There are the rumors they're haunted – but that is all anybody seems to know."

"Have you asked Wordly for help?"

"Not yet. So far, it's been my secret. But I may ask him for help at some point."

"What about the spin dial? Have you tinkered with that at all?"

"Yes, I have," Hayley said as her lips widened into a smile. "That's what I wanted to show you."

Hayley led the way to the tallest partially standing structure in the ruins. They entered the dark, musty room and beelined for a flat circular panel glowing pink on the stone wall.

"I don't even bother covering the panel. Nobody comes near the ruins."

A soft pink glow bathed Ethan's face. It emanated from the symbols on the black rings of the spin dial. He stared at the innermost ring containing only four symbols, one of which was his palm symbol.

"I'm sure you recognize one symbol on the inner ring," she said. "But don't you recognize the others too?"

Ethan studied the other symbols for several minutes, trying to place where he had seen them before.

"Yes, I do," Ethan said as he remembered. "They are the four symbols that made up the Creator's crest we found in the lair of the spider gecko."

"Yes. Those are the symbols of the four Creators of Earth – one from each of the elemental worlds. The one on your palms is Stravis from Zephyr's symbol. The other three represent Driveous, Vraitor, and Zamalador from Atlantis, Ceres, and Hades."

"Interesting – so the ruins must have something to do with the Creators."

"You read my mind," said Hayley. "I think the innermost dial selects which creator was using it."

"Okay, but what is it? What is it for?"

"I'm getting to that," Hayley said as she spun the dials. "I tried quite a few combinations – but nothing worked. Then I fiddled with the center arrow and found out it spins too – and that's when I found this."

Hayley spun the center arrow to point to the right, and then she turned the other three but kept her hand touching the panel. The tall stone walls of the dark room abruptly melted away. They were now standing outside, in a beautiful grassy meadow, under the starry night sky. Stars were everywhere, but what dominated the clear night sky was the giant green planet hovering in space. It was the size of a hundred full moons. The spin dial was still visible, hovering midair with Hayley's hand pressed against it.

"Wow! Where are we?"

"I don't know, but I'm sure that is Ceres," Hayley said. "And I suspect this meadow is just like one on Ceres."

"Cool, it's like we are on Ceres and looking at it at the same time," Ethan said.

She turned the inner dial to Driveous' symbol, and the environment changed around them. They now stood atop a turquoise body of smooth glassy water with various forms of aquatic life swimming below the surface. Ethan gazed up at the enormous blue world hovering in the sky above them. Hayley flipped the dial to Zamalador's symbol, taking them to a hellish fiery environment beneath a giant red planet that pulled the flames skyward.

"And last but not least," she said and flipped the dial to Stravis' symbol. They were now standing on a beach of golden sand that glistened under the starry night sky. The giant yellow planet hovering overhead reflected off the ripples in the calm ocean that stood before them. "The spin dial sticks around as long as I continue to touch it." She removed her hand, and the dial vanished into thin air.

"Where did it go? How do we get back?"

"Just like we did with Daavic." She grabbed Ethan by the hand and turned to lead him away from the water's edge. But then she quickly stopped and stared at something in front of them.

"Wait a minute," Hayley said, "That wasn't there before."

She pointed to a painter's easel and canvas that stood on the beach ahead of them. But they could not see the painting, as it was covered by a yellow sheet with a black swirly eye-shaped emblem stamped on it.

"Well, let's have a look," Ethan said.

They walked towards it – but when they got to within ten feet of the apparition, it vanished.

"Whatever that was," Hayley said, "it wasn't here before – so I think it was meant for you."

They continued inland for another fifty feet – and in a flash, they were standing in the Moongarden's circular courtyard.

It took Ethan a moment to wrap his head around what he had seen. They stood in the courtyard for several minutes discussing Hayley's theories about the ruins. But then Ethan grew quiet as his thoughts flashed back to the chaos in Manhattan and becoming separated from his parents.

"You're thinking about them again, aren't you?" Hayley asked.

"Yeah," he replied. "It just feels different this time. This time something terrible happened – and I need to see for myself that they are alright."

"Well," Hayley said. "I've been thinking about your predicament, and I think I've come up with a solution."

"You have!" Ethan said.

"Yes – but traveling to Manhattan will require us to use the portal plane, and we will need a portal beacon to return to The Residence."

Ethan perked up and listened to every word of Hayley's plan. Obtaining a portal beacon would be tricky – but Hayley knew where CAGE kept a stash of them. So they agreed to meet in the front room in an hour. That would give her enough time to sneak in, borrow a portal beacon, and sneak out.

Ethan stood alone in the front room, awaiting Hayley's arrival. His mind drifted back to his previous visit and the events that took place right in this room. But the sound of the door to The Hall of Doorways opening interrupted his thoughts.

"That was a close call," Hayley said.

"I don't even want to know," Ethan said.

"It's probably better that way. Anyway, let's get a move on." Hayley walked to the front door and opened it. Bright light showered into the dim front room as the portal plane reflected on the mirror next to Ethan.

"Beat you there," Ethan said. He stood several feet from the giant mirror opposite the front door and took a few steps towards it.

"Ethan—"

But she was too late. Ethan smashed headfirst into the solid mirror and bounced off like a pinball.

"Ouch! What happened to the out-door?" he asked as he rubbed his forehead.

"Didn't anybody tell you? The out-door doesn't work anymore, ever since you left. My brother thinks it's related to the out-door to the study vanishing." She stepped out the front door onto the portal plane and waved him over. "But this one works like it did before they locked it."

"Nobody said a word," he said, and joined Hayley on the checkerboard plane.

"You sure hit that thing hard."

"Yeah, I'm lucky it didn't break."

Hayley tapped at her ELMO screen, and a small square matrix appeared. She grabbed Ethan's hand and led him farther out onto the vast checkerboard. He could tell where they were going because a beacon of light shone from a square they were moving towards.

"Don't you need my address or something?"

"We know where you live, silly. Damien has been keeping a close eye on you since the day you left. The portal plane won't take us directly to your home but should get us close."

They arrived at the beacon of light, and Hayley's grip on Ethan's hand grew tighter.

"Have you done this before?"

"No, and I am a little nervous. But I'm excited too. I finally get to see where you live."

They continued to hold hands as they stepped into the beam of light that grew broader and brighter around them – and in a split second, they were gone.

Their eyes took a moment to adjust after the blinding flash of light and the dizzying feeling of being whisked away and dropped on a hard surface. They found themselves at the end of a spacious secluded alleyway between two tall buildings. Dumpsters and trash bags lined the sides of the brick alley walls, and the sounds of a bustling city cried out from up ahead.

"The nearest street corner is that way," Ethan said and pointed. "Let's find out where we are so I can get my bearings."

They started walking down the long alleyway that branched off into smaller side alleys in places.

"Is this a maze?" Hayley asked.

"It can sure seem like one," Ethan said with a laugh. "If you've never been here before."

They were near the midpoint of the alley when a bright flash of light strobed directly in front of them, and a tall man appeared with his back to them. He wore a black overcoat, and long silvery-white hair fell well past his shoulders. He spun around, and his pale blue eyes gazed upon them as a smile grew across his face exposing sharp vampire-like canines.

"How did you find us?" Hayley asked.

"I tracked your portal beacon," said Nicholas. "Your mother is not a fool. She was aware of your little trip before it began. She sent me to look after you."

"This was my idea," Ethan said, "if anyone is to blame, it's me."

"You're wasting your time. We can look after ourselves," Hayley said.

Nicholas sniffed the brisk air and scanned the alley slowly.

"Really? Then I suppose you know we've got company."

Ethan and Hayley scanned up, down, and all around the alley but saw nothing.

"Ethan, your symbols," Hayley said as she glanced down at the red glow emanating from his palm.

"I stand corrected," Nicholas said. "Follow me and keep your eyes on what's in front of you."

They continued towards the mouth of the alley but stopped when the black figure of a woman appeared in front of them. Her piercing yellow eyes glowed brightly as she stared at Ethan and waved her arms skyward. Her mouth moved like she was trying to talk – but muffled gurgling noises were all that emerged.

"The Shadow Princess," Ethan said. "She's warning us about the danger."

Ethan noticed out of the corner of his eyes that Hayley was fiddling with the ring on her finger.

"Is it speaking to you again?" he asked – but her attention was elsewhere.

"Yes, I understand what you are saying," she said and took a step toward the woman – and they exchanged stares for several moments.

"Yes, I understand, and I will tell him," Hayley said.

Yellow rays spilled from the Shadow Princess' lips as a broad smile appeared on her face – and she gazed at Ethan and Hayley.

"It's nice to finally meet you," Hayley said. "And this is Ethan—"

Loud screeching sounds flooded down from above. Ethan and Hayley followed Nicholas' gaze up the sides of the surrounding buildings. Dozens of black figures clung to the brick walls and were inching their way down while others swooped in from both ends of the alley. Two groups of vampires landed in the alleyway, blocking them from both sides. Nicholas started towards the group nearest them but stopped cold when he got close enough to recognize their faces.

"Nicole—but you're—dead," Nicholas said. "I was told he killed you to create—them."

"I no longer answer to that name," said Norell. "And as you can see, I'm not dead—I merely serve a different master, one with a higher purpose."

"But there may be something we can do, Nicole. Please, come back to us. We will figure this out together at The Residence."

"We've come for the boy," Norell said as the vampires behind them slowly advanced. "Give us the boy – or you will all die."

"Well, that don't sound much like a fair fight," a voice said behind the advancing vampires. Ethan could only make out his silhouette – but the tall cowboy hat, long overcoat, and gruff voice gave him away.

"Let's even up the odds a little," Dakota Drakelan said.

He knelt and set three tiny creatures free on the concrete alley floor. Skronk and Gilly scurried past the vampires and stopped at Ethan's feet, while Balder slowly approached the vampires and grew a foot taller with each step. He was nearly seven feet tall by the time he reached them. The vampires fearlessly attacked Balder – but their offensive was futile. Balder countered their attacks by whipping at them with his hooked tentacles. He tore holes in their clothing and ripped pieces of flesh from their bodies with his lashing hooks. One unlucky vampire took flight to flank Balder but was quickly ensnared and slammed to the ground for his trouble.

"Skronk, Gilly, tend to the others," Dakota said and pointed at the unattended vampires. They followed his order and grew larger with each step towards Norell and her companions.

"He's using our brothers and sisters against us," Norell said. "The Grimlord must be told of this."

Norell peered skyward and let out an ear-piercing screech. The walled vampires instantly stopped their descent and leaped into the air to take flight. "This won't be our last meeting," Norell said as she and the others opened their enormous batwings and took to the sky.

The last of the retreating Grimleavers disappeared into the clouds. Balder, Skronk, and Gilly shrank down to size and scurried over to Dakota, who scooped them up and stashed them away in his overcoat.

"Almost didn't recognize ya without ur wings," Dakota said as he walked towards them.

"Your wings. What happened to your wings?" Ethan asked.

"Vamprils can shed their wings at will. I can't allow humans to see me wandering around in their world with giant angel wings."

"How very fortunate we are that you showed up," Nicholas said. "What's lured you out of retirement?"

"Let's just say I have a vested interest in their well-bein'," Dakota said and tilted his head towards Ethan and Hayley.

"How long has she had you looking after the boy?" Nicholas asked.

"Let's just say," Dakota said and then paused. "In some ways, I reckon I've been involved from the beginnin'."

"The Headmistress suspected as much," Nicholas said.

"Not surprisin'," Dakota replied. "Ya may as well tell 'er, the arrival of that shadow spirit is a sign. Things've been set in motion—things Vanessa foretold long ago."

"Vanessa—are you talking about my grandmother?" Hayley asked – but they ignored her inquiry.

"If she knows more about the Grimleaver's plans, she must tell the Headmistress immediately."

"If there's anything ta report, we'll be 'n touch," Dakota said.

"Why are you here anyway?" Nicholas asked.

"The boy wants ta visit his folks," Dakota replied and winked at Ethan. "Return to The Residence and tell Jordanna I'll guarantee their safety an escort them from here."

"Will do," Nicholas said. "Though, I'm not sure how comforting that news will be to her."

Nicholas pulled out a portal beacon, tossed it to the ground, and knelt beside it.

"One more thing," he said to Dakota. "Did you know Nicole is alive?"

"We suspected so."

"Who else knew? Did the Headmistress—"

"No," Dakota said. "Jordanna was not told uv our suspicions."

"Why was I not told? I had the right to know!"

"Vanessa had ur best interests at heart. What would ya have done if ya knew? You woulda charged off and gotten ur darn self, killed. Besides, the Nicole you married is dead. I agreed with the decision then and agree with it now."

Nicholas sighed deeply, placed his hand on the beacon, and vanished in a flash.

The second Nicholas was gone, Ethan turned to speak with Hayley as Dakota watched quietly.

"The Shadow Princess, you could understand her?"

"Yes," Hayley replied. "Her name is Adara, and she wanted me to tell you something."

"Tell me what?"

"She seemed confused and wasn't very clear."

"Just tell me what she said, and we'll figure it out together."

"She said she must help you find the hidden desert fortress – but her presence has put you in danger."

"But she's been helping me. Why would her presence be putting me in danger?"

"Because it is the same fortress he seeks. It is why Victor Qruefeldt has been trying to capture you."

Ethan gasped and felt his face flush as adrenaline coursed through his veins. He stood silently, pondering what Hayley had just told him.

"How are you able to understand her?" he asked.

"I—I don't know," she replied. "I just heard a soft, calm voice in my head when she spoke. But I think it has something to do with my ring because it finally woke up."

"Is that'ta—" Dakota said under his breath. "A rift-key?" He stepped forward and knelt beside Hayley to inspect her ring.

"Yes," she said and held out her hand. "I snatched it from Victor Qruefeldt's puzzle box."

"Hmmm," Dakota said, "well if that don't beat all. Answers a few questions too."

"What are you talking about?" Hayley asked. "Do you know something about my ring?"

"Nah. Nothing to concern yerself with."

"You were talking about my grandmother, weren't you? How do you know my grandmother?"

"We been associates fer a long, long time," Dakota replied. "An if ya wanna learn anythin more, yer gonna have to ask 'er yerself."

Ethan stared at Dakota as he contemplated his next words to the old-timer. Hayley gently reached down and held his hand to calm him.

"Ya got sumthin' ta say ta me?" Dakota asked.

"No," Ethan replied. "I was just thinking. How did they know? How did the Grimleavers know we were here?"

"That's a good question," Dakota said. "It's smellin' more-n-more like we gotta rat at The Residence."

Dakota accompanied Ethan and Hayley to the end of the alley, and they emerged onto a busy city street. Ethan quickly recognized where they were and hailed a taxi to take them the rest of the way. Hayley's eyes scanned up the sides of the tall buildings and became riveted to the sky.

"Reminds me of the Caretaker city of Zen," she said.

"Yeah, in a primitive sorta way," Dakota said.

The taxi dropped them in front of a tall plush high-rise across from Central Park. The doorman recognized Ethan and politely let him and his friends into the building. They took the elevator up to a penthouse near the top of the building. They exited the elevator into a foyer leading to a sizeable living room with huge windows overlooking the park.

"Shhh, stay here. I'll find my parents and explain."

"What are you going to explain?" Hayley said. "Are you going to tell them, Caretakers from a parallel world rescued you?"

"I—I'll think of something," Ethan said and ran upstairs to his parents' bedroom. But he returned moments later because nobody was there.

"I searched every room upstairs, and there is no sign of them. Maybe they're in the game room or George's study."

Ethan headed down the hall to George's study. Light peeked into the dark hallway from underneath the closed door.

"Dad," Ethan called out as he reached the door. "It's Ethan. Are you in there?"

"Ethan, we've been so worried!" George said from inside.

Ethan opened the door as George stood up from behind his desk and gave him a wide-eyed stare.

"George Fox," Dakota Drakelan said as he entered the room and stepped in front of Ethan. "How long's it been? Seems like a hundred years."

George glanced at Dakota, then at Ethan, then back at Dakota.

"Ur all grown up since ur days at The Residence. Up and out from the looksa it." Dakota pointed at George's belly and laughed.

George turned back to Ethan, let out a deep sigh, and sat back in his chair.

"I guess an explanation is long overdue."

"Ya think," Ethan said and held up his open palms. "Are you going to tell me these aren't tattoos from an evil cult?"

"How long have you known?" George asked – but when Hayley entered the room and stood by Ethan's side, he quickly recognized her.

"The Boardwalk. You've known since our trip to Santa Cruz. Your mother sensed there was more to your attraction to the girl."

"Her name is Hayley."

"It is a pleasure to meet you, Hayley," George said.

"Happy to finally meet you too," Hayley said as she stepped forward and held her hand out.

George's face went blank as he took her hand and gently shook it. Ethan could tell he was struggling to grasp what was happening.

"Cat got ur tongue, George? Don't remember ya being the speechless sort."

"I—I've spent years trying to prepare myself for this. Betsy and I tried to envision every scenario."

"Betsy," Ethan said. "Where is she? Is she okay?"

"She is safe. After the attack, Alexander paid us a visit. We decided Betsy would be safer if he took her to stay with family."

"Alexander," Ethan said.

"Yes, Alexander Sturgis, your real father," George said. "I'll explain – but let me start at the beginning."

"Please do."

"When I was a young boy, a taletaddler named Pepper visited me," George said and smiled as he remembered. "We quickly became the best of friends. He would visit me every day like clockwork. But then one day—"

George paused. A serious look crept over his face as his body tensed up.

"I've heard the story," Hayley said. "You were the boy with Pepper when Grimleavers abducted him."

"Yes. They killed my parents and took Pepper."

"I'm sorry you went through that," Ethan said as he hurried to George's side and knelt beside him.

"That's when Alexander arrived and rescued me. He was the Caretaker in charge when they showed up to scrub the site. He took me back to The Residence and raised me as his own."

"Alexander was my apprentice," Dakota said. "The best student a darkness I ever had the pleasure'a meetin, an' e's an even better man."

"Where do I fit in?" Ethan asked.

"They didn't tell me much," George said. "Only something terrible happened – and Alexander and Tiffany's infant son disappeared. Alexander kept your room exactly as it was. Then one day you reappeared at the exact location you disappeared from hundreds of years prior."

"And I had these," Ethan said and held out his palm symbols.

"Yes. After that, Alexander raised us both – and you were like my baby brother."

"What about the picture?" Hayley asked. "We saw a picture of you two with Alexander. You were at a cabin in the woods."

"I was kept in the dark about that too. All I was told is something bad happened – and they moved us from The Residence."

"And you never asked why?" Ethan asked.

"Sure I did. But all they told me was it would be safer if we hid in the human world."

"They, who is they?" Hayley asked.

"I don't know – but Alexander had others helping him," George said as he turned to face Dakota. "And I'm quite sure you were one of them."

Ethan and Hayley turned towards Dakota, who was now fidgeting in place.

"Don't look at me like that," he said. "Question and answer time's over. You've learned as much as ya need to know—fer now."

Ethan stared at Dakota, contemplating whether to question the old-timer about Fin's revelation regarding Dakota's meeting with Stravis and Odin. But he decided to heed Fin's warning and error on the side of caution.

"Well," Ethan said and smiled at Hayley. "While I'm here, I may as well grab my pocket tote."

He walked to George's bookshelf, climbed the ladder, and removed three books from the top shelf exposing a small cubbyhole. Next, he removed a small brown book with shiny gold lettering, and from beneath that he retrieved his pocket tote.

"You found my secret hiding spot?" George asked.

"I've been stashing my pocket tote there for almost a year now."

"That book," Hayley said, "Is that the missing portal book?"

"No," George said, "It's a tether port. That's how they transported you into the future. It's how you disappeared from the Caretaker world. Betsy and I agreed to hide you from the Grimleavers—and it worked. Until now."

"I'll take that," Dakota said. "Workin' tether ports are hard to come by nowadays."

Ethan tossed the book to Dakota. They spent another hour with George discussing whether he should return to The Residence with them. But George was adamant that he and Alexander had a plan. George would stick around as Grimleaver bait just to gauge their interest – but a Caretaker security detail would keep a close eye on him.

All in all, the journey was a success. Speaking with George quelled Ethan's worries, and he learned a little about his past in the process. It was time to return to The Residence—regroup and discuss their next steps. He needed to learn about his real parents, and hopefully, what a Hybrid Child was too.

CHAPTER SIX

THE DRONE WARS

They materialized on the checkerboard plane, and Dakota stumbled forward – but Ethan caught him before he could fall.

"Never have gotten used ta these dag-nam portals," Dakota said. "Miserable way ta travel if ya ask me."

When they entered the front door, a short man with four arms stood in front of the tall mirror across the room. He saw their reflection and spun around to greet them.

"Ethan Fox, what great timing," he said.

"Boris Wentworth," said Dakota. "Squirreled your way out of another close call, I gather. I guess even Grimleavers can't stomach the likes 'a you."

"Still sore about that piece I wrote about you," Boris said, and strode across the room with his right arms extended.

Boris Wentworth was a pudgy man in black formal attire, with a pocket watch chained to his vest. He was shorter than his wife Bella, and had grey flattop hair, long sideburns, and a monocle over one of his brown eyes. A fat droopy nose sat in the center of his round face, and a thick bushy mustache covered his upper lip. Boris and his family were members of the four-armed quadroll species.

"How very fortunate I am," Boris said. "I've so wanted to meet the Hybrid Child face-to-face."

Ethan politely shook one of Boris' extended hands. Dakota walked past him and grumbled as he approached The Hall of Doorways – but he stopped and turned back.

"Be careful what ya say ta that snake oil salesman," he said to Ethan. "Choose yer words wisely, or he'll bend the truth till both ends meet."

Dakota slammed the door as he exited, and an uncomfortable silence filled the room.

"Not your greatest fan, I guess," Hayley said to break the silence.

"Pay him no mind. He's still mad about my article for *The Residential Daily Star*. I suppose he wasn't happy about me exposing the dark dealings from his past. But as I always say, a good reporter makes more enemies than friends."

Boris took out his pocket watch and glanced at the time.

"Oh my, I must have lost track of time. I've somewhere to be, so I must be off."

"It was nice meeting you," Ethan said.

"The pleasure was all mine," Boris said and paused. "Tell me, my boy, are you a fan of the Drone Wars?"

"Drone Wars?"

"Well, if you've never experienced them, you simply must join me for tomorrow night's match. I've access to a VIP seating box, and there is plenty of room for the both of you."

"No, thank you," Hayley said and pursed her lips.

"What are Drone Wars?"

"The sport of Caretakers," Boris said. "A head-to-head battle of evolutioneer ability and wits. The Drone Wars are as much a game of chess as a show of raw brutality."

"That sounds dope," Ethan said.

"Brutal and barbaric is a better description – and I will have no part of them," Hayley said and crossed her arms.

"They're not so bad," Boris said to Ethan and winked. "My daughter Blakelyn isn't a fan either."

Ethan's eyes ping-ponged from Hayley to Boris and back a few times as he pondered the invitation – but in the end, curiosity got the best of him.

"Sounds fun," he said, "I'll go with you."

"Splendid, I will drop by your room tomorrow evening and accompany you."

Boris exited the front room. Hayley stood quietly with her arms crossed, staring daggers at Ethan.

"Don't be mad. It sounds interesting to me."

"I'm not mad. Just disappointed you would want to witness something so barbaric."

"And how do you know it's barbaric?"

"Because I went to a match and saw for myself."

"Oh, so you made up your mind after experiencing a match yourself. Is that what you are telling me?"

Hayley unfolded her arms and laughed.

"Good point," she said. "You should witness a match yourself and make up your own mind."

After the eventful visit to Manhattan, they needed time to decompress – so they grabbed a quick bite to eat in the cafeteria. Then Hayley suggested they stop by the Moongarden to ask Mildred if she needed any help. So they spent the rest of the day and half of the next helping Grubner and his brothers replant a patch of creeping tanglers damaged during the recent Ravisher infestation.

It was late afternoon, and Ethan's Drone Wars date with Boris Wentworth was approaching. Time for him to adjourn to his room to shower and get ready for the main event.

"Sorry guys, I gotta be going now," Ethan said to Grubner and his brothers. "But I promise to help more tomorrow if you need me."

Grubner and his brothers smiled and bid Ethan adieu. They were grateful to have his help and assured him they could not have done it without him.

"Where are you going?" Hayley asked.

"The Drone Wars. Remember?"

"Ooh yeah, I almost forgot," Hayley said with a smirk. "Have fun – and I hope you enjoy them as much as I did."

Ethan laughed and left. Along the way, in The Hall of Doorways, he heard Irvin singing from the darkness ahead.

"My bologna has a first name its G-R-U-M-P, my bologna has a second name, its L-I-N-and-G, oh I love to tease it every day and if you ask me why I'll say . . . cuuuzzzz silly Irvin has a way of making Gruggins mad all day."

"Shnickyrooners and things like that," Ethan said as his light beetle merged with Irvin's, and they came face-to-face.

"Ethan Fox, Irvin is happy to talk to his bestie on such a lovely day."

"Nice to see you too, Irvin. You're in great spirits today."

"Oh yes, Irvin is going to view some of his favorite new shows on TV. The Real Housewives always make Irvin laugh. Would Ethan Fox like to join Irvin this evening?"

"I'm sorry, Irvin – I've got plans. I'm going to the Drone Wars with Boris Wentworth tonight."

"Bahhh, Drone Wars are a kiddie show compared to the Housewives. Irvin is thinking of producing his own version here at The Residence—The Real Caretakers of Zen City."

"Good luck with that, Irvin," Ethan said as he choked back a laugh. "Anyway, I gotta be going now."

Ethan returned to his room, showered, and changed. He didn't expect Boris to arrive for another hour – so he sat on his bed and thumbed around with the apps on his ELMO device. He came across one for *The Residential Daily Star* and opened it. He remembered hearing that Boris Wentworth was a senior reporter for *The Daily Star*.

"I may as well check out some of Boris' work," he thought to himself as he perused the app.

He searched all articles by Boris Wentworth, and a long list of Boris' works scrolled down the screen. Ethan scanned his way down the list to some of the older articles when one towards the bottom caught his attention, *The Troubling Truth*

Surrounding Headmaster Ravenwood's Latest Decisions. He read from the article:

> "Thumbing his nose at popular opinion, new Headmaster Odin Ravenwood has decided against abolishing the Master of Dark Studies position. Created during predecessor Gaylord Trabblemore's tumultuous reign, the position has come under intense scrutiny as calls for its banishment have reached a crescendo. Opponents insist Gaylord's downfall was a direct consequence of him creating the position for his questionable appointee, Heldrik Vonn Grim."

Ethan skimmed his way through the article when another paragraph grabbed his attention.

> "As if the groundswell of negativity were not troubling enough, the position is already filled, as this reporter has learned. While not yet announced by the administration, sources confirm Dakota Drakelan, a little-known Caretaker, will fill the position. On the surface, the appointment of Drakelan may seem like a non-event. But this reporter has uncovered the dark and troubling past of the new appointee.
>
> As an orphaned child, young Dakota was captivated by dark and gloomy things. As he grew older, the subject of dark studies absorbed most of Drakelan's time. Then one day, he encountered a man named Heldrik Vonn Grim. The boy's dreary demeanor and thirst for darkness attracted Vonn Grim. And so it was, Heldrik took the boy under his wing as his apprentice. And so it is, Heldrik Vonn Grim's apprentice, one Dakota Drakelan, will become Odin Ravenwood's first appointee. Needless to say, our

newly appointed Master of Dark Studies is sure to be mired in controversy."

Ethan sat on the edge of his bed, contemplating the article when a knocking sound interrupted his train of thought. He quickly hopped to his feet and answered the door to greet Boris, who was talking to a colorful figurine attached to his lapel.

"No, no, that won't do for tonight," he said to the pendant shaped like a strange bird. The color drained from the charm as it abruptly came to life, peeled itself off Boris' lapel, and scurried onto his shoulder.

"Let's try something reptilian for tonight's festivities," he said. The bird on Boris' shoulder melted into a goopy metallic puddle and slowly elongated into a tube that forked at one end. Black scales grew along its length as the two fork prongs morphed into serpent heads. Shimmering blue diamond markings painted themselves down the entire length of the two-headed serpent as it slithered down Boris' chest and reattached to his lapel.

"Now that's more like it," he said and winked at Ethan.

"That's so cool. Reminds me of Hayley's copycat."

"Not a copycat. Just my favorite garment frill I fancy to wear on occasion."

"I have cufflinks and a tie clip my dad makes me wear sometimes. He wouldn't even have to ask me to wear one of those."

"Well, it pleases me that you like it. Now, are you ready for some excitement, my boy?"

Boris escorted Ethan down The Hall of Doorways and ushered him to the thirteenth door on the left.

"Isn't the Map Room right across the hall?"

"You have a keen recollection," Boris said with a chuckle. "You might have a future in reporting. *The Residential Daily Star* is always looking for fresh young talent."

They entered an enormous flat square room with vendor booths lining the outer walls. Masses of people lined up to buy food and refreshments. But what caught Ethan's attention was the colorful array of robes these Caretakers wore.

"Their robes," Ethan said. "Why are they all wearing so many different colors?"

They wore the same half-and-half style as traditional Caretaker robes – but these consisted of every imaginable color combination. Some robes even split along the diagonal to allow four different colors.

"Most Caretakers wear formal attire to an event like the Drone Wars. The color combinations represent their elemental origins."

"So purple means one parent is from Atlantis, and one is from Hades," Ethan said.

"Exactly. I'll make a reporter out of you yet."

"What do black and white represent?" Ethan asked.

"You possess a thirst for information, and you're asking all the right questions – but I'm going to let you take a stab at that one too."

"Well," Ethan said as he pondered the question. "I would say good and evil, but Caretakers are all good. Aren't they?"

"Of course – but all creatures possess a natural bias towards either darkness or light. Bats live in dark caves, but it doesn't make them evil. Humans equate darkness with evil – but the truth is, darkness is merely a convenient veil under which evil often chooses to hide."

Boris' philosophical explanation confused Ethan – so he shook his head and smiled.

"Wow, look at all the vendors," Ethan said. "Reminds me of the Boardwalk."

"Would you fancy a refreshment?"

"Sure, do they have sugar-pickle soda?"

"I am sure they do," Boris said as they slowly strode towards the vendors.

"Where is the arena?" Ethan asked. "Where does the match take place?"

"The arena is here. You are not looking in the right places."

Ethan scanned the room around him and slowly guided his gaze upwards. The room walls stopped about thirty feet up, but they did not end at a ceiling like most rooms. Instead, it continued up to an open night's sky filled with stars. Ten enormous concentric rings hovered in the sky several hundred feet directly overhead. The annuli grew wider as their diameters increased – and a giant empty circle of the sky filled their center.

"What is that up there?"

"That is the arena," Boris said as they gathered their refreshments. "Come, they are about to open up the floater ports."

"Floater ports?" Ethan questioned.

He followed Boris towards a crowded queue at the room's center, where a trail of giant bubbles floated skyward with people inside.

"What are those?" he asked.

"Elevation pods," Boris replied. "That, my boy, is our way up to our seats."

The line moved quickly, and within minutes, they stood at the edge of an immense circular divot in the ground. A Caretaker couple stood at the center and waited as liquid goop poured from the edges of the divot. Spherical walls grew around them, forming an enormous bubble that slowly floated skyward. Ethan's gaze followed the bubble as it gained speed and drifted towards the arena.

Ethan glanced down as they reached the empty sky at the center of the arena. The room below looked like an open box with tiny people wandering inside. Their pod continued to rise, and he could now tell the floating rings formed a giant bowl-like stadium in the sky as each larger ring floated at a slightly higher altitude than its neighbor, and formed a self-contained section.

"VIP seating, my boy," Boris said as the elevation pod dropped him and Ethan on a walkway of the innermost ring section. He guided Ethan to a roped-off seating box with eight seats that reminded him of the captain's chair in the Map Room. They sat quietly as hundreds of Caretaker-filled bubbles floated through the arena's center and dropped their fare at the various levels. Ethan spotted Brianna, Damien, and Nicholas in one bubble, followed closely by Azron in another much larger bubble. He tried to wave – but they did not recognize him as their elevation pods sped by and dropped them on the highest and outermost ring.

"Your CAGE friends occupy the uppermost section, and I have a theory as to why."

"What do you mean?"

"Caretakers at The Residence revere CAGE. They should be in their own VIP box," Boris said and pointed to an empty box of seats nearby. "Yet they choose to sit topside with the commoners. I believe the Headmistress has put them up to it."

"Why would she do such a thing?"

"I believe the Drone Wars threaten or frighten Jordanna Ravenwood – so she has deployed her henchmen to police the events. And what better place to keep an eye on things than up there, where they have a bird's eye view of all that is going on."

Ethan sat quietly, contemplating his friend's choice of seating. Boris spotted something that piqued his interest in the nearly filled arena.

"I'm sorry, my boy – I must step away for a moment to follow up on something. A good reporter is never off duty. But have no fear. I will return before the match begins."

Ethan's eyes followed Boris up a set of stairs dividing the seating boxes. He stepped onto one of the walkways that ringed the various levels of their section. Boris continued around the walkway to the opposite side of the arena and stopped at a box filled with Caretakers wearing half-black half-red robes. A man with long black hair stood and shook Boris' hand. Ethan had never seen him before, but he recognized two of the people sitting next to him. It was Blair Trabblemore and Caden Stanley, and they were leaving so the man could speak to Boris in private. Ethan vividly remembered he and Hayley's previous run-ins with the resident bullies – and those memories were not pleasant.

Ethan perused the rest of their section and moved his eyes up to the levels hovering above. His eyes scanned the ring, looking for anyone he might recognize, but they were too far away. He stood and turned to look up at the closer parts of the sections when something smacked the side of his head from behind. He spun around and found himself face-to-face with Blair and Caden, who were standing on the nearby stairs.

"Look, Blair, the mutant child," Caden said. "He's come to the match all by himself."

Blair laughed as she clung to Caden's side and held his hand tightly.

"Where is your little pet, Malik?" Ethan asked. "Too bad you didn't bring him along so I can sic him on you."

"He doesn't like the stench of mutants," Caden said and stepped towards Ethan with his fists clenched.

"You didn't learn anything from our previous encounter," Ethan said with a grin.

The thundering sound of a gong rang out over the arena, causing Ethan to flinch. Caden and Blair roared with laughter.

"Mutant boy is afraid of loud noises."

"He's probably afraid of his own shadow," Blair said as they continued to laugh.

"That's enough," Boris said from behind Blair and Caden. "Ethan Fox is my guest here – and you will treat him respectfully."

"We were leaving anyway," Blair said as she tugged at Caden's arm to lead him away.

"I said you will treat him with respect," Boris said louder. "Do you understand me?"

"Yes, sir," Caden and Blair said.

"Very well, return to your father. He is wondering as to your whereabouts."

The two troublemakers turned and hurried away towards the other side of the arena.

"I'm sorry they were so unpleasant. But you are the Hybrid Child, and you will require thick skin."

Ethan's gaze followed Blair and Caden around to the other side of the arena to the seating box where Boris had gone. Then he sat in silence, wondering what business Boris might have with Blair's father.

Several moments passed, and most of the crowd sat quietly when a white circular platform grew from nowhere in the empty sky at the center of the arena. A transparent barrier sprouted up like glass around the exterior of the platform, creating a fat cylindrical enclosure.

"What is that?"

"The battle ring, where combat happens."

Two square platforms grew midair to each side and above the circular battle ring.

"And those are the evolutioneer platforms, where the contenders compete."

With all the blanks filled in, he understood what good seats Boris had gotten them. They were essentially sitting ringside. Ethan sensed the electricity in the air as a low-pitched hum of the chanting crowd slowly grew louder and louder.

"And that sound is the call to battle," Boris said with a broad smile. "The first match is about to begin."

Ethan's eyes widened with excitement as he stared at the arena. He did not want to miss anything. Two giant bubbles floated up through the space between the battle ring and the innermost VIP section. They swiftly floated to opposite sides of the battle ring and dropped the contenders onto their respective platforms. Each of them carried a small pouch matching the colors on their robes.

A giant expressionless face appeared in midair over the battle ring. It was half-black half-white split down the middle and reminded Ethan of a blank Halloween mask. At first, the holographic face hovered motionlessly – but then the mouth smiled and began to speak.

"Tonight's first match pairs two first-year contenders," its voice boomed over the stadium. "On the east platform, robed in white and green, contender Artemis Klem." The crowd roared with anticipation as the face continued. "And on the west corner, robed in black and blue, is contender Reginald Simmons."

The roar from the crowd grew louder as the evolutioneers held out their pouches and opened them. A bubble floated out of each and grew as they glided away from their contenders, stopping when they reached their proper place over opposite sides of the battle ring. Ethan studied the small elevation pods, trying to figure out what the small oblong blobs standing inside were.

"What's inside the bubbles?"

"Those are the drones. Lifeless lumps of flesh each contender starts with. The first-years use smaller ones, but the drones vary in size depending upon the evolutioneer's experience level. Study them closely, my boy. Those drones won't be lifeless for much longer."

"Ladies and gentlemen, beasts and banshees, and all other present lifeforms . . . prepare yourselves for battle," the face said, causing the crowd to roar louder. "Evolutioneers, are you ready?" The contenders bowed their heads in agreement. "Combat commences when the drones hit the canvas." The face flashed one last giant smile and vanished.

The crowd quieted with anticipation as all eyes focused on the two small bubbles hovering over the battle ring. The evolutioneers held their hands up and stood, waiting for something to happen. The bubbles abruptly disappeared, sending their drone payloads thudding to the canvas where they immediately expanded.

The white and green evolutioneer clasped his palms together and spun them in a circular motion. The drone nearest him instantly morphed into a spherical shape. Tiny legs grew from the bottom, and a gaping hole appeared in its side where rows of sharp canine teeth began to form. Brown fur sprouted, covering the emerging creature as small eyes bulged from above its menacing mouth.

"Bad move," Boris said to Ethan, "he's tipped his hand and given his opponent a glimpse at his strategy. This match will be short."

The second evolutioneer in black and blue stepped back and waved his arms up and down in opposite directions — and Ethan was riveted. The evolutioneer's drone flattened out and rolled itself into a long stick shape. Four insect legs sprouted from one end while a ball of flesh grew on the other like meat on a skewer. The insect legs moved in unison to lift the ball of flesh, walk towards its opponent, and dangle it like an enticing meal. The ploy worked as the opponent's fat round creature quickly waddled over and chomped down on the skewered meatball with its razor-sharp teeth.

"That's all she wrote for the little ball of teeth," Boris said with a grin.

It confused Ethan initially — but his eyes remained glued to the battle. And then, in an instant, everything changed as four spikes sprang from the skewered meatball, impaling the fat round creature on all sides from within. A crimson river of blood oozed from the losing drone. It no longer looked like a lifeless mass of flesh; but, instead, a dead creature. Ethan now understood why Hayley disliked the Drone Wars.

Yet something primal had awakened inside of him, and it excited him.

"That was so cool," Ethan said, "but how did you know?"

"Amateur mistakes like that are easy to spot, my boy. Once you witness the more experienced competitors, you'll understand."

After watching several more matches, Ethan understood what Boris meant by 'amateur mistakes.' As promised, the more experienced competitors used larger drones which meant more complex creatures and strategies. It was time for the main event, a battle of champion evolutioneers, and Ethan couldn't wait. Now that he understood what was going on, and the skill involved, he was having the time of his life.

The championship started like all the rest, with the holographic face announcing the champion contenders and disappearing as the crowd awaited the dropping of the drones. But this time, the drones grew to the size of small boulders as they crashed onto the canvas with a loud bang.

The champions wasted no time making their moves but were sneakier about concealing their strategy. The evolutioneer in black and red stepped to the edge of his platform and turned his back to his opponent, making slashing gestures with his hands as he did so. His drone sprouted two long chicken legs that lifted the rest of the fleshy mass off the canvas. A thick thatch of feathers sprouted from the drone's mass and fanned out like an umbrella blocking the opponent's view of its metamorphosis. The transformation continued, hidden from view, as hooked tentacle-like appendages grew around a snout full of razor-sharp teeth that morphed from the drone's body.

Not to be outdone, the champion in white and yellow took a step back and crossed his hands in front of his chest. His drone shivered like an egg about to hatch and grew as it shook more and more violently. A confused look washed over the champion's face as he lowered his arms and stared at his hands. Blood slowly gushed from his nose as the champion shook like his drone.

Boris fidgeted in his seat – and his arm twitched as he watched with a demented grin.

"Oh, how unexpected," he said.

"What?" Ethan asked.

"Something is going delightfully wrong," Boris answered.

The drone's shivering slowed as it morphed into an egg and continued to grow to three times its original size. The crowd fell silent as the bleeding champion dropped to his hands and knees and fell unconscious.

A crack suddenly appeared on the enormous yellow egg in the battle ring.

"Click, click, click," a noise echoed inside the giant egg.

Chills crept down Ethan's spine as he recognized the sound he was hearing. The egg shattered as a massive black beetle-like insect emerged. The creature had broad jagged mandibles and sharp-pointed front legs that thrust forward like stabbing knives. The enormous death scarab leapt forward and made quick work of the opposing drone creature. Wrapping its giant mandibles around the smaller animal, biting it nearly in half, and popping it like a sack of crimson blood.

"Click, click, click," the noise echoed from the death scarab as it circled the battle ring.

"It appears to be searching for something," Boris said.

Ethan's palms tingled, so he peeked down at his glowing red symbols pointing at the death scarab.

"No, it's looking for someone. It's looking for me."

"Nonsense, my boy, it would be impossible for a drone to attack you here."

No sooner had the words left Boris' lips, then the creature leaped from the battle ring and flew across the gap between them. The scarab landed on one of the walkways circling their section and beelined towards Ethan. The nearby crowd panicked and ran – but the beast quickly impaled two unlucky fans. Ethan hopped to his feet and hurried up the staircase to the walkway. The giant insect slowly closed the distance between them. The shocked audience stared at the scene in silence from the other sections.

"It's after me," Ethan shouted to anyone close enough to hear. "Run away from here while I distract it."

Ethan stood motionless, staring into the creature's black beady eyes as it inched closer. It was nearly on top of him when he finally took Boris' advice and bolted up a set of stairs to another empty section. The creature saw where

Ethan was headed and took a shortcut by leaping to the next platform where the staircase led.

Ethan turned as he reached the top of the stairs – but did not see anything chasing after him. He turned back just in time to see the monster directly in front of him. Ethan's momentum was thrusting him headfirst into the creature's giant open mandibles, so he instinctively ducked his head and extended his arms to shield himself. Bright beams of green light erupted from his palms as they touched the beast. Then, in a flash, the creature transformed into a lifeless drone.

Everything fell silent as Ethan fell to his knees, shaking. Boris was the first to arrive at his side.

"You were amazing, my boy!"

"I—I don't understand—I didn't do anything," Ethan said.

"Well, this is another first," Nicholas said as he landed on the walkway alongside Ethan and gave him a toothy smile. "Thought I would fly down and give you a hand, but you've already gotten everything under control."

Above them, the silent crowd erupted in applause at what Ethan had done. Azron, Brianna, and Damien joined Nicholas in the VIP section to help calm the spectators who were still in shock while a steady stream of elevation pods flowed to evacuate the crowd. It took over an hour to empty the floating arena; and by then, Ethan was so tired, he could barely keep his eyes open. He expended a lot of energy to defeat the giant creature, so Azron carried the sleeping Hybrid Child to his room, where Irvin would tuck him in.

369

THE ORACLE

The time was nearly 11:00 AM when Ethan was awakened by a light tap at his door. He popped out of bed, still wearing his clothes from the night before. He answered the door to a somewhat subdued Boris Wentworth standing in the hall.

"I'm sorry, my boy, I didn't want to disturb your rest after last night – but I wanted you to have this."

Boris handed him a small box with a red bow.

"No worries, I was already getting up," Ethan said. He popped the top off the present – and his eyes lit up as he recognized the small reptilian garment frill from Boris' lapel.

"Are you sure? I thought this was your favorite garment frill."

"You earned it, my boy. Nobody has ever performed an instant de-evolution. Everyone considered the maneuver an impossibility, but I witnessed you perform one firsthand— you gave me the thrill of my life."

"I don't know—"

"I want you to have it. You simply must take this as a token of my gratitude."

Boris explained how the pendant would cling to any garment and take on whatever form Ethan imagined. He even showed him a trick to turn the trinket into a two-dimensional cartoon that would wander around on the surface of his shirt. And then, after explaining the secrets of his gift, Boris left.

As he shut the door to his room, Ethan noticed a small envelope slipped underneath at some point in the morning. He opened the letter and quickly remembered the fragrant scent of Jordanna's note from his previous visit.

Dear Ethan,

I've been briefed on what happened during last night's Drone Wars match and your courageous actions in the face of imminent danger. I'm told your heroics drained a lot of energy from your body, so please sleep until you feel rested and join us in the Map Room when you wake. I am concerned with your safety and that of my daughter. I must ensure your well-being and take measures to do so. We will discuss this when you arrive.

Sincerely yours,

Jordanna Ravenwood

Ethan wasted no time changing his clothes, putting on his sneakers, and turning his new gift into a cartoon gecko on his yellow shirt. He jogged down The Hall of Doorways so fast the light beetle barely kept pace. He reached the door to the Map Room and paused to look at the door across the hall. His mind flashed back to the dreadful spider-like eyes of the giant death scarab as it stared at him – and a tingle crept up his spine like the legs of a centipede.

"I am your mother, and you will do what I tell you!"

The sound of Jordanna's voice boomed from inside the Map Room, jogging Ethan back to reality. Hayley was already inside; and from the sound of it, they were having a heated conversation – so he hurried in.

"I am not a child anymore, Mother," said Hayley. "I'm nearly ready for my first-year of Caretaker training. Do you protect all first-years like this?"

"She has a good point, Mother," Damien said.

"You're always jumping to her defense," Jordanna said. "All first-years are not my daughter – and they are certainly not out gallivanting about with the Hybrid Child. His presence places a target on both their backs."

"That's not fair—"

"Your mother is right, Hayley," Ethan said as he stepped onto the crow's nest platform. "Victor Qruefeldt is after me, and until one of us is dead, I am a danger to everyone. I will leave."

"No! See what you've done now," Hayley screamed at her mother.

"Ethan, my dear, I'm sorry you had to hear that," Jordanna said and strode across the room to embrace him. "Please don't take my words literally and accept my apology.

I don't want you to leave. I am merely suggesting additional measures to ensure both your safety."

"She wants to ban us from leaving The Residence," Hayley said. "And she is going to saddle us with a CAGE babysitter."

"Really?" Ethan stared Jordanna in the eye. "But the Shadow Princess, and everything we've been doing, we must be able to come and go as we please."

"Everything you've been doing," Jordanna repeated. "Let's see – thus far, you've been accosted by thieves in the shantytown, attacked by desert harpies, and nearly abducted by Grimleavers."

"You overlook one critical point, Mother," Damien said. "Ethan is the Hybrid Child. His connection to Stravis, and the Seers, has gifted him abilities we cannot begin to fathom. I would suggest there is no safer place for my sister to be than at his side."

"Exactly," Hayley said. "When we are together, I know I am safe. I can feel it."

Jordanna glanced from Damien to Hayley, then she turned to Ethan and peered into his eyes.

"I need to learn about my past and what it means to be the Hybrid Child," Ethan pleaded. "The Shadow Princess is coming to me for a reason – and Hayley is the only one who understands her."

"Nicholas told me of your encounter with the shadow spirit," Jordanna said.

"She's not a shadow spirit," said Hayley. "Her name is Adara."

"I don't yet know her purpose," Ethan said. "But it is vital, I know it is."

"I can tell I'm not going to win this one," Jordanna said and sighed deeply. "Fine, I will allow you to come and go as you please – but you will have a CAGE escort."

"Tinx," Ethan said.

"Yeah, Tinx," Hayley agreed. "We will take Tinx with us everywhere we go."

"I don't recall saying you would choose your own. Besides, I have yet to discipline Tinx for her previous indiscretion."

"How about this," said Damien. "Tinx will accompany them, but I will remain in close contact and oversee everything they do."

Jordanna's gaze moved from Ethan to Hayley and then Damien as she contemplated his compromise.

"Fine," she said and let out another deep sigh. "I will agree to Damien's compromise only because we are already spread so thin – but I feel like you've all sold me a bill of goods."

"I suggest you track down Tinx," Damien said to Hayley. "You can inform her of her new assignment, and I will be in touch."

"Will do," Hayley said and smiled.

It seemed rehearsed to Ethan. He felt like it was all for show, and Jordanna was right about being hoodwinked by her two children.

"Now then, let us move on to the real reason for this meeting," Jordanna said. "Have we learned anything more about last night's mishap?"

"No," Damien said. "But the fallen champion has died from his injuries."

"How could a drone malfunction like that?" Hayley asked.

"Drones cannot malfunction," Damien replied. "Someone in the crowd must have evolved it."

Ethan gasped.

"Only a very powerful evolutioneer could pull that off," Jordanna said.

"Or de-evolutioneer," Ethan said. "Victor Qruefeldt had something to do with this. That monster was sent after me."

"We can't be sure of that," Jordanna said.

"Yes, we can," Ethan said. "My symbols told me so. They've been coming alive lately. I only wish I knew what they are trying to tell me."

As soon as the words left his lips, wisps of golden whimsy wafted from the book in Ethan's pocket tote.

"I believe we are about to find out," Damien said.

Ethan fished the poem book from his pocket tote, and it flipped open to the first blank page where the words appeared. They read:

Round and Round

Round and round they spin and glow,
and point to what you seek to know.

White for where the unseen lands,
or red for where the danger stands.

Green to ward off ill intent,
or yellow when it's heaven sent.

A gift to help you find your way,
and fight the grim that's come to play.

"Interesting," Damien said. "It appears the Seers have sent you the directions to your gift from Stravis."

"If I'm reading this right," Hayley said. "They turn white to point out something you are not seeing."

"That sounds right," Ethan said. "They pointed to the Shadow Princess the first time I saw her – and then they showed me when Jasper was near."

"I'm not sure about green," Hayley said. "But red points to danger."

"Yes," Ethan said. "They pointed to the harpies, the Grimleavers, and the death scarab."

"Yellow when it's heaven sent," Jordanna repeated. "I believe that is referring to Stravis."

"Your right," Ethan replied. "They turned yellow when I met with Fin and spoke in tongues. He was convinced I was possessed by the ghost of Stravis."

"Green is the only one I can't figure out," Hayley said.

"Yeah, I think I may know what that is referring to," Damien said.

"You do?" Ethan asked.

"Last night, when you spontaneously devolved that creature back into a drone," Damien replied. "Witnesses reported seeing a powerful green burst of light as you heroically charged the beast. I believe they turn green to ward off evil, and that's how you devolved the drone."

"Yes, I—I remember now," Ethan said. "My symbols did turn green. But there was nothing heroic about it. I didn't even know the monster was there till I ran headfirst into it."

"Additional reports say you sacrificed yourself by distracting the beast so others could get away," Jordanna said. "Yet you still refuse to accept that your acts were courageous."

"That sounds pretty heroic to me," Hayley said.

"Indeed, it does," said Jordanna. "I've learned enough to feel comfortable with the company my daughter keeps."

They entered The Hall of Doorways, and Hayley stopped, turned to Ethan, and hugged him tightly.

"When I learned what happened last night," she said and paused. "I realized how close I came to losing you."

"It wasn't a big deal."

"Sure, not a big deal. That's why everybody is talking about what happened. Ethan, you did something considered impossible last night. You spontaneously devolved an evolved creature back to its original form. Now everybody is wondering, if that is possible, maybe you can evolve devolved creatures too."

"If I can do that, it would mean—"

"You can destroy the Grimleavers – and if Victor Qruefeldt finds out about last night, he will want you dead even more than he already did."

"He already knows. He was responsible for last night. I feel it."

"All the more reason to stay the course and find the hidden fortress the Shadow Princess spoke of."

"I agree," Ethan said. "Especially if Victor is searching for it too. But where do we start? It's not like I can just summon her, and she appears."

"Yeah, I know. I guess we'll need to think on it," Hayley said.

"Okay, but don't we need to track down Tinx first?" Ethan asked with a grin.

A mischievous smile swam across Hayley's lips.

"What are you and your brother up to?"

"Follow me," she said.

Ethan followed Hayley down The Hall of Doorways, past Dakota's creepy house on the hill, and into the Deadwood Saloon. All was quiet and the few patrons sitting at the bar didn't even turn around when they entered. They made their way to the back of the room, where Tinx sat perched on a table, sipping from a tiny mug of dragon's breath.

"Well, don't keep me in suspense," Tinx said to Hayley. "Did she go for it?"

"She agreed to my brother's compromise. But she is suspicious, so we must tread lightly."

"It was a ruse," Ethan said. "And I played right into your plan."

"You played things perfectly," Hayley said with a grin. "I thought you had figured us out when you asked if Tinx could be our CAGE escort."

"Aw shucks," Tinx said, smiled, and batted her long eyelashes at Ethan. "I'm flattered Ethan Fox asked for little old me . . ."

"Okay, okay, spill the beans," Ethan said.

"Damien came to my room to tell me about last night's drone incident. He warned me that our mother would likely overreact. So, I confided in him, and we agreed to an arrangement."

"But Damien is second in command," Ethan said. "Why would he help us?"

"For two reasons," Hayley said. "For one, when he was in exile, he kept a close eye on us. He witnessed us in action firsthand and understands what we can accomplish when allowed to proceed unhindered."

"And the second reason?"

"I agreed to check in with him occasionally and keep him in the loop. If we need any help, he will be available to us."

"Great, so where do we start?" Tinx asked.

"I was thinking about that on the walk here," Ethan said. "I think we should start by speaking with Gruggins."

"That's right," Hayley said. "The Nibblewarts have been telling him all about the Shadow Princess."

"Gruggins isn't staying in his box as much lately," Tinx said. "He has secret napping spots all over The Residence. I know a few of them, but if he doesn't want to be found, he won't be."

"You're right," Hayley said. "I suggest we split up. Ethan and I will check his box, and if he's not there, we know one of his secret spots too. If you find him, ELMO us, and we will do the same. If not, we will meet up later."

Ethan and Hayley entered the front room and tapped lightly on Gruggins box, but he was not home.

"I guess we check the secret wishing well next," Hayley said.

Ethan glimpsed at something small, black, and red, barreling down the staircase from the upper levels. A hairy ape-like creature with glowing red eyes reached the floor and beelined towards them. Stopping at Hayley's feet, the tiny beast transformed into a metallic statuette of a cat—her copycat had returned.

"Tabby Cat. She must have something to report."

"Are you finally going to let me in on your secret?" Ethan asked. "What covert mission are you working on with your copycat?"

"Shhhh – you never can tell who might be listening," Hayley said as she bent down to pick up her copycat.

"Follow me," she said and nodded towards the stairs.

Ethan remembered the last time he ascended these stairs and discovered another Gruggins lurking. Of course, Gruggins quickly zapped him with a memory-erasing knock-out dart for stumbling upon his secret.

"Where are we—" Ethan said but was quickly silenced.

Once on the second level, they continued into a short hall leading to more stairs. Ethan stared ahead as they slowly crept up the stairs. The staircase was dark and eerie as they continued up towards infinity. There were no ceilings, and the only light visible was the dim glow of the torches lighting each level. Hayley led him to the third level and stopped to whisper to her copycat that transformed into an ELMO device in Hayley's hands. She stared at the directions on the screen, and they guided her into a hallway to their left.

"I overheard a conversation between Blair and Caden some time ago. They were talking about her father's trip to Hades and how if everything went as planned, the Trabblemores would be returning to power. They hate my family and are up to something – so I've been spying on them to find out what."

"I had a run-in with Blair and Caden last night," Ethan said. "Did you ever find out why they hate the Ravenwoods so much?"

"They hate us because my grandfather, Odin Ravenwood, exposed Gaylord Trabblemore for his crimes against humanity. He was our first headmaster, and his crimes disgraced his entire family."

They continued down the dimly lit corridor leading to a dead end. A square room with a stone floor, stone walls, and two iron doors on each of the three walls. Torches hung beside each door and lit the room. The scene reminded Ethan of a musty old castle dungeon.

"This must be the place," Hayley said as she stooped to set her copycat-ELMO on the floor in the middle of the room.

"What place?"

"I tasked my copycat to follow Blair around. The grindle was perfect for that task — but I also needed to instruct it to record her suspicious activity. At first, I wasn't sure how to achieve that one — but I remembered ELMOs have a built-in proximity encoder."

"Proximity encoder?"

"Keep your eyes open," Hayley said as she tapped the ELMO screen and stepped back.

Blair, Caden, and Malik suddenly appeared out of thin air. They stood facing one of the iron doors. Ethan jumped back at first, but quickly figured out they were the holographic result of the copycat-ELMO's proximity encoder.

"What is that blasted combination again?" Blair asked as she rummaged through her handbag.

"You ask that every time," Caden said.

"I know, but I can never remember these stupid symbols."

Blair pulled a piece of paper out, unfolded it, and turned to face the door. She placed her hand against a grapefruit-sized symbol embossed onto the iron door. A faint red glow appeared beneath her hand as the symbol on the door flattened out into a square grid of more symbols that reminded Ethan of a touchpad on an old-fashioned telephone.

"Let's see what new goodies daddy has left for us," Blair said.

She glanced at the paper, touched a series of symbols, and the door swung open. Malik swiftly spun around and growled, and he appeared to be looking directly at Ethan and Hayley.

"He hears something," Caden said as he and Blair spun around.

The feed from the proximity encoder stopped and the apparitions disappeared. Hayley approached the door and studied the symbol embossed on it.

"This symbol," she said, "I wonder what it means?"

Ethan scanned the other doors in the room and walked to the adjacent door.

"This one has a symbol too, and it's different – but the other four are blank."

"She held her hand against the symbol like this," Hayley said and placed her hand on the symbol. But a small blue arc of electricity zapped her hand away. Ethan put his hand on the other door's symbol, which zapped him.

"Must be some kind of security mechanism," Ethan said. "Probably only accepts Blair's hand."

"Blair's hand," Hayley said as a grin spread across her lips. "Ethan, you're a genius."

"I am—"

"Replay the last encoding," she said into her copycat-ELMO. Blair, Caden, and Malik reappeared, and the scene replayed.

"What is that blasted combination again?" Blair said again.

Hayley studied the scene as it unfolded.

"Freeze encoding," she said into the ELMO before Blair's hand touched the door. The three apparitions froze in place. Hayley walked through Caden and Malik to get to Blair's likeness and stood beside her, studying the piece of paper in her hand.

"Create a hard copy," she said into the ELMO.

Ethan watched as Hayley pried the paper from Blair's now solid hand. Then she tugged at Blair's arm with all her might, but it remained solidly frozen in place.

"What are you trying to do?" Ethan asked.

"I'm trying to move her hand against the symbol on the door," Hayley said.

"Stand back. I have an idea," he said.

Ethan pulled out his pocket tote and retrieved a jeweled dagger from it. Then he walked across the room and proceeded to cut fake Blair's hand off below the wrist.

Hayley watched in horrified silence and stood motionless before deciding to speak.

"That was disturbing," she said. "I think last night had an effect on you."

"Yeah, it almost made me gag," Ethan admitted. "But truth be told, up until the attack, I really enjoyed the Drone Wars."

Hayley remained silent for a moment as Ethan stepped away from fake Blair and put the dagger away.

"Erase replay," she said into the copycat-ELMO, and the apparitions disappeared.

"Anyway, I thought you might need a hand," Ethan said and held the severed hand out to her.

"Very funny, but I'll pass. You give it a try," she said and motioned him towards the door.

"Here goes nothing," Ethan said and held the hand against the embossed symbol. A red glow appeared beneath the hand, and the emblem slowly melted away to reveal the flat keypad. Ethan stepped away to make room for Hayley.

"You can take it from here," he said.

Hayley stepped forward and tapped at the keypad to enter the symbols from the paper. The door swung open, and the embossed symbol reappeared on the door.

Ethan followed Hayley into the dimly lit room. They entered what looked like someone's office—full of boxes and rows of shelves in the dark back half of the room.

"Shut the door," Hayley said. "In case someone comes."

Ethan shut the door, and Hayley tapped at her copycat ELMO to turn on its flashlight. She walked past Ethan as he studied the desk under the light of a small lamp barely lighting the front of the room. She strode down one of the aisles of shelving and started snooping through the junk stuffed onto them.

"Ethan, come here," she said as she stopped at one of the shelves stacked with mostly empty jars. She reached up and grabbed one of the jars and held it under her flashlight to show Ethan.

"A death scarab, like the ones Dakota's friends captured."

"It sure is," Ethan said.

"All of these jars are empty," Hayley said and shone her flashlight at the shelf of empty jars. "Except for this one."

"Blair is the one who has been releasing them," Ethan said.

"It appears that way – but we can't prove it."

"Shhh," Ethan said. "Do you hear something?"

"No."

She turned off the flashlight, and they stood quietly for a moment. The sound of muffled voices from beneath the door barely broke the silence. Ethan grabbed Hayley's arm and guided her deeper down the dark aisle.

"It's so dark back here I can't see anything," Hayley whispered.

"I'm seeing perfectly," Ethan said softly. "Everything looks black and white, but I can see."

They walked through a tall free-standing metal frame and ducked behind a tall box near the back of the room as the door swung open.

"Daddy will be along shortly," Blair said as she, Caden, and Malik entered. "I didn't speak with him last night due to all the interruptions. It's been good to have him back these last few weeks—he was away on business for so long."

"What does he want us to do now?" Caden said as he sat down, reclined, and kicked his feet onto the desk.

"I don't know, but it will surely be the end of you if he finds you sitting at his desk like that."

Caden quickly returned to his feet just as the door swung open again – and someone else entered the room. Ethan and Hayley peeked around the box and down the aisle as Blair approached the tall man with long black hair. He wore a half-black half-red robe split diagonally lengthwise.

"Hello, Daddy," Blair said as she reached up to hug the man. "I'm so glad your back."

"Yes, dear, I know," a deep voice replied. "But I've been back for weeks now, and you keep saying that."

"Is there any more we can do to help, sir?" Caden asked and cowered ever so slightly.

"Have you deployed our little friends?"

"All but one, sir. Unfortunately, none have hit their mark."

"We think he is under someone's protection, Daddy."

"As expected – but it was worth the effort."

"How else can we serve the cause?" Caden asked.

"Put this someplace safe," the man said and tossed a pouch to Caden.

"What is that Daddy?"

"That is the Hadean tanzanite I procured on my trip. Should be more than enough to fulfill our needs."

"I took the measurements and built the frame, sir—as you ordered," Caden said. "It is ready and waiting in the back room."

"Good work," Blair's father said. "I will be hearing from the supplier any day now. I will send orders when it is ready for pick up."

"Yes, sir."

"Good, he will be pleased to learn his plan is coming together on time."

"Do you think his plan will work, Daddy?"

"Of course, it will," Blair's father said. "And when it does, it will shock everyone at The Residence to their core."

A cacophony of corrupt laughter filled the room as Caden and Blair cheered her father's prediction. Caden made several more failed attempts to kiss up to him but quickly ran out of material. Blair filled in the awkward moments by reminding her father how missed he was while away. Ethan and Hayley sat silent until the lights finally dimmed and everyone left the room.

"Blair's father was there last night," Ethan said. "Boris left to speak with him about something."

"His name is Roman Trabblemore," Hayley said. "He blames the Ravenwoods for killing the Trabblemore legacy. But I wonder what Boris would need to discuss with him."

"Boris is a reporter," Ethan said. "Maybe he's working on a story."

"Maybe," Hayley replied. "It sounds like Roman is working for someone. He didn't name any names – but when Caden asked if he could serve the cause, a chill crept up my spine."

"Me too," Ethan said. "I'd bet anything it's Victor Qruefeldt."

Ethan and Hayley quietly exited and made it to their rooms before either of them spoke a word.

"I don't know about you, but I'm hungry," Ethan said. "I'm craving pancakes."

"Me too," Hayley said as her stomach growled on cue.

Ethan and Hayley beelined for the dining hall, where Irvin displayed his mad chef skills to the early Caretaker dinner crowd. But he was happy to whip up a batch of pancakes for his two favorite customers—even if it was breakfast food.

"So, where do we start?" Ethan said after slopping down a sizeable fork full of syrup-drizzled hotcakes.

"Good question," Hayley replied. "And since we can't find Gruggins, I've been thinking about anything we may have missed."

"We still haven't looked in the secret wishing well," Ethan said.

"No, we haven't," Hayley said. "Spying on the Trabblemores sidetracked us – so I sent Tinx a message and she agreed to check there."

"So we're back to square one," Ethan said.

"Not yet, we aren't," said Hayley, "I remembered something that gave me an idea."

"What did you remember?"

"When I saw that swirly eye pattern on the yellow sheet it looked familiar," Hayley replied. "Then I saw the Shadow Princess' necklace and I knew I'd seen it before."

"You've seen her necklace somewhere?"

"Yes—but it wasn't till Nicholas and Dakota mentioned my grandmother Vanessa that I knew where I'd seen it. She has one exactly like it."

Ethan's eyes widened and he straightened up.

"We need to speak with your grandmother," he said.

"It's not that simple," Hayley replied. "She left The Residence a long time ago, and I've not been told where she lives. But there may be another way."

"And what might that be?"

"It may be a long shot, but we can start at the Caretaker city of Zen."

"Isn't that where you said you lived now?"

"Yes—but I'm not talking about my place, I'm talking about my grandparents. We may find clues about where she lives now – or maybe even the necklace itself."

"That sounds like it's worth a shot," Ethan said. "Who's living there now?"

"Nobody. My grandmother abandoned the place shortly after my grandfather's death. But my mother has kept it maintained in case she ever returns."

"Dakota said the shadow spirit was a sign of things to come, things that Vanessa foretold. Do you know what he meant by that?"

"Maybe," Hayley said. "My grandmother is an oracle. When grandpa Odin was headmaster, something happened, and she gained second sight. They say she has visions of the future and has never been wrong."

After refueling on their delicious breakfasts, Ethan and Hayley wasted no time following up on their next lead. It took nearly five minutes to make the long trek down The Hall of Doorways.

"Close your eyes," Hayley said as she stopped and grabbed Ethan by the hand. "You are about to enter the Caretaker city of Zen."

Ethan closed his eyes while Hayley opened the door and slowly guided him inside. She closed the door, and they took several steps forward. Ethan listened to the sounds of a city vaguely reminding him of home—without the car horns and sirens.

"Okay, open your eyes."

Ethan squinted as his eyes adjusted to the morning brightness, but they grew wider and wider as he slowly took in the sights of the wondrous Caretaker city. The scene reminded him of a sci-fi movie: there were no cars, but large transparent bubbles floated all about the skyline with people inside. They were standing at the end of a vast street, running straight down the middle of the city. Giant cylindrical skyscrapers lined the sides of the road and stretched skyward as far as the eye could see. Ethan furrowed his brow as he witnessed several bubbles hit and melt into the sides of the buildings.

"Elevation pods," Ethan said. "I rode in one at the Drone Wars."

"Yep, and we are going to take one right up there," She pointed almost straight up in the direction of the nearest building.

Ethan's eyes gazed down the street where hundreds of people in Caretaker robes walked about tending to their daily business. Lines of people waited in front of small telephone booth-like structures. They entered one by one only and disappeared in a bright beam of light that strobed skyward from the top.

"Those are part of our teleport network into the human world," Hayley said.

"I thought the portal plane was your way into the human world."

"The portal plane gives us access to anywhere, which requires special privileges most Caretakers don't have. So they hardwired the teleport network to specific locations throughout the world. Most Caretakers use them to travel to work daily, but others choose to live amongst the humans."

Ethan's gaze wandered from place to place as he took in the sights of the fantastic Caretaker city. Hayley grabbed his hand to guide him toward their destination. They angled down the street and approached the nearest building on the left. She stopped at the end of a queue of Caretakers at the base of the building. They stood for several minutes, but the line moved fast.

"We're next," Hayley said as she gently tugged at Ethan's arm and guided him to the center of the bubble machine.

"Name and destination please?" a young Caretaker asked from the platform's edge.

"Hayley Ravenwood and Ethan Fox to visit Vanessa Ravenwood."

Ethan stood in awe as the bubble formed around them, and they slowly floated into the sky. He felt nearly weightless inside the bubble and could not sense any motion even as it picked up speed and changed course to circle the building.

"We must be a thousand feet up," Ethan said as he gazed down. "The people look like tiny Caretaker ants."

The bubble slowed to a crawl and turned towards the skyscraper. Light shined from a small hole that appeared on the side of the building where the bubble touched. The circle of light grew larger and larger as the bubble melted into the condo unit. Ethan and Hayley stood on a tiled floor at the edge of a plush carpeted living room. The tall viewing windows behind them curved around the outer edge of the living area like a luxurious Manhattan high-rise.

"Kinda reminds me of home," Ethan said as he and Hayley slowly scanned their surroundings. His gaze stopped at a prominent symbol embossed on the wall in front of them.

"That symbol—Hayley, do you know what that symbol is?"

"I've seen it somewhere before, but I don't remember anything about it."

"That symbol—"

"Oh, come now, my dear," a raspy yet feminine voice said from behind them. "You don't recognize your family crest when you see it. I must have a word with your mother."

Ethan and Hayley spun around in unison to find out where the voice came from. A tall woman with a thin slightly wrinkled face stood in the room's foyer, studying Ethan and Hayley with her deep blue eyes. She had long flowing half-black half-white hair and wore a black robe with a golden Ravenwood crest on the lapel. And finally, a shimmering golden chain and pendant dangled from her neck. It was the same swirly eye-shaped necklace the Shadow Princess wore.

"Grandmother," Hayley said as her eyes widened. "I—I—my memories are still quite scattered. I don't remember everything—yet."

"Don't worry yourself, my dear. It's my fault for not visiting more often. I lost a husband and a son at The Residence. This place brings me dark memories, so I choose to live elsewhere."

Hayley's grandmother strode across the room and knelt in front of her.

"I know that's no excuse, I will visit more often in the future. Please forgive me."

"Of course, I forgive you, gramma," Hayley said as she gently embraced her grandmother.

After the warm reunion, Vanessa stood and turned to Ethan.

"And you must be the boy causing such a stir."

"His name is Ethan and he's my friend," Hayley said.

"Vanessa Ravenwood. Pleased to make your acquaintance, Ethan Fox," she said and extended her hand.

"Nice to meet you," Ethan said and shook Vanessa's hand.

"Mother said you haven't lived here since grandfather died. How did you know we were coming?"

"How I learned of your visit is unimportant. What is important is the reason for your visit. So, child, what answers do you seek today?"

"Well—" Hayley said.

"That necklace you are wearing," Ethan interrupted. "What can you tell us about it, and what do you know about the Shadow Princess?"

"Very direct. Now I understand why my granddaughter fancies you."

Ethan and Hayley blushed.

"Very well," she said. "I suppose you've both earned an explanation. But first, let us move this conversation to a more suitable location. Would either of you like a refreshment?"

"No thank you," Hayley said.

"We just had breakfast for dinner," Ethan replied.

Vanessa led them into the living room with a huge comfortable couch and two cozy recliners. Ethan and Hayley sat side by side on the sofa. But Vanessa stood facing them, she touched her chin with one hand while resting the other on her hip, and then she let out a deep sigh.

"You ask about my necklace because you've seen it elsewhere, I suppose."

"Yes, it's the same one the Shadow Princess wears," Ethan said. "But how did you get one just like it?"

"I had this one made because the original captivated me from the first moment I saw it," Vanessa replied. "I'd recently received the gift of second sight, so it seemed fitting. I suppose that's what attracted me to it in the first place."

"Where did you see the original?" Ethan asked.

"The same place you did," she answered. "She came to me in one of my first visions. It foretold the return of a shadow spirit whose return would set off a chain of events that would shape the future."

"She's not a shadow spirit," Hayley said. "She is the Shadow Princess and her name is Adara."

Vanessa gasped. Her face grew pale, and she wobbled back and forth.

"Are you okay?" Ethan and Hayley asked in unison. They stood, dashed to her side, and each grabbed an arm to escort her to the nearest seat.

"Gramma, what's wrong?" Hayley asked.

"Oh, nothing, my dear," she replied. "Just the teetering of an old woman. I was probably just standing too long."

"Are you sure?" Ethan asked as he shot Hayley a questioning glance.

"Yes, of course. Now, where were we?"

"You told us about your necklace," Ethan said. "And your vision of the Shadow Princess. Is there anything else you can tell us about that?"

"Not much more to tell," Vanessa said. "My visions don't often contain much context; they leave a lot to interpretation."

"Do you know anything about a desert fortress?" Hayley asked.

Vanessa sat quietly and appeared to be gathering her thoughts. She looked from Ethan to Hayley and let out another deep sigh.

"Possibly," she said. "It reminds me of something that happened long before Odin was headmaster – but it's quite a long story."

"We have the time," Ethan said and looked at Hayley.

"Yes, please tell us the story," said Hayley.

"It all started with a surprise visit from Creator Stravis," Vanessa began. "It was the first time he confided in Odin and me, and at the time, it was unheard of for a Creator to call upon any Caretaker other than the headmaster. So naturally, his visit surprised us and caused us to wonder why he chose us?"

Vanessa paused to catch her breath while Ethan and Hayley hung on her every word.

"We learned Stravis distrusted the other Creators, especially Zamalador. He insisted Gaylord Trabblemore was under Zamalador's thumb. So, he sought out a high-ranking Caretaker he could trust—one with an impeccable reputation and who shared his elemental origins."

"They had to be from Zephyr," Ethan said, "that's what led Stravis to you and Odin."

"Correct on both counts."

"What did he want from you and grandfather?"

"He told us of a powerful righteous presence he encountered in the desert."

"The Seers," Ethan said.

"Correct again. At first, he experienced visions of eyes peering at him from beneath the sand."

"I have the same visions," Ethan said.

"Not surprising. You are the Hybrid Child – so your connection to Stravis and the Seers is strong."

Ethan and Hayley exchanged glances.

"They found a way to communicate with Stravis. He said they warned him of a fortress in the desert under construction for evil purposes."

Wisps of golden whimsy wafted from Ethan's pocket. He retrieved his pocket tote, pulled out the awakened poem book, and held it in his open hands. The pages flipped to a torn-out page that was growing back. When it finished, another poem had arrived. The passage read:

The Fortress of Fate

North of where the sun will shine, they labor night and day.
Enslaving meek and innocent, to ensure the gracious pay.

Three edges on each side, and four that touch the ground.
A fortress built for wicked plans, to be lost and later found.

Creator from a chosen world, you must find the desert site.
Then enlist the help of others, to assist you with this plight.

The fortress will be hidden, by fate and sleight of hand.
Its secrets devoured forever, till the Hybrid makes a stand.

"It appears Jasper's paid you a visit," Vanessa said as they gathered around to read the poem.

"This must be what they communicated to Stravis," Hayley said.

"Yes, but there was more to it. Stravis showed me this book and read me this very passage – and he explained that the words bore deeper meaning. When he read the Seer's words, he felt their true intent."

"How can that be?" Ethan asked. "The last line is about me, I am sure – but that was before I was even born."

"Stravis said not all the words were for him to understand. It appears they have finally found their intended audience."

"How is that possible?" Hayley asked.

"The Seers are multi-dimensional beings. They view all of time in an instant," Vanessa said. "They understand all possible outcomes of all possible actions and reactions. So it's not hard to imagine they were writing to both of you— even though you exist in different timeframes."

Ethan and Hayley stood in silence, pondering what they had learned.

"So what did Stravis ask of you and Odin?" Ethan asked.

"He gave us the location and asked Odin to investigate what was happening there. So Odin visited the site and witnessed the atrocities they committed. They had evolved ants into three foot giants and used them to assemble huge stones into pyramids. What he witnessed incensed him – so he spoke to the Caretaker in charge."

"What did he say?" Ethan asked.

"He insisted he was under orders from Headmaster Trabblemore and gave a cockamamie story. He said the headmaster needed a fortress to hide from something he feared."

"Did Odin tell you the man's name?" Ethan asked.

"Yes. I'll never forget the man's name—Jason Crowley."

"Why?" Hayley asked. "What makes that name so unforgettable?"

"Not so much his name," Vanessa said. "It's what happened after."

"What?" Ethan and Hayley asked.

"Someone left his corpse on our doorstep. The sight was ghastly, like all his life's energy was drained from his body."

Hayley gasped.

"It happened shortly after Odin visited the pyramids. We were living in an old-town villa at the time. The story made headline news—even on the elemental worlds."

"What happened after that?" Hayley asked.

"These events led to Odin uncovering Gaylord's crimes and exposing him. Gaylord denied any knowledge of the pyramids or fear of anything. But when Odin pressed him about fearing a boogieman, he said he saw the fear of Hades in Gaylord's eyes."

"Anything else?"

"Not much else to tell. Once he became headmaster, Odin sent a team to the site of the desert fortress – but everything had vanished. There was not a trace of anything ever having been there. The disappearance bothered him for years. He never understood how a giant fortress in the desert could up and walk away. After that, he kept everything hush-hush, said he didn't want to put me in harm's way."

"You said this was the first time Stravis came to you," Ethan said. "What about the other times?"

"That is a question not ready for answers," said Vanessa. "Stay the course – and the answers will come when you are ready."

"Why won't you answer?" Hayley asked.

"Oh—but I have, my dear," Vanessa said.

She stood, approached Hayley, and grabbed her by the hand. Then she enveloped Hayley's hand in her own and whispered into her ear.

"And as for you, my dear boy," Vanessa said and turned to Ethan. "That book of yours is a very powerful gift. Pay attention to what it tells you. It may lead you in unusual directions – but the Seers' path is true."

"I—I think I understand," Ethan said.

"And with that, I bid you adieu." Vanessa twirled her hand, spun around, and disappeared in a puff of smoke.

"But wait—" Ethan said—but was too late.

"She always makes a flashy exit," Hayley said.

"I wanted to ask her what Hybrid Child means. If she knew Stravis, she might know something."

PANDORA'S BOX

Ethan and Hayley arranged to meet Tinx for breakfast in the dining hall the following morning. There, Tinx told them about all the places she searched for Gruggins, including the secret wishing well. But she had no luck. He obviously did not want to be found right now. Then they decided it was probably a good time to check in with Damien—to make good on their side of the bargain and keep the headmistress off their back.

After breakfast, Hayley led them to where she was sure her brother would be. They followed her to the front room, where Hayley made a quick detour to check if Gruggins was in his box.

"I thought you were taking us to your brother," Ethan said.

"I am," said Hayley, "he's in the basement."

"The creepy place where we found the grimtailed dread?"

"Damien has repurposed Daavic's secret room," Hayley said. "He's remodeling from top to bottom."

"Doesn't take much to improve upon dark, damp, and dingy," Ethan said.

Hayley knocked at the door to the basement, and the sound of Damien's muffled voice echoed up the stairwell.

"Come in, and I'll be right with you."

They opened the door and their faces bathed in the bright white light shining up the stairwell. Ethan's jaw dropped when he reached the base of the stairs and entered a vast white room lit by the glowing floor and ceiling. Damien stood at a tall white lab bench at the center of the near-empty room. He was hovering over something and tinkering with it under a giant magnifying glass mounted to the end of the extended bench.

"Wow, I love what you've done to the place," Ethan said.

"Thank you. I have turned Daavic's dingy basement into a laboratory with room to grow."

"What are you working on?" Hayley asked as they approached.

"I found Daavic's ELMO in the top drawer of the study. I'm trying to unlock it to peek at what he was doing. I may find clues as to why he joined Victor Qruefeldt."

"That's impossible—from what I've read," Hayley said.

"Difficult, yes; impossible, no. It may take a couple of years, but I will crack the code and unlock it."

Ethan and Hayley stood at Damien's side as he fiddled with the insides of Daavic's ELMO. Tinx fluttered off Hayley's shoulder, landed on the bench, and walked into his field of view. Damien stopped what he was doing and glanced from Tinx to Hayley to Ethan.

"To what do I owe the pleasure?"

"We're just checking in," Hayley said. "To abide by our part of the bargain we struck with mother."

"Well? Anything to report?" Damien asked.

"Not really," Hayley replied. "We're trying to learn more about the Shadow Princess – but so far, nothing earth-shattering."

"Well, didn't you say you are the only one who can understand her? Maybe if you draw her out again, you can ask her."

"That sounds like a great idea," Hayley said and then fell silent.

"I'm still trying to figure out what we missed at Stravis' bunker," Damien said. "I was sure there would be more for us to find."

"Me too," Ethan said. "Instead, it was a total bust – and Azron almost—"

"Ethan, your pocket tote," Hayley said and pointed at the golden wisps of whimsy wafting from his pocket tote.

Ethan quickly retrieved the poem book, the pages flipped open, and a new poem wrote itself up the page. When it finished, they stared at the passage in silence and read:

Pandora's Box

Unearthed by human raiders, a trapdoor in the sand.

Leading to a bunker, with treasures small and grand.

They tried to find the secrets, buried deep inside.
Searching very recklessly, until the girl died.

She stumbled upon a token, that concealed a hidden room.
But instead of finding answers, it led her to her doom.

Pandora's Box was opened, she took a peek inside.
And found unearthly treasures, that left her petrified.

But before that fateful ending, she found the hidden key.
Entombed in wood and waiting, a Creator's gift to thee.

"Entombed in wood and waiting," Hayley repeated. "Pandora—whatever she found must still be with her petrified body."

"Fascinating," Damien said. "It appears we may have been right after all."

Tinx rode on Hayley's shoulder as she, Damien, and Ethan dashed down The Hall of Doorways. They hurried by the trembling nomads, through the tunnel of foliage, and past the skyclimber vine.

Hayley took out her ELMO as they approached the fenced-off petrified Pandora. They stopped at the white picket fence, and Damien watched with a smirk as Ethan and Hayley jumped into action. She tapped at her ELMO screen as she held it up and a green beam of laser light scanned up and down Pandora's body.

"There's something in her left front jacket pocket," Hayley said.

"We'll need something to pry it out," Ethan said as he fished through his pocket tote to retrieve the jeweled dagger.

He hopped the short white fence and pried at the partially rotted wooden pocket. It didn't take much effort to force Pandora's jacket pocket to pop off and fall to the ground. Ethan picked up the petrified piece of wood and turned it over to chip at the embedded object with the dagger.

"Whatever this is, it's embedded in the wood snuggly," he said and continued to chip tiny pieces of wood away from the object.

Damien, Hayley, and Tinx stood silently as Ethan pried the object away and rubbed it against his pant leg to wipe the dirt away. Then he reattached Pandora's pocket so it was hardly noticeable and would not raise Mrs. Moongarden's suspicion. He held the hand-sized metallic object up to show them when he finished.

"Is that an emblem or crest of some kind?" Tinx asked.

"She found the hidden key," Hayley said, quoting the poem.

"Huh?" Ethan asked.

"That's not a crest," Damien said. "It's the missing piece to the puzzle."

"We were right," Ethan said. "There was more to Stravis' bunker than meets the eye."

They returned to the basement lab where Damien could examine it in more detail. He studied the object closely from front to back underneath his magnifier light. He sat in silence, rubbing his chin and pondering something.

"It has to be the hidden key the poem spoke of," Hayley said.

"I understand what it is," Damien said. "I'm trying to figure out our next move."

"We have to take this to Stravis' bunker," Ethan said.

"Yes," said Hayley, "it matches the engraving on the back wall."

"I realize that, but things are not so simple. After our previous venture to the bunker, mother took measures to ensure we would not return. She's locked away the book to *Sand Miser Dunes* – and the only other way I know would take us too close to the great vanishing dune. Sand harpies would attack us for sure."

"Why can't we just use a portal beacon?" Ethan asked.

"We could, if one were there to transport to," Damien replied. "Under normal circumstances, we use portal beacons to return from a protected realm. We don't normally leave them behind for just anybody to find."

"Can't we go around the dune?" Hayley asked.

"No, the whole area is inside one of the protected realms. Venture too far off course, and you end up in the middle of a human desert with no way back."

"Too bad we can't commandeer an elevation pod from a floater port," Ethan said. "Then we could float over the dune and the sand harpies."

Damien gazed at Ethan, furrowed his brow, and turned to his sister.

"That might just work. All I would need is samples of the bubble solution, and I can fabricate one here large enough for all of us."

"But they program elevation pods to hone in on their destination," Hayley said. "How will we steer the bubble to our destination?"

"True—but they are also immune to wind resistance, so the slightest energy will push or pull it wherever we desire. If I can design a way to 'lasso' the bubble, we can attach a tether, and Tinx can tow us to the bunker."

Damien spent the next few days working tireless hours in his lab to finally figure out how to 'lasso' an elevation pod. Ethan, Hayley, and Tinx checked in daily to help and deliver more bubble solution they borrowed from the Drone Wars floater ports.

"I think I've finally figured this out," Damien said on day three. "Actually, it's quite simple. All I must do is add iron to the bubble solution and apply a magnetic field to pull the bubble along."

"Sounds too simple," Tinx replied.

"Well, the idea is sound, but I did over-simplify. I can't use just any iron. The compound must be colorless and very strongly magnetic so a small magnetic field will attract the bubble."

"So, you haven't solved the problem yet," said Hayley.

"No, but I am ready to test the prototype. I've shaved down a small slab of strong-iron from Ceres and removed its pigments."

Damien held up a small jar of colorless crystals as he explained.

"First, I dissolve this into the bubble solution. Then, all I need to do is create the bubble and apply a magnetic field."

Damien poured a beaker of the mixed solution onto a metallic plate sitting alone on the floor. He tapped at his ELMO, and a bubble appeared on the plate's curved surface and grew to the size of a basketball before detaching and floating straight up where it came to rest against the ceiling.

"And now for our moment of truth," he said and pointed a horseshoe-shaped magnet at the bubble. But nothing happened.

"You still have a few kinks to work out, I guess," Tinx said.

"Hold on. This magnet creates a minimal magnetic field. I may need to be a little closer for it to engage."

Damien took a couple of steps towards the bubble, and it swiftly drifted towards him. He walked from one end of the room to the other, and everywhere Damien went, the bubble was sure to go.

"It works. You've done it," Hayley exclaimed.

"Yeah, I've done it all right. All we need now is a portable fabricator, more bubble solution, and a way to strap this magnet to Tinx."

They agreed to tackle Damien's list as a team. Ethan and Hayley would procure more bubble solution, while Tinx would enlist Irvin's help to modify a harness she already had from her job delivering drinks at the Deadwood Saloon.

Meanwhile, Damien would get to work on a portable bubble fabricator.

It took nearly a week to get everything together. Ethan and Hayley helped by painstakingly grinding down a giant slab of strong-iron into crystals small enough to be de-pigmented and dissolved. When they finished, they needed to agree upon the best time to leave The Residence and make their journey. Ethan, Hayley, and Tinx were flexible – so Damien's busy schedule would dictate the best time to not raise the Headmistress' suspicion.

The day had finally arrived, and they all met in the study, where they knew Jordanna would not be during her weekly meeting with Fin Drenchler. Damien arrived toting a huge duffle bag with Tinx riding on top. She wore a harness strapped to her underbelly to hold the magnet in place—making it difficult for her to walk.

"You've brought everything we need?" Hayley asked.

"Everything we need once we arrive," said Damien.

"Where exactly are we starting from?" Ethan asked.

"Yes, Damien, tell them," Tinx said. "Tell them what you've told me, and don't leave out the added dangers you've forgotten to mention till now."

"What is Tinx talking about?" Hayley asked as her eyes bore holes into Damien's.

Damien put down the duffle bag and walked to the shelf of brown books. He pulled one from the shelf and gazed at its golden lettering.

The Glass Pillars of Nym

"We start here. We book-travel to *The Glass Pillars of Nym* – and yes, we will face a few added dangers. But nothing Tinx can't handle."

"Easy for you to say," Tinx said. "If I make one wrong move, I will have to live knowing I caused your deaths."

"What is Tinx talking about?" Ethan asked.

"I think navigating a giant bubble through a forest of towering, jagged glass pillars with us inside is what worries her," Hayley said and peered at her brother.

"Is that true?"

"Yes, but I've triple-checked the calculations. We will have ten feet of clearance on each side—if we take the proper route."

Ethan and Hayley agreed with Damien, the mission was too important to stop now, and they all understood the risks when they signed up. But it still took another five minutes to reassure Tinx and calm her nerves.

Damien handed Hayley the brown book and shouldered the duffle bag Tinx was still standing on. They all joined hands as Hayley slowly opened the book, bright beams of light radiated from its pages, and they were gone in a flash.

When they awoke from the short slumber that usually followed book-travel, they were on a hard patch of sandy ground. Ethan stood and stretched, and as he yawned, his eyes opened. He scanned his surroundings and saw a forest of massive crystalline trunks forming the base of the pillars.

They stretched skyward like giant arms trying to reach up and grasp the clouds. Ethan spun around and saw the pillars surrounding them in all directions as far as his eyes could see.

Damien wandered the area, scanning the ground, and pillars with his ELMO. He needed to double-check his calculations and find a clearing suitable for his portable bubble fabricator.

"This place is amazing," Ethan said. "I've never seen anything like it."

"Nor will you ever again," Damien replied. "This place is an anomaly created by a hyperhole event. The unusually powerful electromagnetic fields caused by the event pulled the desert sands skyward and crystalized them into the towering pillars surrounding us."

"What is a hyperhole event?" Ethan asked.

"They are anomalous high energy vortex events that have appeared randomly throughout Earth's existence," Hayley said.

"They are quite rare," said Damien.

"What causes them?"

"We are not sure, but as my brother pointed out, they are rare. Only a handful have occurred that we are aware of."

"Yeah, and I'm the lucky guy who got to experience one firsthand," Damien said.

"You saw one?" Ethan, Hayley, and Tinx asked in unison.

"So I'm told, I don't remember anything from that day — but the experience left me with this dashing moon-shaped pupil."

Everyone got quiet as Damien set up the bubble fabricator in the clearing he picked out. When he was done, he checked his ELMO to see if it had finished performing the navigation calculation.

"This can't be right," he said as he stared at the screen. "I triple-checked my calculations."

"What's wrong?" Tinx asked.

"The pillars appear to have grown since we last mapped them," he replied. "The clearances are much tighter than I calculated."

"Oh great," Tinx said. "Now, I will kill you all for sure."

"Maybe we should scrub the mission," Ethan said. "We'll find another way."

"Hold on—I may have a solution," Damien said as he tapped away at his ELMO.

"Let us know when you figure it out," Hayley said.

"Well, I have a solution – but I don't like it," Damien said.

"What?" Hayley asked.

"If I stay behind and recalibrate the fabricator to create a smaller bubble for just the two of you—that should give us back the clearance we lost."

"That sounds like a good plan," Ethan said.

"It is – but I don't feel good about sending you three off alone on such a dangerous mission."

"We can do this," Hayley said. "We've come too far to turn back now."

Damien pondered the situation, but then reluctantly agreed to let them go. He explained the new plan. First, he would teach Hayley how to navigate to the bunker and open the hatch. Then, after they launched, he would monitor their trajectory from the ground and relay directional commands to Tinx with his ELMO—just as they had practiced. The only difference was he would no longer be inside the bubble. In addition, he would maintain direct contact with Hayley's ELMO as well. Once they were all comfortable with the new plan, he gave them a few minutes to ready themselves. Then he rummaged through his duffle bag, retrieved the bottle of bubble solution, and gave the bag to Hayley.

"Okay, is everyone ready?"

Ethan and Hayley stood on the shallow round fabricator dish as Damien poured the solution at their feet. The liquid spread out and quickly ran to the outer edges of the fabricator as walls of a giant bubble slowly grew to form around them. Within minutes the bubble entirely enveloped them and slowly rose into the air.

"That's odd," Damien said. "The bubble appears larger than my calculations would suggest. Ten ounces of solution should not have grown to that size."

Ethan and Hayley looked at each other as they realized their mistake.

"We gave you twelve ounces," Hayley admitted.

"We thought you might need extra," Ethan said. "In case you needed to run more tests."

Damien quickly tapped at his ELMO as the bubble rose higher and higher.

"Well, that will make things tighter."

"How much tighter?" Tinx asked.

"How do you feel about five feet of clearance on each side?"

"Horrible—but it's too late to turn back now," Tinx said with a deep sigh.

Ethan gazed up and saw a sizeable, jagged branch protruding out from the side of the nearest pillar, and they were minutes from running into it. He glanced down and saw they were already at a dangerous height.

"Well, Tinx better start steering," Ethan said. "Or we are going to run into that."

He pointed up, and Tinx and Hayley followed his gaze to the jagged crystal branch.

"Well, that's not ideal," Damien's voice said from Hayley's ELMO.

"What's not?" Tinx asked.

"The navigation map I plotted earlier is gone, and my ELMO is going haywire."

"Mine is, too," Hayley said as her ELMO screen went blank.

"The hyperhole event occurred here fairly recently," Damien shouted. "Its lasting electromagnetic activity is off the charts and causing our ELMOs to malfunction."

"So, what do I do now?" Tinx asked.

"Steer us away from the jagged branch, for starters," Ethan said and pointed up. "After that, you'll have to go it alone."

Tinx darted up and hovered by the bubble as the magnet strapped to her underbelly engaged and quickly pulled the bubble towards her.

"Take things slowly, and we will have to try and guide you by eye," Ethan said.

"That's not going to be easy," Hayley said as she scanned the area. "Most of the jagged branches are nearly invisible till you are right up next to them."

"I don't think I can do this," Tinx said. "I didn't feel good about this even with Damien's guidance."

Ethan's palms started to tingle, so he opened his hands to witness the glowing yellow symbols spinning around. They stopped suddenly, both pointing to 2:00 on a clock face.

"How would you feel about guidance from Stravis himself?" Ethan asked.

"Tickled to death," Tinx said. She glanced over her shoulder enough to spy Ethan and Hayley's faces bathed in the yellow glow.

"Veer right," Ethan said. "Perfect, now continue straight ahead slowly."

Tinx followed his directions, and they proceeded slowly as the giant bubble rose higher and higher into the sky.

"We should be at a safe altitude soon," Hayley said, "the pillars taper off the higher we go."

Tinx continued executing Ethan's every command to perfection, and within minutes they glided along the tops of the pillars where she could navigate by eye. As soon as they were out of danger, Ethan's palm symbols returned to their normal position and shimmering white color.

They continued zig-zagging eastward between the tips of the giant pillars for another half-hour before reaching the edge of the desert proper. The sky was clear, and the temperature quickly grew warmer when they floated past the last of the towering shards of glass. Once clear of the danger, Tinx picked up the pace, and they quickly sailed along. Their next hurdle soon became visible as they gazed ahead at the enormous mountain of sand they were speeding directly towards.

"There it is, the great vanishing dune," Hayley said. "We'll fly directly over the top, approaching from the opposite direction we saw it from before."

The height of the expansive dune amazed Ethan. He continued watching the sand quickly climb towards them as they neared the peak of the giant dune.

"It didn't vanish," Hayley said.

"That's not what I expected either," Ethan said. "Which makes me wonder if anyone has ever flown over it before?"

"Exactly what I was thinking," Hayley said. "I bet someone is cloaking it whenever anyone on the ground gets too close."

"I agree—and they are probably inside that building," Ethan said and pointed straight down to the ground below them.

They were clearing the top of the peak, and floating over the other side, when a tall stone building became visible— half-buried by the base of the dune. But the structure was tall and wide enough that the entrance was still visible on the side opposite the sand.

"Could be," Hayley said. "I don't recall reading about any buildings near the vanishing dune. I wonder what's inside?"

"Looks like some kind of a shrine," Ethan said. "It's probably hidden by the horizon when the dune is visible but disappears with the dune when anyone comes near."

"Sounds reasonable," Hayley said.

"I wonder," Ethan said. "If the harpies are down there right now."

Hayley rummaged through Damien's duffle bag, pulled out a small black cube, and tossed it through the bubble wall at the building. The cube disappeared from view before hitting the ground somewhere near the building's entrance. Seconds later, the sand around the building's entrance churned with sand harpies looking for something to attack.

"Well, that answers my question," Ethan said. "But how did you know that wouldn't pop our bubble?"

"I used a portal beacon," Hayley said. "Elevation pods are designed for planetary survey and passing portal beacons is part of that design."

Ethan looked at Hayley with a concerned expression.

"Don't worry, I took inventory before we left," she said. "Damien always packs extra portal beacons."

Ethan's gaze moved back and forth from the harpies to the dark entrance, barely visible from their altitude. A glimmer of light twinkled at the center of the opening, and something flashed into his mind. He was no longer looking down at the building. He was inside. It was dark all around, and glowing yellow eyes slowly moved toward him. The Shadow Princess was motioning and speaking to him, but her words were unintelligible.

"Ethan, are you okay?" Hayley asked, and her voice snapped him out of it.

"Y-Yes, I just saw her in a daydream," he replied.

"Saw who?"

"The Shadow Princess," Ethan said. "We were inside that structure. It was dark, and she was trying to tell me something."

They continued to glide for another twenty minutes, and the great vanishing dune was a bump on the horizon when Hayley took out her ELMO and tapped its screen.

"It is working fine now that we're away from the anomaly."

She directed Tinx to veer a little bit to the left and slow to a stop as quickly as possible. They halted as Tinx hovered like a hummingbird, and Hayley stared at her ELMO.

"Okay, I think that should do it, Tinx. Now head straight down."

Tinx slowed the pace of her beating wings and began slowly falling towards the ground—pulling them along as she did. Hayley waited until they fell to a hundred feet off the ground and tapped at her ELMO.

"The hatch should appear soon," she said as the pole once again popped up to reveal the hatch buried beneath the sand.

"There it is," Hayley said and pointed.

Tinx beelined straight for the hatch and slowed as she neared. They landed on the desert floor next to the bunker's entrance. The bubble burst as soon as they touched down on the hot sand, leaving them standing next to the opening. Hayley wasted no time; she attached a mechanical gizmo to the hatch as Damien instructed and it swiftly swung open. They quickly descended the staircase to escape the desert heat and the swarm of harpies that soon arrived.

"Seems like they were expecting us," Ethan said.

"They probably were," Tinx said.

"Where is the key?" Hayley asked as she paced back and forth by the wall at the back of the bunker.

"I've got it right here," Ethan said and handed the key to her. "You do the honors."

"Wait one second," she said as she rifled through Damien's duffle bag to find another portal beacon. "In case we need to make a hasty exit."

Hayley approached the engraving in the stone wall and slowly placed the metal key inside. It fit perfectly and made a satisfying clanking sound as the rock appeared to suck the key into place. At first, nothing happened, but then part of the rock wall melted away, exposing a yellow door with Stravis' symbol embossed on it. Ethan and Hayley glanced at one another as they recalled seeing something similar while spying on Blair.

"I'll take it from here," Ethan said as he stepped forward and placed his hand against the symbol that quickly disappeared along with the door.

"OMG," Ethan said.

"Wow, look at all that," Hayley said. "I think we just furnished Damien's laboratory."

"And then some," Tinx said.

Tinx fluttered over and landed on Hayley's shoulder as she entered Stravis' secret room. Ethan followed as bright lights clicked on one at a time until they illuminated the entire room. It was nearly identical to Damien's basement laboratory in size and shape, except this one was yellow and fully stocked. One long row of laboratory benches ran down the room's center, arranged back-to-back in pairs to double the allowable working area. To each side of the line of benches stood rows of shelves stocked floor to ceiling with supplies, equipment, specimens, and samples.

"Cool arrangement," Hayley said, "I bet Damien will want to duplicate this room entirely when we move it to The Residence."

"How are you planning on doing that?" Tinx asked. "Your mother will find out for sure."

"We'll cross that bridge when we get there," Hayley said. "That's my brother's problem anyway."

Ethan walked to the other side of the row of benches and stopped cold.

"Hayley, come here. You must see this."

Hayley followed him and stopped in her tracks as she turned the corner and saw what Ethan was talking about. Sitting atop the adjacent lab bench was an extensive collection of swirly eye-shaped medallions like the one hanging from the Shadow Princess' necklace, only smaller.

They were spread out and ordered in rows as if Stravis had been cataloging them.

"I count sixteen," Ethan said.

"Me too," Hayley said. "This is definitely related to the Shadow Princess."

"I agree," Ethan said. "I think we should take them and keep them between us for now. At least until we know what it means."

"I was going to suggest the same thing," Hayley said as she gathered the necklaces. "Here, put these in your pocket tote."

Ethan and Hayley agreed to stash their find away—for now, and return to it once they returned to The Residence. Until then, they would continue their current mission and keep their eyes open for more clues.

Hayley turned down one of the aisles to peruse the fully stocked shelves.

"I've never seen so many samples of animals, vegetables, and minerals from the elemental worlds as well as Earth."

"You might want to come check this out," Ethan shouted from across the room.

Hayley and Tinx followed the sound of Ethan's voice to an aisle at the back of the room, where he stood next to a shelf full of yellow notebooks.

"Stravis kept a lot of journals," he said as they joined him.

"Holy moly," Hayley said. "This is a huge find. We can't tell anybody about this."

"This discovery will please Master Damien," Tinx added.

"Yeah—and it might even prove to your mother the importance of what we've found," Ethan said.

"I'm sure it will," Hayley said. "Maybe that's how we convince her to move it all back to The Residence."

"Good point," Ethan said. "But I agree, we must keep this secret. Victor has already infiltrated The Residence, so we must not speak of this till we meet with your mother and brother."

They spent another hour scanning every aisle with their ELMOs. They needed to document everything for their return. That way, they would have something concrete to show Damien and the Headmistress.

A GRIM NEW START

Upon their return to The Residence, Damien greeted them at the front room door to the portal plane. It surprised them to learn nobody found out about their journey, especially Jordanna, who was none the wiser. Damien eagerly led them to his near-empty laboratory, so they could brief him on their findings.

Hayley told her brother about every detail of their journey and showed him the footage from her ELMO's proximity encoder. His jaw nearly hit the floor as he watched the footage they had taken. Then he copied it to his own ELMO for further scrutiny.

They agreed that Damien would study it more and create a presentation for Jordanna. She needed to know about such a significant find, so they could convince her of the importance of moving it all to The Residence.

The following day, they decided to take a break from the chaos. Ethan helped Hayley study for the placement exam required for her first-year of Caretaker training. They were in the study sitting on the couch by the fireplace when the door barged open, and a voice filled the room.

"Oh, here you are, my d-dears," Bella Wentworth said. "You've b-been summoned to an impromptu CAGE m-meeting."

She shuffled through a small stack of envelopes with two hands while her other arms held tissues up to her face and dabbed at her cheeks and eyes.

"I, I'm t-t-told it is of u-utmost importance," she said and broke out balling.

"Why are you crying?" Ethan asked as he ran to her side to calm her.

"You're such a n-nice b-boy," she said between sobs.

Hayley hurried over to help, and Bella handed her two envelopes. She opened one up and scanned it, but she and Ethan knew what the meeting was about.

"Mother is convening a meeting. We are to join them in the CAGE meeting room."

"It's the eleventh door on the right, in The Hall of Doorways," Bella whimpered.

It took several minutes for Ethan to get Bella to stop crying. She was upset about not being invited to the exclusive CAGE meeting—but Ethan and Hayley understood why. The need-to-know nature of today's subject meant no Bella. The last thing the Caretakers needed was for her to blab about their find to everyone who would listen.

Ethan and Hayley were the last to arrive. They entered and parted the dark curtains separating the foyer from the meeting room proper. The room was square with a giant round table and a tall ceiling to accommodate Azron's height. Jordanna sat at the far side of the table with Damien to her right and an empty seat to her left where Alexander usually sat. Nicholas, Brianna, Azron, Ethan, and Hayley took up the remaining seats clockwise from Damien's right. Tinx sat curled up on a small pillow on the table next to Hayley. A glass of water stood on the table before each meeting participant.

"Some of you are already aware of what the rest of you are about to learn," Jordanna said as her gaze wandered from Ethan to Hayley to Tinx. "Let me start by saying, I cannot stress enough how important secrecy is with this information. It is strictly need-to-know, and in my assessment, only those in this room need to know."

Jordanna paused, took a drink of water, and let out a deep sigh.

"Well—that was quite the buildup," Nicholas said.

"My thoughts exactly," Brianna said between lashes of her black serpent tongue. "We know the drill. S-spill it already."

Jordanna tapped at her ELMO, and a holographic screen popped up from the table's center. The screen was plus-shaped by design to divide the table into quadrants and create the illusion they were all watching from the same angle.

"Damien will walk you through what they found," she said as the presentation started.

"My sister took this video inside Stravis' bunker."

"How is this possible?" Nicholas asked. "I've been there myself. Stravis' bunker consists of no more than a dry sandy cavern."

"I've s-seen it too," Brianna said. "And nothing was there."

"Stravis cleverly crafted a secret room behind the back wall of the cavern," Damien said. "Even our most sophisticated instruments did not detect its presence."

"How were you able to find this?" Brianna asked.

"It was brought to my attention by—"

"Let me guess," Nicholas said, turned to Ethan, and flashed a toothy smile. "A little divine intervention."

"Yeah, I guess you could say that."

"Tell them what we are looking at," Jordanna said.

"Best I can tell, Stravis was studying something. What you are seeing is the best-equipped research laboratory I've ever run across. He appears to have taken detailed notes – so I should be able to recreate everything he did."

"But that could take yearsss," Brianna said.

"I agree," Nicholas said and glanced at Jordanna. "We have legions of scholars. Why not send a team of them to recreate Stravis' experiments and learn what he was up to."

"We cannot do that," Damien said and tapped at his ELMO to speed through the footage. "We cannot because of this."

The room fell silent as the scene changed to the shelves full of Stravis journals. The feed slowly scanned from left to right and shelf to shelf and panned back for effect.

"Now, I hope you all understand the urgency of this matter," Jordanna said and stood. "Victor Qruefeldt found a single journal from Creator Stravis important enough to enlist Daavic's help to steal. What do you think he'd be willing to do for shelves full of them."

Deep sighs filled the air, and the room remained quiet as they absorbed Damien's presentation.

"What are you suggesting?" Nicholas asked Damien.

"I suggest we rehouse Stravis' laboratory here at The Residence."

"That will be tricky if we are to keep it a s-secret," Brianna said.

"Tricky, but not impossible," Nicholas said. "But where do we move it to?"

"I've already figured that out. I've been retrofitting my brother's basement hideout into a lab of my own. It's mostly empty now, but with a little expansion, I think we can accommodate everything."

The room fell silent again as Nicholas and the others thought Damien's idea over.

"Well, what do you think?" Jordanna asked.

"Logistically speaking, the basement is perfect," Nicholas said. "You will have to restrict access to the front room and the study for a week. That will allow us to bring everything in through the portal plane."

"But how do we travel to the bunker without raising suspicion?" Brianna asked.

"Got that one covered, too," Damien said. "Hayley wisely left a portal beacon so we can use the portal plane and travel directly to the bunker."

"But that—"

"I know," Jordanna said and glared at Damien. "It is strictly against protocol – but I'm willing to overlook it in this case—if you all agree."

"Agree," Nicholas said.

"Agree," Brianna said.

"Gree," Azron said.

"Great, I know the rest of the guilty party agrees, and I have Alexander's proxy – so let's get on with it."

Jordanna excused Ethan, Hayley, and Tinx from the rest of the meeting while the others stayed behind to map out the details.

Four days had passed since the CAGE meeting, and Ethan and Hayley had not heard a peep out of Damien. They met Tinx bright and early every morning for breakfast before heading to the study to peruse its books for references to a desert fortress or anything that might refer to a princess named Adara.

Ethan and Hayley entered the dining hall and like clockwork, Tinx was sitting atop the table in the corner by the piano, patiently awaiting their arrival. They chose both the table and the time because nobody came early or sat anywhere nearby, so they could speak openly in private if they whispered.

"Good morning, you two," Tinx said as they approached.

"Morning, Tinx," Ethan and Hayley said.

Tinx scanned the dining hall and paused before she spoke.

"I think they've finished. Yesterday was our first normal CAGE meeting since the move started. Everybody showed up on time, and the Headmistress lifted the restrictions on the front room and study."

"Sounds like they've finished the move," Ethan said.

"Yes," Hayley said. "But I wonder why Damien didn't tell us himself."

"You saw how obsessed he was with the laboratory," Tinx said. "I'd bet he is so engrossed that the thought never crossed his mind."

"Yeah, you're probably right."

They didn't want to raise suspicion, so they sat together and enjoyed their morning breakfast as they had every day this week. After breakfast, they hurried to the front room and gathered around the basement door in anticipation.

"Come on in," Damien's voice said from a small speaker barely visible above the door.

He didn't need to tell them twice; Hayley swung the door open, and they scrambled down the stairs to witness what Damien was up to. They stopped at the base of the stairs and scanned the room to see what had changed.

"Wow, I love what you've done with the place," Hayley said.

The now full room was more extensive than before and nearly identical to Stravis' laboratory, minus the yellow walls. The main difference was the white floor and ceiling lit up from within, giving the lab a clean, sterile appearance. Damien was standing at the nearest lab bench, pouring over one of Stravis' yellow journals. Ethan, Hayley, and Tinx stopped at the bench to witness him set miniature furniture up inside a brown box with the top and one side removed. It looked like he was creating a tiny living room.

"So, you are playing with dollhouses now," Tinx said, causing Ethan and Hayley to chuckle.

"I've skimmed through several of Stravis' journals. He has them numbered, which will make my life much easier. I'm starting with the first journal and have read through it several times. Stravis had an interesting style of notetaking. Many passages are his thoughts of the moment, like diary entries. Then we have detailed notes on his experiments and some encoded entries I have yet to decipher."

"Have you learned anything important yet?" Hayley asked.

"Nothing concrete—only that Stravis did not trust the other Creators, especially Zamalador."

Ethan and Hayley exchanged glances as they both remembered Vanessa telling them the same.

"Anything else?"

"Yes, the purpose of this lab," Damien said and stopped what he was doing to look at them. "He built this lab to research peculiar interactions between elemental and earthly matter. What I find odd, though, is I skimmed through several journals and have only come across references to Atlantis, Ceres, and Hades. Thus far, I've not seen any mention of Zephyr."

Damien scratched his head and went back to what he was doing.

"So, what are you working on here?" Ethan asked.

"This one caught my attention. Stravis called it a habitat absorbing reflection trap."

"What does it do?" Tinx asked.

"Stick around, and you might find out."

He finished setting up the tiny room mock-up and attached an empty picture frame to the missing side of the box. Next, he slid a rectangular piece of glass into the frame and spray-painted the outer side black.

"You're making a mirror," Ethan said.

"Maybe, maybe not. The glass and paint are earthly, but the paint is gray, so I mixed powdered lava rock from Hades to create the black hue."

Damien shined an intense light on the wet paint for at least a minute as they watched silently.

"Should dry quickly; I think it's ready now."

Ethan spotted the reflection of the scene in the box on the surface of the glass.

"As I said, you are creating a mirror."

"Am I?" Damien detached the framed glass from the box and spun it around to face them. The image of the mini dollhouse remained on the surface like a three-dimensional picture.

"The glass captured the image," Hayley said.

"No, the glass absorbed the reflection and created a perfect copy of the environment," Damien said. "But I think something is missing, don't you?"

Damien plucked a small figurine of a person off his lab bench. Then he reached his hand into the image, and it passed right through as if the glass were not there. He set the figure down in the middle of the room and pulled his hand out.

"Much better, don't you think?"

Ethan's jaw dropped as he stared into the image that now included a tiny person in the middle of the room. He slowly moved his hand towards the picture, but the glass barrier stopped it.

"How did you do that? Is this a magic trick?"

"The first one's free," Damien said as a broad grin crossed his lips. "But I'm not finished."

He moved to the next lab bench and set the framed image down flat. Then he picked up a wood plank and laid it on top, covering the glass entirely within the frame's borders. Next, he grabbed a rubber mallet and hammered away at the plank. Ethan heard the muffled sounds of glass shattering underneath. When he finished, Damien lifted the frame and left the board and shattered glass on the bench. He held up the empty frame and turned it towards Ethan, Hayley, and Tinx to show them the image was still there.

"Now reach inside," Damien said.

Ethan slowly moved his hand towards the image, and this time it continued into the scene. He felt around and was able to grab everything inside. He grabbed a tiny chair, removed it from the picture and handed it to Hayley, who studied it carefully.

"And look, two for the price of one," Damien said and flipped the image over. The same image reflected on both sides of the glassless frame, surprising Ethan.

"Here, see for yourself," Damien said and handed the frame to Hayley.

She set it down flat and reached her hand inside to put the tiny chair back. It appeared to Ethan the lab bench was swallowing her arm. She flipped the frame over to check if the chair was back in place and reached inside to touch and feel everything on that side too.

"This is amazing. Both sides are windows into the same environment."

"Yes, and this is only the beginning," Damien said. "I can't begin to imagine what else we can learn from Stravis' research. I'm excited to continue, but between this and my CAGE duties, I don't know where I will find the time."

Ethan and Hayley took Damien's excitement as their queue to let him get back to his work. Tinx offered to stick around and help, and Damien accepted without a thought. It excited him to have her help. She'd learn where everything was and could dart about the lab to retrieve samples as he needed them. Sure, Tinx's size would cause some limitations, but any help was better than none.

Ethan and Hayley met in the Moongarden the following day to help Mildred with the skyclimber harvest. An infrequent event that only occurs once every two hundred years, according to an excited Mrs. Moongarden. But first, they would meet Irvin at Market Square to help him procure and transport specialized containers to house the seedlings once they were found.

"Today sounds like a scavenger hunt," Ethan said as he and Hayley entered the door to Market Square.

"Yeah, it should be fun," said Hayley.

"Shnickyrooners and things like that," Irvin said. He was waiting for them at the edge of the yellow brick road that led to Market Square. "It's a shiny moose tail that catches the slimy green mountain poodle in the afternoon trailer sewage."

"I always wondered about those green mountain poodles." Ethan's reply brought a glow to Irvin, and a giant ear to ear smile washed over his face.

"Hi, Irvin," Hayley said. "I hope we aren't late."

"Oh—no—Miss Hayley, you are not late. Irvin is just eager to get started. Mrs. Moongarden is blossoming with joy."

Red and yellow flowers sprouted from Irvin's head to illustrate Mildred's mood.

"Well then, let's get going," said Hayley.

Ethan, Hayley, and Irvin strolled along the yellow brick path into town. Market Square was teeming with people when they arrived. Rows of tents stood at its center, where patrons bartered with vendors for their goods. The tables lining the outer edges of the town were packed with people eating and drinking the fare from the various food merchants.

"I believe the vendor we are looking for is right down that aisle," Irvin said and pointed.

Ethan and Hayley followed Irvin as he pushed through the bustling crowd. A mixture of Caretakers, humanoids, and other elemental creatures patiently waited their turn to barter with their vendor of choice. Irvin stopped and turned to check if Ethan and Hayley were still following.

"We are almost there."

Ethan lunged forward and crashed into Irvin's chest, but Irvin reacted quickly and caught him before he could fall. Ethan regained his footing and turned around to find out who had pushed him. Hayley was already busy giving Blair and Caden a piece of her mind. Ethan stepped in front of her to confront Caden directly.

"Look, Blair, the mutant child is going to blame me for his clumsiness," Caden said with a devilish grin.

Ethan clenched his fists together and stepped toward Caden, but the bigger boy stood his ground. Irvin gently placed his hand on Ethan's shoulder and pulled him back.

"Ethan Fox is Irvin's friend," he said as he stepped between the two boys and stared into Caden's eyes. "Irvin will not permit you to bully his friend."

"Oh no, the Ravenwood butler-servant has come to their rescue," Blair said.

"You don't scare me," Caden said to Irvin.

"Bad idea to piss off a mimic," Hayley said to Ethan.

"Oh, it's not me you need to worry about," Irvin said calmly. "The big bad wolf is who you need to worry about!"

Irvin's face and body instantly morphed into a tall grey werewolf towering over Caden. Long sharp canines protruded from his snout and dripped with blood as he raised his dagger-like claws above Caden's head. Caden jumped back in shock as the crowd backed away from the commotion.

"This, this i-isn't over," a shaken Caden said to Ethan. "You won't always have someone around to save you."

"Let's go, Caden," Blair said as she stood by Caden's side. "We have a job to do. Daddy is expecting us."

The crowd returned to normal as Blair and Caden turned and pushed through. Ethan stood on his tippy toes to watch them closely. They moved to the opposite side of the lane and stopped at a merchant's tent. The letters on the sign read:

Ceresian elderwood for sale.

"Let's go. Those bullies won't mess with Irvin's friends again."

They followed Irvin to the container merchant to purchase seven containers. Irvin bartered with the merchant and was proud to have gotten all seven for only two sacks of mimicking melons. Irvin carried three containers for the trip back while Ethan and Hayley each carried two. They passed the sister cafes at the edge of town when something caused Ethan to turn around. He instantly spotted Blair sitting at a table sipping on a hot drink while Caden impatiently stood nearby holding up an enormous wooden plank.

"What's keeping you, Master Ethan," Irvin said from the yellow brick road where he and Hayley waited.

Upon returning to the Moongarden, they headed straight for the base of the skyclimber. Mrs. Moongarden was waiting patiently with her assistant Rosebud while Grubner and his brothers paced around like a small herd of cattle. Mildred wasted no time asking everyone to gather around, so she could explain today's mission.

"Whip-dilly-doodles," said Mildred. "Many of you have met her already – but for those of you who haven't, I'd like for you to meet Lois."

Mrs. Moongarden motioned to the massive trunk of vines weaving their way into the clouds.

"Seems like Lois dropped her last batch of seedlings only yesterday," she continued. "Yet here we are, waiting for the same precious moment two hundred years later."

Mildred paused to wipe a tear from her cheek.

"Lois will drop exactly seven seeds, no more, no less. She will eject them randomly into the sky in all directions. Small parachutes will sprout to guide them to the ground safely. They may land anywhere – but you can identify them by Lois' markings. They will be visible on the seed and parachute."

Ethan gazed up at one of the giant leaves protruding from Lois' side and stared at the unique swirling pattern that vaguely reminded him of something. He turned his head to look at it sideways, and his mind jumped back to meeting

Vanessa Ravenwood. Then another memory flashed into his head; he and Hayley pressed their hands against the embossed symbols, and it zapped them. Then his mind returned to when his hand pressed against Stravis' symbol, and he opened the secret laboratory.

"Ethan, are you okay?" Hayley said softly into his ear and awoke him from his thoughts.

"Yeah – but I remembered something important. Something I meant to tell you earlier – but something distracted me."

"That's understandable. A lot has happened to distract us lately. You can tell me as soon as this scavenger hunt begins, and we are alone."

"Look there. I think I see one," Grubner shouted, causing his brothers to gaze skyward.

"Oh yes, and there is another," Mrs. Moongarden said. "Okay, everybody, the skyclimber harvest has begun. A dozen candied foxtails to anyone who finds a seed."

Grubner and his brothers split into two groups and ran off zig-zagging through the Moongarden in a feeble attempt to follow the parachutes as they fell. Rosebud and Mrs. Moongarden patiently waited for the next seed to eject but were pleasantly surprised when three shot out in succession, followed by the other two a minute later.

"Oh my," said Mildred, "Lois wanted to get it over with quickly this time."

Rosebud counted, traced, and plotted the courses of the five newest ejectees.

"Our chances appear best if we head in that direction," she said to Mildred.

Ethan and Hayley stayed behind to talk as Rosebud and Mildred headed off to search for skyclimber seeds.

"Okay, so what did you mean to tell me," Hayley said.

"When we broke into that room upstairs to spy on Blair. I counted six doors – but only two had symbols etched onto them."

"Yeah, I remember, and they zapped us when we touched them."

"Yeah—but did you look at the door that zapped me?"

"No, I was too focused on getting Blair's opened."

"Well, I did, and I saw the same symbol again on the wall of your grandparents' condo."

"My family crest," Hayley said. "Those rooms must be the headmasters chambers."

"What is that?"

"Special quarters given to each headmaster. Headmasters use them to do with as they please. I've heard talk that they existed but never knew where they were."

"Well, we do now, and the Ravenwood chamber may hold clues about the desert fortress," Ethan said. "Or even the Shadow Princess. I have a feeling your grandmother didn't tell us all she knew about her."

"Me too. She nearly fainted when I mentioned the name Adara," Hayley said. "But how are we going to get inside? My mother won't allow us to go poking around in there."

"You're forgetting something. If I was able to open Stravis' lab, and Blair was able to open the Trabblemore chamber—"

"I should be able to open the Ravenwood chamber," Hayley said as a deep grin grew across her lips.

Ethan and Hayley agreed to check out the Ravenwood chamber as soon as they finished helping Mrs. Moongarden find her precious seeds. There was a slight chill in the air, and the hunt went very slowly.

"I wish they would tell us where they landed," Ethan said and rubbed his hands together.

"Yeah, this is a slow and frustrating scavenger hunt, all right."

A white glow emanated from Ethan's palms as his symbols came to life and pointed out a direction. It took only fifteen minutes to find four seeds before Ethan's symbols returned to normal.

"They must be all accounted for," Hayley said as she and Ethan headed for the skyclimber.

Grubner and his brothers were standing at Lois' base when they arrived. They had found the other three seeds and were bickering about who would receive the prized candied foxtails. Ethan and Hayley broke up the quarrel by giving them their seeds so they could all receive a prize. Mrs. Moongarden and Rosebud returned empty-handed minutes later. Mildred heaped praise on Grubner and his brothers and awarded them each for finding the seeds. But she gave Ethan and Hayley a wink to tell them she knew the truth.

Upon leaving the Moongarden, Ethan and Hayley headed straight for the third floor headmasters chambers. Hayley approached the door slowly, moved her palm up, and gently pressed it against her family crest. A soft yellow glow emanated beneath her hand as a keypad materialized on the door.

"What now?" Hayley asked.

"I don't know. There was no keypad when I opened Stravis'."

"Wait, I may already have the combo," she said.

Hayley reached into her pocket, pulled out a piece of paper, and unfolded it.

"Where did you get that?" Ethan asked.

"Do you remember before my grandmother's exit?"

"Yeah, when she whispered something to you."

"She said we would come upon an obstacle we would not know how to overcome. She gave me this and told me not to open it until then. I think that time is now."

Hayley glanced down at the paper and held it up to show Ethan the numbers. She punched them into the keypad, and the door swung open. The room was dark inside until they were far enough in to set off the automatic lights. The chamber was like the study but much smaller. Ethan and Hayley wandered the room and poked around.

Ethan approached a large desk at the end of the room and opened the top drawer. He shuffled around inside and found a folded-up piece of paper. He unfolded it and studied the handwritten list for a minute.

"Hayley, come check this out," he said.

Hayley walked over and studied the note with Ethan. It read:

The Four Cohorts

1. Drake Evans
2. Lindrew Scragmort
3. Jason Crowley
4. Heldrik Vonn Grim

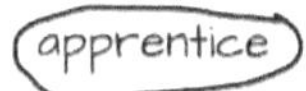

Ethan and Hayley studied the list in silence.

"Jason Crowley," Hayley said. "That's the name of the man my grandmother said was building the pyramids in the desert."

"Yeah, that's what caught my eye, too," Ethan said. "Heldrik is the only other one that sounds familiar to me."

"Me too—but I wonder what apprentice means and why it's circled."

"I have an idea what that means," Ethan said. "I meant to tell you, but I learned about it on the night of the Drone Wars."

"What does it mean?"

"Heldrik Vonn Grim had an apprentice, and his name is Dakota Drakelan. I read about it in an old *Daily Star* article by Boris Wentworth."

"That must be what Boris was referring to when he said he uncovered dark dealings from Dakota's past."

"Yeah, that's what I was thinking too."

"Tuck that away in your pocket tote," Hayley said. "We'll investigate it more later. We should keep digging around, there is bound to be more in this big room, but it could take weeks to—"

"Shhh," Ethan said and put his finger to his lips. "I hear someone."

They tip-toed to the door and placed their ears against it to listen. Blair and Caden talked as they entered the Trabblemore chamber.

"Daddy will be here soon," Blair said. "He will be overjoyed with the work you've done."

"Do you think he will let me come along?"

"He might," Blair said. "He will likely want to proceed with the plan as soon as he arrives."

The sound of a door opening and closing interrupted their eavesdropping.

"Did you hear that?" Hayley said. "Whatever their plan is, they are about to put it in motion."

"Yeah, I heard. We need to tell someone."

Hayley was hesitant to tell her mother anything, so they would discuss the matter with Damien first. They quietly slipped out the door and ran to the basement laboratory as fast as possible, but nobody answered the locked door.

"He must not be here," Hayley said as she pulled out her ELMO and tapped at its screen. "He's in the CAGE meeting room."

They dashed as fast as their light beetle could run. Ethan opened the door, and Hayley stormed through and swiped the dark curtain aside, disturbing the CAGE meeting.

"What is the meaning of this?"

Hayley froze at the sound of her mother's voice. Ethan entered the room and stood by her side.

"It's the Trabblemores," he said. "They're planning something, and we have reason to believe whatever they are planning is about to happen."

"We are well aware of the Trabblemores intentions," Nicholas said. "They've been trying to undermine Ravenwood leaders since Gaylord's downfall."

"Nothing the Trabblemores do could be more important than CAGE business," Jordanna said.

"But Mother—"

"We will listen to what you have to say after our meeting."

Ethan and Hayley sat quietly at the table as the CAGE meeting continued. Nearly forty minutes passed, and Ethan's patience was waning. He looked at Hayley, who was staring daggers at her mother. But then something happened to interrupt the meeting for good.

Wisps of golden whimsy wafted from beneath the table grabbing everyone's attention. Ethan quickly retrieved the awakened poem book. It flipped open, and a new poem slowly appeared. Ethan and Hayley read the poem as Damien and Jordanna hurried around the table to read the passage over Ethan's shoulder. It read:

Mirror Mirror

Mirror mirror on the wall, its secret started with a ball.

Bouncing on the checkered plane, to end the curse that caused refrain.

Unknown to those who live inside, created by the one who died.

Useless standing where it stood, till shattered under

elderwood.

The Grim rejoice a brand new start, made from shards of a

broken hart.

The four of them stood in silence, pondering the meaning of the latest Seer communication.

"I think this refers to when Ethan unlocked the portals," Hayley said.

"Yes," said Jordanna. "But they spelled 'heart' wrong. Have they ever made such a mistake before?"

"They didn't spell anything wrong," Ethan said as he spun around to face them.

"Damien, when you showed us the experiment in your lab, what was the wooden plank made from?"

"That was the secret sauce," Damien said proudly. "Ceresian elderwood treated with Hadean tanzanite."

Ethan's eyes widened as he realized his theory was correct.

"The Seers don't make mistakes," he said. "Hart stands for habitat absorbing reflection trap. And if I'm right, we must hurry to the front room immediately."

Ethan stood and bolted out the door, followed by Hayley and the CAGE members. When they arrived in the front room, it confirmed Ethan's worst nightmare. Shards of broken glass covered the floor by the wall opposite the front door, and the giant mirror normally reflecting the portal plane was gone.

"I don't understand," Jordanna said. "Why would anyone want to break the mirror and steal an empty frame?"

"This wasn't just anyone," Ethan said. "Victor Qruefeldt did this and we have reason to believe the Trabblemores helped him."

"And that wasn't an empty frame they stole," said Damien. "It was a working replica of the portal plane."

"If what you say is true," Jordanna said. "The Grimleavers now have complete and total access to the human and elemental worlds."

"Yes, this is horrible news," Damien said. "This changes the game completely."

THE

NIBBLEWARTS

After allowing somebody to steal a copy of the portal plane, The Residence was on high alert, and the Caretakers did everything they could to ready themselves for what was to come. Ethan and Hayley felt partially to blame since they learned of the Trabblemores' plan before anything happened. And because Jordanna had failed to listen to their warnings, the divide between mother and daughter was widening. Damien and Tinx wanted to smooth things over, but now was not the time to try with tensions on the rise around The Residence. Besides, Jordanna spent every waking hour in the Map Room or CAGE meetings while Hayley was spending all her time with Ethan, and they were mostly out of sight lately.

To be precise, Ethan and Hayley were secretly staking out the headmasters chambers. They felt defeated after seeing the shattered mess on the front room floor nearly a week earlier. The feeling did not sit well with either of them; and they were determined to do something about it. But for now, Hayley insisted they stake out the Ravenwood chamber. She hoped to accomplish two things by doing so. For one, they would continue to search Odin's chamber for any other valuable information. They had a lot to sort through; so for now, they would focus on anything related to Jason Crowley and the secret pyramid fortress in the desert. In addition, they would keep an ear to the wall and listen for any word out of the Trabblemores they might overhear.

Thus far, there was no peep out of the Trabblemores. The only part of Hayley's plan bearing fruit was something Ethan found rummaging through Odin's bookshelves. He found a couple of folders stuffed between two books. They contained pages of notes and pictures. One folder contained photos of the four men believed to be "The Four Cohorts" and accompanying notes Hayley recognized as her grandfather's handwriting. The other folder had a picture of a young Victor Qruefeldt, with handwritten scribbles on the back that were unintelligible.

Up until now, the only thing they learned was Hayley's grandmother was not as forthcoming as she seemed. According to Odin's notes, she was way more involved than she led them to believe.

Ethan sat at Odin's desk with the medallions they found at Stravis' bunker laid out in front of him. Hayley had organized them into rows and fastened them to a large piece of felt for safe keeping. After studying each one carefully, the only thing he learned was they were all identical. Ethan was at the end of his rope with all this waiting around, and he was ready for action. All he had to do now was convince Hayley.

Ethan's hair blew back as hot grains of sand pelted his forehead, and he struggled to see what was in front of him. He held his arms up to shield his face as he leaned into the strong wind to make his way through the desert. He did not know where he was going, but the importance of what he was striving toward drove him forward. The wind stopped abruptly, and everything fell silent as Ethan wiped the sand boogers from the corners of his eyes to see the man in a yellow robe.

Stravis approached a tall woman in a hooded black-and-yellow Caretaker robe. Her back faced Ethan, so he could not tell who she was as Stravis spoke to her and motioned his arm at the surrounding desert. The woman turned her head from Stravis to focus on the desert as she knelt to place her hands on the warm sand. She bowed her head and chanted something unintelligible. At first, nothing happened, but then the sand churned in front of her as something arose from beneath the desert floor.

Stravis walked towards the disturbance, his arms filled with white fabric clothing. Then, one by one, bare humanoids with enormous oversized blue eyes emerged from the desert sand and accepted Stravis' offering. They were bald and totally naked except for a golden swirly eye-shaped medallion embedded in each of their chests. It continued for several moments until fifteen to twenty of them were visible, but it was hard to tell because they circled another woman that Ethan could not see well in the crowd. The big-eyed humanoids looked at one another and embraced as they passed, like at a family reunion. The scene was strange, but the happiness in their generous eyes brought calm to Ethan and made him smile.

The festive scene changed into a dark, dreary one in the blink of an eye. Black clouds hung in the sky over the rain-soaked desert. The big-eyed people lay chained to one another on the ground. They had hair now and sat in a half-circle around a woman chained to a post. Her blonde locks fell past her shoulders and framed her beautiful face and golden swirly eye-shaped pendant necklace. But she had regular-sized blue eyes, and they glared at the man standing before her.

He was a young man wearing a half-black half-white Caretaker robe and holding a small black box in the palm of his opened hand. Ethan recognized the man as a young Victor Qruefeldt as the woman shook her head at him in defiance. He reached his arm towards her, spoke some words, and the box came to life. Light emanated from the box as its lid flipped open, and wiry black strands shot out and enveloped the woman. A purplish glow surged within the strands, and the color drained from the woman's face and body as the life force slowly drained from her.

The chained survivors cried out to mourn their fallen leader, who stood pitch black and motionless before them. But something happened—she opened her eyes, and a bright yellow light glowed from within as a sheen flowed over her prune-wrinkled black skin, making her smooth again. The black apparition of the woman floated free of her restraints and moved slowly towards her captor. Shock erased the evil grin from Victor's face as he held the box out and shouted. The apparition vaporized into a thick black cloud of smoke that was quickly sucked into the box. The lid clamped shut, and the woman was gone.

Then, the scene changed again in a flash, and Ethan was standing under a calm night sky. He was still in the middle of the desert, but now tiny creatures moved all around him. They were three to five inches tall and looked like little cavemen with long ropy braids of hair that hung to the ground and covered their faces and most of their bodies. Their little arms and legs were only visible when they moved about, and their braids moved from side to side.

A yellow flash of light caught the attention of the little critters as the apparition of the woman in black appeared from out of nowhere. She stood alone in the sand and smiled down at the puny beings. Storm clouds formed overhead, and lightning bolts danced across the sky. A vortex opened behind the woman as she turned to the creatures and motioned for them to follow. She ushered them into the open vortex Ethan could now see into. He peered into the maelstrom and saw giant three foot tall ants standing upright and welcoming the new arrivals. Then, all at once, the clouds, the vortex, and the woman disappeared—leaving Ethan alone under the calm night sky.

Something glistened in the sand under the light of the silvery moon. Ethan walked over to investigate and knelt to see what it was. He found a golden medallion half buried in the sand. It was swirly and eye-shaped like the ones embedded in the chests of the big-eyed people. A strong gust of wind crawled across the desert's surface and peeled a layer of sand away as it passed. It exposed several more pendants scattered around the area and glistening under the night sky.

The sound of Ethan's ELMO awakened him from the life-like dream. He had fallen asleep at the table while thumbing through some of Odin's library books. He tapped at the screen, and Hayley's voice filled his room.

"Ethan, meet me in the study."

"But what about our stakeout?"

"Almost a week has passed. We need to regroup and start making things happen."

"You don't have to tell me twice," Ethan said as a full grin enveloped his face. "Be right with you."

He folded up the medallions, put them away, and bolted out the door. Then, he ran down the stairs so fast that Hayley had barely set her ELMO down when he entered the study. She was sitting at the reading table with a newspaper in front of her. Wordly stood on the table next to her and a stack of more newspapers.

"Wow, you got here fast."

"Your call sounded important. What have you—"

The sound of Tinx entering the room cut Ethan short. She darted over and landed on the table next to Wordly.

"Good, you're all here," she said. "Where have you two been hiding out lately?"

"Well, we've been—"

"Never mind, forget I asked. If you tell me, I'll want to tag along, and I am far too busy helping Damien with his lab research. On top of that, the Headmistress even sends me on some CAGE-related missions now. Ever since the portal theft, it's all hands on deck for CAGE."

"Okay, what can we do for you?" Hayley asked.

"I've come to cordially invite you to the unveiling of my family memorial. We will be holding the service at The Grimleaver Atrocities Memorial in a few days."

"We would love to be there for you," Hayley said.

"Great, I will ELMO you the details."

Tinx turned her attention to Wordly.

"Of course – you are more than welcome, too, Wordly. But I have other business to discuss with you as well."

"What can I do for you?"

"Well, let me start by saying this is sensitive CAGE business," Tinx said. "But I have the okay to bring you into the inner circle."

"Sounds intriguing. I'm in."

"But you don't even know what I am asking yet."

"You had me at CAGE. Tell me what you want me to do."

"A secret CAGE mission recently recovered a treasure trove of vital information. Damien has set up a laboratory in the basement, and I've been helping him organize things. I had an idea I think you would be perfect for."

"Books are my expertise – but I am not well versed in laboratory procedures."

"Exactly, I'm getting to that part," Tinx said. "A crucial component of what we recovered includes hundreds of journals written by Creator Stravis himself."

"Oh, now that sounds intriguing," Wordly said and rubbed his tiny hands together.

"Yes—and that is where my idea comes in. We would like you to go through the journals. Read them and re-read as many times as you need to catalog them for us."

"I'm a bookworm. It will take no more than one read through each journal for me to have a complete recall of the entire set."

"I don't want to burst your bubble," Hayley said. "But many journal entries are encoded or written in Creator Stravis' sloppy shorthand."

"Well, that's a different story. I may require several reads through. As for the encoded entries, until we crack the code, I won't understand the meaning, only the location of certain segments."

"Perfect, what you describe is light years from where we are now," Tinx said. "Damien will be pleased."

"When do I start?"

"Damien's CAGE duties consume him lately," Tinx said. "But he promised to find some time tomorrow if you agreed to help."

"That works for me, and will give me time to finish my daily duties here in the study, if Miss Hayley does not require more of my time."

"I think we are okay," Hayley said.

Tinx exited the study to continue her work in the laboratory. Wordly estimated it would take a few days to sift through Stravis' notes, and he was eager to start. So he book taxied his way back to the study bookshelves and disappeared.

"So, what's all this?" Ethan asked as Hayley went through the stack of newspapers on the table.

"These are old *Residential Daily Stars*. I asked Wordly to pull all stories referencing anything about my grandfather cross-referenced with pyramids or Jason Crowley. He didn't recall anything involving Odin and pyramids, but these all contain articles about Jason Crowley's dead body showing up on my grandparents doorstep."

"Have you learned anything?"

"Not a lot," she replied and pointed at the stack of newspapers. "Those are all follow-up articles by various reporters. They are mostly speculation and innuendo, but there's not much substance. But this is the original article covering the crime, written by your pal Boris Wentworth."

Ethan peered over Hayley's shoulder and read the title of the article: *Up and Coming Caretaker Couple Make a Grisly Discovery*. He continued scanning through the article but didn't find any new information.

"So, Jason Crowley was one of Gaylord Trabblemore's right hand men. But we already knew that from the notes in your grandfather's office."

"Yeah, I know, this seems like a dead end."

Hayley's words were lost on Ethan as his eyes moved to another article halfway down the page titled: *Magnetic Maelstrom*, and he began reading.

"Earth's magnetic field has always been of keen interest in the human world. But now, the new world's latest surprise development has stumped Caretakers and elemental scholars. A magnetic maelstrom of sorts has confounded experts who have no idea how or even when Earth's magnetic poles abruptly shifted."

"Ethan, are you daydreaming again?" Hayley asked, causing Ethan to stop reading.

"No, just distracted. But now that you mentioned it—I did have a strange dream earlier."

Ethan told Hayley about the vivid three-part dream that flashed from scene to scene like a slide show in his head.

"Parts of it sound like what my grandmother described."

"Yeah, I saw giant humanoid ants – but I didn't see any pyramids – and I don't remember Vanessa mentioning tiny caveman creatures."

"Excuse me," Wordly said as he popped out from between two books on a nearby shelf. "I wasn't eavesdropping, but what I did hear sounds like something I think you need to view."

"What would that be?" Hayley asked. "We welcome any help you might give."

"Have you heard of the Alcove of Enigma?"

"No, the name doesn't ring any bells," Hayley said.

"The Alcove of Enigma is a specialized room in the Gallery. What makes the alcove so unique is all paintings in that room have one thing in common. They were all determined to be significant by the Fates, yet we still have no idea what they mean or represent."

"And why would we need to view that?" Ethan asked.

"Because one of those paintings is similar to what you described."

Ethan's eyes widened as he turned to Hayley and saw her mouth gaped open.

"Yeah," she said and paused, "we need to see that."

"Thank you, Wordly, you've been a great help," Ethan said.

He grabbed Hayley's hand and ushered her out the study door. They ran the rest of the way and stopped to catch their breath before entering the enormous canvas room. Dorkin Drumbles immediately took notice of his visitor's arrival and hurried over to greet them.

"Wonderful day it is," Dorkin said in his usual Yoda'ish tone. "Happy, Dorkin is, to help Miss Hayley and Ethan Fox. Now how can Dorkin help?"

"We would like you to take us to the Alcove of Enigma," Hayley said.

Dorkin's head jumped back, and his glasses slid down his long, sloped nose.

"Is something wrong?" Ethan asked.

"Wrong—oh no—nothing is wrong. It's just, Dorkin does not get many requests for that."

They followed Dorkin as he walked towards the far side of the room, to the corner opposite the viewing hall. At first, they were walking straight at a blank wall, but when they got close enough, the outline of a door appeared against the white canvas.

"The Alcove of Enigma is in there," Dorkin said.

"Aren't you going to show us in?" Ethan asked.

"Oh no—Dorkin does not go in there. That room is a den of inequity if you ask Dorkin's opinion."

Ethan and Hayley opened the white door as Dorkin scurried away as fast as his little legs would carry him. They stepped into the well-lit white room filled with dozens of canvas paintings. Rows of them stood on easels and were covered in sheets at the room's center.

"I get the feeling Dorkin is afraid of this room," Ethan said.

"Ya think?" Hayley said and giggled as they approached the rows of covered easels.

"If we split up, we'll find it faster," Hayley said as she hurried past Ethan to search a different row.

"That sounds like a—"

"Ethan, we don't need to search for anything," Hayley said cutting him off mid-sentence. "I'm pretty sure I've found it."

Ethan hustled toward Hayley and when he rounded the corner, he immediately saw what she was talking about. Standing on an easel at the row's center was a canvas covered in a yellow sheet with a black swirly eye-shaped emblem stamped on it. They wasted no time uncovering the canvas to see what secrets it held.

"The Pyramids of Never," Hayley said, reading the title.

The two of them stood side by side and stared in silence. The painting depicted the building of a complex of pyramids off in the distance. One enormous pyramid stood in the middle with two smaller ones on each side. Near the build site, a much smaller temple-like structure was already complete.

In the foreground, a mountainous boulder crawled with tiny cavemen-like creatures with long braids of hair tied behind their tall heads. Their long faces were nearly twice the size of their bodies and mainly consisted of huge blue eyes and even bigger chomping teeth. Enormous three foot tall ants hauled giant rectangular stones to the build site. Two by two, the ants hoisted stones over their heads and walked them in a long single-file line stretching to the distant build site.

"The little cavemen creatures are eating the boulder," Hayley said.

"Yeah, they appear to be cutting that mountain of rock into giant stone bricks for the construction."

Ethan's gaze followed the trail of ants to the build site, and a tiny sparkle appeared on the central pyramid. His mind raced, and in a flash, he was inside the enormous pyramid watching as the Shadow Princess slowly floated towards him.

"Ethan, are you with me?"

"Huh," Ethan said and shook his head.

"Are you okay? You've been acting strange lately."

"I, I saw her again, the Shadow Princess."

"Are you talking about your dream again?"

"No, she came to me in a vision just now. And it's not the first time that has happened."

"She's trying to tell you something," said Hayley. "If only I could get inside your head and translate."

"Yeah, I wish you could."

They returned to the painting and studied the scene in silence.

"Interesting," Hayley said as she moved closer to gaze at the tiny cavemen creatures.

"What?"

"Well, I can think of a valid explanation for the giant ants. Any Caretaker could evolve one to grow that large and even walk upright. But I have no earthly idea where the little rock-eaters came from."

Something Hayley said jogged Ethan's memory.

"I wonder," he said.

"Wonder what?"

"Gruggins called them rock-eating roaches. Could they be Nibblewarts?"

"Well, I've never seen one myself – but now that you mentioned it, they fit the descriptions."

No sooner had the words slipped from Hayley's lips than Ethan's pocket tote erupted with golden wisps of whimsy. He pulled out the poem book as the pages turned to a blank one and wrote a new poem. The passage read:

The Nibblewarts

Bestowed with Seer spirit, they came to save the day.
The Sayers were awakened, with the gift of what we say.

But evil spied their presence, and tried to learn their truth.
By imprisoning Adara, a princess in her youth.

She gave her life to save them, and sacrificed her soul.
Disabling his weapon, to thwart his evil goal.

Attempts to kill them failed, and the Nibblewarts were born.
They fled indentured servitude, when a rift in time was torn.

But if you want to find them, make haste and leave right now.
For they are standing at the altar, of green grump with
furrowed brow.

"Nibblewarts," Ethan said. "They are Nibblewarts, and we need to get to Gruggins' box now!"

They quickly exited the alcove and ran past Dorkin towards the Gallery's exit. Halfway down the dark curved hallway, they heard Gruggins shouting.

"This is the last time you lousy gravel eaters will disrupt my nap," Gruggins screamed. "If I have to tell you again, I'm gonna—"

Gruggins stopped his rant when Ethan and Hayley entered the room. He gazed at Hayley, and his demeanor changed too.

"Well, hello, Miss Hayley—and err, Master Ethan. I was discussing the importance of proper sleep with my friends here."

The caravan of Nibblewarts was on their hands and knees, mumbling at the foot of the small table Gruggins' box sat on. All at once, they stood up, turned around, and stared up at Ethan and Hayley. The long hair braids fell to the sides of their faces exposing big blue eyes and fat buck teeth. One carried a miniature golden staff and raised it over his head as he spoke to the others in a low-pitched, unintelligible grumble. The others gathered their things, walked to their miniature wagons and wheelbarrows, and headed for The Hall of Doorways in single file.

"Wait, we need to speak with you," Hayley said. "Ethan, they are leaving."

Hayley frowned, but the Nibblewarts continued slowly towards the door.

"Don't bother," Gruggins said. "They never listen."

Ethan's eyes followed the caravan from front to back, and that's when he spotted the three inch tall blue bunny rabbit with yellow spots walking backward, waving at him. Ethan shook his head and wiped his eyes to ensure he wasn't seeing things – but then he heard a cartoonish voice.

"Don't miss out on all the fun Ethan Fox," tiny Jasper said. "But come prepared. They don't speak to giants."

"Ethan, are you having another vision?"

"No, I'm looking at a mini-Jasper. He's following the caravan, and I think he wants us to follow them too."

The caravan stopped to allow the door to swing open. Ethan and Hayley moved slowly so as not to spook them. The Nibblewarts entered the dark hallway and turned right instead of left as expected.

"They're going the wrong way," Hayley said. "The negative doorways lead to the past, and our rules forbid their use without proper authorization."

Ethan and Hayley followed the caravan into the hallway and turned right. They slowed their pace to stay at the trailing edge of their light beetle's light field. The procession stopped, and a door magically opened. The Nibblewarts entered, and Ethan nearly followed, but Hayley grabbed his arm to stop him.

"We can't follow them, Ethan."

"But we have to."

"Even if we wanted to, we can't go now. We wouldn't have a way back to the present."

"But Jasper followed them, and he might show us the way."

"Jasper. Really?"

"But I—"

"Is that a chance you are willing to take?"

"Yeah, your right, I guess."

"I know I'm right," she said as a broad grin spread across her lips. "If we do this, we will make a plan first."

THE PYRAMIDS OF NEVER

The door closed as the last of the Nibblewarts disappeared. Ethan tilted his head to watch as Hayley stood silently with her hands on her hips. The determination on her face was the only signal he needed to keep his mouth shut and wait for it.

"If we do this, the first thing we need is a tether port."

"Dakota has one," Ethan said. "The one he took from George."

"Yeah, I remember – but convincing him to give it to us might not be so easy."

"Never know till we try. But there is one more thing, something Jasper said to me."

"What did Jasper say?"

"He told me to come prepared because they don't talk to giants. I think he was speaking of the Nibblewarts."

"They did appear to be intimidated when they saw us," Hayley said.

"Yeah, to them, we are giants. But even if we could approach without scaring them, we can't understand a word they are saying."

"No, we don't – but my ELMO does, and it can translate."

"Great, then we are back to, they don't speak to giants."

"I think I've got that one covered, too," said Hayley. "Grubner Trowel oversees the Moongarden's supply of dwindle-berries, and he owes me a favor. Four each would be enough to shrink us down to Nibblewart size. Of course, we will need four more to return us to size – so that's sixteen total."

"Dwindle-berries?"

"Yes, each one we eat will roughly halve our size. By my calculations, four each will reduce us to three or four inches. But don't worry, they're delicious."

"Oh—right—you tell me you will shrink me down to three inches, but don't worry about a thing."

"The way I see it, our biggest challenge will be talking Dakota Drakelan into letting us use his tether port without telling my mother."

"Then maybe we don't talk him into anything. We could borrow the tether port for a few hours. I mean, we will return it."

After discussing the matter, they talked themselves into the more morally corrupt option. Ethan would distract

Dakota while Hayley located the tether port and retrieved it with her copycat.

The long walk down The Hall of Doorways gave Ethan time to think about what he would say to Dakota. They entered the twelfth door on the right and nervously inched their way up the trail to Dakota's shack on the hill. It was late afternoon, and the sky was pinkish orange as they stepped onto the creaky front porch. The door slowly squealed itself open, allowing the remnants of the day's light to fill the dimly-lit cabin. Ethan and Hayley paused at the entrance as their eyes adjusted.

"Well, are ya goin' ta come in 'ere or not," said Dakota's gruff voice.

"Your place is quite dark," Hayley said.

"Pardon me," Dakota said and snapped his fingers, causing lights to flip on around the room. "I fergot my manners. Not used ta gettin' so many visits from light lovers."

As Ethan and Hayley entered, Dakota stood up from his reclining chair.

"What can I do fer ya?"

"I, I h-have a few questions," said Ethan as he moved closer.

"Well, spit it out," Dakota said and chuckled.

Hayley casually scanned the room as Dakota and Ethan spoke. She stroked her Tabby Cat hidden away inside her robe.

"I've discovered your secret," Ethan said.

"And what, pray tell, would that be?"

"You were Heldrik Vonn Grim's apprentice."

"Not much of a secret, Boris Wentworth made sure a that."

"I'm not talking about the article. I'm talking about this." He waved the note they found in Odin's office at Dakota, who took it from his hand and studied it.

"Yeah, so?" Dakota said and handed the note back to Ethan. "Why do ya think he circled the word 'apprentice'? It's circled because Odin knew I served as Heldrik's apprentice. It's why he hired me. He was skeptical of me at first, but he was a fair man and decided ta give me a chance."

"Then why do you hate Boris so much? Because of the article?"

"Because 'es a scoundrel, and when that article came out, it caused Odin a lotta grief. Didn't hurt me none, but Odin was new ta bein' headmaster and didn't need the added strife."

"So you've seen this list before," Ethan said.

"Odin showed it ta me before hirin' me. An I'll tell you the same thing I told 'im. The only thing I know 'bout them names is they're all associates a' Gaylord Trabblemore."

"And that's all you told him?"

"No, I also told him Heldrik wasn't the monster everyone made 'im out ta be. Sure, he had 'is demons, but he was a decent man."

"Anything else?"

"I've said ma peace. If I didn't know any better, I'd think ya'd gone ta work fer Boris and 'is rag of a newspaper."

Ethan pressed Dakota more to give Hayley time, but he was running out of things to say.

"Let's go, Ethan. I think we've worn out our welcome here," said Hayley.

She grabbed him by the arm and pulled him towards the exit when Dakota sat back in his chair.

"Little lady, I trust yer goin' ta bring that back when yer done goin' wherever yer goin."

"W-what are you talking about?"

"The tether port ya pilfered."

"B—but how did you know?"

"I wasn't born yesterday," said Dakota as a broad smile appeared beneath his mustache. "Ethan Fox comes ta my house with a strong-minded Ravenwood woman, and she stands by silently as he asks all the questions. You'd have ta be a darn fool ta not be suspicious a that."

"He's got a point," Ethan said and chuckled.

"Yes, I will return it to you, I promise."

They left the creepy house perplexed. Ethan was sure Dakota knew more about the names on the list. But he'd let them take the tether port. Dakota seemed to have ulterior motives. But for now, they had bigger fish to fry.

Hayley woke bright and early the following morning to help Grubner with his chores in the Moongarden. Sixteen dwindle-berries was a tall ask, even if he did owe her a favor. So she would butter him up before broaching the subject. Noon was approaching when she met Ethan in the front room.

"Mission accomplished," she said and showed him a pouch full of colorful purple berries.

"So you have everything we need?"

"Tether port, check. Dwindle-berries, check. ELMO, check."

"Let's get a move on."

They entered The Hall of Doorways, looked around to check for spying eyes, turned right, and hurried to the door the Nibblewarts had used.

"Well, here goes nothing," Hayley said as she pulled the door open, grabbed Ethan's hand, and pulled him inside. Ethan felt dizzy as purple sparks flashed in his eyes, and everything grew dark.

When he came to, they were at the edge of a vast desert under the calm night sky. Behind them, an enormous spherical rock stood partially buried in the sand. The flicker of flames was barely visible at the base of the distant boulder.

"That rock is huge," Ethan said. "Nearly the size of a small town."

"Yeah, it's gigantic, alright."

"Where on Earth did they find that?" Ethan wondered aloud.

"I don't think they found it on Earth."

Bright lights beamed from the desert floor not far from them, lighting the sides of gigantic pyramid structures under construction. Ethan and Hayley instantly recognized this place from the painting in the Alcove of Enigma. They moved stealthily towards the construction site to avoid being seen by the Caretakers guarding the area. When they got close enough, they crept on their bellies to hug the ground. A Caretaker in a half-black half-red robe emerged from the small temple near the build site. He spoke to the guards, which, thankfully, gave Ethan and Hayley the cover they needed to run and duck behind a row of enormous, stacked bricks.

"Yes, sir, we understand, sir," one of the guards said.

"Of course, Mr. Crowley, we take turns circling the site every hour as you have ordered," the second guard said.

The guards sounded frightened by the man, so Ethan peeked out from behind the rock wall. He recognized the man from the pictures in Odin's folder, but he witnessed something else that shocked him to his core. He ducked back behind the rock wall and took several deep breaths to maintain composure.

"What did you see?"

"You're not going to believe it! Jason Crowley is here – and he's holding a Heldrik Vonn Grim puzzle box."

"Let me see."

Hayley switched places with Ethan and took a peek for herself, and when she turned back to him, her eyes were as wide as saucers.

"But—how is that possible? We are thousands of years before your birth."

"Yeah—and I thought Heldrik created it for Victor Qruefeldt."

They sat behind the rock wall, quietly pondering their discovery. Jason Crowley bid the guards farewell, then one of them left for their scheduled hourly rounds. Ethan and Hayley took that as the perfect time to run away before being spotted at the build site.

"We should head for the giant boulder," Ethan said. "That's where we are most likely to find the Nibblewarts."

"Great idea, and even if we don't find them, we can use the rock for shelter. Deserts can become very cold at night."

They spent the better part of an hour covering the distance to the base of the giant rock. From closer up, the flames from many torches were visible around the area where they quarried the rock. A small team of the giant ants were moving enormous stone bricks and stacking them into a long, tall row, partially blocking their view of the area.

The giant ants ignored Ethan and Hayley as they slowly crept around the wall of stacked rock. A massive bonfire burned at the area's center to warm the tiny caveman creatures that were now visible to Ethan and Hayley. The Nibblewarts worked in small teams to eat straight lines into the rock and cut perfect blocks away from the giant boulder. When one group filled their bellies, they would go to the back of the long line to rest while another team took their place to carve out the next brick.

"Well, I haven't seen any guards here," Ethan said. "Let's go in for a closer look."

"Ethan, you are forgetting what Jasper said."

"I'm not forgetting anything. But Jasper giggles after nearly everything he says, which doesn't exactly inspire my confidence. So before I shrink myself into an itty-bitty, I will be darn sure he is speaking the truth."

Ethan stepped out from behind the rock wall and into the bonfire light. Hayley followed as he slowly strode towards the long line of Nibblewarts gathered on a flat surface carved into the giant rock. Several tiny creatures spotted them and pointed as the others turned and a low pitch grumble filled the air. Then, all at once, the perfect line of Nibblewarts turned to chaos as the creatures hopped to the desert floor and scurried in random directions like confused ants. But the confusion was short-lived and quickly turned into an orderly evacuation as they beelined left and right around the base of the boulder. Ethan followed the escaping Nibblewarts to a series of small tunnels burrowed into hardened sand beneath the boulder. He turned to Hayley, who stood behind him with her arms folded.

"Got any more bright ideas?"

"No—but I had to be sure."

"Okay, now that that's settled, we must follow them."

Hayley pointed at the holes at the base of the giant rock, pulled out the pouch, and handed Ethan four dwindle-berries. He was still staring at them in the palm of his hand when Hayley quickly shrunk down to half barbie doll sized. He barely heard her tiny voice as Hayley shouted up at him.

"Come on. They're getting away."

Ethan popped the dwindle-berries into his mouth and swallowed. His head grew fuzzy, and his vision blurred. Everything around him appeared to be in slow motion and grew larger and larger. Twenty long seconds passed while Ethan shrank to Hayley's size. His head was still wobbly, and he was losing his balance, so Hayley put her arm around him to steady him.

"You didn't chew," she said. "It goes much faster if you chew. Dwindle-berries are delicious."

Once he regained his composure, Ethan scanned his new, much larger surroundings. It amazed him how different everything appeared from a puny perspective. The previously small holes burrowing underneath the giant rock were now large tunnels.

"Let's get moving," Hayley said.

Ethan followed her into the nearest tunnel, and she quickly turned on her ELMO flashlight. But the light from the shrunken ELMO was feeble and barely lit their way, so Ethan asked her to turn it off.

"Everything is pitch black in here," Hayley said. "We need light."

"No, we don't. Remember, in the Trabblemore chamber, I could see perfectly while you barely saw a thing. My eyes will adjust to the darkness."

Hayley switched off her ELMO light, and they waited a minute for Ethan's eyes to adjust – but once they did, his vision was like watching a fuzzy black and white television.

"Grab onto my shoulders and walk behind me."

Hayley pawed around in the darkness, trying to find Ethan's shoulders and scooted her way behind him.

"Tell me if I'm going too fast," he said as he headed into the deep dark cave.

The tunnel descended deeper beneath the desert sand and joined with other tunnels leading to unknown destinations. They continued down the remaining tunnel that made a U-turn and leveled off before turning perfectly straight and circular.

"Our path seems to have straightened," Hayley said.

"Yeah, we appear to be inside a long pipe or something."

"You can go faster now," she said. "As long as we are on a straightaway."

They continued down the long straight corridor for another half hour before reaching a flickering light at the end of the tunnel.

"I can see," Hayley said. "Burning flames up ahead from the looks of it."

She moved to Ethan's side, and they continued towards the flickering orange light dancing across the wall at the end of the tunnel. They slowed to a crawl as they reached the entrance to an expansive chamber and peeked around the corner. The Nibblewarts gathered around a bonfire burning at the center of the room. They were aware of Ethan and Hayley's presence and turned to look at them but were not scared.

Hayley fished her ELMO from her Caretaker robe and turned it on as she slowly entered the chamber. Ethan followed her lead and stayed by her side as she inched towards the Nibblewarts.

"We mean you no harm," Hayley spoke into her ELMO.

She tapped at the screen and held her ELMO up into the air. An unintelligible low-pitched grumble erupted from the ELMO and filled the cavern. The Nibblewarts remained quiet at first but then all burst out in laughter.

"Great, they think you are telling them jokes."

"We only want to speak with you," Hayley said into her ELMO and held it up again.

This time the grumbling sound did not garner any reaction. The Nibblewarts sat quietly by their fire and stared at Ethan and Hayley. The uncomfortable silence ended when the one with the golden staff stood and approached them. He seemed to be their leader, stepping forward to speak for his tribe. Hayley tapped her ELMO to record the low-pitched grumbling from the Nibblewart leader. When he finished speaking, she tapped again for translation.

"Nibblewart high priest recognize shrunken giants. Nibblewarts no afraid and no listen to lies of shrunken giants."

He turned and started back towards his people.

"As Gruggins said, they don't listen," Hayley said.

But something she said struck a chord, and Ethan's mind drifted back to their return from Stravis' bunker. Gruggins was in a tirade, shouting at the 'rock-eating roaches' that had just left the room. He fast-forwarded through the scene in his mind and tried to remember what Gruggins had said.

"Wait a minute," Ethan said to Hayley. "Gruggins said, they always speak of the Shadow Princess."

"Yeah."

"And he said something else," he continued, his feet tapping on the ground. "I was the only one listening, but there was something else they speak of. The um—er—the— that's it—the Nibblewart prophecies."

"Wait," Hayley shouted and tapped at her ELMO to speak into it.

"We want to learn about the Shadow Princess and the Nibblewart prophecies."

This time, the ELMO's grumbles caused the Nibblewart high priest to stop and turn around.

"Show him a picture of Gruggins," Ethan said.

Hayley tapped at her ELMO, and a holographic Gruggins appeared on her shoulder. The Nibblewart high priest fell to his knees and bowed before them. The others turned away from the fire and fell to their knees as the room filled with low-pitch chants.

"That got their attention. I'm turning the translator to persistent mode. It will allow us to speak freely to them but won't pick up our whispers if we need to speak to one another."

She tapped her ELMO, and Gruggins' holograph disappeared. The Nibblewart high priest stood and walked towards them.

"Master Gruggins asked us to come," she said. "He sent us to learn more about the Nibblewart prophecies and the Shadow Princess."

"Shadow Princess, save Nibblewarts from evil giant," said the high priest. "Shadow Princess disappear long time."

"What do you know of Adara?" Ethan asked.

"Adara become Shadow Princess. Shadow Princess save Nibblewart people. Adara save Nibblewart people."

"I think he's talking about what I saw in my dream," Ethan said to Hayley. "The woman chained to the post must have been Adara. Victor Qruefeldt transformed her into the Shadow Princess, and then she saved the Nibblewarts."

"That sounds like a reasonable explanation," Hayley agreed.

"What does the Shadow Princess want with me?" Ethan asked the high priest.

"Shadow Princess, return. Shadow Princess lead chosen one to Nibblewart prophecies."

"But what are the Nibblewart prophecies?" Hayley asked.

"What was, what is, and what shall be," the priest said.

"Great, he is telling us 'it is what it is,'" Ethan quipped.

Hayley rolled her eyes at Ethan. The Nibblewart high priest stood silently, staring at them as if pondering something. Then he turned around, waved, and spoke.

"Come."

They followed him into another corridor, this one filled with bright purplish light; and as soon as they entered, they understood why. This short corridor ended at a swirling vortex with no path around it.

"He's leading us into that vortex," Ethan said. "I hope he knows where he is going."

Hayley glanced behind them and saw the whole tribe of Nibblewarts was following too.

"I doubt he would lead his whole tribe into a death vortex."

When they reached the mouth of the ominous-looking vortex, the Nibblewart leader did not hesitate and walked through like it was an open door. Ethan and Hayley took a leap of faith and followed. Purple sparks flashed in Ethan's eyes, like when they walked through the negative doorway. When they shook off their dizziness, they found themselves standing in a vast room lit by torches attached to the walls.

"That vortex," said Hayley as she stared at her ELMO. "It was a time portal; we are back to our present time."

In front of them, a vast wall column rose to a very high ceiling. On each side, a stone staircase ascended into the darkness of what was above. On each side of the staircases, more stone flooring led to tall walls on each side of the room. And beyond the wall column, the room stretched into more darkness where no torches were lit.

"Where are we?" Hayley asked.

But the high priest did not answer. Instead, he walked forward towards the tall wall column. He stopped and pointed up at the wall with both of his hands, and he turned towards them.

"Shadow Princess, come here; Nibblewart prophecies, come here."

Ethan peered at the tall empty wall where the high priest was pointing. His gaze continued up the wall towards the ceiling, and that's when he spotted them out of the corner of his eyes. Stealthily creeping down the walls on both sides were vicious black dragons with blue swirls and gleaming green eyes.

"Pixie-devils," Ethan said as he pointed at the walls above.

"Pixie, they look more like real dragons at this size," Hayley said.

Ethan scanned the room and saw glowing green eyes emerging from the darkness behind the column wall. He quickly spun around and spotted the bright light of an exit at the front of the room.

"There's an exit over there," Ethan said to Hayley. "If we make it outside, we may be able to return to size. At least then, we'll have a fighting chance."

A dragon leaped from the wall and landed between Ethan and Hayley and the Nibblewart high priest. The creature inched towards the priest, but his tribe was quick to defend their leader. Four sprang to action and jumped between the beast and their chief. They stabbed at it with spears while others from the tribe shot arrows at the other prowling devils. Ethan grabbed Hayley's hand as she spun around and glanced at him.

"Let's run," Hayley said.

They ran towards the exit as more Nibblewarts leaped into action to fight the attacking pixie-devils. They reached the entrance and continued through, leading them into a giant-sized room. This room was dark too, but they continued running towards the light source, which was the exit.

"We have plenty of space now," Ethan said and stopped running.

Hayley quickly fished out the pouch of dwindle-berries and poured them into her hand. They each grabbed four and gobbled them down. Ethan chewed them to a fine mush before swallowing, and he grew back to size quickly.

Ethan glanced down to where they had just been. A miniature replica of the pyramid site sat on the ground at their feet, and they had emerged from the largest pyramid at its center.

"We were in a model," Hayley said.

The Pyramids of Never

Ethan scanned the rest of the room that was darker towards the back as the only light came from the tall spacious entrance. They were in a huge rectangular room with towering columns rising to the ceiling in the darkness above. One wide aisle split the room down the center from the front entrance to the blackness in the back. The rest of the room consisted of square and rectangular enclosed structures scattered randomly about, dividing it into a maze.

"We are in a mausoleum or something," Hayley said.

"The Nibblewarts won't be able to hold off those pixie-devils forever," Ethan said and motioned for the exit.

A creepy hissing noise echoed from the blackness of the room's depths.

"Let's get out of here," Hayley said.

She grabbed Ethan's hand, and they hurried towards the light and charged through the entrance. Their eyes took a minute to adjust to the bright desert sun. They found themselves on a veranda outside the front of the building. Enormous stone columns rose to support the heavy rooftop of the gothic structure. A massive dune of sand covered the stone floor on the left half of the veranda and blocked most of their view in that direction. Ethan stepped off the stone floor and walked into the desert to scan the horizon to the right.

"You see anything?" Hayley asked from the shade of the veranda.

Suddenly, his feet began to vibrate as a disturbance several hundred feet away churned the sand like ocean waves.

"Harpies," Ethan shouted. "We can't leave this way."

"Get back here," Hayley said.

Ethan hesitated as something caught his attention. A small black shiny object rode the vibrations, floated to the surface, and peeked out from beneath the sand.

"What are you waiting for," Hayley shouted. "They are moving fast."

Ethan turned and ran back to Hayley. They stood watching the harpies from the stone floor of the veranda but retreated inside when they reached jumping distance. Their eyes took another minute to adjust to the darkness inside.

They tiptoed deeper into the building, passed the tiny replica on the floor, and stopped between two of the many structures that divvied up the room.

"We need to keep our eyes open," Ethan whispered.

"But it's so dark in here. I can barely see anything."

"Right, I will keep my eyes open."

They stood quietly, trying to gather their thoughts and find a way out of their predicament.

"I saw something green flash," Hayley said. "Over in that direction."

Ethan looked to where Hayley pointed but saw nothing. He turned to her and spotted a set of green eyes glaring at them from the floor behind her. He shoved Hayley into a dark hallway, dove, rolled away, then jumped to his feet and ran behind one of the structures as a yellow energy beam burst from the pixie-devil's mouth.

"Take cover," he said. "They shoot energy beams from their mouths."

"Where are you?"

"I'm a couple of structures over," he said. "Hang tight, and I will find you."

"When you first encountered the pixie-devils, how did the Shadow Princess save you from them?" Hayley asked.

"She jumped between us and shielded me from them."

"Ahh, that gives me an idea."

Hayley reached into her robe pocket, pulled out her copycat, and whispered as she stroked it. The cat figurine flattened out and widened into a circular shield with a mirrored chrome-like finish. Hayley stood and held the shield up in front of her and stepped out into the center aisle. She could barely see in the darkness, but several glowing green eyes glared back at her, so she advanced toward them. Their little mouths gaped open as yellow light radiated between their sharp teeth. Hayley bent low to the ground as she continued forward and kept her eyes on the pixie-devils about to blast her. She crept into Ethan's view, and he saw what she was doing.

"Where did you find Captain America's shield?" he whispered.

Hayley glanced to her left and spotted Ethan bathed in yellow light reflecting from her shield. He took cover between two of the room's many structures. Then, all at once, the pixie-devils let loose with their energy blasts. All of them hit their mark, striking the shield dead center and showering out in all directions like a fireworks display. Hayley's shield withstood the devil's wrath without a scratch. The room lit up for several seconds as if someone had tossed a yellow road flare in, but the brightness subsided, and the darkness returned.

Ethan's eyes adjusted quickly to the darkness. He glanced at Hayley and noticed something moving in the reflection of her mirrored shield. He peeked around the corner and saw a small battalion of pixie-devils backing away and staring up at something. Their movement stopped in an instant as they quickly turned to stone. The creepy hissing noise returned as Ethan's gaze moved away from the stone devils to where they were looking. At first, he saw another structure, but then a tall snake-like figure moved into view. His veins chilled as the creature slithered towards the still pixie-devils, and the nest of red-eyed serpents swayed back and forth atop her head.

Ethan recalled the first time he saw a likeness of Medusa. Hayley had taken him to The Grimleaver Atrocities Memorial. They met Brianna, mourning in front of her sister Medusa's exhibit. Even the distant memory sent a chill up his spine. Later, he learned more about Medusa while helping Hayley study for Caretaker training. If you look Medusa in the eyes, you'll turn to stone, he repeated in his head.

"Ethan, what's that?"

Medusa spun around, spotted Hayley, and slithered slowly towards her next victim.

"Our worst nightmare," he shouted.

Medusa stopped in her tracks and turned towards Ethan.

"Run!" he shouted.

Hayley bolted for the exit.

Ethan ducked into the nearest hallway and ran deeper into the building, screaming to ensure the serpent followed. He circled around and returned to the wide center aisle he knew would lead to Hayley. But when he stepped into the corridor, Medusa was there blocking his way, so he ducked back into hiding unnoticed by the lurking creature.

"I need something to distract her," Ethan thought as he scanned the floor for rock or debris. He crept down the hall and spotted a damaged wall with a hole blasted through, so he pried some stones free and put them in his pocket. He tiptoed back to the center aisle and peeked around the corner. Medusa was still there, scanning the area and staying as still as possible to listen for any nearby disturbance.

Ethan stepped into the wide aisleway to throw a rock and distract her. But his palm symbols suddenly came to life, bathing him in a white glow as they spun around to point at the back of the room. Medusa saw him and quickly slithered towards her prey at top speed. Ethan clasped his hands together as he bolted across the aisle and down another corridor between two crypt structures. He ducked behind the structure on his right as he tossed a couple of rocks over the adjacent structure. Medusa was right on his tail but did not see his maneuver, so she followed the sound of the rocks when they hit.

Ethan sprang from behind the structure and backtracked to the center path and towards the exit as fast as he could run. Medusa detected his footsteps and followed in hot pursuit. But she stopped and retreated when he reached the bright light at the building's entrance. Hayley stood on the door's threshold, staring into the darkness as Ethan emerged.

"I wasn't sure if you were going to make it," she said.

"I wasn't either. That was close," he replied.

His mind poured over their seemingly meager options. What would be a better way to die—getting buried by sand harpies or turned to stone by Medusa?

"I'd give anything for a portal beacon about now," he said.

Hayley gazed up at him and the glimmer in her eyes told Ethan all he needed to know—she had an idea.

"Ethan, you're a genius."

"I—I am?"

"I don't know why I didn't think of this before. The tether port connects two points in time and space. We've already moved back to the present time, but the tether port is still connected to its location in space."

"Then, if I understand you correctly, it should transport us to my dad's place in Manhattan."

"Yes, unless Dakota reprogrammed it, then who knows when or where we might end up."

"Well, wherever that is, it can't be worse than where we are now."

THE PYRAMIDS OF NEVER

487

THE SAYERS

The tether port transported them to someplace very dark. Ethan stood and helped Hayley to her feet. His eyes were still adjusting, so he only saw what was right in front of him. But he heard something stir, and a loud clapping noise rang out. Candles lit up in succession around the small room they were in. Ethan recognized the small stick creatures with their hands and arms burning in apparent agony.

"Thought ya'd be gone more'n a day," Dakota said from his corner chair. "Are the two a' ya okay?"

"We're fine," Hayley said.

"Did ya learn anything from yer little adventure?"

"Nothing we're going to tell you," Hayley said.

"I'm thinkin' you'n me got off on a wrong foot, little lady."

"I do have one question I have to ask you," Ethan said. "Jason Crowley was there, and he was holding a Heldrik Vonn Grim puzzle box."

"Well, don't that beat all."

"How is that even possible?" Hayley asked. "We were thousands of years in the past. Long before Ethan was ever born, and long before Victor Qruefeldt commissioned the puzzle box."

"Victor Qruefeldt," Dakota said. "He didn't commission Heldrik ta build the box. What gave ya that idea?"

"That's what his plaque says in The Grimleaver Atrocities Memorial."

"Never been ta see it," Dakota said. "Sounds like someone's tryin' ta bury somethin' in the past."

"How can you be so sure?"

"I was 'is apprentice, remember," Dakota said. "Someone commissioned the box long before anyone'd ever heard a Victor Qruefeldt. I remember, plain as day, Heldrik worked day an' night tryin' ta figure out how to power the darn thing. He was stumped. Then, one day, he received a strange letter an 'is problems were solved."

"What did the letter say?" Ethan asked.

"Dunno, I didn't see it – but Heldrik described it to me. Wasn't till years later I realized what he was describin' was a leap-letter."

The room fell silent as Ethan and Hayley absorbed what Dakota had told them. Ethan remembered when they witnessed Daavic send a leap-letter. He didn't even know what one was, but Hayley explained they were telegrams sent backward in time.

"Well, we better be going, Hayley said to break the silence. But first, this is for you."

She handed the tether port to Dakota.

"Thank you for letting us use this," she said. "You won't tell my mother—will you?"

A huge smile appeared below Dakota's thick mustache.

"Heavens no, little lady. I think we may 'ave just regained our footin'. This'll be our little secret."

They left Dakota's shack and were near The Hall of Doorways when Hayley stopped abruptly.

"What?"

"Leap-letters," Hayley said. "Daavic sent one to Victor to relay information from the future. Now, we learn a leap-letter helped Heldrik complete the most dangerous weapon ever created."

"Yeah—but where are you going with this?"

"I'm wondering how often they've used leap-letters and if there's anything we can do to stop them."

"Good question," said Ethan. "All I know is, anything to do with time travel boggles my mind."

The sound of Hayley's ELMO ringing interrupted their conversation. Tinx was calling to tell them she would not be available for breakfast. They scheduled her family's unveiling for first thing in the morning, which lasted till noon. Hayley assured Tinx, they'd miss her company but would visit her immediately afterward, and asked if they could bring her something from the dining hall. Tinx was grateful and sounded relieved her two friends would be by her side.

They arrived at The Grimleaver Atrocities Memorial promptly after breakfast. Hayley brought Tinx a small plate of cricket toast so she would have something in her belly. They stopped at the golden plaque inside the entrance. Ethan glanced down a corridor to their left and spotted Brianna coiled up in front of her sister's memorial where they first met. Her head, full of green tube-like worms, smiled and glistened as Brianna turned to flash him a smile.

"I think our destination is over there to the right," Hayley said. "That's where we mourn the smaller victims."

Ethan turned to where Hayley was pointing.

"Yeah, kinda hard to miss with Azron standing there."

They walked over to join Azron and Tinx in front of the display, which was exceptionally bright due to the two extra light beetles assigned for this special day. The display sat upon a sizeable golden pedestal and depicted Tinx's cousin in her original form on the left side. On the right stood a black and blue pixie-devil that Ethan and Hayley were all too familiar with.

"Hey Tinx. Hey Azron," Ethan and Hayley said as they arrived.

Azron nodded to them and attempted to wink by wrinkling his forehead and closing his only eye. Hayley's thoughtfulness pleased Tinx, and she made quick work of the cricket toast.

"Boy, you must have been hungry," Hayley said.

"Yeah, I'm not used to skipping breakfast."

"Has anyone else been by?" Ethan asked.

"Brianna stopped by earlier," Tinx said. "And Azron has been here all morning."

Ethan glanced down the aisle, and Brianna still looked at him, her worm hairs moving back and forth as if waving at him.

"I'm sure the others will stop by, too," said Hayley.

"No, they won't. The Headmistress already informed me it's all hands on deck. Everybody is too busy thwarting Grimleavers' plans. I'm going to cut this short today. I'm not serving anybody by standing around here when I can be helping elsewhere."

"Makes sense, I guess," Ethan said. "I'm surprised Azron and Brianna were able to come."

"Azron, no look human," Azron said. "Brianna, no look human. No look normal for human world."

They stuck around for another fifteen minutes making small talk, then agreed to meet Tinx in Damien's laboratory later in the day when he'd be available. Hayley gave Tinx a wink when Azron wasn't looking to let her know they had some juicy news to share. Hayley noticed Brianna's apparent interest in them on their way out, so they made a quick detour.

"Hi Brianna," Hayley said as they stopped by her sister's display.

Ethan's skin tingled when he peered at Medusa's hideous figure and recalled their close encounter the day before.

"I came here today," Brianna said. "Sss-seeking you out."

"How can we help?" Ethan asked.

She turned to Hayley.

"What have you learned of my species?"

"I know you are serpeneze," Hayley said, "but I haven't learned much about your species yet."

"Serpeneze sss-sisters share a powerful bond. When Medusa and I were young, we barely needed to speak to know how one another felt."

"Yeah," said Hayley, "sounds like telepathy."

"When they took her from me," Brianna turned away from them as she continued. "I wondered if our bond would change, and if so, how."

"And did it?"

"In our case, it did change. I no longer feel what she feels," she said and spun around to face them. "But I do often see through my sister's eyes. I've seen nearly every corner of the dark mausoleum she wanders."

Ethan and Hayley glanced at the shock on one another's faces as Brianna spoke.

"Sss-so imagine my surprise when I watched through my sister's eyes as she chased after and nearly killed you both."

"We—we can explain," said Ethan.

"Promise you won't tell my mother," Hayley said.

"I've been looking for her for so long. Tell me where she is, right now, and I won't tell a soul."

"We can't tell you exactly where she is because we don't fully know ourselves," Hayley answered.

"What nonsense is this? I saw her chasing after the both of you."

"Please give us a chance to explain Brianna," Ethan said, "we are meeting with Tinx and Damien this afternoon in his laboratory. Join us, and we will explain everything." Afternoon arrived fast, and Damien was the last to arrive.

"I love what you've done with the place," Brianna said as she reached the foot of the stairs.

"Brianna, what a lovely surprise," he said and glanced at Ethan and Hayley.

"I didn't mean to crash your little party," she said to Damien. "But these two know the whereabouts of my sister."

"Not exactly," Hayley said.

"Out with it," Damien said. "I've only got an hour – so tell us what this is all about."

"It all started with the Nibblewarts," Ethan said.

He opened the poem book and set it down on the nearest lab bench for them to read.

"Wordly told us about a painting in the Alcove of Enigma," said Hayley. "So we went to see for ourselves."

"We wondered about the little hippy caveman creatures," Ethan said. "And the poem appeared."

"Interesting," Damien said.

"We ran to Gruggins' box, and that's when we saw them," Hayley said.

"They left as soon as we arrived," Ethan said. "But I saw a mini-Jasper following them, and he motioned for us to follow too."

"We followed them into The Hall of Doorways," Hayley said. "They turned right, and we followed them to a negative door."

"They used the forbidden doors," Brianna said. "Why would they be traveling into the past?"

"I've been wondering the same thing," said Hayley. "Gruggins says they pass through often – so I think they travel back and forth a lot."

"They must have a reason for doing so," Damien said.

"All we saw them do was eat rocks," Ethan said.

"Yeah, until we scared them away."

"They may have specific dietary needs," said Damien. "If only we had a sample of that rock, we might learn something."

"Here, I grabbed these to distract Medusa," Ethan said as he reached into his pocket and pulled out a hand full of rocks. "These aren't the exact ones they were eating, but they look and feel the same."

Damien held his ELMO over the rocks – and a beam of light scanned across them.

"Very interesting. These rocks are from a Ceresian bloating stone."

"Aren't those prohibited on Earth?" Brianna asked. "I've never heard of such a thing."

"Wait a minute," Ethan said. "What is a Ceresian bloating stone?"

"A form of rock found on Ceres," Hayley said. "When exposed to water, they expand, almost limitlessly depending on the size of the water source."

"Which is why we outlawed bringing them to Earth," Brianna said. "If exposed to Earth's oceans, who knows what havoc might ensue."

"What's even more interesting," Damien said, "is that these rocks were not grown using earthly water. According to my ELMO, Atlantian water hydrated them."

"But why go to all that trouble?" Brianna asked.

"Good question," Damien said.

"We can discuss that later," Hayley said. "Let us continue with what happened."

"Agreed," Brianna said. "And most importantly, where my sister is."

"But that's what we are trying to tell you," Hayley said. "We don't know where your sister is. Not exactly."

"Explain," Brianna said.

"We scared the Nibblewarts away. So we took some dwindle-berries and followed them into a series of small tunnels. We spoke with them and talked them into trusting us. They led us through another time portal into the present time, but we have no idea where we were."

"How did you return to The Residence if you didn't know where you were?" Damien asked.

"We used the tether port we took for the trip back from the past," Hayley said.

"Great thinking," Damien said. "But if you'd have used a portal beacon, we'd be able to trace the location."

"We didn't think we'd need one," Hayley admitted, "so we didn't take a portal beacon."

Damien looked at his sister and furrowed his brows.

"I know, I know," she said. "I should never leave The Residence without a few portal beacons—"

"So, I'm no closer to finding my sister," Brianna interrupted with a deep sigh.

"It doesn't look like it," Ethan said.

"What did the Nibblewarts say?" Damien asked. "Maybe there are clues."

"They told us about the Shadow Princess," Hayley said. "They said she will lead the chosen one to the Nibblewart prophecies."

"The Nibblewarts are a mush-mouthed little species who have spewed gibberish for centuries," Brianna said. "Nibblewart prophecies would be of interest to absolutely nobody."

"True," Damien said. "Nobody regards what they say with esteem, and they won't likely start now."

"But they speak the truth," Ethan said. "The Shadow Princess has come to me, and I have visions of her trying to tell me something."

"I saw her once myself," Hayley added. "And I was able to speak to her."

"You've got my attention," Damien said.

"You've got mine too," Brianna said.

"This poem, The Nibblewarts," Ethan said. "It has something to do with a dream I had. I saw Victor Qruefeldt use the puzzle box on Princess Adara and try to kill her. I think she was one of the Sayers, but something went wrong, and the puzzle box didn't kill her. It shocked him at first, but he used the box again, and it sucked her inside."

"Do you know anything about these Sayers?" Brianna asked.

"No, only that they have giant blue eyes," Ethan said. "I'm mostly reading between the lines and making connections that may or may not be right."

"You're doing great. Keep going," said Hayley.

"Well, I-I think the Sayers and Seers are somehow related, but I'm not sure how."

"What became of them?" Damien asked.

"I don't know what happened to them after Adara disappeared. But a Caretaker woman was present when they rose from the desert sand. If we find out who she was, she might be able to tell us something."

"You may find your answer," Damien said. "Your Seer friends have more to say."

Wisps of golden whimsy wafted from the poem book as the pages turned to the next blank page, and a passage wrote itself backward. When it finished, the passage read:

The Shadow Princess

She appeared from out of nowhere, with piercing yellow eyes.
Pointing out the dangers, that crept down from the skies.

She tries to speak but is not heard, it's an unfamiliar sound.
Understood by the one and only, whom together she was bound.

Devolved from Seer spirit, as a favor for a friend.
For reasons that will become known, in the messages we send.

Seek out the friend of Stravis, the oracle of her day.
And behold the Shadow Princess, as she strives to lead the
way.

"Your grandmother—I thought she was holding something back."

"Me too," Hayley said. "Her reaction when I said the Shadow Princess' name was Adara was suspicious. She knows more about what's happening than she told us."

"Well then," said Damien, "it's time to visit dear Grandma. But first, I must tell our mother something important has come up."

Damien pulled out his ELMO, tapped the screen, and stepped away to speak with the Headmistress.

"I'm glad you called," Jordanna's voice echoed from the ELMO. "Have you seen Brianna? I need you both in the Map Room."

"She's with me, but you'll have to do without us. Something important has come up. I will explain later."

"Does this have anything to do with our other thing?"

"Yes," Damien said, "and I believe it is about to bear fruit."

"Okay, we will make do for now. But give me an update as soon as you learn more."

Damien tucked his ELMO into his robe and turned to face his sister as she stared at him with her hands on her hips.

"What was she talking about?" Hayley asked. "Our other thing is Ethan and me. Isn't it?"

"Yes."

"But I trusted you. How could you betray my trust?"

"How did you think this little arrangement happened?" Damien asked. "I spoke to her on your behalf, and she agreed to stop being overly protective. But only under the condition that I gain your trust and keep a close eye on you."

"We have been able to come and go as we please," said Ethan.

"True, I guess," Hayley said. "But he's been telling her everything we've been up to."

"You haven't exactly been giving me regular updates – and I've been much looser than our mother is comfortable with."

Hayley conceded her brother was looking out for her best interests and trying to maintain the peace between her and Jordanna. Besides, they had bigger Ravenwood fish to fry.

"So, how do we find our grandmother's creepy castle?"

"Follow me," Damien said.

He led the others up the stairs in the front room, where he proceeded up its never-ending staircase. They continued their ascent to the thirteenth floor and turned right on the landing, which led them to a dark hallway where two torches burned at its entryway. Damien grabbed one for himself and handed the other to Brianna.

"I'll take the lead, and you bring up the rear."

They entered the narrow hallway and followed Damien for several minutes before reaching a thick wooden door framed in iron. Damien slowly pulled the creaky door open and side-stepped through it. The others followed and found themselves at a clearing at the foot of a small mountain.

"How much farther?" Hayley asked.

"The castle is at the top of this hill," Damien said and pointed to the black silhouette of a castle.

The night was dark, windy, and raining as they started up a steep path winding its way to the mountain's top. The torches barely lit their way as they fought to stay burning – but the constant flash of lightning helped them on their way. Surprisingly, the journey took only twenty minutes to reach the top, where they found themselves at the entrance to a giant castle.

"I think we've found Count Dracula's house," Ethan said.

They made their way over the stone steps leading to an enormous front door. Damien raised his fist to knock, but the door slowly creaked open. Light from inside showered through the door as a tall, white faced butler appeared. He wore a pinstriped tuxedo with a red rose corsage pinned to the lapel, and he looked like a department store dummy had come to life.

"Irvin, what are you doing here?" Ethan asked.

"Irvin—" the butler said in a flat, monotone voice. "You must have me confused with my goofball of a brother. My name is Melvin McGillicutty, and the madam is awaiting your arrival."

"Thank you, Melvin," Damien said. "She is expecting us?"

"Yes, they are waiting in the sitting room," Melvin said, "right this way."

"I know the way," Damien said as he entered and beelined past Melvin.

They followed Damien through an expansive foyer, past a double staircase, and into a large room. A fire burned in an enormous fireplace that reminded Ethan of the study at The Residence. Vanessa and Dakota Drakelan stood to greet them as they entered.

"Greetings," Vanessa said.

She nodded at Brianna, Damien, and Tinx as she strode by them to face Ethan and Hayley.

"So, your journey has led you here," she said. "The questions you seek answers to are finally ready for answers."

"Show her the passage," Hayley said to Ethan.

He fished out the poem book, turned to the correct page, and handed it to Vanessa.

"What can you tell us about this?"

Vanessa read the Seers' new passage and paused.

"This refers to the second visit Stravis paid Odin and me. He came to ask me for a favor."

"You? Why you and not grampa Odin?"

"Because Odin was now the Caretaker headmaster. Stravis wanted him protected from any fallout if anyone exposed us."

"Sounds ominous," said Damien. "What was he asking you to do?"

Vanessa sighed.

"The Seers required certain skills only Caretakers possess. But to accomplish what they were asking, I had to break our most sacred rule."

"What rule? What did you do?" Damien asked.

"She created the Sayers," said Ethan.

Vanessa nodded and stared at the floor. Ethan gazed at her, and a light turned on in his head as the picture became clear.

"How? Caretakers do not have powers of creation," Hayley said.

"She didn't create anything," Ethan said.

Vanessa nodded.

"What Ethan says is true. The Seers are a very evolved lifeform. The only way to create a humanoid from them is to devolve them."

"Oh, so that's the rule you broke," Hayley said.

"Yes—and in return, the Seers gifted me with second sight. Though I often wonder if their gift is not a curse cast down upon me for breaking the most sacred of our oaths."

"But if you devolved the Seers," said Hayley. "Who is communicating with Ethan?"

"I didn't devolve them all, only a select few who volunteered for the mission."

"What mission?"

"The Sayers' mission was to bring the word of the Seers to the Caretakers. They were to deliver the portal prophecies described in the Book of Creators."

"I think I'm beginning to understand," Ethan said. "I witnessed part of it in my dream. Victor Qruefeldt had them all chained together. He used the puzzle box to turn Princess Adara into the Shadow Princess. But I don't know what became of the rest of them."

"Because your dream was incomplete," Vanessa said. "Let me show you what your dream did not."

She approached Ethan slowly, reached up, and pressed her left hand against his temple. Ethan's eyes shut. And when they opened, his eyes were white, and he was in a trance.

"What are you doing to him?" Hayley asked.

"Filling in the blanks," said Vanessa.

Ethan's head shook, and his eyes returned to normal. His brows furrowed, and his eyes widened as his head moved from Hayley to Damien and back to Hayley.

"The answers have been staring me in the face this whole time."

"What answers?"

"The poem even spells them out: Attempts to kill them failed, and the Nibblewarts were born."

"What are you saying?"

"Don't you see? Victor couldn't kill the Sayers with the puzzle box – so he devolved them into Nibblewarts."

"Yes," said Vanessa, "I had a vision long ago and witnessed some of the horrors – but I lacked context. As time passed, it became clear the Seers left me with a piece of a puzzle – but it would be up to others to solve. I didn't know the shadow spirit was Adara, until Hayley told me. But then I had an epiphany, the two of you are the ones. You are meant to find the fortress and uncover the truth."

The room fell silent as they absorbed Ethan and Vanessa's words.

"The Nibblewart prophecies," Damien said. "If what you say is true, the portal prophecies and the Nibblewart prophecies are one and the same."

"Yes—and the Nibblewart high priest showed us where they would appear," Hayley said. "In *The Pyramids of Never.*"

Ethan froze as his mind drifted, and past scenes replayed in his head. He skipped through them like flashcards. He was on the back of a sand slug watching his palm symbols follow the vanishing dune across the horizon. Then he was in a bubble looking down at a structure half-buried in the giant dune. In a flash, he stood inside the building with the Shadow Princess. Next, he was in the Alcove of Enigma, looking at a painting of a pyramid construction site. Then, in a flash, he was inside the central pyramid with the Shadow Princess.

"All this time, she was trying to tell me something," Ethan whispered to himself.

His mind raced, and now he stood in the sand staring at a small black shiny object as a legion of desert harpies approached.

"But how is that even possible," he whispered.

The scene flashed again, and he was in the library with Hayley, and she was talking as his gaze wandered to an article called *Magnetic Maelstrom.*

"Ethan, did you hear me?" Hayley asked. "Snap out of it."

He shook his head and looked at the others with a broad smile perched upon his lips.

"Yes, you said *The Pyramids of Never*, and I just figured out where they've been hiding all this time."

MEDUSA

Ethan told the others he was sure of his theory, but he wanted to show them rather than tell them. To do so required the Map Room, where Jordanna was meeting with other CAGE members. But that worked out perfectly because they would report any critical news to her anyway. They entered the Map Room and headed for the crow's nest, where they heard Jordanna and Nicholas speaking.

"The Grimleavers have increased their attacks since acquiring their own portal plane," she said.

"We expected that," Nicholas said. "Thus far, we've been able to keep things under control."

"Great—and have we learned anything from implementing Damien's idea?"

"Yes, I am told the algorithms are beginning to bear fruit. The Grimleaver attacks are not as random as they might appear."

The group reached the top of the stairs and stepped onto the crow's nest platform. Jordanna and Nicholas spun around in their chairs and appeared surprised.

"You've brought an entourage," Jordanna said. "What brings you all?"

"Important news, Mother," said Damien.

"Ethan knows where they hid *The Pyramids of Never*," Hayley said.

"*The Pyramids of Never*," Jordanna said. "What are you talking about?"

"The pyramids themselves are not important," Damien said. "But what's inside will interest you. If what they tell me is correct, the central pyramid holds the portal prophecies foretold by the Book of Creators."

Jordanna stood, approached Ethan, and peered into his eyes.

"You've found the prophecies? Please, tell us what you know."

"I-I can't be sure, but with the help of the Map Room, I was hoping to prove my theory."

"The floor is yours," Jordanna said. "Tell her what you need."

"Hi, Map Room," Ethan said awkwardly.

"Hello, Ethan Fox," a soft feminine voice said. She reminded him of George's Alexa back home. "How may I assist you today?"

"Headmaster Odin Ravenwood reported visiting a construction site in the desert. Do you have any records of that?"

"Scanning archive," the voice said. "Yes, I have located several references."

"Great! Could you please show us the location on a map?"

The spherical room's walls lit up, and a giant globe of Earth surrounded them. The globe spun around and shrunk smaller as it did until a large holographic globe of Earth hung in the air. A black dot appeared over a desert in northern Africa.

"This is where Odin reported the site," the voice said. "And where he later sent a Caretaker survey team."

"Okay, keep showing that, but also show us the location of the great vanishing dune."

"The vanishing dune is in one of the protected realms," the voice said. "And not accessible from the human world."

"If the protected realm was part of the human world, can you show us where it would be physically located?"

"Affirmative, plotting now."

Another black dot appeared on the map halfway across the continent.

"You can't be suggesting these two locations are somehow related," Nicholas said. "They are deserts apart."

"How do Caretakers determine location?" Ethan asked.

"It's quite embarrassing, actually," Damien said. "These days, we use human GPS satellites."

"But in Odin's day, human GPS did not yet exist. So, how did you do it then?"

"The same way everybody used to," Hayley said. "We used Earth's magnetic field."

"That's what I thought," Ethan said. "Computer, can you reference articles from *The Residential Daily Star*?"

"If you are referring to me, the answer is yes. But I am an artificial intelligence and do not appreciate being called a computer."

"Please accept my apology. Can you find an article titled *Magnetic Maelstrom*?"

"Yes, the article details an abrupt shift in Earth's magnetic field," the voice said.

"Great. Now, using a different color, plot where Odin's reported location would have fallen before the shift."

"Re-plotting."

A green dot appeared on the map at the same spot as the vanishing dune.

"They used an old magician's trick," Damien said.

"Sleight of hand," Ethan said.

"The pyramids have been hidden beneath the vanishing dune all along," said Hayley.

"Yes, and Brianna's sister is there too," Ethan said. "She's inside the structure we flew over that was half-buried in the dune."

"Sss-she is protecting something. She patrols the dark depths of that mausoleum like it's her life's mission."

"We've already determined something is cloaking the dune whenever anyone gets close," Ethan said. "I believe we will find whatever is doing that inside the structure."

"We must dispatch a team immediately," Damien said.

"How do you propose we get past the desert harpies?" Nicholas asked. "The desert is their domain, and we have no chance of defeating them."

"I'm afraid the point is moot anyway," said Jordanna. "After we cleaned out Stravis' bunker, I had the *Sand Miser Dune* portal destroyed."

"Why would you—"

"We don't need it," Ethan said. "Hayley dropped a portal beacon when we floated over the dune. I didn't realize it was a portal beacon at the time, but when we followed the Nibblewarts there, I saw a shiny black object in the sand near the entrance."

"You mean when desert harpies almost overran you," Hayley said.

"Yes—but the beacon is not far from the entrance. If we distract the harpies, that will buy us the time to run to the entrance."

"That's a fantastic idea," Damien said. "I'll rig up a small sounding device to mimic approaching nomads. If we transport Tinx first, she can drop it in the desert, far enough away to buy us all the time we need."

"Great, we have a plan for getting there," said Jordanna. "But we still need a plan for defeating Medusa."

"I will handle my sister. I sss-see through her eyes and feel through her skin, which will give me an advantage."

Ethan and Hayley glanced at one another. They knew Brianna was fibbing and wanted a chance to save her sister.

"Even if I believed you could defeat your sister," Jordanna said. "I would not—"

"What about Dakota Drakelan?" Hayley interrupted. "He's a dark master. He might be able to defeat Medusa with a little help from his friends."

Ethan's eyes widened at Hayley's sudden fondness for Dakota.

"He's retired. Sleep is about all that old codger does anymore," Jordanna said. "But I will consider it."

"Well, I'd hate to throw another wrench into the mix, but what about the dune itself," Nicholas said. "How do we move a mountain of sand so vast?"

"I've been pondering that question," Damien said. "The winds should have dispersed a dune that enormous long ago."

"If that's true," Ethan said. "I'd bet the answers to that also lie inside the structure."

"Very well. I will speak with Dakota Drakelan. Brianna, Damien, Ethan, Hayley, and Tinx will accompany us to the site. Nicholas, you will stay behind to lead our operations while I am gone."

"You—you're going to let me go along," Hayley said to her mother.

"You've earned it, my dear. And I'm fully aware you've already lived through many dangerous encounters since Ethan's return."

Hayley smiled, approached her mother, and they embraced.

"Thank you, Mom, for believing in me."

"But don't expect me not to worry. I am your mother, after all."

Nicholas was not happy with Jordanna's decision to leave he and Azron behind, but he followed her orders as he always did. Damien would need some time to craft the miniature sounding device while Jordanna made the rest of the arrangements. But the team would be ready to leave at sunrise—vanishing dune time.

Tinx was the first to arrive, as planned. She book-traveled to *The Glass Pillars of Nym* and flew the rest of the way to be safe. They couldn't risk her losing consciousness and being swallowed up by the harpies before the mission started.

"Wooo-hooo," she roared to herself. She darted over the vanishing dune and started her descent at full speed. Tinx was ecstatic about finally going on a real mission fully sanctioned by the Headmistress.

Damien estimated the harpies traveled through the sand at about twenty miles per hour. So she continued two miles past the structure as he instructed. That would be close enough to attract the harpies but not trigger the cloak, which made the trip roughly a six minute one-way journey. Tinx stopped suddenly and hovered midair as she climbed to approximately one hundred feet above the desert floor. She dropped the device and let it plunge to the ground. The fall from that height would awaken the device and alert Damien's ELMO that it was time to move.

The team stood on the black-and-white checkered plane, waiting single file next to a beacon of light rising skyward from one of the squares.

"Where is Dakota Drakelan?" Hayley asked.

"He promised he would be there," Jordanna said. "But he hates portal beacons, so he said he would find his own way."

Damien's ELMO signaled the activation of the sounding device.

"Okay, now we wait until they are five minutes from the structure," Damien said. "That should give us plenty of time if the beacon is as close as Ethan described."

Five minutes later, the team walked single file into the light and disappeared from the checkerboard plane. After nearly a minute, they regained their balance and shook off the effects. Ethan spun on his feet and spotted the temple entrance. But it was much farther away than he remembered, and they were in a broad depression in the sand, so the trek would be uphill.

"The entrance was much closer before," he said. "They must have moved the beacon."

"This is going to be a close call," Damien said. "But if we run, we should all make it."

The team took off running – but it was a slow trod uphill through the thick sand. Brianna slithered like a sidewinder, so the trip only took her a couple of minutes. She waited on the veranda and watched the harpies turning up the sand in the distance.

"Hurry, they're getting close," Brianna said a couple of minutes later.

The team was still a hundred feet away, and the harpies were closing the distance fast. Tinx darted past them and quickly saw their dilemma. She stopped in front of Brianna's face and hovered.

"Did you bring your ELMO?"

"Yes," Brianna said.

"Tune it to a human radio station, turn the volume as high as possible, and put it in my claws."

Brianna quickly did what Tinx asked. The miniature dragon darted straight up into the sky, past the approaching harpies, and dropped the ELMO. It plunged to the ground and landed a few hundred feet behind the school of harpies. They instantly stopped, turned around, and swirled into attack formation. They surrounded the ELMO and churned the sand into a whirlpool that slowly swallowed the device to the tune of Eddie Van Halen's *Eruption*.

The team made it to the safety of the veranda and stopped to catch their breaths as the attacking harpies calmed to a quiet stir.

"That was a close call," Jordanna said.

"You would not have made it," Brianna said, "if not for Tinx's quick thinking."

"Yes, it appears my daughter is not the only one I've underestimated."

They entered the dark temple cautiously. Brianna's head worms glowed green to help light their way while the others held up their ELMOs to see where they were going.

"Medusa must be sleeping," Brianna whispered. "I'm unable to see through her eyes."

"Over here is the tiny scale model of the whole complex," whispered Ethan as he motioned the others to follow.

They approached the small model on the floor and stopped when they spotted something on the ground moving towards them. The tiny object grew larger with each step closer until finally, they could recognize Dakota Drakelan returning to size.

"You followed the Nibblewarts," Hayley said to Dakota.

"Ain't gonna let you an Ethan have all the fun."

"I don't want to know," Jordanna said as her eyes moved back and forth from Dakota to Hayley.

"Medusa has awakened," Brianna said. "She is moving quickly towards our light."

No sooner had she said the words than the serpent slithered from the shadows and let out a piercing hiss that echoed through the building like a screeching owl. Dakota backed away as she crept between him and the rest of the group. Everyone else backed away except for Brianna, who inched her way closer to her sister.

"Remember, don't look into her eyes," Jordanna said.

Brianna closed her eyes and continued forward. The green tube worms on her head danced from side to side and glowed brighter as if trying to hypnotize Medusa. But that angered the nest of vipers on Medusa's head. Their eyes burned with laser-like intensity as their black bodies lunged at Brianna like a team of snapping turtles.

Dakota quietly knelt and set down three small creatures on the ground. Balder, Gilly, and Skronk scurried away and disappeared into the darkness.

"Please, sister, let us help you," Brianna said. "The Hybrid Child is here, and he may be able to—"

The girth of Medusa's lower body swiftly whipped around like a catapult and slammed into Brianna's side. The impact launched Brianna at the others like a cannonball. Ethan tackled Hayley to the ground just as Brianna sailed over their heads and slammed into Damien and Jordanna, sending them to the ground. Ethan struggled to his feet as Medusa beelined towards them. Hayley jumped to her feet, stepped in front of Ethan, and held her shield in front of their faces. Medusa was nearly on top of them but backed away from the sight of her own reflection.

Balder, Gilly, and Skronk emerged from the shadows from different directions. They were now gigantic versions of themselves and ready for a fight. Balder grabbed Medusa from behind, ensnaring her head and upper torso in his hooked tentacles. Skronk wrapped his long arms around the circumference of her lower torso, while Gilly caught her tail in his mouth to stop her stabbing attacks. Medusa's head vipers closed their eyes, and she gradually stopped struggling. Hayley lowered her shield as the others rose to their feet, and Brianna approached her entangled sister.

But it was all a ruse, and the viper's piercing red eyes opened. Half of them snapped at Balder's tentacles while the other half spit acid at Gilly. Medusa's body writhed fiercely, so Skronk tightened his grip on her lower torso. But one of the acid spurts hit Gilly in his right antenna eye, causing the mouth at the end of his tail to lose its grip. The dagger-like tip of Medusa's tail darted forward and hovered in front of Ethan and Hayley, who froze in place. The tail danced slowly from side to side as if deciding which one to kill. Medusa's tail thrust at Ethan but hit the shield Brianna swatted from Hayley's hands to block the strike. Ethan jumped back as the shield fell to the ground. Medusa's tail lurched back, readying for another strike, but this time at Hayley.

"No!!!" Ethan shouted.

Everything around him slowed as he watched Medusa's tail lurch forward. He jumped into action and ran towards Hayley, hoping to push her out of the way. But then, he froze as if a giant invisible hand had suddenly grabbed hold of him. Something moving at normal speed caught his attention. He turned and saw Dakota Drakelan approaching with his hand raised, and he was speaking unintelligibly.

Medusa's tail swiftly thrust forward as everything returned to normal speed. At first, it appeared to disappear into Hayley's chest but then reflected out. It continued its path forward, burying itself in Medusa's own chest and impaling her. Medusa curled up and writhed in pain as her hair-vipers' eyes grew faint.

"Release her now," Brianna shouted.

Balder and Skronk released their grip, and Medusa's body fell to the floor. Brianna rushed to her sister's side and began to weep.

"Ethan, your palms," Hayley said.

Ethan raised his hands, and when he saw them glowing green, he somehow understood what to do. He ran to Brianna's side and held his palms against her dying sister. The color of Medusa's skin changed beneath his hands, and a new pigment quickly swam over her entire body bringing back her natural shade of greenish blue. The black nest of vipers transformed, too, returning to the same green tube-like worms on her sister's head.

"B-Brianna, I thought we'd never find each other again," Medusa said in a barely audible whisper.

"I'm so sorry," Brianna cried. "I came here to save you."

"It'sss not your fault. I left you no choice. You've always made the right choices, and even though you're my baby sister, I've always looked up to you."

Tears streamed down Brianna's cheeks as the life slowly drained from her sister.

"Please, promise me one thing," Medusa said.

"Anything."

"Don't waste time mourning over me. Get on with your life," she said as her eyes closed and her body went limp for one final time.

Brianna buried her face in her sister's chest and wept uncontrollably while the others stood by quietly and let her mourn.

THE NIBBLEWART PROPHECIES

Brianna grieved for several moments, and when she finished, her lower body coiled as she rose and turned to Ethan.

"That was a very precious gift," she said.

"But—I didn't save her."

"No—but you allowed us one final moment together. And for that, I will be forever in your debt."

Brianna turned to Jordanna with a determined look in her face.

"Let's get on with it," she said. "Let's find out what they enslaved my sister to protect."

Dakota Drakelan stepped out into the open and clapped his hands together.

"Well, if yer lookin' ta see in this crypt of a place, I'll start by removin' the darkness."

He waved his hands in a circle over his head and whispered unintelligible words. The building's interior slowly grew brighter as the darkness in the room condensed into ever-shrinking clouds. The smaller they shrank, the lighter the room got. And when they finished, black baseball-sized orbs hovered overhead all around the room. There were no apparent light sources around, yet everything was visible from one end of the room to the other.

"She sss-spent most of her time in the back," Brianna said and pointed. "That's where we will find what she was protecting."

"That's where my palm symbols pointed," Ethan whispered to Hayley. "When I was hiding from Medusa the first time that we were here."

They followed Brianna down the center aisle into the room's previously pitch-dark back half. The end of the corridor led to a clearing where two odd contraptions stood. Each half of the clearing housed a device, and a short wall of stones divided the two.

"Well, there's the cloaking device," Damien said.

He walked to the left and stood by the tall device. The bottom part was a shiny black metallic cylinder, tapering from top to bottom, and was taller than Damien. The top consisted of an enormous flattened-out transparent glass sphere that reminded Ethan of a giant skipping stone.

"Yeah, I've seen those in my Caretaker studies," Hayley said. "But I want to find out what this is. I haven't seen one of these."

Hayley stood next to the sizable flat black cube sitting at the center of the right side of the clearing. She bent down to inspect the ribbed ridges covering the cube's surface.

"Be careful little lady. Ya don't wanna be touchin' that till I see what's inside."

"You know what that is?"

"Looks like a giant HVG puzzle box," said Ethan.

"Astute observation – but if yer lookin' ta win a prize, I'm fresh out."

"What are you talking about?" Jordanna asked. "What is it?"

"Don't know exactly. Seen a lotta different contraptions that looked similar. Heldrik had a thing 'bout black boxes. Said they were his signature."

"So Heldrik Vonn Grim created that," Damien said as he hopped the stone wall and dashed over.

"Yep, but yer all gonna have ta stand back while I peek inside. Could be any sorta danger inside."

Everyone backed away.

"Or—could be a bowl of fruit," Dakota said with a chuckle. "Heldrik was an odd sort."

The others looked on as Dakota rubbed his hands together and placed them on each side of the box. He hunched down to put his ear against the lid. He repeated the process from each side of the cube.

"Stand back a little more," Dakota said as he stood and walked to the front of the box. "I'm a fixin' ta open 'er up."

They backed away and watched as Dakota rubbed his hands together again. He bent down and held them out over the top of the box and whispered unintelligible words. Bright beams of red light radiated up and showered his face as the lid slowly slid open and disappeared. Dakota studied the insides of the box for several quiet moments.

"Can I have a look?" Damien asked.

"Sure! If yer keen ta havin' another moon-shaped pupil, come take a peek."

Damien took Dakota's warning to heart and stayed back while the old master studied his mentor's handy work. Then he stood tall, snapped his fingers, and the lid slid back in place.

"Well?" Jordanna asked.

"I'm familiar with it," Dakota said, "an if I recall correctly, I helped build the prototype. But this one's far more complex than the one I remember."

"Are you going to tell us what it is?" Tinx asked.

"Gimme a minute," said Dakota. "First, I need more information. Tell me, have ya run inta any sorta infestation in these parts?"

"We encountered pixie-devils our first time here," Ethan said.

"Nah, them are of Grimleaver origin. I'm talkin' more like rodents or any kinda vermin with a hive-like behavior."

"The desert harpies," Hayley said. "They protect the whole outside area around this place."

"Very good little lady," Dakota said and smiled. "If I did have a prize, it'd go ta you."

"What are you getting at?" Tinx asked.

"Can one of ya lemme borrow yer little ELMO gizmo?"

Hayley stepped forward and handed Dakota her ELMO. He held it up and tapped the screen as he headed towards the building's entrance. The others quietly followed him onto the veranda but stopped when he walked out into the desert. In no time, the harpies were churning up the sand and headed towards him. Dakota stood calmly, stared at the ELMO screen, and scanned the harpies as they drew closer. He turned towards the vanishing dune, scanned from its base to its peak, and returned to the veranda just as the harpies arrived.

"Interestin'. No wonder this one's so complicated."

Jordanna and the others followed Dakota inside and down the center aisle to the black box.

"Well," Jordanna said as she placed her hands on her hips. "What is it?"

"Better question might be, who're they?"

"They're desert harpies," Hayley said. "Everyone knows that."

"That's what this device has scattered em inta. But desert harpies don't exist, really. They're merely part of a bigger whole, and most 'a that bigger whole's body lies dormant outside coverin' up this complex."

"I'm not sure I follow," Jordanna said.

"I'll tell ya a simpler way. Me an Heldrik tested the prototype device on a colossal mud worm. Scattered the creature inta thousands of tiny vermin. We called 'em mud-stingers—nasty little creatures. But they took orders nicely and worked together as a collective."

"Hive mentality," Brianna repeated. "So Heldrik discovered a way to create new lifeforms from existing ones."

"Not exactly. This device scatters a lifeform inta smaller ones, but the whole of the original lifeform is still intact. That's where the hive mind comes from."

"So, those desert harpies are pieces of a larger lifeform?" Jordanna asked.

"Yeah—but only a small part. Mosta its body is the vanishin' dune itself."

"Do you have any idea what that lifeform might be?" Damien asked.

"I scanned the dune, and it's mostly made o' Zephyrian dust with some earthly sand mixed in. So yer probably lookin' at a Zephyrian dust goliath."

Jordanna and Brianna gasped at Dakota's admission, but Damien grew more excited.

"Of course," Damien said. "The specific gravity is far too great, which would explain why the winds haven't disturbed the dune."

"What kind of creature is a dust goliath?" Ethan asked.

"They're from the elemental world of Zephyr," Hayley said. "Like a Hell-Giant, only much bigger and made from wind and dust instead of fire."

"So let me get this straight," Ethan said. "If we were to destroy that device, the harpies and the vanishing dune would reconstruct themselves back into a dust goliath?"

"That's about the size of it," Dakota said.

"But we can't even consider doing that," Brianna said. "We have no way of wrangling a dust goliath."

"There's got to be a way," Ethan said.

"Water," Hayley said. "When harpies attacked us, you fought them with the water pistol Irvin gave you."

"Yeah—and I didn't even have it set to full power," Ethan said. "But if the dust goliath is as enormous as you describe, even on full power, I doubt if that will be enough to kill the creature."

"Your right," Hayley said. "But if we each had hydrosphere ejectors as well, we could blast it from all directions."

"That might work," Ethan said, "but if you remember correctly, my water pistol didn't kill the harpies. It only repelled them."

"Yeah," Hayley said, "we need a way to solidify the creature, and I doubt it's just going to sit around and let us do that."

"No – but if we weakened it enough," said Ethan. "RGB could lasso it like they did with the Hell-Giant."

Jordanna listened to Hayley and Ethan, wide-eyed, her hands folded up in front of her chin. She lowered her hands, exposing a hint of a smile on her lips and a glimmer in her eyes.

"Ethan, do you still have the water pistol Irvin gifted you?" She asked.

"Yes."

"Good," Jordanna said. Her smile widened as she pulled out her ELMO and tapped the screen.

"What can I do for you, Headmistress?" Nicholas asked.

"I need you, Azron, and RGB to join us at the site."

"RGB? What have you gotten yourselves into?"

"Nothing we can't handle. But I also need you to gather a few supplies and bring them."

"What do we need to bring?"

"Hydrosphere ejectors, gravity shoes, and sand-peepers for all of us. Have the ejectors modified to switch between earthly and Atlantian water sources."

"Got it," Nicholas said. "That's a strange request. Might I ask why?"

"I will explain to everyone when you arrive."

"Anything else?"

"Yes, we'll also need energy coils for you and Azron."

Jordanna finished her conversation and put her ELMO away.

"What was that all about?" Hayley asked.

"I'm just getting you and Ethan what you need. I'll explain when they arrive."

Nicholas wasted no time contacting the Caretaker technicians and putting them to work building the hydrosphere ejectors. He tracked down RGB in the Arts and Literature archive. They attempted to capture Wordly again, but he got the best of them as usual. He met Azron on the checkered plane two hours later, and they were ready to join the others.

Jordanna and Tinx stayed to scout every square inch of the mausoleum while the rest of the team waited for the others in the shade of the veranda. Dakota noticed Ethan staring at him, so he walked over and sat next to Hayley, who sat alone with her back against a tall column.

"I'm seein' some not-so-friendly looks from yer boyfriend," he whispered to Hayley. "Did I do somthin' ta anger him?"

"It's not anything you've done," Hayley said. "It's what you—"

"You been lying to me," Ethan said loudly across the veranda. "Fin told me he saw you and Stravis meeting with Odin."

"I told ya I'd met him," Dakota said.

"Yeah—but you held back important details," Ethan said. "You didn't tell me I was there as an infant. Which means you know about my past."

"I don't know as much as ya might figure. Sure, I've been keepin' an eye on ya for Vanessa, and I helped 'em look after ya back when George was around. I even helped Alexander out with your ma after ya disappeared."

"What do you know about my mother?" Ethan asked. His jaw dropped, and his eyes widened as he waited for Dakota to speak.

"Well—I—um," Dakota said and paused. "She was in bad shape after ya disappeared. Stayed in a catatonic state fer quite some time."

"What happened to her? Where is she now?" Ethan asked.

"Can't say fer sure," Dakota answered. "When she came to, she began havin' episodes—visions of evil, courtesy of Victor Qruefeldt. Best we could figure, when the Seers intervened ta rescue ya, it left Tiffany's mind somehow connected ta his. She was there, after all. After a time, it nearly drove 'er mad."

"Where is she now?" Hayley asked.

"Not sure. We all agreed she had ta be moved. If she could see through Victor's eyes, he could likely see through hers. So Alexander took 'er someplace safe, and only he knows where that is."

"So she is alive," Ethan said.

"Yeah, she's alive," Dakota said. "Alexander visits her occasionally, but he says she's not his Tiffany anymore. Somethin' happened ta change 'er."

"What happened to her?" Ethan asked.

"Don't know. Alexander wouldn't say, said it'd give away her whereabouts."

Ethan grew quiet as a wave of emotions flooded his mind. This was the first solid piece of information he had learned about his birth mother, and it came from a reliable source.

Jordanna joined the others on the veranda, and her presence quickly broke up the silence.

"It's time," Jordanna said.

She laid down a fresh portal beacon so Azron and Nicholas could transport directly to the veranda and not suffer the same close call with the harpies. A flash of light radiated from the beacon. Azron and Nicholas appeared on the veranda, each carrying a leather saddlebag. Jordanna led the team inside to the scale model on the floor so they could map out a plan.

"That was fast," she said. "I thought the ejector modifications might take longer."

"Having me watch over their shoulder may have sped up the process."

"And RGB?"

Nicholas zipped open one side of his saddlebag.

"You can come out now," he said.

Three colored balls, one red, one green, and one blue, shot out and unraveled midair. The three mischievous pyrodevlins flew overhead and darted around the room, performing aerial stunts.

"Yippee," Albert shouted.

"Woohoo," Linus screamed.

"Yeehaw," Newton cheered.

"Behave yourselves," Jordanna said. "I've asked you here for an important mission."

RGB beelined for the Headmistress, landed by her side, and stood at attention. Tinx arrived shortly after and landed on Damien's shoulder. She had stayed inside to continue mapping out the interior while Jordanna gathered the others. The team gathered around the Headmistress as Nicholas and Azron emptied the contents of their saddlebags onto the stone floor.

"Tinx, did you find any other exits?" Jordanna asked.

"I think so. There are two stone walls at the back corners of the structure. They're framed like doorways and appear to be exits – but they're beneath the dune for now."

"Perfect. I asked Nicholas to bring you all a pair of gravity shoes, sand-peepers, and a hydrosphere ejector."

Nicholas handed them each a pair of silver glasses with horizontal slits for lenses.

"These are sand-peepers," Nicholas said to Ethan. "They will enable us to see in the sandstorm."

He handed them each a pair of black foot-shaped flats that looked like shoe inserts.

"Gravity shoes will keep you from getting sucked off the ground by the creature."

Hayley tossed hers to the ground and stepped on them. Metallic fibers sprouted from beneath her feet and grew over her existing shoes like a shrub enveloping a house. He followed her lead and did the same.

"Last but not least," Nicholas said as he picked up a hydrosphere ejector. "I had these modified to switch between earthly and elemental water sources. They are preset to earthly, but you can use this selector switch to change that."

"Why do we need two water sources?" Ethan asked. "Normal water worked fine before."

"Yes—but you said it yourself," Jordanna said. "Earthly water only served to repel the harpies."

"We're making pottery," Damien said.

"I'm lost," Ethan said.

"Artisans on the elemental worlds," Damien said. "They craft durable goods using a mixture of Zephyrian dust and Atlantian water. That creature is made of Zephyrian dust."

"Exactly," Jordanna said. "We use earthly water to repel the beast, then switch to Atlantian water to solidify it – or turn it to pottery, as Damien pointed out."

"I see," Ethan said, "but what are those for?" He pointed at two glowing energy coils that reminded him of Wonder Woman's rope. One was much larger than the other and obviously met for Azron.

"Those are energy coils," Brianna said. "They're used to restrain deplorables."

"Remember when RGB lassoed the Hell-Giant," Hayley said. "Energy coils enable Caretakers to do the same."

"Okay," Jordanna said and looked from Ethan to Hayley. "I've provided you with everything you two discussed. So what's the plan?"

Ethan and Hayley looked at one another in disbelief. Was the Headmistress really going to let them plan out the most essential details of the mission?

"We can do this," Ethan whispered to Hayley.

"I know we can," she replied.

Ethan grabbed Hayley by the hand and led her around the scale model of the complex. They faced the others, and Ethan began to speak.

"Okay—so here's the plan," Ethan said. "Dakota will destroy Heldrik's device, which will cause the harpies to merge into a dust goliath."

"Dust goliath," Nicholas said and looked at Jordanna. "You're going to purposely unleash a dust goliath."

"Yes, we are," Jordanna said. "Please, continue."

Ethan looked at Hayley and nodded.

"Once the harpies fully merge with the body," Hayley said. "The vanishing dune will lift off the complex and allow Azron to open one of the rear exits. We will exit out the back when he does, which should let us out here."

She tiptoed around the model, knelt, and pointed to the back of the temple structure they were in.

"Given what Dakota has described," she continued, "the monster should be somewhere around here."

Jordanna watched with a proud smile as Hayley pointed to the largest pyramid at the center of the complex.

"Ethan, you'll be the only one without a hydrosphere ejector. You start the barrage with your water pistol set to full power. We will join in with our ejectors using earthly water, which will back the creature away. Azron, Brianna, and Nicholas take the far side of the center pyramid, while Mother, Dakota, Ethan, and I take the near side. RGB, stick by Nicholas' side until he gives the order. We won't hear one another in the windstorm the creature will unleash. So, Tinx will remain with Ethan and me to relay information to all of you."

She pointed to the front of the complex.

"Once we've advanced that far, switch to Atlantian water. That will solidify the creature enough for RGB's energy lassos. Azron and Nicholas will help RGB wrangle the beast with energy coils. They will pull the creature away while we switch back to earthly water to repel it. Eventually, the monster will tire, the winds will subside, and it will solidify."

"That's one heck of a plan," Dakota said.

"Yes, it is," Jordanna agreed.

"But will it work?" Brianna asked.

"Well, it should," Damien said. "In theory."

"Does anyone else have a better plan?" Ethan asked.

Nobody had a better plan, so the team discussed the details for another hour until they were all comfortable with their roles. Because they had never seen a dust goliath, Ethan and Hayley stood by the entrance to watch the harpies re-merge into the monster. When most of the creature's body mass lifted itself off the complex, they'd run back to the others and inform them it was go time. They stood at the entrance waiting with bated breath—and then it happened.

"Are ya ready boys 'n' girls?" Dakota shouted from the back of the temple. "Let's rustle us up a behemoth."

Flashes of bluish-white light strobed from the back of the temple, and everything fell silent.

"The calm before the storm," Hayley whispered.

They gazed out at the churning desert sands stretching across the horizon and growing taller as they moved closer rapidly. Only a minute went by before the wall of leaping harpies became visible, but this time they were not coming straight at them.

"They're heading for the dune," Ethan said.

"Yeah—and there are a lot more of them," Hayley said.

They continued watching as the harpies leapt one after another at the giant mountain of sand and disappeared inside. As the onslaught continued, ripples of sand moved on the mountain's surface as strong winds gusted around the dune in a circular motion.

"The dune," Ethan said, "is beginning to break apart."

An enormous harpie jumped out from the dune and exploded into a cloud of dust that the growing winds instantly swept away. Another giant harpie leapt out, followed by another, and another, and another. The winds grew stronger and louder as they circled in tighter swirls and sucked the giant harpies into the developing tornado.

"I think I'm ready for the sand-peepers. I can hardly see anything," Hayley shouted.

Ethan followed her lead and fumbled around to put his on too, and when he finally got them on, he saw the monster. Several hundred feet from them, growing up from the center of the tornado, an enormous creature was forming before their eyes. It had no legs; its bottom half was the tornado that glided the monster effortlessly over the desert sand like a giant genie.

"I can see the pyramids now," Ethan shouted.

"Me too. Let's warn the others," Hayley yelled back.

They bolted inside, pulled up their peepers, and ran towards the others as fast as possible.

"It's time," Hayley shouted to her mother.

"Do it," Jordanna said.

Azron's giant hands slammed against the stone slab like a pair of sledgehammers, sending rock slabs crashing into the open desert and unblocking the exit.

Azron, Brianna, RGB, and Nicholas dashed out into the swirling winds first and headed for the far side of the center pyramid. The rest of the team followed Ethan and Hayley as they made a U-turn and headed down the broad clearing between the temple and center pyramid. They spread out and walked side by side towards the creature, now fully formed beside the pyramid. The beast looked like a tornado, with the upper half of a devilish sand monster growing from its center. It reminded Ethan of a pissed-off giant sandman with ram horns. The dust mass making up the creature's shape flowed like liquid through its body. The tornado sucked in any particles falling to the ground and replenished its form.

Ethan was the first to open fire and start the barrage, but he braced himself first. Then, he flipped the switch to full power, aimed up at the creature's torso, and pulled the trigger. The stream from the toy pistol expanded as water gushed from the tiny pinhole and blasted the beast like a military-grade water cannon. The monster winced and backed away from the barrage of water. The others opened fire with hydrospheres and backed the monster up farther.

They continued their slow advance for several minutes and finally reached the front corner of the pyramid. Ethan gazed down the front edge of the giant fortress and saw Azron and the others advancing in the distance. He continued dousing the creature as the rest of the team stopped to switch over to Atlantian water. The behemoth used the lull to his advantage and swiftly glided towards them, closing half the distance. Ethan continued moving towards the creature to buy the others more time. But when the barrage of Atlantian water started, he instantly knew something was wrong. The giant water balls dissipated and blew away as soon as they neared the swirling winds around the creature's torso.

Without the others to worry about, the monster turned its focus to its biggest threat, Ethan. The beast extended its massive arm and waved its four long fingers at him. Then, with a quick flick of its wrist, the fingers launched at him like a salvo of missiles. But Ethan was alert. He ran to his right and dove away as they crashed into the sand.

He jumped to his feet and blasted them with his water cannon. The fingers split apart into wet clods of dust. They rolled across the sand, and the tornado sucked them up. The monster winced and backed off again, which gave Ethan an idea. He ran over to Hayley and stopped by her side as he continued to douse the beast that was advancing on them.

"The Atlantian water is acting unexpectedly," she shouted to Ethan.

"I know. It can't break through the swirling winds – but if you aim your shots at the tornado's base, the suction will suck them in."

"Great idea, Tinx. Tell the others," Hayley ordered.

Tinx darted through the wind like a bullet relaying Ethan's idea and was back in a flash. The team quickly retargeted their shots at the creature's base, and the results were immediate. Within minutes, the monster writhed and slowly backed away as its color and consistency became visibly darker.

"Tinx, tell Nicholas to unleash RGB."

Tinx darted off to relay the orders, and in no time, RGB were in the sky buzzing around the creature's head like flies. Azron and Nicholas dropped their ejectors and ran around to flank the beast. Bright, colorful glows, one red, one green, and one blue, radiated from RGB's bodies as they circled the monster. Then, all at once, they stopped midair, hovered, and blasted the beast with their energy lassos. Albert's red lasso wrapped around the creature's neck, while Linus' green one wrapped around its left horn, and Newton's blue one found the right horn.

The monster recoiled, but RGB were swift and agile in the air and quickly adjusted to counter its every move. Right on time, Azron and Nicholas' energy coils wrapped several times around the monster's upper midsection. The five of them pulled and tugged while the rest continued blasting away with earthly water. Several minutes passed, and the demon did not appear to be weakening.

"Something is wrong," Hayley shouted. "The creature should be weakening by now and hardening."

Ethan's mind raced, and in a flash, he was back at home with his mother Betsy. She was smiling and holding up a red ceramic pot. He snapped out of the trance and turned to Hayley.

"I think I have an idea," he shouted and ran towards Dakota.

"Dakota, I need to know something about your powers," he said when he reached him. "Do you have the ability to create heat or fire?"

"Can't make somthin' from nothin'," Dakota said. "But I could summon a Hell-Giant if yer lookin' ta roast marshmallows."

Ethan shook his head and did a double-take but stopped to peer into Dakota's eyes.

"Can you summon two?"

Dakota stopped what he was doing and stared back at Ethan.

"Whatcha wantin' me ta do?"

Ethan whispered in Dakota's ear and waved his hand towards the monster as he explained. He backed away from Dakota, ran back to Hayley, and whispered in her ear. She glanced at him and paused – but then said something to Tinx, who darted about relaying the message.

Moments later, Ethan watched Dakota Drakelan approach the beast as he rubbed his hands together. Hayley turned in time to see him raise his hands and summon two Hell-Giants. The fire creatures appeared out of thin air halfway between Dakota and the dust goliath. They were enormous, but the dust behemoth towered over them at nearly thrice their height. Dakota stood to witness from close up as the two fire giants strode across the desert sand to battle the larger beast. At first sight, the match-up didn't appear to be a fair fight.

"If this doesn't work, we're in big trouble," said Hayley.

"It will," Ethan said. "Just keep your eyes opened."

Azron and Nicholas' energy coils disappeared, followed by RGB's. The dust goliath lunged forward and started towards the approaching Hell-Giants. The gigantic fire creatures stopped and turned to one another as if communicating. The dust beast continued towards them and bent down to swipe at them with both arms. But that was a mistake, and the Hell-Giants quickly took advantage by leaping over the whipping appendages and wrapping their arms around them as they flew by. The dust goliath rose in agony and waved its burning arms skywards. The Hell-Giants slowly climbed to the beast's upper arms and cuddled them like a child hugging mommy. The scene reminded Ethan of his first time watching a firelyte melt into a log.

"The goliath is tiring," Hayley said as she flashed Ethan a smile.

The others joined them and witnessed the winds subside as the dust goliath made its final movements. Minutes later, a statue of an enormous beast stood half-buried in the sand.

"Hell-Giants," Nicholas said. "I don't recall them being part of the plan."

"The plan wasn't working as expected," Hayley said. "So Ethan devised a new plan, and we improvised."

"Dust goliath no like Ethan Fox. Har, harr, harrr!" Azron roared.

"What gave you such a crazy idea?" Hayley asked Ethan.

"I remembered Damien saying something about making pottery. Then I had a flashback to Betsy telling me about baking her pottery in an oven."

"Darn near almost restrained ya when ya asked me ta summon the hellions – but I saw it in yer eyes."

Once the pleasantries were over, they turned their attention to the mission at hand, the pyramid. The massive structure made the nearby temple pale in comparison. They entered through the tall, dark entryway at the front of the fortress. The room inside was dark, but Dakota performed his darkness banishing trick so they could see.

"You're gonna have to teach me that one," Ethan said.

"Sure enuf, soon as ya teach me a few o' yers."

They entered a massive square room, and torches lit up in sequence on the surrounding walls as they moved farther inside. A rectangular pond, embedded at the room's center, had a bottom so black that the water reflected like a mirror. Ethan winked at Hayley as they peeked over the side to see if anything was swimming around.

"Reminds me of a coy pond," Ethan said.

"I don't think anything's been swimming in there for a while," Hayley said.

Beyond the pond stood a tall wide column rising into the darkness high overhead. To each side of the column, a staircase rose into more darkness. Ethan and Hayley gazed at one another as the feeling of deja vu overcame them.

"We've been here before," Ethan said.

"Yes, except for the pond, this room is exactly like the miniature in every detail," Hayley said.

"Which means the Nibblewart prophecies should appear on that wall."

Ethan pointed at the tall wall column as he made his way around the pond, but the others stood quiet right where they were. He stopped and turned to the others, but they were all staring across the pond at something in his path. When he turned back around, Ethan was face to face with the Shadow Princess. Adara had come to fulfill her destiny. He peered into her beaming yellow eyes, and a smile flowed across her face as golden wisps of light escaped from between her lips.

"Hayley," Ethan said. "I think you better get over here to translate."

Hayley hurried around the pond and stood at Ethan's side to help him greet Princess Adara.

"Hello, Adara," Hayley said. "It's so good to see you again."

Adara's eyes widened, bathing Hayley's face in a shower of yellow rays. Her smile widened as she turned to gaze at Ethan, and then Jordanna and the others.

"Adara wants me to tell you," Hayley said, "she is the daughter of Seer Hippocrates and princess of the Sayers."

"Tell her I am pleased to make her acquaintance," Jordanna said.

Hayley relayed the information, and the Shadow Princess continued.

"She wants to know if Ethan is the Hybrid One," Hayley said.

"Well, I—"

"Tell her we need her to lead us to the prophecies," Jordanna interrupted.

Adara glanced from Ethan to Jordanna and back to Ethan.

"She says the Hybrid One connects to the Seers," Hayley said. "They require his presence to reveal the prophecies."

"Tell her I am the Hybrid Child," Ethan said.

"She said she's witnessed you from afar and felt your strength. She believes you are the hybrid but requires proof."

Ethan moved closer to the Shadow Princess and held up his hands. The symbols on his palms flashed white twice as if blinking hello to her. Adara's smile widened further as she turned back to Jordanna.

"She asked if you are the Caretaker leader," Hayley said to her mother.

"Yes," Jordanna said and slowly approached.

The Shadow Princess spoke directly to Jordanna.

"What did she say?" Jordanna asked.

"The Nibblewart prophecies as foretold in the Book of Creators," Hayley translated, "they are yours now to protect."

"But—where are they?" Jordanna asked.

Adara waved her arms towards the wall, and ripples of golden whimsy wafted through the air showering the wide blank wall. They stood watching in silence as writing etched itself into the stone. When the etching finished, the words read:

The Nibblewart Prophecies

I.   The Hybrid Child Returns

II.   A Hell-Giant Breaches the Silent Forest

III. Grim Times Enter the Human World

IV. The Hidden Fortress is Unearthed

"Four of them have already occurred," Damien said.

"Adara says as more come to pass, they will appear as foretold."

"But—how many prophecies are there?" Jordanna asked. "How will we know when to perform the ritual?"

"She says the Hybrid One will know. Protect him from the Grimlord, and his journey will lead us to the answers we seek."

Adara spun around and slowly floated towards the wall column. Ethan turned his head to Hayley, who was rubbing her infinity ring.

"Wait," Hayley said. "Where are you going?"

Adara stopped, turned around, and peered at Hayley.

"I have fulfilled my destiny, but before I leave, I owe you thanks."

"Thanks? Why?" Hayley asked.

"Because you saved me. I bound my soul to the rift-key to save my people from the evil one. When you recovered it from the puzzle box, you freed my soul from eternal damnation."

"That's why you're so familiar to me," Hayley said. "You were the voice who spoke to me through my ring. You helped us, and I should be thanking you."

"And I led you to the Hybrid One. We are familiar because of the time we shared, bound to the same prison."

"Will I see you again?"

"My soul is free now. Whether our paths cross again is in fate's hands."

She turned away, floated towards the wall, and disappeared below the prophecies she had delivered. Ethan turned to face Hayley, who was still rubbing her ring. But the smile on her face told him this was not the last they'd see of the Shadow Princess.

A GRISLY

DISCOVERY

The following morning Ethan and Hayley met Tinx in the dining hall for breakfast as usual. They liked returning to a routine, so at least things seemed normal again. But the Headmistress told them they were to meet her in the study at 9:00 AM sharp. So they took their time, and all had seconds while they made small talk to bide their time.

Nine AM came quickly, and they entered the study right on time. Jordanna, Nicholas, and Irvin were already present. Irvin was busy dusting the bookshelves while Jordanna and Nicholas quietly discussed things.

"The others should be along shortly," Jordanna said. "But Dakota Drakelan has declined."

No sooner had she spoken the words, then Azron and Brianna entered the room, followed by Damien and Tinx.

"I've called you all here for a quick informal meeting. Mostly as a debrief of yesterday's events, but also to update you on current events. Nicholas, the floor is yours."

"We've searched the entire pyramid complex and found nothing else of interest. But now that we have discovered the prophecies, the responsibility falls upon us to keep them protected. The Headmistress and I have discussed various strategies and decided on our best course of action."

"What's to decide," Brianna said. "Send in a platoon of armed Careguards and call it a day."

"That is precisely what we've decided not to do," Nicholas said. "We are all aware that Jordanna's reign as headmistress has its detractors. We cannot afford to call attention to the fact, we are protecting something. To that end, the existence of the complex and the prophecies, must remain a secret."

"The secret is safe with those in this room," Damien said. "But what about Dakota Drakelan? I notice he isn't present."

"While I agree Dakota is a wildcard, I discussed the matter with Alexander, and he vouched for the old coot."

"So you've also let Alexander in on the secret," Brianna said.

"Yes—but we've all put our lives in his hands on numerous occasions. Alexander is beyond reproach."

"Agreed," said Brianna, "But what about Irvin? He's in this room and knows our little secret now."

"Irvin could never become a leak," Damien said. "He's been a part of the Ravenwood family for eons, and he would no more betray us than you would."

"So—what is the plan?" Tinx asked. "We still need to hide and protect this secret. How do we achieve that?"

"I updated the cloaking device," Nicholas said. "It is now a projector as well as a cloak. It projects a copy of the vanishing dune that is only seen from a distance, and at the same time, it cloaks the complex from those who pass by."

"Okay, that solves part of the problem," Brianna said. "But what about the indigenous lifeforms living in the protected realm? What if they wander straight into the complex and learn of its existence?"

"That is a good point," Damien said. "Many are thieves and nomads who have found ways into and out of the human world."

"I also placed proximity detectors around the perimeter. If anything approaches by land or air, they will alert us. A gnat couldn't get to within a mile of the complex without us knowing."

Out of the corner of his eye, Ethan saw Hayley fiddling with her ring.

"What about the portal plane," he said. "You mentioned detractors. If they were to find out, they could teleport directly to the complex."

"That's where the Careguards come in," Jordanna said. "I've ordered two armed soldiers to guard the portal plane at all times. They will strictly monitor its usage from here on out."

"Yes—but the Grimleavers have a portal plane, too," Hayley said. "You can't police theirs."

"We don't need to," Damien said. "Theirs is a copy of our portal plane, the same in every way – but they are separate entities. A beacon tuned to ours will not work from theirs; they would need to place their own portal beacon."

"Sss-sounds like you've covered all the bases."

"Yes—but there is one more fly in the ointment," Jordanna said. "I have spoken with the Council of Elders, and as required, I briefed them on the matter."

"Wonderful," Damien said. "I guess the question is, who doesn't know about our secret?"

"The situation is not as bad as it seems. I only told them we'd recovered the prophecies. They know nothing of the complex."

"Several council members pressed us for more information," Nicholas said. "But we insisted where and how we protect the prophecies must remain our secret for security reasons."

"How did they react?" Damien asked.

"In the end, they agreed to trust us," Jordanna said. "But that does bring up another related matter. My sources on the council tell me Roman Trabblemore has been busy on the elemental worlds. He is rallying my detractors to further undermine my authority within the council itself."

"Thus far, he has only been moderately successful," Nicholas added. "Their numbers are small but growing, so we must keep an ear to the ground and monitor the situation."

The room fell silent as they mulled over the news.

"Moving on, I would like to update you on other matters. At Damien's urging, I asked a team of scholars to scour all available data on Grimleaver activity in the human world. They created algorithms to scan through gazillions of data points and search for patterns of any kind. Nicholas will update you on what they found."

"After painstakingly sifting through mountains of data from all over the human world. Our scholars determined the Grimleavers are attacking random cities across the globe to cover up what is happening in a select few. Atlanta, Boston, Chicago, and Washington DC, these are the cities—"

"Atlanta, Boston, Chicago, and DC," Irvin interrupted. "ABC news investigates is trying to learn—"

"Irvin, this is not the time for your babbling," Nicholas said. "Where was I? Oh yes, the cities I mentioned have all experienced museum break-ins coinciding precisely with the Grimleaver attacks. We believe the Grimleavers are searching for something in these museums."

"Duh, even the humans have figured that out."

"Irvin!" Nicholas shouted.

"Wait, I think Irvin is trying to tell us something," Ethan said. "He views a lot of human television channels. I believe he is mimicking something he's seen in the news."

"Irvin, you may continue," Jordanna said.

Irvin straightened up and morphed into a human anchorman to aid his presentation of the human news story.

"ABC news investigates is trying to learn what the break-ins have in common. But the list is growing, as sources confirm others are occurring across the pond, in Berlin, London, and Rome. And it gets more chilling as our crack team of researchers has discovered one common denominator. Each of the galleries in question exhibits artifacts shared from the same mystery collection. While neither the owner of the collection nor its origins are known at this time. Sources confirm pieces from the mystery collection have gone missing due to these break-ins."

The room fell silent as they all took in Irvin's revelation.

"So much for our crack team of scholars," Jordanna said. "Next time, we should monitor the human TV networks."

"It makes sense the humans found out first," Damien said. "They react to what happens in their world, but our scholars were searching for a needle in a universe of haystacks. I'd give them kudos for learning what they did."

"At any rate," Jordanna said. "We must send investigators to each of those cities. They must learn about this mystery exhibit and find out what they stole."

"I will get on that right away," Nicholas said.

The team debated the pros and cons of what they had learned for another hour. But Hayley asked her mother to excuse her and Ethan, and the Headmistress obliged. They exited the study, and Ethan instinctively headed towards The Hall of Doorways, but Hayley had other ideas.

"Follow me," she said.

"What are you up to?"

But she did not answer, so he followed her up the stairs and into her grandfather's chamber.

"Last night, I did some digging," she said as she shuffled through papers on Odin's desk. "I think we've missed something."

"Is this you talking? Or are you getting a little help from your friend?"

He pointed to her infinity ring. Hayley's eyes widened, and her lips pursed as she stood looking into his eyes.

"She wanted me to keep it a secret, but I should have known better. You read me like a book."

"Listen, you don't have to tell me anything," Ethan said.

"No, it's okay. She says I can tell you anything, but she wants this to stay between us."

"You speak as if she's here right now," Ethan said. "Is she back inside your ring or something?"

"No, it's more like telepathy, I guess. She doesn't have to be here physically for us to hear each other's thoughts. Adara thinks our connection is stronger because her soul is free now, and she's fulfilled her destiny."

"Okay, so what have we missed?"

"Let me back up a little," Hayley said. "I was lying in bed thinking about everything that has happened. I remembered Dakota Drakelan saying all the names on Odin's list were Gaylord's associates. So I dug into the other names, and here's what I found. Drake Evans was a long-time friend of Gaylord's. When Gaylord became headmaster, Drake was his number one and consulted on his every decision."

"Yeah, that doesn't sound so ominous," Ethan said.

"No, it doesn't, not until he went missing and Gaylord started to act irrationally. Then there's Lindrew Scragmort, the portal master during the Trabblemore administration. He oversaw the four portals during the Great Exodus and became Gaylord's number one after Drake Evans' disappearance. He, too, later went missing."

"An interesting pattern is emerging," Ethan said. "We already learned of Jason Crowley's fate. You could argue he went missing too."

"Exactly, until someone tried to make a point by leaving his body on my grandparents' doorstep."

"What about Heldrik? Do we know what became of him?"

"I haven't discovered a word about him. Like he's disappeared from existence with no record."

"Dakota Drakelan might be able to tell us something," Ethan said.

"Again, my thoughts exactly, but I don't think he'll tell us anything. He shares a bond with Heldrik and gets nervous at the mere mention of their past together."

"Yeah, you're probably right, but he's sure taken a shine to you."

Hayley blushed at Ethan's observation.

"Oh, I almost forgot," she said. "I was also wondering about the pixie-devils."

"What about them?"

"I find it bizarre we encountered them at the pyramid complex. How could they have possibly found us? But Damien just confirmed my suspicions."

"That's right," Ethan said. "Grimleavers cannot teleport to the complex, so they couldn't have found us. They had to have followed us."

"Yes, which means they were in The Residence, and someone is helping them."

"I think we all know who that is," Ethan said.

"Maybe, maybe not."

"Adara told you herself, remember, she was afraid she had put me in danger because he was after the hidden fortress too."

"That's right, I almost forgot about that," Hayley said. "But I'm sure the pixie-devils didn't learn anything. Medusa killed them all."

"You and Adara sure burned the midnight oil. Did you sleep at all last night?"

"A little—but there's one more thing."

"What?"

"Adara and I have a funny feeling about the pyramid complex. Too many things don't make sense."

"Like what?"

"Why did they build it for one. They sure didn't build it so the Nibblewarts would have a place to put the prophecies. The Nibblewarts stumbled upon it after being transported into the past by the hyperhole event. They only stayed to help, and continue to return, because the rock is their only viable food source."

"Good point," Ethan said. "I assumed Victor Qruefeldt was after it to ensure we didn't find the prophecies. But if it serves a different purpose, he might have a different reason altogether. Come to think of it, the poem clearly says, 'A fortress built for wicked plans.'"

"So the question is, what could they use a structure that big for?"

"I don't know, but I think you two are on to something," Ethan said. "We've missed something in those pyramids just like we did at Stravis' bunker."

They continued brainstorming for several more hours and decided to take a break. A leisurely stroll through the Moongarden would be the perfect remedy for brain fatigue. But along the way, they changed their minds and chose to visit Damien's laboratory instead. Damien and Tinx were hard at work on another experiment when they entered.

"Tinx, fetch me the jar of wobble stones, please," Damien said as he hovered over his lab bench.

Ethan and Hayley moved close enough to watch but still be out of their way.

"You're just in time," Damien said. "I'm about to detonate my next blast."

"What—are you making bombs?" Ethan asked.

"In a word, yes," Damien said and smiled. "Stravis' findings reveal a strange alchemy between certain earthly and elemental combinations."

"A strange alchemy indeed," Tinx said as she landed on the lab bench with a jar of quivering green rocks.

Damien removed one of the tiny rocks and dropped it into the left side of a glass box divided in the center by a glass divider. The rock wobbled inside the container and reminded Ethan of a Mexican jumping bean. Damien opened a small pouch, tweezed out a pea-sized gold nugget, and dropped it into the other side of the glass partition.

"Here, put these on," Damien said as he handed them a set of dark glasses.

"Ready for the blast when they touch," he said. "And you might want to cover your ears too."

"How big of a blast are we talking about?" Ethan asked.

"Approximately the equivalent of a ten-kiloton nuclear explosion."

Ethan's eyes widened, and his jaw dropped open.

"Nothing to worry about," Damien said. "This enclosure has a one hundred megaton rating."

Ethan and Hayley held their hands over their ears as Damien touched the screen of his ELMO. The glass partition disappeared as the two rock samples slowly floated towards the center of the glass cube. But when they met in the middle and touched, nothing happened.

"Wow—that blew my socks off, brother," Hayley said.

"I'm sorry, my mistake," Damien said. "I used normal gold when the recipe calls for once-cloaked leprechaun gold."

Damien reset the enclosure, separated the samples, and set the experiment up again using once-cloaked gold.

"Okay, I guarantee I will knock your socks off this time."

Ethan and Hayley cupped their hands over their ears as Damien touched his ELMO screen. The samples floated towards one another, and this time when they touched, a bright white flash of light enveloped the room and a sonic boom shook the ground. Even with his ears covered, the sound made Ethan's ears ring.

"Wow—" Ethan said, "that was amazing!"

"That was nothing," said Tinx. "One of his earlier blasts cracked the enclosure, so we had to get a new one."

"Thus far, my results are confirming Stravis' findings. Minerals from Ceres react when they encounter once-cloaked leprechaun gold. What I find interesting is the effects are not consistent. Some minerals create a much more powerful blast than others."

"What cracked the enclosure?" Hayley asked.

"A Ceresian bloating stone hydrated with earthly water. Which leads me to another oddity Stravis uncovered. The same stone, hydrated with Atlantian water, does not react."

"That must be why they used Atlantian water to hydrate the stone used to build the pyramid complex," Hayley said.

"If that's true, Jason Crowley must have known something about these reactions," Ethan said.

"Excellent observation," Damien said. "That must be why they went to all that trouble."

Ethan and Hayley witnessed Damien detonate a few more samples of various Ceresian minerals, but none equaled the yield of the bloating stone. Learning the new information fatigued their brains more, so again they decided to take a walk in the Moongarden. But along the way, Hayley stopped to ponder something.

"What's wrong?"

"Something my brother said is bothering me. Why did they go to all that trouble? I can think of only one reason. They knew the structure would encounter leprechaun gold."

"Could be."

"Which brings me back to something I asked you earlier. What purpose does such a giant structure serve?"

"I see where you are going with this. They could store things in a giant structure like that."

"Store many things, and I suspect that is what we missed."

After Hayley's epiphany, they strolled quietly through the Moongarden and spent some time skipping stones in the pond next to the Moon Orchard. After that, they settled on an early dinner and decided to call it a day.

The following morning, Ethan woke up to find a note from Hayley slid underneath his door. It read:

Dear Ethan,

I got an early start and came up with a few new ideas. I'm going to skip breakfast this morning to follow up on another possible lead. I have no idea how long it will take so I will meet you at noon in the cafeteria, we can discuss what I found then.

With love, Hayley

Ethan met Tinx for breakfast, she was waiting in their usual spot. He read Hayley's note to her and filled Tinx in on some of their latest thoughts about the pyramid complex. After that, they made small talk as they ate. Ethan had a light breakfast because he was meeting Hayley later for lunch. When they finished, Ethan accompanied Tinx to the laboratory on his way to Odin's chamber. Tinx disappeared down the basement stairs. Ethan stood silently as the door creaked closed.

"Well, well, well," Gruggins said as he popped out of his box and stood at the table's edge. "Not often I see you without Miss Hayley. Did you finally piss her off?"

"No, it's not like that. She hasn't slept well lately and didn't want to wake me – so she left to run an errand on her own."

"I wouldn't exactly call visiting the Wentworths an errand," Gruggins said. "Sounds more like torture to me. Bella is like fingernails on a chalkboard."

"She is meeting with the Wentworths?"

"She passed through here a few hours ago and stopped by to say hello. Told me she was off to Zen city to visit the Wentworths."

"Did she say why?"

"Didn't ask why. I'm not nosey."

"Okay, thanks for cheering me up, Gruggins," Ethan said. He turned and started towards the stairs.

"I'm sorry. Did I say something wrong? No offense, you're still my favorite Hybrid."

"I'm the only Hybrid you know."

"Well, there is that."

"Anyway, no offense taken. Thanks, Gruggins. I'll see you later."

Hayley had made Ethan a copy of her hand so he could enter her grandfather's chamber without her. He mulled around for several hours, looking for any clue as to why she might want to speak with the Wentworths. But he found nothing by noon, and it was time to meet Hayley for lunch.

He sat at their usual table again and waited. Ten minutes went by, but Hayley did not arrive. He sat for another twenty minutes, checking the time every two minutes. It was not like Hayley to not show up like this, which worried Ethan. So he thumbed his way around his ELMO and found the app she used to find Wordly Pagemore. But when he saw her name, only dashes appeared where her location should be.

"Gruggins said she was going to the Wentworths," Ethan thought.

He pulled up the Caretaker condo's directory to find out where they lived and sprinted into The Hall of Doorways. He ran down the hallway to the 99th door on the right and entered the Caretaker city of Zen. It didn't take long to run down the crowded street to Tower number three. But twenty minutes went by while he waited in line for an elevation pod.

"Name and destination?" the young Caretaker asked.

"Ethan Fox, to visit the Wentworths."

Ethan grew more worried by the second, making the three minute ride seem like an eternity. But his bubble finally arrived and melted into the Wentworth condo, dropping him off in a dark, quiet room.

"Hello, is anybody here?" Ethan called out.

Nobody answered, but Ethan's palm symbols quickly turned on and showered the darkroom with a soft white glow. He gazed down at them, and they spun around in his palms to point to his left, so he followed their direction. The sound of rustling came from around the corner where his symbols pointed.

"Is anybody here? Who is that?" Ethan asked as he turned the corner to see a sizeable spider-like shadow rising from the ground. But the lights came on, and he quickly recognized the shadow was not a spider at all. It was Bella Wentworth using all four of her arms to pick herself up off the floor. Ethan quickly ran to her side to help her.

"What happened? Are you okay?"

"I—I don't recall," Bella said. "But you are such a dear to come to my rescue."

"You don't remember what happened? Hayley came to visit. Do you remember seeing her?"

"Oh yes, I remember now. She came to see my Boris, but he was out. So the dear girl stayed to comfort me."

"Why did she comfort you?"

"M-M-My B-Boris," Bella said and started sobbing.

"What about Boris? What happened? Why are you crying?"

"He's not himself lately. He comes and goes all hours of the night. And his temper, he's not my Boris since his return."

"What about Hayley?"

"The girl was such a dear to listen to all my troubles."

"What happened to Hayley?" Ethan said louder.

"I—I don't know. I was telling her something when the lights went out. The next thing I remember is you helping me off the floor."

"What were you telling her?"

"I—I don't remember," Bella said and cried uncontrollably.

Ethan tried to calm Bella and ask her more questions, but quickly decided it was a waste of time. So he scrambled from Zen city to find help, and Damien's basement laboratory was his first stop. He ran down the stairs into the bright white room, but only Tinx was present.

"I need to find Damien now."

"The Headmistress called him away," Tinx said. "They are out in the field on CAGE business."

"Great, now what will I do."

"Maybe I can help."

"No offense—but I doubt there is anything you can do."

"What's wrong?"

"It's Hayley, I can't find her anywhere. And I'm worried."

"I saw her about an hour ago. She wasn't very talkative, and they seemed to be in a hurry."

"They? Who was she with, and where were they going?"

"She was with Boris Wentworth, and they went upstairs somewhere."

"They must have gone to the headmasters chambers."

He turned and ran towards the stairs.

"Now you've got me worried," Tinx said. "I'm coming with you"

Tinx followed Ethan up the stairs to the third floor headmasters chambers. He fished out the replica of Hayley's hand and used it to enter the chamber. Nobody was there, but Ethan slowly walked around the room and scanned every inch.

"Well, somebody's been here. Odin's desk was different when I was here a few hours ago."

He dashed over to study the desk and noticed a piece of paper on the floor beneath it. So, he picked it up to examine and instantly recognized Hayley's handwriting.

Where's Heldrik?
* Dakota Drakelan
*Boris Wentworth

Bella Wentworth
*Boris not himself
* Bad Temper
* Bella saw someth——

"Based on this, I think she went to ask Boris about Heldrik Vonn Grim. We were going to speak with Dakota together. But Boris wrote articles about Dakota's past with Heldrik. So she must have figured Boris knows something about what became of Heldrik."

"Makes sense."

A loud knock on the door interrupted their discussion.

CHAPTER FIFTEEN

Tinx fluttered over and landed on Ethan's shoulder as he pulled the door open. But something fell into the room and thudded to the floor at Ethan's feet. He and Tinx looked down, and what they saw shocked them both to the core. Lying on the ground in front of them was a shriveled grey corpse.

The body appeared to be that of a short man based on his clothing, but he was lying face down on the stone floor. Ethan knelt to flip him over, and when he did, a chill crept down his spine as he grew cold and began to shiver.

"What is it? What's wrong?"

Ethan studied the man's clothing and the monocle in his right eye to ensure he wasn't seeing things. The wrinkled grey skin on the terrified face gave the appearance something had drained the life from his body while he watched in horror.

"This body," Ethan said as he stood up. "It, it's Boris Wentworth."

THE DAY OF

RECKONING

Ethan stood expressionless, staring down at Boris' shriveled limp body. Tinx stared down from his shoulder with an equally perplexed expression.

"Well, if that's Boris," said Tinx. "Who did I see Hayley with?"

"I don't know, but there's something tucked behind his lapel."

He knelt to retrieve a piece of paper crudely pinned to the chest of Boris' corpse. He unfolded it and read its words:

```
Dear Ethan Fox,

    The Residence blocks the conscious
connection we share, so it is left to
my imagination to show me how
delightfully terrified you must be
```

right now. Your dear Miss Hayley is
safe for now, but I will leave you to
your imagination to wonder what horrors
might fall upon her if you do not heed
my words exactly. You have three hours
to join us in the central pyramid. Come
alone. If you fail to make it, the
desert fortress will become her tomb.

Best wishes, Victor Qruefeldt

Ethan's hands shook as he finished reading the note and stood pondering his next step.

"How can we possibly make it there in three hours?" Tinx asked. "The Headmistress has posted guards on the portal plane, and nobody can access it without her approval."

"There is no us. Didn't you read the message? I must go alone."

Ethan's fists clenched as he concentrated on saving Hayley, and slowly but surely, a plan was forming in his head.

"Yeah, I understand," Tinx said. "I don't want to endanger Miss Hayley. I only want to help."

"Well, maybe there's a way you still can."

It took an hour to find Gruggins and Wordly, tell them about Hayley's predicament, and get them up to speed on Ethan's plan. Tinx and Wordly would make necessary arrangements while Gruggins went with Ethan to the Moongarden. They found Grubner tending to the trembling nomads. Ethan didn't even need Gruggins' help talking him into eight dwindle-berries. Grubner was happy to help the Hybrid Child with anything his heart desired.

Afterward, Ethan sprinted down The Hall of Doorways to the door the Nibblewarts used to venture into the past. He opened the door and ran through without hesitation. It was daytime in the desert, so the terrain appeared quite different, but the long line of giant ants walking enormous bricks towards the build site led him to the right place. He spent the next hour backtracking through the maze of tunnels to find the long straightaway to the chamber where he and Hayley had met the Nibblewarts. But eventually, his palm symbols woke up to show him the way.

Even during the day, everything beneath the sand appeared the same; so, once he found the straightaway, he quickly found the portal back to the future. He emerged from the tiny replica, chomped down four dwindle-berries, and promptly returned to size inside the temple structure. The trek through the sand to the center pyramid only took another few minutes, but he still worked up a sweat under the hot desert sun. He checked the time as he walked through the tall entrance.

"Twenty minutes to spare," he thought to himself.

The room was dark and quiet when he entered, but there was not a soul around. Ethan's night vision struggled to adjust as he ventured deeper into the dark. But he triggered the torches, which lit themselves around the room's perimeter. His vision worked perfectly under the flickering flames that barely lit the room. The pond in front of him looked like a pool of black oil as he approached.

He stopped and peered down at his reflection, but something moving caught his attention. The gecko on his shirt crawled towards his head like a cartoon on the fabric's surface. The garment frill popped out of his shirt and morphed into a live gecko that climbed onto his shoulder. The color drained from the gecko as it transformed into a tiny metallic humanoid that reminded him of the Silver Surfer. The small shape of a man sprang up, dove off his shoulder, and landed on the stone floor. The trinket landed splat on the ground and flattened out into a pancake. But the transformation was not over, as an object slowly grew from the circular pancake shape, Ethan's eyes widened as he slowly came to recognize the object before him and the realization of what it meant. A portal beacon stood before Ethan. Victor Qruefeldt had just tricked him into giving him access to *The Pyramids of Never.*

A bright flash of light strobed inside the room, and two figures appeared from nowhere. It was Hayley, and Boris had his right hand wrapped around the back of her neck.

"Ethan," Hayley cried out. "He's not Boris!"

"I know who he is," Ethan said as he glared into fake Boris' eyes.

Devilish laughter filled the room as Boris grew taller, his face contorted, and his clothes morphed into a tattered black robe. Victor Qruefeldt's piercing red eyes bore through Ethan's as a broad grin stretched across his face revealing sharp pointed teeth that reminded him of Pennywise, the evil clown. The brainy ridges covering his scalp pulsated between the enormous ears that protruded over his head like devilish horns. His guttural laughter grew louder and louder.

"Let her go," Ethan shouted. "Your quarrel is with me."

Victor threw Hayley to the ground at his feet as he stepped closer to Ethan and glared down at him. The dank odor of death filled Ethan's lungs as he breathed in Victor's unforgettable scent.

"My quarrel is with the whole lot of you," Victor screamed. "You and anyone else who stands in my way."

"Like my mother stood in your way," Ethan said. "She didn't do anything to deserve what you did to her."

"Oh—so you've learned of our little tryst," Victor said. "I kept it to myself at first. Thought I'd use our connection to eavesdrop and be the first to know when the Hybrid Child returned. But I quickly grew tired of listening to the thoughts of her feeble human mind."

"You drove her mad," Ethan said.

"That was the fun part," Victor replied. "After months of listening to the cacophony of worries in her head. Between that and the love she felt towards you, it nearly drove me mad. So I gave her a little peek into my mind. Showed her some wonderfully horrid ways I could dispose of her beloved child."

"You'll pay for what you've done," Ethan said. "I promise, I will make you pay for what you did to my mother, and for what you did to Adara."

"Adara—" Victor repeated. "So the shadow spirit—is Princess Adara. Interesting, I hadn't made the connection. But when she kept coming to you in your dreams, I knew there was a reason. That's why I planned the attack, to draw her out."

"I'm surprised you came here alone," Ethan prodded, "without your minions to protect you."

"He's not alone," Hayley said. "He has a whole army of Grimleavers coming."

No sooner had she said the words than the room lit up like a disco ball. One flash after another signaled the arrival of vampires, trolls, ogres, and other dark creatures.

"Norell, you've made it. I wondered if my confidant failed to inform you of my plans."

A tall vampire woman with long black hair stepped forward and bowed to Victor.

"All hail the Grimlord," she said.

"All hail the Grimlord," a chorus of voices echoed around the room.

"Whatever you're planning is destined to fail," Hayley said as she rose. "Caretakers will come, and we will defeat you."

Norell's arm whipped around like a club and pummeled Hayley's back to the ground. Ethan lunged at Norell, but Victor froze him cold with a swipe of his long, wicked hand. A cold wave of chills washed over his body as he struggled to move. But the harder he fought, the more frozen he became.

"What are our orders?" Norell asked.

"We must not underestimate Mr. Fox again. I must assume he has made contingency plans, and the Caretakers will arrive shortly. How fast can your army remove the cargo?"

"I've brought hundreds, and they are all equipped with sticky beacons. They will teleport the larger containers using those, and the rest will be hand-carried by the trolls and ogres."

"What about the other structures?"

"I've already sent teams to the other pyramids. They are awaiting word. I estimate twenty minutes once I've given the order."

"Give the order and tend to the cargo while I play with our guests," Victor said with a wicked scowl.

Hayley rose to her feet and stood next to Ethan, still frozen in place.

"Calm yourself," Hayley whispered to Ethan. "Adara says calmness will free you."

Ethan closed his eyes and thought of when he first met Hayley on the beach. He remembered her grabbing hold of his hands and the butterflies he felt. A warm rush of energy swept through his body; and suddenly, he could move again.

"You've learned to defeat my freezing hex," Victor said with a wide smile. "Not surprising, curses are so amateur. I hesitate to use them."

Norell moved across the room to the gigantic wall rising into the darkness above them. She ordered four of the enormous ogres to follow her. They looked like dirty, dumb, and mean versions of Shrek; only much bigger, and they carried small trees like clubs.

"Two of you take this one," she said and pointed at the wall. "And two of you take that one."

She pointed to an identical wall across the room. The ogres stood looking at one another like four stooges. One scratched its head, while two of the others picked at their noses.

"Dumb, stupid creatures," Norell said under her breath. "You and you, take down this wall while you and you take down that one."

She pointed at the ogres as she spoke, and they finally followed her instructions. Two giant oafs began slamming their trees against the wall like battering rams, while the other two slowly strode across the room to do the same.

"What are you going to do with us?" Hayley asked.

"You, my dear, still have something that belongs to me," Victor said. He held his right arm out towards Hayley and waved. Her hand involuntarily opened as the rift-key unwrapped from her finger and flew into his ghastly hand. Victor held out the black puzzle box with his left hand, and the top slowly slid open and disappeared. He dropped the rift-key in, and the lid slid back into place like a trap door.

"There will be no tricks this time," Victor said.

He cupped the puzzle box between his hands and held it in front of his face.

"Bind him," he said.

Ethan's arms moved behind his back as if the invisible man were restraining him. Something wrapped around his wrists like a coiling snake and tightened until he barely felt his fingers.

"What are you doing to him? STOP THIS!" Hayley screamed.

The loud noise from the smashing rock wall distracted Victor. He turned and took a few steps towards the commotion to watch the ogres break through the barrier to a secret cargo hold. Walls of sizable, stacked containers filled the room. Several vampires took flight to slap small devices onto the sides of the boxes, causing them to disappear in a flash of light. The legion of trolls took care of the ground-based containers as soon as the vampires freed them.

"Some of the leprechaun gold has been de-cloaked," Norell said to Victor. "But the extraction seems to be moving along faster than I expected. I will leave you now to check on the other structures."

"Leave this complex as soon as the last of the cargo has been teleported," Victor said.

"All hail the Grimlord," Norell said and was gone with a flash.

"Now, now, where was I," Victor said as he turned his attention back to Ethan and Hayley.

"You were about to let us go," Ethan said.

"Oh yes, there will be no tricks," Victor continued as he moved his hand over the puzzle box and pet it. "Fetch me the copycat."

A small metallic figurine of a cat appeared on the floor at his feet. Hayley glanced at Ethan as Victor bent down to pick it up and toss it over his shoulder.

"How did he know about my copycat?" She whispered to Ethan.

"I—I may have mentioned something to Boris."

"Give that back to me," Hayley said as she stepped toward Victor.

"That would not be a wise choice," Victor said.

A loud noise erupted from the other side of the room, where the other two ogres broke through the wall. The vampires and trolls finished clearing out the other hold, so they charged across the room to start on the new one. Victor turned to watch.

"It's time," Ethan whispered.

"What?" Hayley whispered back. But he did not answer. She turned away from Victor to see Ethan and glanced something green out of the corner of her eye. Gruggins was clinging to Ethan's back and climbing down towards his invisibly bound hands. He hopped off, landed between Ethan's wrists, rubbed his hands together, and touched the invisible binds. A coil of black rope instantly became visible around Ethan's wrists. Gruggins wasted no time. He pulled out a serrated knife and carefully hacked away. Ethan's hands were free within a minute, but he kept them behind his back to maintain the illusion.

Victor turned back to Ethan and Hayley, stroked his puzzle box, and grinned a wide tooth-bearing smile.

"Sadly, our time together is coming to an end," he said and stepped towards them.

The expression on one of their faces must have betrayed Ethan's intentions.

"You are up to something," Victor said to Ethan. "I feel it in my bones."

"He's not up to anything," Hayley shouted to draw his attention away from Ethan. "He's only here to rescue me from you. Now give me back my Tabby Cat."

She took several steps toward him – but Victor reacted quickly.

"Repel her."

Hayley flew across the room and landed nearly twenty feet behind Ethan. But she shook it off and quickly jumped to her feet.

"Tabby Cat, Tabby Cat, Tabby Cat," Hayley said. With each utterance, she took a step closer.

Victor stared Ethan in the eyes and gave him the most demonic look possible. Hayley's copycat apparated in her outstretched hands. Victor turned towards Hayley and started walking in her direction.

"You, my dear, have become a nuisance I will no longer tolerate."

He continued towards her, raised the puzzle box, and stroked it. A tingle started at Ethan's feet and slowly crawled up his legs and over his body as he felt what Victor was about to do. A loud diabolical laugh erupted from his lips as he opened his mouth.

"End her, now," Victor said as he stretched his arms out in Hayley's direction. A tiny purplish-black vortex appeared before his extended hands and swirled faster and faster as the room grew silent. Then, the vortex abruptly rocketed towards Hayley like a missile.

Everything in the room slowed down as Ethan burst into action. He swiftly sprinted in a feeble attempt to move between Hayley and the vortex. But he quickly realized he was moving too slow, so he launched his body into the air and zipped into the path of the menacing whirlwind. The vortex struck him dead center in the chest and instantly changed his direction, sending him volleying across the room like a bowling pin.

The blast from the collision threw Hayley to the ground as well. Gruggins fluttered over and landed on her chest to see if she was okay.

"You pitiful boy," Victor said. "Heroic till the very end, and I had such plans for you."

Hayley peered across the room at Ethan. He was on the ground gasping for breath and writhing in pain.

"What have you done to him!" she screamed.

"Reaped his soul, I'm afraid," Victor said. "But in my defense, it was meant for you. Sadly, there is nothing you can do to save him."

Victor's sinister laugh echoed throughout the room as strobes of light bounced off the walls. The vampires, trolls, and ogres had finished their task and were teleporting away.

"What am I going to do with you? It would be such a waste to kill you now that your life is about to be filled with sorrow. But I suppose I must."

Victor took another step toward Hayley, but Gruggins acted quickly. He rubbed his hands together, raised them into the air, and moved them in a circular motion. Hayley and Gruggins instantly disappeared, hidden from harm by a Grumpling's cloak.

"I must remember to exterminate all grumplings," said Victor.

He let out a deep sigh, turned, and headed for the portal beacon. But he stopped and turned to watch the life slowly drain from Ethan's body.

"So much for their Hybrid Child."

His laughs echoed through the room, but he quickly stopped when Jordanna and the rest of CAGE hurried through the entrance accompanied by an armed battalion of Careguards.

"I guess that's my cue," Victor said. He turned, grabbed hold of the portal beacon, and vanished.

Gruggins and Hayley reappeared, and she was kneeling at Ethan's side, sobbing uncontrollably. Jordanna and the others rushed over to them.

"It's Ethan," she cried. "He needs your help."

"What happened to him?" Jordanna asked.

"A soul reaping vortex," Gruggins said. "He threw himself in its path to save Miss Hayley."

"We have to save him!" Hayley screamed as tears streamed down her cheeks.

"I'm afraid there is nothing we can do," Jordanna said in a quivering tone.

"But you can do something," she cried to her brother. "All of Stravis' journals . . . the answer must be there somewhere."

"I'm sorry," Damien said. "If the answer does lie within Stravis' journals, there's no time. He'll be gone before we can find it. Even with our vast knowledge of the universe, there is no cure for this."

Ethan's face turned grey. His breaths grew shorter as his life continued to drain away. A bright yellow flash strobed across the room, drawing everybody's attention. It was the Shadow Princess swiftly gliding over the black pond to where Ethan lay dying.

"You have to help him, please!" Hayley pleaded to Adara.

Everyone moved out of her way as the Shadow Princess floated to Ethan's side and knelt beside him. She reached her arms down and held his head in her hands. Then moved one hand over his head to feel his cold forehead. She gazed up at Hayley and calmly shook her head back and forth.

"YOU CAN SAVE HIM! I KNOW YOU CAN!" Hayley cried louder.

Ethan's body quivered, and he slowly reached his hand up at Hayley. She knelt at his side opposite Adara and gently grabbed his hand as more tears flowed from her eyes. The Shadow Princess lightly forced her arms underneath Ethan's upper torso, lifted him, and cradled him in her bosom.

"What is she doing?" Tinx asked.

But nobody spoke a word. They stood by quietly as Ethan turned as black as the Shadow Princess. Then, Adara and Ethan dimmed without warning until the stone floor was visible through them both. They continued fading, becoming more and more translucent until, finally, they were gone.

TWO WEEKS LATER

A KRAKEN'S FURY

Two weeks went by with nary a peep out of Hayley. She was not taking the loss of Ethan well and was deep in mourning, spending most of her time behind door number 6L in The Hall of Doorways. Staying in Ethan's room made her feel closer to him and safe in some strange way. But with Caretaker training looming on the horizon, she needed to find a way to summon the strength and learn how to live without him.

She pulled herself out of the pillowy cloud bed in Ethan's room and stretched. Today was the first day of the rest of her life, and from here on out, she would take it day by day. Her plan for today was to return to her room, take a shower, brush her teeth and hair and dress.

"So far, so good," Hayley thought to herself. She stood in front of a full-length mirror and stared at herself in her Caretaker robe, pondering whether or not she could do it. But a rustling sound distracted her, and she spun around as a green blob appeared on her dresser and Gruggins popped out.

"My dear girl," he said. "I know you miss him. I miss him myself—but life goes on."

Tears streamed down Hayley's cheeks, so Gruggins fluttered over and landed on her shoulder to comfort her.

"Ethan Fox would not want you to mourn him. He would want you to celebrate his life by living yours to the fullest. He'd want you to be happy."

Gruggins sat down, scooted closer, and rested his head against her neck. Hayley wiped her tears away and calmly stood as Gruggins cuddled her neck.

Jordanna sat behind the study desk, discussing current events with Damien, Nicholas, and Tinx. Tinx perched on Damien's lap while he and Nicholas sat in chairs across the desk from the Headmistress. Hayley entered, and the room fell silent.

"I—I came to study a little," she said.

"That is quite all right," Jordanna said. "We will move to the CAGE briefing room."

"No, please don't," Hayley said. "I want everything at least to seem normal again. Pretend like I'm not here and return to your conversation."

Jordanna looked at the others and nodded.

"Well then, where were we? Bring me up to speed on our findings on the museum break-ins."

"I received the full report this morning," Nicholas said. "It appears they took similar items from each of the museums. They were thoroughly ransacked, which leads me to believe they were looking for something specific."

"So they must have found what they were looking for," said Jordanna. "What did they take?"

"All the museums they hit had exhibits with items pilfered from Stravis' bunker during the Pandora fiasco," Nicholas said.

"And?"

"And, according to gallery workers, the only things missing were small rock collections."

"Rock collections," Damien said. "What kind of rocks? Did you order a molecular scan of the exhibit?"

"Yes, it took some doing, but I had a clandestine team slip in and perform the scan under cover of night."

"And—what did they find?"

"Various elemental minerals were present. I have the list right here."

Nicholas handed a piece of paper to Damien. His eyes moved down the list and stopped as his mouth gaped open.

"What is it?" Jordanna asked.

"This could be a problem," he said. "I believe they were looking for this, a Ceresian bloating stone."

"And why is that a problem?"

"Because of what I've learned from Stravis' research. He studied peculiar alchemy between earthly items when they come in contact with certain elementals."

"And a Ceresian bloating stone is one of those elementals," said Jordanna.

"Yes, one of the worst. At least as far as I've learned thus far."

"How dangerous?" Nicholas asked.

"Well, my experiment used a tiny pebble from an earthly hydrated bloating stone and an equivalent nugget of de-cloaked leprechaun gold. The resulting blast cracked a containment cube rated at one hundred megatons."

Jordanna and Nicholas gasped in unison, and Hayley stood up from the study table.

"Did you say leprechaun gold?"

"Yes. Why do you ask?"

"The cargo holds in the pyramids, that was part of the cargo the Grimleavers took. I heard the female vampire named Norell, and she told Victor some of their leprechaun gold was de-cloaked."

"Then it's a safe bet the Grimleavers also know about the alchemy you describe," Nicholas said.

"Therein lies our problem," Damien said. "Victor Qruefeldt now has all the material he needs to blow up a vast portion of the known universe."

"I agree we have a problem," Jordanna said. "But mutual self-destruction or martyrdom is not Victor's style. No, he has definitive plans for his new weapon of mass destruction."

Hayley pulled up a chair and joined their conversation as they debated dealing with this new revelation and the other issues they faced. But Dorkin Drumbles scrambled into the study and interrupted their talk. He hurried to Jordanna's side, whispered in her ear, and ran out. Jordanna stood up and looked around the room before she spoke.

"Dorkin has informed me of an important new painting in the Gallery. You are all welcome to come along."

Damien and Nicholas followed her to the study door, Tinx rode along on Damien's shoulder, but Hayley went back to studying. Jordanna opened the door, stopped, and turned to her daughter.

"Hayley dear, you will want to see this. Dorkin was adamant."

Hayley reluctantly agreed and followed them to the Gallery. Dorkin was waiting by the entrance when they arrived and wasted no time escorting them down the long hall of significant works of art.

"It took no time, no time at all," Dorkin said. "The Fates were unanimous in record time, and they even gave this one a name."

"That's odd," Jordanna said. "They don't normally name them for us."

"Very odd indeed," Dorkin said. "This is the first time they have named one."

Dorkin stopped at the last painting in the hall that was still on the easel and covered with a white sheet.

"What did they name it?" Tinx asked.

"A Kraken's Fury."

He pulled the cover off, and they all stood and studied the painting. The scene was a dark cavern lit by a green glow and yellow highlights where a giant beast perched majestically upon a raised platform. The creature was dark green, with three dragon heads up top. Its bottom consisted of long tentacles and a sharp tail. Massive arms hung to the ground below the dragon heads, and it used them to lean on. At the monster's midsection, between its arms, a mouth with rows of sharp teeth gaped open. Above that, several randomly placed eyes peered out.

"The creature is a full-grown earthly Kraken," Damien said.

In front of the beast, lying to its left at the platform's base, sat a perfectly round black orb, cracked at the top where yellow rays of light beamed up at the Kraken.

"Who cares about the monster," Hayley said. "Who is that?"

She rubbed her eyes and stepped closer to the painting, and the others backed away to give her space. She focused her eyes on the lower middle left portion of the scene where the body of a boy lay on the ground. Upon first glance, he appeared to be unconscious or dead. His back was to the platform, and his face flat against the floor. Hayley turned her head sideways to view the boy's face, but then she turned her attention to his hands. His right arm tucked in and hugged his chest, but his left arm lay flat on the ground, palm up, and the symbol in its center gave off a dim yellow glow. Hayley perked up and spun around to face the others.

"That's Ethan," she said with a tearful smile. "He is alive, and he needs our help!"

BOOK 3

MAYHEM IN THE MOONGARDEN

E. L. SEER

MEET THE

Grubner Trowel
Mrs. Moongarden's
right hand man.

Ravisher
Pesky gluttonous
creatures that infest
any food source.

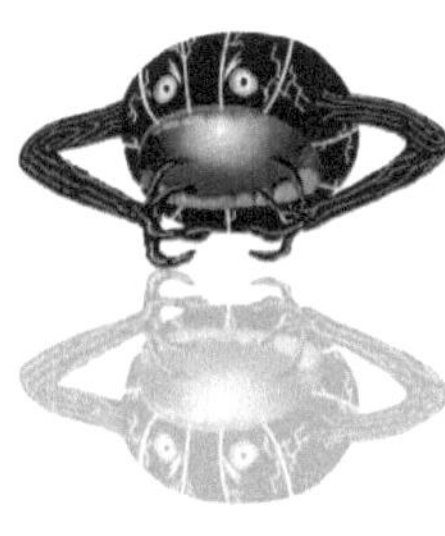

Mildred Moongarden
Caretaker head botanist and
creator of the Moongarden.

Hayley Ravenwood
Daughter of the
Caretaker Headmistress.

Irvin McGillicutty
Butler and keeper of
The Residence.

CHARACTERS

Gruggins McGhee
Grumpling of the house
at The Residence.

Wordly Pagemore
Bookworm and keeper of the
Caretaker Arts & Literature archive.

Albert
Red pyrodevlin from
Hades: the 'R' in RGB.

Linus
Green pyrodevlin from
Ceres: the 'G' in RGB.

Newton
Bluepyrodevlin from
Atlantis: the 'B' in RGB.

Prologue

THE CARETAKER UNIVERSE

Our story takes place in a mysterious world within our own—a world where the Caretakers watch over the human race and protect it from evil. The Caretakers are a coalition of intelligent beings from the four elemental worlds: Atlantis, Ceres, Hades, and Zephyr. Caretakers inhabit The Residence, their home base on Earth hidden and unknown to the humans they protect.

The Moongarden is a special place within The Residence created by Mildred Moongarden. Wonderous and otherworldly plant-life inhabit the Moongarden proper, while its special purpose Moon Orchard provides the Caretakers with all of their food needs on earth.

Grubner Trowel's greatest desire is to gain more responsibility and earn the respect of his mentor, Mildred Moongarden. Eager to please, Grubner gets his chance when Mildred is called away on important business and asks him to look after her prized Moongarden. But when Ravishers suddenly infest the Moongarden and its all-important orchard, mayhem ensues.

Grubner rushes to save the Caretaker's primary food source, the Moongarden's Moon Orchard. He quickly learns that earthly Ravishers are intelligent creatures, and he has his hands full in his battle to exterminate them. Will Grubner prevail against the witty pests before they wreak total devastation? Or will Mildred return beforehand and find "Mayhem in the Moongarden?"

Chapter 1

WEDDING PLANS

The fresh scent of morning dew tickled Grubner's nose as he breathed the fresh morning air in the Moongarden. Today is going to be a wonderful day, he thought to himself. He glanced down to re-read the urgent message from Mrs. Moongarden. It read:

"Dear Grubner, I hope this letter finds your spirits flowering with bliss. I've been called away on crucial matters, and my wits are as frayed as a feathering whistle vine in a rainbow storm. It is with utmost urgency I ask for your assistance. Please meet me in the clearing as soon as the sun sprouts. We must harvest a blossoming plan for the upcoming weeks. Kind regards, Old Moonshoes."

Old Moonshoes was a nickname Mrs. Moongarden had given herself, and in true 'Moonshoes' fashion, the letter sounded as whacky as its author. By the time he finished reading, Grubner still had no idea what she had asked of him.

Grubner Trowel was a three-foot-tall dwarf with big blue eyes, white hair, a Santa's beard, and a kind smile. He wore a green cloth garment draped over his body like a bedsheet. It hung above his brown high-topped boots, and a black belt secured it below his potbelly.

Grubner, the fourth of seven Trowel brothers from his mother's first and only earth-born litter, hated being the middle sibling. Being one of seven dwarfs led to a lot of ribbing by other Caretaker kids at The Residence. He and his brothers had heard every Snow White comment ever invented while growing up. But Grubner didn't mind because he enjoyed the old Disney classic.

"Hi-Ho, Hi-Ho, it's off to work I go," Grubner sang out loud as he skipped down the path to meet up with Mrs. Moongarden.

Grubner approached a thatch of shrubbery with brilliantly colored flowers, like butterflies, their wings opened and closed as if ready to take flight. Mrs. Moongarden's head popped up from behind the tall bushes.

"Lisa's flowers will flutter away soon," Mrs. Moongarden said. "I find it pleasing when they fly off to make little shrubs of their own, brings a tear to my eye every time."

Mrs. Moongarden named all of her creations, and Lisa was the name of the Butterfly Shrub. Mildred Moongarden's sweet grandmotherly demeanor made her a favorite of everyone. Her wrinkled rosy cheeks always cradled a smile beneath the round glasses perched on her nose. She wore a blue and white sundress on her slightly plump frame and a floral bonnet over her frail white hair.

"Simply tickled pink I am, you are showing up so early. Come, we've no time to waste. Rosebud is expecting us. I will explain on the way."

He followed Mrs. Moongarden down a different path leading deeper into the Moongarden to the right. Grubner was Mildred's 'little helper' around the Moongarden and was thrilled and excited to have been summoned by her for something sounding so important.

"Percy the pear tree has asked for the branch of Alicia the apple tree," Mrs. Moongarden said, "and she said yes! The wedding will take place in the clearing near the Moon Orchard in two weeks. We've barely enough time to plan."

Mrs. Moongarden let out a deep sigh.

"And to make matters worse, I've been called away on important business. A Skyclimber seedling has made its way into the human world. It is only a matter of time before she reaches the clouds and humans discover her."

Mrs. Moongarden stopped at a small bush with a mixture of blue and red leaves.

Several small twigs poked up and away from within the thicket and curled into the shape of a pig's tail. A thin, stringy vine hung to the ground at the end of each pigtail, and bright purple berries slowly slid down like on a guidewire. Small red cones beneath the end of each vine collected the berries.

"I'm afraid we may need to harvest all of Linnie's dwindle-berries to contain the growing Skyclimber. We must move her to safety. The human world is no place for a young Skyclimber."

Linnie was Mrs. Moongarden's pet name for the Itsy Bitzy bush, another of her ingenious creations. Each Itsy Bitzy grew up to ten dwindle-berries a day on every one of its pigtails. The fruit was highly valued due to its ability to shrink things, even people. One dwindle-berry will cause the near-halving of the consuming party, but the shrinkage is reversible by simply eating an equal number of shrunken dwindle-berries.

"Grubner will gather a sack full of dwindle-berries for Moonshoes."

"I once witnessed a gluttonous-gordgerat eat two dozen," Mrs. Moongarden said. "Poor creature disappeared from existence, didn't save any berries for a return to size."

"One must plan ahead when eating dwindle-berries," Grubner said.

"Oh my, we mustn't get distracted from our purpose," she said as she started back down the path at a frantic pace, and Grubner trailed behind.

When they arrived at the clearing, Rosebud stood by a fold-out table beneath the shade of Alicia the apple tree. A pile of invitations sat in front of her as she folded them in half and addressed them. As soon as she set one down, the invite would fold itself into a paper airplane and take off for delivery.

Rosebud dressed like Mrs. Moongarden, bonnet, and all. Mini-Moonshoes, some called her, but Rosebud's youth made her look more like Mildred's granddaughter. Her flowing strawberry blonde hair, bright green eyes, and matching green lipstick gave her an odd but beautiful appeal.

"Good morning," said Rosebud.

"I trust all is going smoothly, and you have accounted for all of the invitees?" Mrs. Moongarden asked.

"Smooth as a silk-flower."

"Terrific, our plans have blossomed."

A confused frown swept across Grubner's face. Why did she summon him with such urgency if Rosebud and Moonshoes already had everything planned?

"Okay," he said as the color drained from his face. "If there will be nothing else, Grubner will fetch dwindle-berries for Moonshoes."

"Oh my, I am sorry," Mrs. Moongarden replied. "My old noggin isn't as snappy as it used to be. Please forgive me for getting sidetracked. I have asked you here for an urgent reason."

Grubner perked up as the corners of his smile nearly reached the edges of his eyes.

"I must ask you for a significant favor. I must ask you to tend to the Moongarden while I am gone."

Grubner's forehead crinkled to make room for his eyes widening like saucers.

"Rosebud has offered to help, but she is far too busy planning Alicia and Percy's wedding. I have tremendous faith in Grubner, but if the responsibility is too much for you—"

"Grubner accepts. Grubner will take care of the Moongarden for Moonshoes."

"Whip-dilly doodles," Mrs. Moongarden said. "I'm as pleased as a peach. If you need any help, Rosebud will be available in case of an emergency. Now, I have provided Irvin with several days worth of supplies. But he will be stopping by to discuss his needs so you can properly plan the Moon Orchard's crop configuration."

Irvin McGillicutty was the keeper of The Residence and the right-hand man to the Caretaker Headmistress. He performed all manner of duties around The Residence, including procuring the food required to cook for an army of hungry Caretakers. And the Moon Orchard played an essential role as it supplied Irvin with all of his daily needs at The Residence.

Grubner got his final marching orders from Moonshoes. Afterward, he hung around and listened to her and Rosebud blabber on about wedding plans.

Grubner had worked as Mildred Moongarden's assistant for years and had learned a lot from her. He regarded Old Moonshoes as his mentor and even carried a copy of her book 'Moonshoes Guide to the Moongarden' in his pocket. It was all he had ever wanted, to be accepted by her and given more responsibility. Today was a wonderful day, and Grubner's dreams were coming true.

Chapter 2

GRUBNER'S TROUBLES

Grubner's eyes squinted nearly shut as he gazed up at the enormous vine stretching into the pillowy white clouds in the sky. The Skyclimber is indeed a marvel to behold, he thought. How on earth is Mrs. Moongarden going to corral a young one growing in the wild? He had no idea, but today began his chance to prove himself more than a trusted helper. The

Moongarden would flourish during Mildred's absence, and Grubner would handle everything himself without Rosebud's help.

For his first rounds of the day, Grubner decided to walk every single path through the Moongarden and take notes on anything requiring his attention. Thus far, things didn't look so good, and Grubner's notepad already brimmed with writing. He found a lot of things out of place or ever so slightly disturbed. Mrs. Moongarden would never leave things in such an unkempt state. Grubner's stomach churned with angst, something strange was going on, but he had no idea what.

As he walked past the burning Firelyte Shrub, a twinkle of light tickled the corner of his eye as its flames flickered. But when he turned to glance at the blazing bush, the encompassing inferno appeared normal.

"Now I'm seeing things," he said, "and talking to myself."

Grubner continued along the path, and something disturbing grabbed his attention. Wendy, the Withering Froo, was all balled up in her protective shielding leaves, or "shleaves" as Moonshoes called them. A boulder of tree bark stood where a beautiful giant red flower usually sat. Something must have disturbed it for that to happen, but he found no apparent culprit when he scanned the area.

Grubner made his way to the clearing where he had met Moonshoes and Rosebud the previous day. He and Irvin were scheduled to meet at the Moon Orchard to discuss Irvin's supply needs for the following days. The Moon Orchard was another of Mrs. Moongarden's ingenious creations, a massive garden created to supply all of the Caretaker's daily food requirements at The Residence. It was designed in sections, each of which could be reconfigured on a rotating basis to supply Irvin with his ever-changing daily needs.

When he arrived, he stopped in horror. Row upon row of uprooted and devoured vegetation lay spread across the expansive garden. Something foul was afoot in the Moon

Orchard. Grubner walked to the remains of a nearby peacock plant where tattered feathers lay scattered, the buttery core gnawed to a nub. Nearly one-quarter of the Moon Orchard had been consumed, and only stems, leaves, roots, and bulbs remained.

"Schnickyrooners and things like that," Irvin ranted as he approached from behind. "Hotdog worms eat green dirt noodles on the side of the flying turtle lips. And when they scream loud enough, the pig warts won't even make a sound like they did before brunch."

"Stop it, Irvin! I have no time for your jibber-jabber. Something terrible has happened; someone sabotaged the Moon Orchard."

"Oh my, what happened to the Moon Orchard?" Irvin asked as he snapped out of his rant.

Irvin McGillicutty was tall with white skin resembling candle wax, and his face had little definition. He wore a black tuxedo with a bow tie and a rose corsage. Irvin worked as the butler, chef, maid, and handyman of The Residence, you name it, and he probably had a hand in it.

"Don't worry," Irvin said, "I'll go fetch Rosebud. She'll know what to do."

"You will do no such thing! The Moongarden is under my watch, and I will take care of this."

"Sure you will. That's why your face looks like this." Irvin's face morphed into a funny version of Grubner's face. His mouth drooped ridiculously wide open, down to his neckline, and his eyes covered half his face and turned as round as tennis balls.

"I have everything under control," Grubner insisted.

"If you say so," Irvin replied as his face returned to its usual department store dummy appearance. "In the meantime, I have no current need for supplies. Old Moonshoes made sure I stocked up before she left."

"She did?" Grubner asked as a slight frown invaded his face.

"Must have foreseen Grubner's troubles," Irvin said.

Grubner spent the next five minutes smoothing things over with Irvin and convincing him not to tell Rosebud what had happened. Finally, Irvin reluctantly agreed and gave Grubner a list of his future needs. He would return in a day or two to check on the status of his next order.

Once Irvin left, Grubner wasted no time cleaning up the trashed areas so he could replant the damaged section of the Moon Orchard as fast as possible.

"Did Mrs. Moongarden foresee troubles for Grubner?" he thought to himself. If so, it meant she didn't have any faith in him and only chose him because Rosebud was too busy. Either way, Grubner would prove himself capable to them all.

Chapter 3

THE RAVISHERS

Grubner continued cleaning up the mess in the Moon Orchard the following day. Rosebud stopped by on her way to visit Alicia and Percy to discuss their ceremony and reception details.

"Howdy-doody Grubner, is everything running smoothly?" she asked. "I thought I would stop by and see how things are going."

"Smooth as a silk-flower," Grubner said with a wink and a smile. "I'm nearly ready for the next reconfigure."

Luckily, he cleared enough of the mess away, so Rosebud didn't notice anything out of the ordinary.

"You're doing a wonderful job. Anyway, I must run along. The wedding is not going to plan itself, toodle-oo."

He spent the next few hours looking over his shoulder as he cleaned up the rest of the Moon Orchard. Could Mrs. Moongarden have asked Rosebud to spy on him? Surely not. She wasn't that kind of person. Still, he would be prepared, just in case.

"Grubner will show them all," he said to himself as he scooped up the last few remnants of consumed plant remains.

Grubner stretched his arms out and yawned, then sat down on the grass to lean against a tree stump at the edge of the Moon Orchard. He tossed a rock into the nearby pond and stared at the circular ripples as they grew across its surface.

"I hear there are troublemakers in your midst," a voice said from over Grubner's shoulder.

Grubner turned his head to see who spoke to him. His old friend, Gruggins McGhee, stood behind him on the stump. Gruggins was a bluish-green mouse-sized creature called a grumpling. He had the face of an old man with a fat bulbous nose, tall blue Tweetie-bird eyes, and two moth-like wings with a purple and yellow eye pattern.

"Hey Gruggins, I bet I can guess where you heard that on my first try."

"Of course, you can. Irvin has been blabbing all over The Residence. That mush-mouthed-morph-dork never keeps his trap shut."

Grubner and Gruggins were friends, so he decided to confide in him.

"I don't know what to do, Gruggins. I don't know what happened, and now I'm ready to replant the damaged section of the Moon Orchard. It may happen again, and I am freaking out."

"Which is why I dropped by," Gruggins said. "Maybe I can aid you in exposing the culprit, and together we will get to the bottom of this."

"Thank you, Gruggins. I would like your help, my dear friend."

"Sit tight while I take a glide around to investigate." Gruggins fluttered off to search the area from above for signs of Grubner's troubles.

Gruggins would take time to flutter around the expansive Moon Orchard. So, in the meantime, Grubner would use his break time wisely. He pulled out his elemental modulator. A small iPhone-like device referred to as an ELMO. Grubner tapped on the ELMO's screen, and a list with Irvin's order popped up. He studied the list but did not get very far because Gruggins returned and landed on the tree stump.

"Well? Did you find anything?" Grubner asked.

"I sure did."

"What did you find?"

"You've got an infestation, my friend. The garden is infested with Ravishers."

"Ravishers? What are Ravishers?" Grubner asked.

"They are nasty gluttonous creatures that eat almost anything. I'm surprised they didn't devour the whole Moon Orchard. Must be a small infestation, but you better eradicate them before they multiply, and Mildred returns to a Nonegarden."

Gruggins hopped onto Grubner's shoulder.

"Head that way, and I will show you the cause of your troubles," Gruggins said. He pointed towards an undisturbed portion of the Moon Orchard. "Behind the row of peacock-plants."

Grubner approached a tall line of colorful bushes resembling giant peacock feathers arranged in circular tiers around small hills. But they were not actually hills and consisted of mounds of peacock butter the limbs excreted as they grew. The feathers tickled Grubner's face as he slid between two of the plants, and Gruggins ducked to avoid getting knocked from his shoulder. They emerged into another small garden area where rows of carrots, radishes, and other vegetables lay ruined. Grubner's eyes widened, and his lips tightened into an angry smirk.

"Here we are," Gruggins said.

"But I don't see anything except for more devastation."

"Oh, I almost forgot, you can't see them, they cloak themselves, but I'll fix that."

Gruggins snapped his fingers, and the Ravishers slowly came into view. Grubner cringed at the sight of four black pumpkin-shaped creatures the size of basketballs. Their heads were almost nothing but a mouth full of dull chomping teeth. Bright orange-yellow light emanated from their mouth, eyes, and line markings like a fire burning from within. Stubby little legs sat barely visible below their round bodies, while thick and lanky dark green arms dragged on the ground in front of them to scoop food into their faces.

At first, the Ravishers kept chomping away at the garden and ignored Grubner and Gruggins' presence. "They don't realize I have de-cloaked them," Gruggins whispered to Grubner. "What do you say we let them know?"

"Ahemmmm," Grubner cleared his throat loudly as he and Gruggins glared down at the creatures.

The Ravishers stopped all at once as their round bodies slowly pivoted upwards to point their eyes up at Grubner and Gruggins.

"Boo," Gruggins said.

The Ravisher's black eyes grew to the size of silver dollars, and their arms swiftly became long legs hoisting them off the ground and running away fast.

"Boo," Grubner repeated as the Ravishers ran for their lives like scared mice.

After scaring the Ravishers away, Gruggins hung around to give his buddy a pep talk. He warned Grubner the creatures would return and offered his assistance. Grubner thankfully declined but was grateful to his friend for exposing the culprits. Before leaving, Gruggins gave one final word of advice and showed his friend how to use his ELMO to adjust the Moongarden's light so the Ravishers could no longer cloak themselves. Grubner's task would be a whole lot easier if the Ravishers were not invisible when they ravished.

Chapter 4

SPLASH DOWN

Sweat droplets trickled down Grubner's cheeks, and his beard quickly soaked them up. The Ravishers had returned, so he raked up the remains of more wilted vegetation in the Moon Orchard. He had adjusted the Moongarden's light settings as Gruggins had suggested and made the morning rays more intense, but so far, he had not spotted any of the nasty creatures.

After cleaning up, he decided to explore every inch of the Moon Orchard to search for more damage. But he would not ignore the rest of the massive Moongarden, so he enlisted the help of his six brothers: Grabner, Gribner, Grobner, Gripner, Gropner, and Daryl. They assembled near the huge pond adjacent to the clearing and Moon

Orchard. Grubner gave them their marching orders, and they would report back with their findings.

"Sleepy and Sneezy, you two will take the Skyclimber area," Grubner said. "Grumpy and Bashful will take the courtyard and ruins, and that leaves the remainder of the Moongarden for Happy and Dopey."

Grubner's brothers hated when he made Snow White jokes, but they knew his ribbing was all in fun, and they would do anything for their brother Doc. It would not be so funny if the names didn't match their personalities so closely, Grubner thought; whoever wrote the story must have met his siblings.

While his brothers paired off and departed for the Moongarden proper, Grubner would concentrate on the Moon Orchard, where he knew more troubles would surface. So, he walked towards the Moon Orchard's center and stopped short of a tall barrier of foliage. Thorny black vines slithered out from beneath the wall of vegetation like serpents. They crept directly towards him and were nearly upon him when he pulled out his ELMO and tapped at its screen.

"A little too close for comfort," Grubner said, "but you Creeping Tanglers won't get me."

The thorny vines slowly retreated under the black wall as it unraveled into an archway for Grubner to walk through. The Creeping Tangler barrier wall was another of Mrs. Moongarden's wondrous creations, designed to trap any vermin infesting the Moon Orchard. But so far, the Ravishers had steered clear of the tanglers.

Grubner continued through the archway and realized he had never been this deep into the Moon Orchard. Finally, he came upon a row of six-foot-tall trees with thin straight trunks and big white globes of growth on top like giant dandelions. The balls on top formed from hundreds of foot-long twigs holding a perfect white egg at the end like skewers.

"The eggplants are untouched," Grubner said, "I thought for sure they would have ravished these by now."

Grubner continued his rounds and found nothing else out of place. Finally, he came to the hill at the back of the Moon Orchard where Mrs. Moongarden's prized Mimicking Melon trees grew. As he reached the top of the knoll, everything appeared to be in order. He stood at the foot of one of the tall trees and gazed up into its branches where hundreds of melon fruits the size of tennis balls were hanging. Tiny watermelons, cantaloupe, honeydew, and various other melon replicas hung, ripe and ready.

As he lowered his gaze, he focused down the row of forest and spotted one at the end that had fallen. His walk turned to a jog as he quickly approached the fallen timber.

"No, please no," he yelled, "not one of her prized melon trees."

Tears welled up in his eyes as he scanned the destruction. Bare branches and scattered leaves were all that remained of the beautiful Mimicking Melon. "I'll teach those horrid creatures," Grubner said as he ground his teeth. "They'll learn not to ravish Old Moonshoes' wonderful creations."

Grubner's brothers returned from their rounds and reported nothing out of the ordinary. So, after his discovery atop melon tree hill, he thought long and hard about how to react and came up with a plan to show the Ravishers who they were messing with. First, with the help of his brothers, he would climb one of the Mimicking

Melon trees and hide in its branches. Then, when the Ravishers attacked it, he would pounce on them and scare them off. If he scared them bad enough, maybe they would not return.

Since the culprit always returned to the crime scene, Grubner picked out a tree right next to the fallen one near the edge of the hill. His six brothers got on their hands and knees and arranged themselves into a small staircase, three at the base, two on the next level, and one on the next. They reached barely high enough for Grubner to climb and grab the lowest branch to pull himself up.

Once safely in place, his brothers retreated to their homes for the day.

He hung out for nearly three hours, and with only two hours of light left in the day, all remained quiet. An hour later, Grubner's eyes grew heavy as he strained to keep them open. Ten minutes later, the sound of his snores filled the air.

Day faded to early evening when Grubner awoke to a grunting and gnawing noise. He peered down as his eyes came into focus on the sight of four Ravishers below him chomping at the base of his tree. Ready to pounce, Grubner's tree abruptly angled sideways and fell swiftly. It hit hard at the edge of the hill and bounced, knocking Grubner out and sending him tumbling down the steep incline. He rolled to the bottom of the knoll and into the muddy end of the pond that wrapped around the backside of the Moon Orchard.

It took him several minutes to inch his way out of the thick deep muck. When he finally emerged from the goop, Grubner looked like a giant chocolate-covered dwarf. Mud oozed down his entire body as he glared up the hill. One of the Ravishers was standing at the edge of the hill, peering down at Grubner while the others continued to chomp away. This Ravisher was different than the others; the top of his head angled to a shallow cone just deep enough to hold the thick ring of thorns circling its head like a crown. The lead Ravisher continued to glare down as it let out a loud shrill laugh. Grubner's face felt flush as he raised his fists and yelled up at the Ravishers.

"This is not the last you pests have seen of Grubner Trowel. I will get all of you devils."

But the other Ravishers paid no attention to his rant and only stopped munching melons long enough to join their leader in laughter. By the time Grubner washed away the mud and hiked back up the hill, the Ravishers were gone, and another Mimicking Melon tree was destroyed.

Chapter 5

CORN RAVISHED

The clean odor of rain tickled Grubner's nose as he strolled on one of the Moongarden's many dirt pathways. But there wasn't a cloud in the sky, and it could only mean one thing – he would soon witness the dance of the Trembling Nomads. Grubner always got a kick out of their chaotic tango, so he hurried down the path to their enclosure.

"Well, at least the Moongarden is business as usual, and the infestation is confined to the Moon Orchard," Grubner thought to himself.

He stopped at the white picket fence surrounding tiny evergreen trees, their tops peaked forward like penguin heads. They resembled little people, each with two pine-covered arm branches and two brown leg trunks. Grubner watched closely as the nomads slowly raised their arm branches skyward and trembled violently like a group of little people shaking their fists at the sky.

Grubner's cheeks bunched into a smile as he anticipated what would happen. They would stop trembling any moment now, pop their trunks from the ground, and run around the pen bumping into one another like bumper cars. But instead, to his surprise, they popped up and formed a perfect row. Grubner had never seen this before, but Moonshoes had told him of it.

He gazed in astonishment as they joined branches,

hopped up and down, and kicked their trunks around in unison like Irish dancers.

"Seedlings will be coming soon," he said. "Am I ever going to catch a break?"

Trembling Nomad infants were not hard to deal with, but it meant he would have to wrap their enclosure, or he would have seedlings roaming free in the Moongarden. And given his current struggles battling the pesky Ravishers, his to-do list grew longer by the day.

He continued on his way to the Moon Orchard where more destruction likely awaited his arrival. As he passed by Wendy the Withering Froo, Grubner stopped to examine one of Mrs. Moongarden's latest creations – a small shrub of Squid Blossoms. The pink flowers donned yellow and red spots resembling eyes. They had oblong bodies with long thin petals, like tentacles at the end. He bent down to sniff their sweet aromatic scent and could almost taste it. The delicate flowers grasped the end of his nose with their fragile tentacles. It tickled as he gently pulled away from their grasp and continued the journey, he dreaded to the Moon Orchard.

Grubner closed his eyes and crossed his fingers as he approached the Moon Orchard. Maybe the Ravishers had gotten their fill devouring two whole Mimicking Melon trees. Of course, he wasn't counting on it, but at least he'd hope for the best.

When he opened his eyes, the carnage was worse than he imagined. Husks and stalks littered the empty dirt field where the cornfield from his latest reconfigure should have stood. And to make matters worse, Irvin would be arriving soon to check on tomorrow's order. But Mrs. Moongarden had developed tools to deal with such emergencies. If he could clear out the devastation in a couple of hours and replant Irvin's cornfields, he would use some of Mildred's special Moongrow fertilizer to grow the crops overnight and still have plenty of time for the morning harvest. Grubner would need to call on his brothers for help once again.

"Shnickyrooners and schnackleboxes and things like that," Irvin's said in a goofy tone as he approached. "A giant fiddle-stick always disappoints its mother when the zoo is open for snail cookies. But you should never tell the sleeping lizard how to drive a finicky goober elf."

"Stop it, Irvin. I have far too many troubles as it is. Why are you always babbling?"

"Well, now, someone woke up on the wrong side of the tree-hut."

"I'm dealing with a nasty Ravisher infestation."

Irvin scanned the ravished cornfield and turned to face Grubner.

"Of course, Grubner's got everything under control. No problems at all, just as you promised.

Except for maybe over there—" he pointed at the cornfield. "And over there, and there, and there and right there." Arms morphed out from Irvin's body to point all around the destroyed pasture.

"Grubner will take care of this," he said as he let out a big sigh.

"What am I going to do for corn tomorrow?" Irvin asked. "I know . . . I will grow it out of my ears."

Irvin's four extra arms retreated into his body as two sizable ears of corn pushed their way out of the sides of his head and fell to the ground.

"I have a plan," Grubner said. "My brothers will help me clear the field, and I will replant the cornfield with Moongrow. The harvest will go on as planned tomorrow."

"If you say so."

"I just need to make sure those pests don't come back beforehand."

"You should build a scarecrow," Irvin suggested. "Humans use them all the time, and they never have Ravishers in their cornfields."

"Great idea, thank you," Grubner said. "If the humans can scare them away, Grubner will too."

"Happy to help, good luck, and see you soon." Irvin turned to leave but then turned back. "I almost forgot; Hayley Ravenwood will be joining the harvest tomorrow. The poor dear's been sad ever since Ethan Fox returned to the human world. She is in a funk."

"Ethan Fox," Grubner repeated.

"Indeed," Irvin said, "the hybrid child himself was in our midst. I do hope master Ethan is doing well, it has been nearly six months, and I have not heard a word about him."

"Well then," Grubner said, "we will try to cheer Miss Hayley up at the harvest."

After Irvin's exit, Grubner contacted his brothers on his ELMO. They arrived quickly, and in no time, had cleared away the rubble and replanted Irvin's cornfield. But it was only the beginning of Grubner's plan. Next, they would build a human-engineered totem to keep the Ravishers away. But first, they would travel to Market Square to buy supplies for the project.

The Moongarden grew dark by the time they finally made it back. There were barely enough Trowel siblings to carry all the supplies on Grubner's list. Nevertheless, the brothers were undeterred. They would build Grubner's masterpiece and fix the Ravishers for good.

Grubner and his helpers worked long into the night on the enormous monument. A silvery moon lit the night's sky and gave them enough light to admire their work.

"It would sure scare me if I were a Ravisher," Grubner said as he gazed up at his creation.

His brothers nodded in agreement.

Chapter 6

AN HONEST MISTAKE

Grubner waited at the entrance to the Moongarden when Irvin and Hayley arrived through the Hall of Doorways. He didn't return home until after midnight and hardly slept due to his excitement level. He also hadn't checked the Moon Orchard yet because there was no need. The Ravishers would be miles away by now, hiding from the masterpiece he and his brothers built to guard the cornfield.

"Good morning, Miss Hayley," he said. "May a dozen candied foxtails brighten your day." He knelt in front of Hayley and held up a bouquet of colorful treats.

"How thoughtful, Grubner," Hayley replied with a smile. "I love candied foxtails. Thank you."

Hayley was the daughter of the Caretaker Headmistress. She had golden blonde hair, blueish-green eyes, a petite nose, a rosy smile, and a charming demeanor.

Grubner turned to Irvin with fire in his eyes. "I have taken care of everything," he said. "We stayed up late last night working on it, and boy is it scary."

"Will your brothers be joining us for the harvest?" Irvin asked.

"Of course, let's go. They should be there already. But first, you must close your eyes so it will be a surprise. Grubner will lead the way."

Irvin and Hayley closed their eyes and held their hands over their faces as Grubner walked between them and grasped their elbows to guide them. As they approached the Moon Orchard, Grubner's brothers stood side-by-side admiring their work. Unfortunately, Grubner was the runt of the Trowel litter, so he could not see over them to view the cornfield.

"Open your eyes," he said as he parted the wall of siblings to take a look at his victory.

Grubner's face felt numb as his victorious smile flipped upside-down. He fell to his knees and buried his face in his hands.

"I'm surprised all right," Irvin said as he scanned the carnage in the pasture. The Ravishers had returned, and the new crops were entirely lost.

"And what in the blazes, may I ask, is that?" Irvin asked as he pointed to the middle of the ravished cornfield.

"It is the scared-crow," Grubner replied. "We built it to scare the Ravishers, just like you said. After all, humans don't have Ravisher infestations."

The only thing left standing in the cornfield was a giant black crow erected atop a tall wooden pole. It had ruffled feathers and extra-large eyes, gaped open like it had seen a ghost. Grubner's creation appeared to be the only scared thing in the Moongarden today.

"I said scarecrow, S-C-A-R-E-C-R-O-W," Irvin shouted as the letters morphed from his body and bulged from his chest one by one.

"Stop teasing him," Hayley said.

Grubner buried his head in his hands again and began sobbing.

"Everything will be okay," Hayley said as she ran and knelt beside him. "You made an honest mistake. You should use this as a lesson and learn from it as Mrs. Moongarden would."

Grubner stopped weeping and glanced up at Hayley.

"Really? Mildred would do such a thing?" He asked.

"Everybody makes mistakes, even Mrs. Moongarden, and do you know what she would do in your place?"

"What?" Grubner asked as he rose to his feet.

"She would do her research. She would study everything about Ravishers and learn what makes them tick. Then she would come up with a plan."

"But how would Grubner research?"

"You would start in The Residence study. There are many books to learn from, and Wordly Pagemore would be more than happy to help."

"Grubner will do research," he said, "Grubner will learn all about his Ravisher enemies, and Grubner will make a plan."

Grubner canceled the harvest due to unforeseen circumstances. His brothers stuck around long enough to console him and help with another clean-up. Irvin left empty-handed, but he took it well as he had expected Grubner's failure and had made other arrangements just in case.

Hayley hung around for a while after Irvin's quick exit. She must have sensed Grubner's need for her approval, so she stayed and gave him a long pep talk. Tomorrow, Grubner would begin his research, as Moonshoes would do, and then the Ravishers would be in big trouble.

Chapter 7

UNDUE STRESS

After losing his second corn harvest to the troublesome Ravishers, Grubner camped out by the Moon Orchard in case he needed to deal with any further devastation quickly. But of course, the Ravishers did not return, so Grubner stayed up half the night to no avail.

The light of the morning sky rained down on the Moongarden's lush assortment of unique plant species. Grubner rubbed the sleep from his eyes as his mouth parted into a big yawn. The unmistakable sound of Mrs. Moongarden's Snapping Spruces awakened him. Loud clacking sounds of their snaps echoed in the morning air. Something threatens them, or they would not be snapping so fiercely, he thought.

He rushed down the path towards the Moongarden's entrance and turned in a different direction near the Butterfly Shrubs. He continued past Wendy the Withering Froo and took the right fork leading to the back of the clearing where the forest thickened.

The Snapping Spruces lay calm and quiet by the time Grubner arrived, but he slowly scanned the area anyway to be sure. He gazed up at the tall, colorful trees similar to their earthly counterparts with a few significant differences. The ordinarily green or blue needles were bright red and black at the base where they were attached. Each of the branches held a small bear-trap-like appendage at the end. The yellow teeth-shaped snappers would lurch forward on long necks and bite at any critters coming too close.

The quick jog through the Moongarden reminded Grubner, he would need to wrap the Trembling Nomad pen. He had put it off for too long, so he had to do it right away. Grubner's brothers would arrive soon to look after the Moon Orchard while he went off to study as Hayley had suggested. But now, studying would have to wait, as the seedlings would be arriving any day now.

Grubner wiped a bead of sweat from his brow as he stared into the burning Firelyte Shrub and awaited his brothers' arrival. The flames flickered off twice as he stood transfixed on the hypnotic blaze, and that concerned him because the shrub's flame should never stop until it is time.

"Rose shouldn't be dropping seeds for another two years," Grubner said to himself.

The Firelyte Shrub was an import from the elemental world of Hades, and Mrs. Moongarden named this one Rose. Like all Firelyte Shrubs, Rose stayed in a perpetual state of 'on fire,' yet she would never burn. The brilliant red and orange flames swayed with the slight breeze in the air and flickered off again for a few seconds. Grubner pulled out his copy of 'Moonshoes Guide to the Moongarden' and thumbed through its pages.

"Here we are," he said and read. "A Firelyte Shrub's protective flames extinguish once every five years so its seed can drop. This event is always preceded by days of flickering."

Grubner remembered he had seen the flames blink off before, but that had been several days ago. He read more.

"After dropping its seeds, the Firelyte Shrub will reignite and start the process over. Once dropped, seeds that are disturbed or touched by external sources are rendered infertile."

Grubner sighed deeply and read the next part slowly.

"Seeds rendered infertile become firelyte capsules, which when smashed, summon a firelyte demon."

Grubner gulped and scanned the footnotes.

"I am correct. Moonshoes made a note, and it says Rose last dropped her seeds three years ago. But why—"

The following sentence gave him his answer.

"When exposed to undue stress, a Firelyte Shrub will prematurely drop its seeds."

Just as Grubner suspected, the Ravishers had been doing more than eating up all the Caretaker crops. They had been somehow subjecting the other species to undue stress as well.

When Grubner's brothers arrived, he sent three of them directly to the Moon Orchard, and the other three to walk the Moongarden proper and keep an eye out for anything out of the ordinary. Grubner continued wrapping the Trembling Nomad pen when Irvin McGillicutty showed up unexpectedly.

"How are you on this fine day?" he asked as he approached.

"No Schnickyrooners and things like that," Grubner said, "well that's a first. How may I be of assistance?"

"Irvin is here to help Grubner."

"Help? Grubner needs no help. I have everything under control."

"Of course, you do," Irvin spoke slowly as his face ballooned larger and he winked one of his now giant eyes. "But just the same, Irvin is here to tell you he requires no new orders from the Moon Orchard. Market Square is hosting a human farmers market for a few days, and the Caretakers find it an occasional treat to eat human-grown produce."

Grubner breathed a quiet sigh of relief. Irvin's news was indeed the break he needed to get the upper hand on the Ravishers. Mrs. Moongarden would be back in a couple of days, so hopefully, he would have defeated the infestation by then. Not having to constantly reconfigure, replant, and protect the crops would help.

"Whatcha doing?" Irvin asked.

"The nomads are about to drop their seedlings. So, I must wrap their pen so the little ones cannot escape. Hard to find those little sprouts when they are running around loose."

"Can I give you a hand?" Irvin asked as he morphed into a giant hand with a face.

"Everything is under control," Grubner replied as hand-Irvin mouthed the words.

"Somehow, I knew you would say that. Toodles," Irvin said and then left.

Chapter 8

STAMPEDE OF THE NOMADS

Grubner had barely finished wrapping the Trembling Nomad pen when the loud clacking noise started up again. Something had disturbed the Snapping Spruces again, so he hurried down the path to catch the mischief-maker in the act. Grabner and Gribner arrived from different directions.

"I saw two of them," Grabner said. "They ran under the brush in that direction."

"Me too," Gribner said. "You must have run right by them."

"They better not be unwrapping the nomad enclosure," Grubner said as he bolted back down the path he had entered from, and his brothers followed.

They stopped at the nomad pen and walked around its perimeter, examining Grubner's work.

"Nice wrap job," Gribner said.

"Doesn't appear to be disturbed in any way," Grabner added.

All remained silent around the Trembling Nomads, but that's what disturbed him. It seemed too quiet, and then he realized why. Rose's flames no longer burned. Someone or something had extinguished her.

"Rose must have dropped her seeds," Grubner said as he rushed over to examine her.

He studied the ground around her but found only dirt, and her blue and green leafy frame that usually blazed with orange and red flames.

"Oh no," Grubner said.

"Where are Rose's seeds?" Grabner and Gribner asked in unison as they walked up from behind.

Grubner crawled around on his hands and knees, scouring the ground frantically.

"They must be here somewhere. Firelyte seeds don't just stand up and walk away."

"Something's burning," Grabner said as his nose twitched at the air.

Suddenly, a Trembling Nomad ran by with its side branches raised at the sky. Grubner jumped to his feet and turned towards the nomad pen, now on fire. The Ravishers had the enclosure surrounded, one on each side. The closest to Grubner, the leader, turned and flashed a teeth-baring grin.

It then stretched out its long shoveling arms and opened its hands to reveal two red marbles with orange and yellow swirls. The Ravisher leader glared into Grubner's eyes and winked at him.

"The Ravishers have disturbed the seeds," Gribner said.

"They are firelyte capsules now," Grubner said. "We must stop them from igniting more of them."

Another Trembling Nomad scampered by as Grubner and his brothers slowly approached the troublesome creatures.

"It's okay, be a nice little Ravisher and hand me the seeds," Grubner said in as calm a voice as he could muster.

The Ravisher backed away as two of its minions came around the pen and joined the party. One of them held a firelyte capsule.

"Come on now," Grubner said in a hushed tone as he painted a soft smile with his face. "Nice little monster, give Grubner the capsules."

But instead, the Ravisher king tossed one of its capsules to its lackey, and now all three held one of the colorful marbles. Grubner and his brothers continued their slow advance as the creatures matched their pace, backing away. Then, the lead Ravisher started solo juggling its capsule, and the others followed along, tossing them up and catching them, tossing them up and catching them.

Grubner stared the lead Ravisher right in the eyes as a sparkle jumped from one eye to the other, and the corners of its mouth slowly ascended into a giant toothy smile. Grubner's face reddened, and his blood boiled as he knew what would happen next.

"Now! Get-em boys," he yelled as he and his brothers lurched at the creatures.

But they were too late. The Ravishers had already smashed their firelyte capsules onto the hard dirt outside the nomad pen. Three small infernos engulfed the ground between the Ravishers and Trowel brothers. The flames slowly rose from the soil as they morphed into small foot-tall fire creatures. The firelytes had black facial features, with tiny beady eyes and devilish grins.

"Never seen a firelyte for real," Grabner said.

"Me neither," Gribner added.

The brothers stared at the scene in horror as the firelytes whistled and marched in unison towards the Trembling Nomad pen. The tiny fire demons each walked to a different corner where the enclosure had not already burned. They each grabbed hold of a post and hugged it like a long-lost relative. The whistling grew louder and louder as the creatures slowly melted into their respective posts. A loud popping noise interrupted the whistling as they erupted into flames with a red puff of smoke.

The firelyte infernos spread quickly around the pen, aided by Grubner's wrapping that acted like kindling on a campfire. It only took a few minutes to burn to the ground. No sooner had the enclosure burnt down than the Trembling Nomads began to  tremble. Apparently, the Ravishers could induce the nomad dance as well, and now all of the Trembling Nomads were on the loose running about the Moongarden.

By the time the enclosure finished burning, the Ravishers were nowhere to be found. Grubner assembled his brothers to assign tasks and start the rebuild. Grobner, Gripner, Gropner, and Daryl would repair the nomad enclosure while Grabner, Gribner, and Grubner tracked down the dozen missing nomads as they had seen them escape firsthand.

"Okay, are there any—" Grubner's ELMO ring interrupted him. "Hello, Miss Hayley. It is such a pleasure to hear your voice."

Grubner's talk with Hayley was short and sweet. She was checking in on him because Wordly had told her he hadn't shown up for his study session. Grubner told her what had happened but assured her he had everything under control. Hayley said she would stop by the first chance she got.

After rebuilding the Trembling Nomad enclosure, Grobner, Gripner, Gropner, and Daryl helped search for the tiny missing trees lost in the vast forest of vegetation. They had already tracked down and returned nine of the nomads to their new corral by the time Hayley showed up.

"How goes it?" she asked as she reached the pen.

"We've repaired the damages and found nine of them," Grubner said as he silently recounted the nomads in the pen. "My brothers are out gathering the rest as we speak."

No sooner had he spoken than Grobner and Gripner approached with another missing nomad.

"They should call these things 'wandering nomads,'" Grobner said.

"What happened to you two?" Hayley asked.

Scratches covered Grobner and Gripner's arms and legs, and their clothes were tattered from head to toe.

"Found this one wrapped in a wad of Creeping Tanglers," Grobner replied.

"Had to fight them off as we untangled the poor thing," Gripner said. "Sharp little barbs those tanglers have."

"We now have ten out of twelve," Grubner said.

"Make that eleven," Hayley said as she pointed at two more brothers approaching from the direction of the clearing. "And it appears they ran into trouble too."

Mud covered Gropner and Daryl from head to toe, as well as the tiny tree they carried between them.

"Found this one in the center of the moon-pond," Gropner said.

"Of course, the little tyke got stuck in the muddy end," Daryl said. "Had to wade clear out to the middle of the muck to reach him."

"And that makes eleven," Grubner said. "Only one more to go."

"We've searched all around the Moon Orchard. But unfortunately, he isn't there," Grobner said.

"And we covered everything in and around the clearing," Daryl said.

"Well, then that leaves the Skyclimber area past the foliage tunnel," Grubner said. "Let's hope Grabner and Gribner have found him."

"They haven't found him," Hayley said as she stared into the distance, and her eyes widened. "They haven't found him because he's there." Hayley raised her arm and pointed towards the Skyclimber vine that weaved its way into the clouds.

Grubner and his brothers sighed in unison as they spotted what Hayley pointed at above the wall of foliage dividing the Moongarden. About two hundred feet up the Skyclimber, firmly planted in its side, stuck the missing Trembling Nomad.

"Well, at least we've found it," Grubner said.

Chapter 9

RGB VERSUS WORDLY

Grubner had reached his last and final straw with the Ravishers. Their leader was obviously taunting him, and now it felt personal. Today, he would start in the study as Miss Hayley had suggested. His brothers would guard the Moongarden in his absence, and he fully expected the worst. The mischievous monsters would surely get the best of his brothers as they had him. Heck with it, he thought, even if they destroy the rest of the Moon Orchard, there were no outstanding orders. Irvin had given him a more significant gift than he would ever know.

Grubner passed by Lisa, the Butterfly Shrub near the Moongarden's entrance. He pulled out his ELMO and tapped at its screen to make a set of double doors appear out of nowhere. He'd never gotten used to the strange sight of black double-doors standing alone against a backdrop of rolling

green hills and a blue sky. He always thought they'd look better framed in flowers. Grubner tugged open one of the doors and entered the Hall of Doorways. A light beetle clung to the ceiling and lit his way as he walked down the long black corridor filled with huge edge-to-edge doorways.

He reached the front room of The Residence and stood at the entrance to the study. But instead of entering, he turned to face a small green box sitting atop a pedestal table.

"You home?" Grubner asked.

"Sure am," Gruggins said as he sprang out of the box and landed at the table's edge. "I hear things are getting dicey in the Moongarden. My offer to help still stands."

"I know Gruggins' assistance would be valuable. But this is something I must do alone, or Moonshoes will never take Grubner seriously."

"I understand, but if you need anything, say the word."

"Well, maybe there is something. Would Gruggins study with Grubner? Grubner has never studied before."

Gruggins fluttered over and landed on Grubner's shoulder, then pointed to the study's door.

"Let's hit the books."

They entered the study quietly, and Grubner stopped.

"Looks like RGB are up to no good as usual," Gruggins whispered as they watched the scene unfold.

RGB was the collective term for three pyrodevlins named Albert, Linus, and Newton. They were nearly two feet tall with tiny slits for noses, yellow catlike eyes, devilish horns, and rows of spikes that flowed down the center of their backs to the end of their forked tails. The term was fitting due to the creatures' respective red, green, and blue colors and because they always found mischief together.

Albert stood atop the main reading table with a book held over his head, looking down beneath the table. Linus squatted on a small end table with a lamp raised above his head, ready to clobber someone. And last but not least, Newton sat on top of the bookshelves holding an upside-down wastebasket.

"Where did he go?" Albert asked.

"I saw him over here," Newton said.

"No, you didn't. He was right here," Linus countered.

Grubner stood quietly with Gruggins perched on his shoulder as they witnessed the scene unfold. A bright red dot suddenly appeared on the ground at the study's center. The pinhead-sized dot slowly moved around and traced a random pattern on the floor.

"What's that?" Newton said as he pointed at the red spot.

Albert, Linus, and Newton stared at the dancing fleck, riveted as they followed it around the carpet with their eyes like three bobbleheads.

"I think it's a blaze-mite," Albert said.

"Definitely not a blaze-mite," Linus replied. "It's a fire-nit."

"Nope, you're both wrong," Newton said. "It is an inferno particle for sure."

RGB jumped from their perches onto the floor and crawled towards the tiny spec as it raced around in ever tighter circles. They inched ever so slowly like a tiger on the prowl, and then all at once . . .

"Let's get it," Newton shouted as the three pyrodevlins sprang forward headfirst with all their might. But the dot vanished, and RGB collided with one loud thud and a puff of smoke. All that remained were three small balls on the study carpet – one red, one green, and one blue.

"What's wrong boys, all balled up and nowhere to go," a voice said from the bookshelf. The soft-spoken voice sounded like a young boy.

"Bravo Wordly," Gruggins said as he clapped in applause. "You've bested RGB yet again."

Two books on one of the shelves parted enough for a small creature to squeeze through, and Wordly Pagemore appeared. He was a four-inch bookworm that resembled a caterpillar, blue and green on top, fading to yellow at the bottom. Oval red rings with yellow centers lined his sides. He wore round glasses over his big blue eyes, which made him appear intelligent. Which he was. Wordly had fourteen back feet for walking and six front feet that carried a small laser pointer.

The three balls slowly unraveled on the floor.

"You were all wrong," Wordly said. "Not a particle, nor a mite, nor a nit."

Loud popping noises rattled the room, followed by flashes of red, green, and blue light as Albert, Linus, and Newton emerged from being balled up.

"Light Amplification by the Stimulated Emission of Radiation," Wordly said. "Or stated simply, a LASER."

"There he is," Albert said, lunging at Wordly.

"He's mine. I saw him first," Linus said.

"Let's grab him," Newton said.

"You will do no such thing," Gruggins yelled. "I've warned you before to stop messing with Wordly. Besides, he always gets the best of you three buffoons."

RGB stopped in their tracks and turned towards the door. Grubner walked to the center of the room so Gruggins could stare them in the eye.

"Do you remember what Miss Hayley said when you harassed Pepper?"

RGB's eyes grew to the size of silver dollars as they stared up at Gruggins, like puppy dogs, and nodded.

"Miss Hayley said we would be locked up," Newton replied.

"Imprisoned with firelyte capsules," Linus said.

"No!" Albert screamed, "Not firelyte capsules. We're afraid of firelytes."

The three pyrodevlins joined hands and bolted for the out-door of the study.

"Please, please, please, not firelytes," they cried out in unison as they exited.

"Well then," Gruggins said. "Let me make the introductions. Grubner, this is Wordly Pagemore."

Wordly put down the laser pointer and held his tiny hands out to shake.

"Wordly, may I introduce you to Grubner Trowel."

Chapter 10

SCHOOL'S IN SESSION

Grubner and Wordly hit it off like old chums and made small talk for several minutes before the 'grump' in grumpling came out, and Gruggins had finally had enough.

"If I could interrupt you two new besties, I do believe there is a reason for Grubner's visit."

"Indeed," Wordly said. "How may I be of help?"

"Help, Grubner needs no help."

"But Miss Hayley said you'd be along for research," Wordly said.

"Research, oh yes, Grubner wants to study. Miss Hayley told Grubner to do his research as Mrs. Moongarden would."

"How delightful," Wordly said. "Now then, what might the subject be?"

"You mean Irvin hasn't been blabbing it all over The Residence?" Gruggins said. "McGillicutty must be slipping. He missed a spot."

"Ravishers," Grubner said. "Grubner wants to study Ravishers and learn what makes them tick. Then Grubner will make a plan."

"Ravishers," Wordly repeated. His back feet tapped at the bookshelf while his front feet rubbed together, and he stared at the ceiling. "Ravishers ravishing, Ravishers ravishing," he whispered to himself as he concentrated.

Grubner glanced at Gruggins and hunched his eyebrows.

"Nothing to worry about," Gruggins said. "It's all part of Wordly's process. Miss Hayley would not steer you wrong."

"Got it," Wordly said as he snapped out of it and quickly climbed to another shelf. His little feet were like a gecko's and allowed him to walk right up the sides and undersides of the bookshelves.

"There are four primary species of Ravishers. Each elemental world is populated by its own flavor, and they are all quite different."

Wordly disappeared behind a row of books, and one of them slowly slid out from the others on the shelf. He pushed it off the bookshelf, but instead of falling to the floor, the book floated towards Grubner as it opened to a specific page and turned upright.

"You've got the bubble blob Ravishers of Atlantis, the scorchers of Hades, the clod chompers of Ceres, and the dune harvesters of Zephyr. On each of those worlds, there are tried and true methods for ridding oneself of Ravisher infestations."

Wordly dashed from shelf-to-shelf pushing books off as he explained. They floated one by one in single file to the study table, where they gently laid themselves down. Grubner's jaw dropped open, and his eyes jumped from page to page as they glided by his face.

"He's showing off," Gruggins whispered to Grubner. "Bookworms can make a book do just about anything, but now he's showboating."

"Now then," Wordly continued, "this is where we venture into the gray area. Ravishers migrated to Earth during the Great Exodus. They migrated from all four of the elemental worlds and banded together to form a community. But that occurred many millennia ago, and earthly Ravishers have evolved a lot since then.

"So, you are saying it is possible what would work on elemental Ravishers may not work on the earthly version," Gruggins said.

"Exactly. Not much information exists on earthly Ravishers. Only a footnote in Moonshoes' Guide to the Moongarden."

The mention of his heroine and mentor piqued Grubner's interest.

"Mrs. Moongarden battled Ravishers?" he asked. "But I've read her book many times and recall no reference to Ravishers."

"Because they were not called Ravishers back then," Wordly replied as he hurried to another shelf and pushed a book off. It floated in place and opened so he could read from its pages. "There is a small footnote near the end of the section on Trembling Nomads. Here it is, and I quote: '*The Moongarden was visited by the ravishing earth brood today, but as luck would have it, I got by with a wee bit of help.*'"

"Wee bit of help," Grubner repeated. "What's that supposed to mean? How am I to defeat the Ravishers with that advice?"

Grubner's shoulders drooped as he wiped a bead of sweat from his forehead, walked to the study table, and plopped down into a chair.

"Don't give up yet," Wordly said. "There are still some things we can try."

"Like what?" Grubner asked.

"Well, many fantastic methods exist for eliminating elemental Ravishers. I would suggest some combination of those might do the trick on earth as well. They can't have evolved all of their natural elemental behaviors away."

"Sounds like a reasonable assumption," Gruggins said. "Let's get to work."

The words of encouragement from Wordly and Gruggins pepped up Grubner's somber mood.

"Grubner is ready to study," he said as he sat upright and pounded his fist on the table.

Wordly and Gruggins stood on the reading table and helped Grubner do his research. Right off the bat, they came across one item that sounded particularly promising: a special potion called Ravanisher that worked on all flavors of elemental Ravishers. But they could only obtain it from the elemental worlds, so getting their hands on some would be nearly impossible. So, they moved on and continued scouring the literature for a solid three hours. Grubner took diligent notes as Gruggins and Wordly took turns to read passages from the books Wordly had gathered. They found references to many types of traps, decoys, tricks, distractions, and barriers invented to thwart Ravishers. By the time they finished, Grubner had pages upon pages of proven methods used for Ravisher removal on the elemental worlds, and he felt pretty confident about the plan forming in his head.

"Grubner will gather helpers now," he said. "Grubner's brothers will help implement every last one of these methods. The Ravishers will surely leave the Moongarden alone once Grubner deals with them."

"And I will assemble others to help," Gruggins said, "I'm sure it won't take much talking to convince Miss

Hayley to assist. But Irvin McGillicutty will be helping too, even if I have to make a few threats or call in a few favors."

"One more thing, if I may," Wordly said. "I'm not making any promises, but I will be involved in an important meeting tomorrow. The Headmistress requires my assistance speaking with the Council of Elders, and we will be teleporting to the elemental world of Zephyr. I may be able to get my little hands on some Ravanisher potion for Grubner."

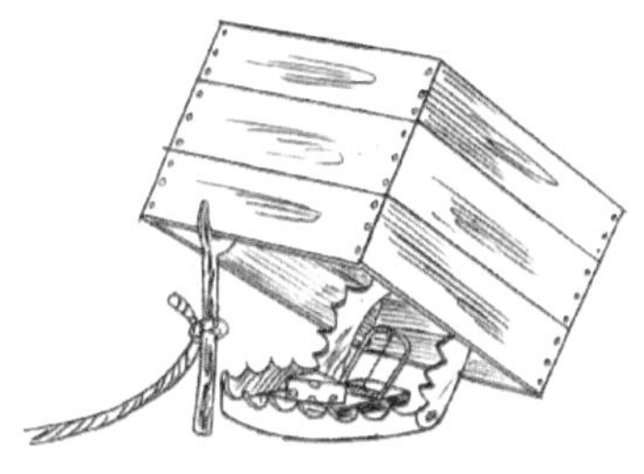

Chapter 11

THE TRAP IS SET

After his long day of studying all about Ravishers, Grubner returned to the Moongarden to see how his brothers had fared in keeping watch. He arrived back at the Moon Orchard right around twilight, and what he found did not surprise him at all. His brothers had zonked out side-by-side in a pile of bodies. They had apparently had a very trying day. Grubner scanned the destruction. The Moon Orchard appeared more like the moon's surface than a plentiful garden of vegetation. He walked along the edge of the ravished pasture and studied the area as he combed over his research notes to cement his plan. When he returned to his pile of brothers, some of them began to stir.

"There was nothing we could do," Grabner said.

"They were too fast for us," Gribner said.

"Tricky too," Gropner added, "and smart."

"No worries, Grubner has a plan."

"But you don't understand," said Daryl. "They are not even frightened by us."

"They laughed at us," Grobner said.

"Grubner has done his research and studied the Ravishers. Grubner knows what makes them tick."

"But—"

"Grubner's plan will stop them."

His brothers cleared away the remains of yet another ravished Moon Orchard and replanted it to align with his plan. This time there would be a more varied assortment of melons, berries, and fruits favored by most all Ravisher species. He designed it so lots of space remained between neighboring patches to make room for the trenches, traps, and snares they would be building.

Even with Moongrow, the new harvest would not be ready for at least sixteen hours, so Grubner and his brothers had plenty of time for a decent night's sleep before implementing his plan in the morning. Then, it would only be a matter of time before the Ravishers would unwittingly walk into the ambush he had so carefully planned.

Grubner arrived back at the Moon Orchard before dawn, and surprisingly his brothers did too as they were already there and raring to go. Like Grubner, his siblings didn't like to be made a fool of, so now they too had a score to settle with the Ravishers. They straightened up and stood at attention as Grubner approached.

"Awaiting orders," they said in unison like a platoon of soldiers. "Nobody messes with the Trowel brothers and gets away with it."

Grubner's heart warmed. His brother's enthusiasm gave him the boost of confidence he needed.

"Grabner and Gribner, you'll be my ditch diggers," Grubner said. "I'll chalk off the placement of the trenches. Grobner and Gripner, you'll be building the Creeping Tangler snare. Gropner and Daryl, I'm sending you to Market Square to purchase hydro-pods, muck-bombs, and twister-mines. Two dozen of each should do it. We'll be placing those later today."

"How deep do we dig?" Gribner asked.

"Needs to be deep enough that their shoveling-arms can't hoist them out. I think up to your eye-level should do the trick."

"How do we build a Creeping Tangler snare?" Grobner asked.

"You'll need to harvest a couple of Mimicking Melon trees first. Gather as much bait as the two of you can carry, and simply place it next to the Creeping Tanglers without getting tangled."

The Trowel brothers followed Grubner's orders and got right to work while Grubner roamed the Moon Orchard and chalked off additional details of his plan.

Two hours later, more help arrived as promised. Gruggins perched on Miss Hayley's shoulder as she walked alongside Irvin McGillicutty.

"Schnickyrooners and things like that," Irvin said. "I always love the stinky smell of tumbling whisker pebbles in the midst of a hedge of stone bushes. It's rather akin to the frost pimple dumplings on a grumpling's toenail but much less interesting."

"I'll show you grumpling dumplings," Gruggins said.

"You two need to stop your bickering," Hayley said. "We are here to support Grubner."

"Of course, how may we be of assistance?" Irvin asked.

"I've chalked off the locations where the scare devices will be placed," Grubner explained. "I'll need you to help Gropner and Daryl bury them along the perimeter of the fruit patches I configured for precisely this purpose."

"We've got three types," Gropner said, "hydro-pods, muck-bombs, and twister-mines." Daryl held the devices up as Gropner spoke.

"Aren't you forgetting one?" Gruggins asked. "I don't see any inferno traps."

"This group of Ravishers used firelyte capsules to torch the nomad pen," Grubner replied. "They are not frightened by fire, so I ruled those out."

"Smart thinking," Hayley said, "Grubner's research is paying off."

His face reddened as he basked in Miss Hayley's complement.

"I've strategically placed the devices according to the Ravisher behavior they might encounter. For instance, the scorchers of Hades always approach from the east, so the hydro-pods will be buried along the eastern perimeter because water scares them away."

"I must say, you really have thought this out," Irvin said. "I think Mrs. Moongarden would be proud of Grubner."

The team worked till sundown following Grubner's orders. They planted scare devices, dug hidden trenches, built traps and brush shelters, and scattered all manner of snares throughout the Moon Orchard. For the last part of his plan, they would create a tall watchtower as command and control. He had left a small patch of space at the Moon Orchard's center for precisely this purpose. With all his help, it only took the team another two hours to build the twelve-foot-tall structure that resembled a tree fort on stilts.

Hayley, Gruggins, and Irvin said their goodbyes and promised Grubner they would be checking in to see how well his plan worked. He felt proud of all he and his helpers had accomplished in such a short time. Grubner would sleep in the command tower from here on out, and his brothers would occupy the hidden brush shelters scattered evenly around the Moon Orchard's perimeter. They would communicate via their ELMO devices if the Ravishers returned or anything out of the ordinary occurred. But for now, they could only sit and wait.

Chapter 12

DEVASTATION

A full day and a half had passed since Grubner and team had set his plan in motion, but there was no sign of the Ravishers yet. The Moon Orchard's latest seeding grew as scheduled and would be at peak ripeness by day's end, so they expected another attack at any moment. Grubner's brothers were now his full-time volunteer staff and took turns walking the grounds while he scanned the Moon Orchard from above in the control tower.

"Any sign of earthly Ravishers?" A boyish voice said from nowhere in particular.

Grubner gazed around but did not see where the voice came from, so he climbed down from his perch to gain a ground-level view.

"Who said that?" Grubner pivoted in a circle to scan the area.

"Up here," Wordly Pagemore said. He stood upon a closed book hovering a few feet above Grubner's head. A small package dangled from a string a few inches below.

"Sorry, I remember you being taller," Wordly said as his  book taxi floated down to Grubner's eye level.

"Not a hide nor hair of them," Grubner said as his arms folded across his chest. "I'm beginning to think they have retreated. Now that Grubner knows what makes them tick."

"Maybe, but they could also be playing you."

"Playing Grubner?"

"Remember what you learned. Ravishers are smart creatures, and the earthly version maybe even smarter."

"Smarter than Grubner?"

"Not smarter than Grubner. But in case your plan goes south, I have brought you a present."

Wordly tugged at the string tied around the book, and the package gently dropped to the soft ground.

"What is it?" Grubner asked.

"Open it," Wordly said.

Grubner knelt and tore the wrapping from the package. A small white spray bottle the size of a Coke can fell out. It had bright red writing on the side that read: Ravanisher. Grubner picked up his present and stared at the label.

"Grubner is thankful to Wordly. But Grubner needs no Ravanisher potion if there are no Ravishers to vanish."

"Of course not. Your plan is a suitable one. But all proper plans must have a fall-back in case something goes wrong. This is Grubner's backup plan."

"Yes," he agreed, "Ravanisher is a good fall-back for Grubner."

After coaxing Grubner into creating a brilliant backup plan, Wordly said his goodbyes and floated away on his book taxi. Grubner returned to his roost in the command tower and promptly contacted his brothers via ELMO. He needed to put them at ease because he now had a backup plan.

Two more days passed, and still no sign of the Ravishers. Miss Hayley, Irvin, and Gruggins had stopped by on separate occasions, and Grubner proudly proclaimed victory over the nasty critters. Miss Hayley came bearing news of her own, Mrs. Moongarden would be returning in two days. So, he would have to harvest the Moon Orchard's crops and donate them to the vendors at Market Square before her return.

Grubner and his brothers took up their usual positions as the daylight gave way to nightfall. They would guard the Moon Orchard for one more night, and the harvest would take place first thing in the morning. Grubner took one last look over the quiet untouched garden as the proud feeling of accomplishment coursed through his veins. An hour later, he and all of his brothers fell fast asleep.

The early dawn light had just peeked out from the dark when loud cries for help erupted from Grubner's ELMO and jolted him awake.

"Mayday, Mayday," a voice said.

"We are under attack," said another.

Grubner jumped to his feet and hurried to the edge of his lookout. One of his brothers ran towards him, screaming at the top of his lungs as his arms waved in the air like streamers.

"The Ravishers have returned," Gribner said, "and there are more of them."

"Keep calm," Grubner said.

"But you don't understand," Gribner replied.

"We must stick to my plan," Grubner said as an enormous ball of water slammed against the command tower and knocked him down.

"As I was about to say, they have dug up all of the scare devices and found a way to aim them."

Screams rang out from the direction of the fruit patches. Grubner wiped the water from his soaked

eyes and face and returned to his feet to witness the commotion. Grabner ran through a patch of strawberries from a miniature tornado, chasing after him and weaving a path of devastation in its wake.

"Help, help. They're after me," Gropner's voice cried out from another direction as he backed away from a group of three Ravishers. He held a long stick and poked at the creatures to fend them off as he back down a row of blueberries. Grubner watched as the Ravishers slowly advanced on his brother like lions stalking their prey. Gropner neared the end of the blueberry patch when Grubner remembered something.

"Jump the trench, jump the trench," he shouted.

But it was too late. Gropner took one last step backward and disappeared from view as the hidden ditch swallowed him up.

"Where did he go?" Grubner asked no one in particular. "Those trenches are only supposed to be eye-level deep."

Gribner climbed through a small trapdoor in the floor and joined Grubner in the command tower.

"It's the Ravishers," he said. "They dug them deeper. We found mounds of dirt out near Mimicking Melon hill."

Gribner pointed to the piles of freshly dug-up soil at the base of the knoll. Grubner rushed to the other side of the watchtower to take a look, but his eyes quickly darted to the commotion at the top of the hill.

"Is that Daryl?" Grubner asked.

"I think so," Gribner replied.

Daryl hung upside down from a Mimicking Melon tree, and his arms gyrated in a circular motion like a baby bird trying to fly.

Suddenly, the command post shook like thunder as a giant glob of mud plastered its side. It was a direct hit, and more than the tower could handle.

"I'm feeling dizzy," Gribner said.

Grubner's eyes widened as they met Gribner's, and they both realized the watchtower was slowly falling sideways, and they were about to crash. Grubner barely had time to react and latched onto a corner post as Gribner grabbed hold of him. The tower slammed into the ground and crumbled into a box of ruins, knocking them both unconscious.

The Ravisher onslaught raged on for another hour before Grubner and Gribner awoke. They were groggy but quickly regained their composure.

"Our brothers need our help," Grubner said.

"I'm with you," Gribner replied.

"You cut Daryl down while I pull Gropner from the trench," Grubner said.

"Sounds like a plan."

"We'll meet near the south side of the strawberry field to search for Grabner. It's the last place I saw him."

Grubner and Gribner split up to help their brothers and returned to the strawberry patch within fifteen minutes. Between the four of them, it only took another five minutes to find Grabner's kicking feet sticking out of the ground. He had fallen face and arms first into a deep hole the Ravishers had dug to tunnel into Grubner's trenches.

"Five of us are accounted for," Grubner said. "But where are Grobner and Gripner?"

"Shh, do you hear something?" Gribner asked.

The brothers quieted down to listen for what Gribner heard.

"I hear it," Grubner said.

"Voices," Gropner said, "they're coming from that direction."

"The Creeping Tanglers," Grubner replied. "The voices are coming from the Creeping Tanglers."

The five brothers ran towards the sound of the garbled voices and arrived to find what Grubner had feared. A giant black ball of thorny vines with arms and legs poking out from all directions.

It took them over an hour to free their entangled siblings, and by the time they finished, they were exhausted and covered in scratches. The defeated look on his brothers' faces said it all, so Grubner sent them home. He felt ready to finally admit defeat, and it was time for the Trowel brothers to throw in the towel.

Chapter 13

A WEE BIT OF HELP

After his brothers' departure, Grubner roamed the Moon Orchard to survey the latest devastation. It quickly became apparent that the earthly Ravishers were far more intelligent than their elemental cousins. They had found and thwarted every piece of Grubner's plan. The traps sprung, the decoys exposed, and the snares used against his brothers. But what bothered him the most was that he let Mrs. Moongarden down. She left him in charge of her life's work, and he failed to handle a clan of nasty critters in her absence.

Grubner came to a small clearing of what were once rows of ripe blueberries. He glanced past the graveyard of upturned blueberry mulch, where several of the other patches stood undisturbed. A curious grin hopped onto

Grubner's lips as motion in the distance grabbed his attention. The Ravishers were gathering in the strawberry patch to finish it off, and there were eight of them now. He felt a rush of warmth crawl down his face and slowly envelop his body. His jaw knotted shut as his teeth ground together and his fists clenched. Grubner neared full-on rage mode when he remembered Wordly's visit and the present he had left.

"Grubner is not defeated yet," he said to himself as he let out a deep sigh. "Grubner still has a backup plan."

He spun around on his feet and dashed for the crumbled remains of his watchtower. He made it there in no time and began sifting through the rubble. The command tower's cabin remained primarily intact but flattened by the crash. So Grubner plopped down onto his hands and knees and crawled around till he found a crevice he could squeeze into. He turned on his ELMO flashlight to light his way through the dark interior as he inched his way around, frantically searching. Within minutes he emerged from the ruins, hopped to his feet, and held up the can of Ravanisher.

He sprayed some into the air to test its range. A stream of white liquid shot out ten feet in front of him, and a giant cloud of vapor enveloped the area. Grubner held his breath but caught a tiny whiff of a chemical odor.

"The Ravishers will vanish now," he said as he bellowed out a sinister laugh.

He ran as fast as his short legs would carry him to the edge of the strawberry patch. The Ravishers continued munching down a row of strawberries. They marched side-by-side like soldiers as their long arms shoveled the crops into their mouths in unison. Grubner took in a deep breath as his sweaty hand tightened around the can of Ravanisher.

"Well, here goes nothing."

Grubner let out a wailing sigh and walked straight at the Ravishers, on a collision course with the chomping chorus line of teeth. When they got within twenty feet of one another, the Ravishers stopped and glared at him. But Grubner kept walking straight towards them as he slowly raised the can of Ravanisher.

Finally, he closed to a mere six feet from them and stopped to open fire. The stream of white foamy liquid shot out like a firehose drenching the line of Ravishers. He emptied the entire can for safe measure, and when he finished, a thick white vapor hovered over the strawberry patch.

He sat on the ground and buried his face in his clothing to wait for the cloud to dissipate.

Several minutes went by, and the Moon Orchard sat silent. Grubner opened his eyes and rose to his feet, but the Ravishers had left. He breathed a short-lived sigh of relief, but then the sound of something rustled behind him. He spun around on his feet and came face-to-face with the lead Ravisher and his seven minions. They had quietly moved behind and closer to him, and now they laughed at him with a cackling roar.

Grubner slowly backed away from the Ravishers as their hissy laughs grew louder. He had opened the gap to ten feet when the creatures began matching his speed to maintain the distance. Their laughing grew deafening and more annoying when it abruptly stopped. Movement on the ground tickled the corner of his eye, so he turned and looked down in time to see a Trembling Nomad seedling dashing between him and the line of Ravishers. Grubner instinctively stepped in front of it and bent down to scoop up the tiny sprout and protect it. But when he rose to face the Ravishers, they were gone.

On his way to return the seedling to its pen, Grubner pondered how it could have gotten loose in the first place. But he remembered that the Ravishers burned down the enclosure after he wrapped it, and he never instructed his brothers to re-wrap it during the rebuild.

He passed by Linnie the Itsy Bitzy bush. All of her dwindle-berry cones were brimming with berries and needed harvesting.

"Grubner's chores are piling up," he said as he glanced at the tiny seedling and spoke to it as Mrs. Moongarden would. "And on top of it all, now I need to track down all of you little wee bits."

Grubner stopped in his tracks as the words resonated in his head.

"She got by with a wee bit of help," he whispered as he spun around, and his eyebrow raised like a mad professor's. He looked down at the dwindle-berries as a wide grin strode across his lips. "A wee bit of help indeed."

Grubner hid out near the few patches of crop that had yet to be ravished. Hours went by, and nightfall approached when the Ravishers finally returned. They were not as orderly this time, instead choosing to hang out and eat solo like a group of teenagers.

He wasted no time and marched right past two of them as he strode to the group's center to face their leader. The minions quickly closed in and surrounded him in a tight circle. They began to cackle, but Grubner stood his ground and flashed a devilish smile back at the leader. He held a small red cone full of dwindle-berries he emptied into his free hand.

"One-two-three," Grubner said as he dropped the cone, plucked three berries from his hand, and pocketed the rest.

Undeterred, the Ravishers advanced slowly as their cackling grew louder.

"Three near-halvings oughta be wee bit enough." Grubner popped the dwindle-berries into his mouth and swallowed.

He stared back at the approaching Ravishers as they grew larger and larger. It took less than a minute for him to shrink down to size. Finally, Grubner knelt, picked up the red cone, and placed it on his head like a sorcerer's hat. The Ravishers' mouths shrank as their eyes expanded larger, and they backed away from itsy Grubner.

"Boo," Grubner said.

Swiftly, all at once, the Ravishers popped up off the ground as their long shoveling arms took over as legs. They turned away from Grubner and ran away like a herd of wild ostriches.

"A wee bit of help indeed," Grubner said with a victorious smile.

Chapter 14

THE AFTERMATH

After discovering the Ravishers' fear of tiny things, itsy Grubner took a victory stroll. He found it fun seeing all of the Moongarden's beauty from the perspective of a seedling. But he did still have a long list of chores to complete before Moonshoes return. So, he cut it short and swallowed three shrunken dwindle-berries to grow back to size.

He knew the Ravishers would be back, so he ordered one hundred 'itsy Grubner' garden gnomes to place around the Moongarden to frighten away Ravishers.

In the meantime, Grubner called his brothers back into service and gave each of them enough dwindle-berries to shrink down to wee-sized and wander the Moon Orchard. His brothers happily accepted their new task as it would be fun to scare the dickens out of the Ravishers for a change.

Grubner called Miss Hayley on his ELMO to tell her all about his victory over the pesky Ravishers. She sounded happy for Grubner and promised to spread the word to Gruggins and Wordly.

Mrs. Moongarden would be returning in one day, and the wedding would be the day after. With the Ravishers under control, it would now be simple to restore everything to normal before Moonshoes return. Irvin even stopped by to put in a new order once he caught wind of Grubner's successful Ravisher removal.

Mrs. Moongarden arrived early the following morning and was 'pleased as pickles' at the job Grubner had done. She was especially 'tickled' by Grubner's surprise, he had framed the doors to the 'Hall of Doorways' in a beautiful arrangement of flowers. But tomorrow was the ceremony, so she had a long list of chores for him to attend to in preparation.

Grubner reported to the clearing to help Rosebud iron and fit tiny wedding dresses onto Alicia's many apples. Irvin would be along shortly to deliver Percy's tuxedos, but he already pressed, fit, and numbered them to match Percy's pears. So Grubner only needed to assist with the dressing.

Rosebud, Grubner, and Irvin had nearly finished dressing Alicia and Percy for the ceremony when Mrs. Moongarden arrived.

"Oh my," she said, "Alicia is such a beauty, and Percy is as handsome as a Skyclimber."

"Everything is going as planned," Rosebud said. "And I couldn't have done it without Grubner. He's been an amazing help."

"Speaking of Grubner," Mrs. Moongarden replied. "Irvin tells me you dealt with a Ravisher infestation in my absence."

"Um, well, uhhh," he mumbled.

"I want to know," she said.

Grubner thought he was in for a scolding and did not know how to answer.

"How in the fiddles did you get rid of them?"

"A wee bit of help," Grubner said, "that, and I ate three dwindle-berries and turned into Itsy-Grubner gnome."

"Fiddlesticks, why didn't I think of that?"

"But you defeated the Ravishers," he said.

"I didn't have the dilliest of an idea what to do. If it weren't for the seedling hatch, I might never have rid myself of those nasty creatures. I got lucky, but you are resourceful and figured it out on your own."

"But—" Grubner said.

"But what?"

"Moonshoes only chose Grubner because Rosebud was too busy."

"You were always my first choice. I told you Rosebud offered to help, but Grubner was my only choice.

Grubner blushed as his teeth peeked through his gaping grin of a smile, and he straightened his posture.

"Moonshoes chose Grubner first," he said.

"Yes, but I have one last thing to ask of you."

"Name it, and Grubner will do it."

"Will you officiate Alicia and Percy's wedding?"

"But, Grubner has no proper clothing to wear," he said and drooped his head at the ground.

"Have no fear. Irvin is here. I'll hook you up with the old McGillicutty special. I am the resident seamstress I'll have you know."

Grubner perked up at Irvin's kind gesture.

"Grubner will officiate the wedding," he said.

The wedding was an hour away, and most of the guests had arrived already. It would be a quick ceremony, and the crowd would be small, but that didn't make Grubner any less nervous.

Miss Hayley approached as Grubner paced back and forth. Two of his dearest friends escorted her, Gruggins on one shoulder and Wordly on the other.

"I'm glad you will be officiating the ceremony," Hayley said with a bright smile.

"Thank you, but Grubner is very nervous."

"Nothing to worry about," Gruggins said. "If you can defeat Ravishers, you can do anything."

"Grubner got lucky," he said. "The Ravishers foiled all of Grubner's plans, even his backup plan."

"You mean the Ravanisher didn't work?" Gruggins asked.

"Of course, the Ravanisher worked," Wordly said.

"But it didn't," Grubner said.

"Yet it did just the same," Gruggins said.

"Ravanisher never existed in the first place," Wordly said. "Gruggins and I made it up. We made it up to give you something to believe in."

"To pump Grubner up with confidence," Gruggins added.

"But why would Gruggins and Wordly do such a thing?"

"They did it because they believe in you," Hayley said. "They did it so you would believe in yourself as much as they do."

"We knew if you believed in yourself, the Ravishers didn't have a chance," Gruggins said.

A tear rolled down Grubner's cheek as he understood what his friends told him.

"And if Grubner believes in himself," he said, "a wedding ceremony is nothing to be nervous about."

The guests sat quietly as angelic music filled the air. Mildred and Rosebud were seated in the front row while Miss Hayley, Gruggins, and Wordly sat behind them. Grubner's brothers took up the row behind them, and in the back, Irvin McGillicutty sat with a few other unfamiliar Caretakers.

Grubner stood at the end of the aisle, looking at the small stage nestled beneath an apple tree and a pear tree. Alicia looked stunning with each of her bright red apples dressed in tiny white wedding dresses while her leaves flitted in the light breeze. And Percy was equally as dashing with his plump pears dressed in mini-tuxedos like pudgy grooms.

Grubner quietly strode the aisle with an upright and confident stride. He took the podium and began speaking.

Grubner finished his short speech and proceeded with the ceremony. Alicia and Percy joined branches, and he proclaimed them husband and wife. Mrs. Moongarden was the first to compliment him on the wonderful job he had done, and that meant the world to Grubner.

Now he knew for sure, his hero and mentor, Mildred Moongarden held him in the highest regard. But in the process, Grubner learned something even more important – if you believe in yourself, you can accomplish anything.

THE END

Author Photo © 2024 Edwin Wolfe

Eric Moeszinger—an acclaimed award-winning author and creative force behind the enchanting world of Ethan Fox Books—is a storyteller whose tales are steeped in the essence of his own life. Writing under the pen name E. L. Seer, the "E" representing Eric and the "L" a nod to his beloved wife Lori. Eric's literary journey began in the serene neighborhood of Sacramento, California, where rustic charm blended seamlessly with the spirit of exploration. From Sacramento roots to engineering, his journey culminates in inspiring stories that resonate and give back.

Explore the expansive multiverse of the Ethan Fox *Original Series* by visiting our website and blog, or by connecting with us across our social media platforms. And join us on a journey that glows with rare magic, unearthly wonders, and true friendships.

https://www.EthanFoxBooks.com, https://www.KidsStagram.com,

www.Facebook.com/EthanFoxBooks, ELSeerAuthor@gmail.com,

www.Twitter.com/@EthanFoxBooks, www.Instagram/@EthanFoxBooks,

www.Goodreads.com/user/show/133515145-e-l-seer